THE ARCHIVES OF *Biatre*

Keri Dyck

LifeRich Publishing is a registered trademark of The Reader's Digest Association, Inc.

LifeRich Publishing books may be ordered through booksellers or by contacting:

LifeRich Publishing
1663 Liberty Drive
Bloomington, IN 47403
www.liferichpublishing.com
844-686-9607

ISBN: 978-1-4897-3250-7 (sc)
ISBN: 978-1-4897-3241-5 (hc)
ISBN: 978-1-4897-3254-5 (e)

Library of Congress Control Number: 2020924428

Print information available on the last page.

LifeRich Publishing rev. date: 12/28/2020

This book is dedicated to my mom, who taught me how to write.

ABOUT THE AUTHOR

Keri was always known as a storyteller to the children in her church. One day, she decided to start writing them down and see where it took her. She currently lives with her parents, four younger siblings, a little red dog, and lots of plants. You can find her on Instagram @writer_girl_19.

I

"And tell them I hope they sleep well," continued Prince Adhemar.

"Aye, Yer Highness." Katira curtsied as well as she could without dumping the full chalices in her hands. "As ye wish."

His Royal Highness scrutinized her, nodded once, then abruptly turned. His pewter cape swirled behind him as he strode away, leaving the servant girl to her task. She turned also, heading toward the farthest room in the wing.

The wide hallway was beautiful. The candles in the wall sconces sent flickering shimmers through the crystals hanging about them. The unsteady lights illumined the empty sockets of the carved busts mounted on pillars, making them look alive. Portraits lined the walls, too, of the royal family, bedecked in crowns, furs, and jewels aplenty.

It was strange, that the world used to work this way. Some people were born into royalty and died there too, no matter what they were like. If they were honourable rulers, the people loved them; if they were tyrannical beasts, the people were too scared to do anything about it. It was strange how others, simply because of their ancestry, were born into poverty and servitude.

Nowadays it was different, of course. Rank did not have much to do with anything. Now it was all about money. But there again, some people made it, and some did not. It was strange and yet perfectly normal—it was the luck of fate. Or was there perhaps a God who decided such things?

A sharp light glinted in the corner of her eye, reminding her of the cameras. She shook the thoughts away as she reached the door. She was not employed to philosophize.

Katira tapped the door gently with the toe of her shoe. An unfamiliar servant opened it from within, his wide shoulders barring the entrance.

"State your intentions," he demanded.

She held the chalices out to him. "Some refreshments and the wish of a good night's rest to our visiting royalty, from His Highness Prince Adhemar."

One of his eyebrows cocked, suspicious, but he reached for the chalices nonetheless. "Tell His Highness that King Willhem and Queen Marielle send their gratitude," he said and shut the door. Some footsteps and quiet words were exchanged. There was a gentle thump, most likely a traveling bag being moved. Katira stood there for a few more seconds before turning back to the kitchen. Doubtless there would be more work to be done in preparation for tomorrow.

The cook had the fine idea of cooking the potatoes slowly overnight so they would be ready to be hashed for breakfast first thing, without him having to get up so early. Katira knew that he would get up early anyways; it was his duty to achieve a perfect meal, on time, thrice a day, not to mention always being ready for teatime and private refreshments.

She didn't mind humouring him. Getting supplies was never a burden. To cross the garden to the storehouse, to descend into the cellar that smelled of earth and harvest, was all a pleasure enhanced by the moon and stars. The walls of stone could not hold them out the way they did everything else. She closed the kitchen door behind her, took a deep breath and smiled, then let it out in a song.

> *"Pick her some calamint, fresh e'er to be,*
> *Elecampane, to sweeten the air*
> *Mistletoe, for the future so bright*
> *And myrtle, for the young and the fair."*

A cool breeze let her syllables play on them before floating away like so many fairies into the nighttime mist.

"But pick for me bluebell, to bloom o'er my grave
With laurel, my story to keep
And thyme, to be true, and ne'er forsake
Alas, time 'tis for me to sleep."

The song came to an end as she opened the door to the little building on the far side of the garden. The brick enclosure echoed her last word, and she left the door open behind her. An oil lamp mounted on the wall lit her way down the stairs. She found the potato bins, filled her basket, and walked up the stairs, leaving the light behind her. Tunes started flitting through her brain as she kicked the door shut, but her load was heavy. The mood was not right, either, for some reason. Her footsteps made the only sound.

A beam of light poured into the darkness from the crack in the kitchen door. The closer she got, though, the more something blocked it—something, something tall, that had not been there before. Katira's steps slowed as she drew nearer, and when it turned, she stopped completely. The glittering eyes that shone out from under that hood could only belong to one man.

"Yer Highness." She curtsied, keeping her head down. "What can I do for ye?"

He ignored her question. "You took them the wine?"

"Aye. Their Majesties send their thanks."

"Are you sure they drank it?" The tone in the prince's voice was strange. He was always so silent and morose; but now that he was speaking, it seemed as if his entire dark essence was trying to bleed out in those words.

Katira couldn't help the shudder that ran down her spine. "I do not know, Yer Highness. Their vigil took the chalices from me." She felt like she should have added something else, but she didn't. This was making too much sense. It was all she could do to not let him know that she understood.

He analyzed the naive expression on her face for an agonizing minute, then turned toward the rosier section of the garden, boots clicking on the stone path. Katira stood among the rows of vegetables and watched him go.

2

Queen Vivian strolled the length of the room, smiling as she took in the rows of manned computer screens covering live footage from the castles. "Any good scenes today?"

"Not from Biatre, ma'am," Miss Director answered, walking at her side. "As you know, a good deal of the castle staff is on leave while the king and queen are absent. The royal advisor had the day off, and Prince Derek did nothing but fence and read. Here in Taklin, though, we had Soldier Twenty-Seven stumble, as you requested, and he got whipped for it."

"How did he take it?"

"We had him under control the whole time, so very dramatically."

"Excellent. Crowds love a good whipping."

"Ma'am, aren't you worried that they'll tell someone outside on their off months? Obviously, they don't remember details, but they know enough to get suspicious."

"No, I am not worried in the slightest. You see, I am very invested in my actors. I know all about them—just like I know all about you. I know what can break you. Therefore, I am not worried at all." Queen Vivian walked to the section of screens that monitored her own castle. "Then what about our current project?"

"Fairly well. Your son, Adhemar, was more than willing to play his part, but he was too zealous. I think the servant girl's onto us."

"As we supposed."

"It's too bad, really; she would've made a good editor. She has a good head for drama."

"She's got an even better face. You know what to do."

Miss Director nodded, mentally listing the paperwork she would need to forge and then file with the Canadian government. The girl would have been good behind a camera, but she was even better in front of one—so there she would stay.

3

First reality. Those words were the only thing taking shape in Katira's brain. She managed to hold on to the basket she was carrying and stumbled inside. The faces all blurred together as she searched them, looking for the housekeeper. *There she is.*

"Miss Director!" Katira hefted her load onto the nearest table and spoke in a hushed tone. "Miss Director, may I speak with you for a moment?"

The woman in question was always busy, but her arched brows rose slightly. She placed a hand on her hip and waited.

Katira grabbed her arm and whispered, "First reality."

Miss Director stared blankly at her. "What are ye talking about, child?"

"First reality," she repeated, enunciating her words more clearly. "I want out."

The woman shook her head. "Ye're speakin' nonsense, child. Back to yer chores."

Katira stumbled back, glancing around at the other servants. A few eyes sparked with recognition and then fear, and Katira realized what was going on. Her hand withdrew from Miss Director's arm. She searched the ground, then shut her jaw. "I am sorry, ma'am. I was frightened by the shadows in the garden. I have been rambling nonsense. Pardon me." Katira curtsied and walked back to where she could busy herself in her work. As she moved, thoughts whirled in her head. *Miss Director lied to me. There isn't a way out. I am to be filmed for international television, as a servant in a grand castle, for the rest of my life. I have to get away.*

The last bit of the evening passed without any incident. Had Katira been trying to fool the other servants that her blunder was because of a fright, she would have acted embarrassed. But she was more concerned with fooling Miss Director, so she maintained a sad, confused look: helpless, hopeless, and entirely despondent. It wasn't hard. That was how she actually felt—except the burning desire to get away. That she kept well hidden.

Since the servants slept on the floor, there was no creaking of the mattress as Katira rolled off her blanket. Since there was only a curtain in the doorway, there was no squealing of hinges as she slipped past. Since everyone had worked hard that day, no one was watching the kitchen. And since no one used the garden at night, no one watched as she climbed the stack of barrels and crates, tiptoed to the edge of the storage shed, and jumped over the stone wall.

The landing was hard. As soon as she recovered her breath, she rolled to the base and waited for someone to call out, or come running, but no one did. Miss Director must have taken her cover story of a fright in the garden as a sort of apology and hadn't had her watched. It seemed too good to be true.

Her white nightdress was not exactly camouflage in the darkness, but it wasn't like she had much choice in the matter, so she pressed on, keeping in the shadow of the trees lining the road. As soon as she was out of the castle's sight, she began to run. The tree line broke. The worn dirt path became hard asphalt, and houses began lining up. The darkness was interrupted by fluorescent street lights that gave everything an eerie glow. Instead of birdsong and rustling branches, the music and ruckus of a nearby bar grew louder, then faded as she passed it too.

She realized that she hadn't missed the modern life as much as she had thought she would. Working in the castle hadn't been that bad. It was being stuck there that terrified her. Especially after being the one to bring those drinks to the king and queen, with everything in the castle being filmed...

They could very easily edit that footage and use it against her. She had to get away.

A tall building rose on her right. The street lights played off the bright-coloured, peeling paint. The doors were locked, but she knew the one counsellor who would give her a chance: Miss Eillah. She had a room on the bottom floor: east side, third from the road. Katira glanced over her shoulder. That unnerving feeling of being followed was not going away.

She rapped on the window, gently. Twice. For a second nothing happened, then the curtains shifted. Eillah! Her eyes widened and her mouth opened, but she reached out and unlatched the window, then pulled it open.

"What are you doing here, Katy?"

Katira was already halfway through the window. "I've got to go," she panted. "I need to leave." She landed on the floor, then looked both ways out the window before shutting it and pulling the curtains across. She stared at the counsellor before her face crumpled. "Where can I go? What do I do?"

Eillah caught her in an embrace, stroking her messy hair with one hand. "What happened?"

"They're going to blame me for the assassinations of King Willhem and Queen Victoria. I need to hide."

She pushed Katira to arm's length. "They'll look for you here."

"I know." The girl shook her head in desperation. "I'll have to go somewhere else, like out of the city, probably out of the province. Maybe Nunavut or something. I don't know how, but—"

A rumble grew outside: the sound of horses galloping on pavement. A voice demanded entrance, and the receptionist on night shift must have allowed it. A fist pounded the door. Eillah shoved Katira toward the bed, and she dove underneath.

The knock sounded again, then the door was forced open. Before the lead soldier could state his intentions, Eillah spoke.

"I'm sorry, sir, I was just coming to open the door. I'm still half asleep."

"I'm sure." His voice was sarcastic. "Where is she?"

"Who, sir?"

"Katherine Shultz."

"Oh, you mean Katy? She went into foster care a few months ago. You'd have to check the records to see where; I'm not authorized to give out that kind of information."

Katira could almost hear the soldier glowering, then there was a shuffling noise. Another soldier spoke.

"She's under the bed, sir." Boots thumped over. The number Four was printed on both sides of the heels, bold and black.

Katira clenched her jaw but did not close her eyes. She curled up in the corner and tried to shrink, so desperately, but the soldier stooped down and took hold of her leg. She grabbed the bedpost, but her sweaty hands slipped on the iron. He yanked her out. Taking her shoulders, he stood her upright, roughly, and pulled her hands behind her back. Another soldier supplied rope. Their firm hands dug into her arms.

Eillah was protesting something, something about orphan protection by law, but Katira couldn't make out her words. The soldiers weren't listening either. They dragged her out of the room. The last glimpse she caught was the bright poster on the wall, and Miss Eillah's face wet with tears. The door slammed shut between them.

She didn't scream. It was useless. So was fighting. Her wrists were already chaffed by the rough rope, and her arms and shoulders would bruise soon.

"Left." The soldier numbered Four shoved her in that direction. The whole contingent turned in perfect unison, keeping her in the centre of the square formation. They marched on, back to the castle. She panted, her much shorter legs having a hard time keeping up. It was taking so long. She wanted to faint. This all seemed surreal. It could have passed for a dream—or rather, a nightmare.

A drone buzzed around her from behind, and she glanced up. Its camera was extended, zooming in on her face. She shot it a nasty glare. She hated it. That drone had followed her. They had known that she was going to run, and were turning it into a whole drama. She had played right into their hands.

A siren cut the night air, then stopped as a police car blocked the parade. Two men in blue uniforms stepped out. Katira opened her mouth only for a soldier to stuff a gag in it.

"What is going on here?"

A soldier with the number Seventeen on his chest stepped forwards, motioning to one of the drones. "Filming a scene for *Castles in Time*. We were informed that there would be no interruptions."

"That's funny. It must not have made it onto the schedule." He cast his eyes over the group, landing on Katira. Tears welled in her eyes as the gag tickled the back of her throat. She tried to scream now, but it came out as a muffled groaning sound. He looked back at Seventeen. "Is she here willingly?"

"Of course. I have the paperwork on me, if you'd like to see it." He took a few folded sheets from inside his uniform coat and handed them over.

The officer flipped through the pages, checking all the necessary signatures, then looked at Katira again. She pleaded as hard as she could with her eyes. "She's very convincing."

Seventeen broke into an easy smile: an expression Katira had never known he was capable of making. "She's one of our best. Now, if you don't mind, we'd like to get this scene done before her hours are up. Junior actors' regulations, you know."

"Of course. Good night."

The officers left Katira to her fate. The soldiers started up their march again. If it had been hard to keep up before, it was even more difficult now. The gag kept her from catching her breath. She stumbled. Black spots began to dance in front of her eyes, and with a few more steps, they took over entirely.

4

Not a soul was to be seen down the hallway, neither prisoner nor guard. The bars on the window wouldn't budge. Neither would the door. Katira shook them, throwing her whole weight against them, but nothing. Knocking on the stones was no good either. Halfway down one wall, the blood started dripping from her knuckles. She grimaced and straightened while shaking her hand out, then did a double take. If she stood just so, a glint of hazy morning light from the window shone off a piece of something in the mortar between two stones, about waist high. She stooped to take a closer look at it, and it... moved?

She should have known. It was a camera. They were filming her. Of course. A flashback hit her so hard she stumbled backwards. An episode of *Castles in Time*. The show she had auditioned for.

Prince Adhemar, the dark, brooding heartthrob of the show, had been struck by a maid. Her name had been Elisa. Rumour said she was only defending herself. She had been in this very cell. Those stains on the floor, in the corner, there, were where she had lain and bled out after a beating. The guards had dragged her back because she didn't have the strength to stand up.

Katira began to shake. Fans had been so impressed by how well the scene had been played: the effects were so lifelike, the girl was such a good actor, the bloody wounds looked so real!

She felt the horror seep through her bones. They would say the same about her fate. Maybe she could say something, explain what was happening—but no. Everything was edited. No one would hear. If she were to fight, it would only make her look more guilty.

But what if she were to play along?

A tear escaped one eye as she leaned her head back on the wall she had fallen against. The camera hummed a bit, no doubt zooming in on whatever its operator thought could be of use: the tear trickling down her cheek, the pale arms wrapped around her knees, the lips whispering to herself, "I was only doing what I thought was right." Her voice cracked beautifully. "How did it come to this?" She buried her head in her knees.

She needed more tears, but they would not come. Fear was dry. She needed sorrow, reflection, sadness... She pictured Miss Eillah's face as the door closed, the tears that had been streaming down her face. But then the poster caught her attention: the poster that had been behind her, the bright words. What had they said? According to purpose, or something. She had asked Miss Eillah about it once. Oh, yes: *"And we know that all things work together for good to them that love God, to them who are the called according to his purpose"*. The head counsellor hadn't liked it, but Miss Eillah had fought that the other counsellors were allowed to display their respective religions, so she could too.

It was strange how those words were imprinted on her mind, like a tattoo. The thought that, if there was a God, he could turn around any circumstance for good. For those who loved him, anyways. For those he called, but she had said that all were called. And he always had a purpose. It was a neat thought, and to be honest, it would have been comforting. But she didn't love him, so there was no hope, was there?

That was another thing Miss Eillah had said. There was always hope. The most hopeless situations were God's favourite, because that was where he could show himself. *Just like any movie,* she had explained. *It always gets as bad as possible so that the good has to prove itself.*

She shook herself. Yes, those thoughts were nice, but she had a pressing concern at the moment. What could she do to make the audience pity her? To make Miss Director pity her? She started to rock back and forth, but was too tired to keep that up and leaned back against the cold stone.

Haunting melodies were her favourite. Perhaps they would do the trick. The words were not coming to her, though. She needed to portray the sadness, the hopelessness of being rendered guilty of someone else's crime. She still couldn't believe what was happening, and yet at the same time, it was so brutally real.

That was it!

"My dreams come to life
Phantoms floating near
Reality not what it seems to be
I wish to awake, but find—"

A key clicked in the lock at the end of the hall. Her song caught in her throat. The door swung open on rusty hinges, and boots clicked on the floor. Her palms began to sweat. Her breaths were coming short and rapid. The soldier with the Four came around the corner. A ring of skeleton keys jangled while he used one to open the padlock hanging on the door.

"Let's get this over with," he growled.

Katira opened her parched mouth and whispered, "What?"

He only stared at her, no pity in his firm lips and cold grey eyes. There was no way a normal man could be so void of any soul, was there?

She stood, shaking. Her cold muscles were stiff. Four had untied the ropes around her wrists when he had thrown her in before, no doubt so that she could smell hope, but now he bound them behind her back again. Her knees threatened to give out underneath her. He grabbed her shoulder, pinching her hair down. She gave a little cry as the strands tugged on her scalp, but he pulled her forwards with him, down the hallway. They were going in the opposite direction than he had come in. Her heart was thudding again—not racing, but deep, slow throbs that seemed to take so much effort. She wondered how long her chest would be able to keep it inside.

They got to the only door at the end: a huge, iron enforced door with the bars on the inside. Katira didn't understand why until Four pushed her through into the blinding morning sunshine.

She was in the arena.

Four slammed the door and the bars fell into place behind them, metal jarring on metal. Her eyes adjusted to the light, but the only thing she could see was the wooden platform in the middle of the sandy floor. In front of her were the steps. Her balance was precarious with her hands behind her back, but there was no choice other than to ascend. One. Two. She tripped. Her head cracked against a corner, and for a second, stars danced in front of her eyes. Four jerked her up. She swayed. Sticky red blood dripped over her brow and trickled right next to her eye. Up she went anyways, propelled by an unrelenting hand, to see her fate.

Here on top of the platform were three different edifices. One end hosted a pillory, the other a whipping post. But in the middle, facing the crowd, was a noose. It swirled around in the gentle breeze. Katira froze, then bolted. Four grabbed her wrists and yanked them up, backwards, past her shoulders. Pain shot through her entire body. She screamed. He held her there. She was shaking violently before he dropped her.

Two more soldiers marched up the steps then. They picked her up off her knees and stationed her on a barrel while Four pushed a set of steps beside her and climbed up. He placed the noose around her neck and tightened it. Katira began to pant for breath, tears streaming down her face. She pulled and struggled, whimpering, but they held firm. Four descended the steps and pulled them away. The guards released her arms.

Four kicked the barrel.

5

Katira gasped for breath, choking on the air while trying so desperately to drink it in. Her chest heaved, but it felt like there was a mountain crushing her lungs. Where was she? Her eyes were open, wide, but everything was dark.

Then the floor tilted beneath her, and she rolled against a wall. The floor tilted? A crash sounded by her ear, but a wet, splashy crash. Again. Water. She was on a ship.

She was not dead.

Slowly, the pressure began to lessen, and she could breathe normally. The rolling waves made her slightly nauseous. She rolled over onto her stomach and swallowed the bile that rose in her throat. They had taken the ropes off her hands again. She pushed herself up into a sitting position. This made her dizzy again, so she leaned against the wall and closed her eyes.

A memory surfaced from the dark haze that was her mind. Dark eyes, underneath a thin circlet of gold on dark hair. A figure had stood up from among the royalty. With an arrogant, sneering tone, he had declared that she deserved a fate worse than death.

Katira shuddered. Prince Adhemar was so powerful, so creepy, so… so good at his game. He had played his cards well. If she were to protest against anything, the "proof" they had against her would secure her death. Now wherever she was going, there would be no escape.

Dry eyes were the strangest feeling. Everything that could go wrong had, yet there were no tears. It was as if she had already cried her limit; that there was nothing else left in her. She felt empty. Void. Her eyelids fluttered shut, too exhausted to care anymore.

But sleep could not hold memory at bay.

"So, Katherine, you don't have any siblings… do you have a lot of friends?"
"Not really."
"Why not?"
"Well, I talk to people, but I'm always busy with homework or reading something."

Miss Director *tapped her pen on her clipboard, then looked up again at her newest candidate.* "Your transcripts show good grades in your drama and music classes. I took the liberty of watching the plays your school put on. Your portrayal of Ophelia especially was quite good."

"Thank you. I do like tragedy. Also, in every production that I did not have a part, I was in the soundtrack choir."

"Did you ad lib at all?"
"No, I stuck to my lines. I'm sure I could if I needed to, though."
"Well, we'll see. About your singing. Did you have any solos?"
"A few."
"What style?"
"It varied with my role."
"Try one, right now. Let's say a lonely girl in a grand castle."
"Umm…" The first thing that came to mind was a little string of words, an idea that had been floating in her head for a while.

"Will you rescue me
Will you set me free
From this cage I've made
All around me
Will you come to me
Will you—"

Miss Director *smiled.* "Yes, that is fine, just fine. What about a dish maid?"

"Pots and pans, forks and spoons
Plates and cups, laugh and swoon
Giggle, chatter, dishwater splatters
But hurry, the chef is here soon!"

"And what about a lover?"

"Take me in your arms
And never let me go
Whisper in my ear
And hold me oh so close
Let me hear your heart
Beat so soft and slow—"

She took a breath to continue the song, but the words failed her, and she dropped it.

Miss Director actually seemed quite pleased. "Obviously avoid anything modern but sing every chance you get."

Katy nodded. "When do I start?"

Miss Director shot her an impatient glance. "Your application says immediately."

"I guess I'll grab my stuff, then."

"That won't be necessary. Everything you need will be provided."

"But—"

"You applied for this, Katherine. Don't you want it?"

"I do."

"Then there is nothing you need. Do you have any questions?"

"Um, how long is the course?"

"You will be completely immersed in medieval culture until you have proven your ability to stay in character. Once you are convincing, we'll give you your certificate and bring you back to the orphanage."

Katy nodded. This complete change was what she wanted.

"We will have to do something about your name, though. Your preferred nickname 'Katy' is rather unromantic. You need something with more depth. We could stick with Katherine, your given name, and call you Kitty for short?"

"Actually, I did think about this. What about Katira? Then they could still call me Kati."

"That sounds good." Miss Director held out her hand.

Katira shook it.

6

The door rattled as someone unlocked it, then pushed it open. It was a ship boy, probably one of the rigging monkeys. He plopped a dish down in front of her.

"Thanks," Katira managed, blinking away the dregs of a useless sleep. She felt like there was a rock lodged in her skull.

The boy's eyebrows raised. "Prisoners don't usually thank me."

"I guess you have some very unmannerly customers." Katira took the wooden bowl. It felt good to talk out loud. Everything in her mind was a jumbled mess.

"They don't usually get such good food, either. Be careful." He walked toward the door.

"Wait!" she cried. "Why especially?"

"You're getting good treatment. Means they need you for something." He fished the keys out of his pocket and left her in the dark. Katira heard the key click in the lock, then his footsteps away.

She felt around for the bowl and picked it up. They hadn't given her any utensils, but it had looked to be a thick soup or stew of some kind. Easy enough to drink without making a huge mess—except when the floor tilted again.

Nothing else happened for the next few hours. And the hours after that. Nothing. This gave Katira time to think, and that would have been nice, if she hadn't already thought everything in every direction and still not figured anything out. She was bored. What the boy had said was interesting. Terrifyingly foreboding, but interesting. She was still bored.

Katira stood up and stretched. She began to pace, but it was pitch black and her balance was trippy, so she kept a hand on the wall. Another few hours passed before the door opened again. It was the boy.

"What happened to you?" Katira asked. His left cheek was red and swollen, forcing the eye above it half shut.

He shrugged and grinned carelessly, putting another bowl of food down and taking her empty one. "Commander had a fit again."

"Ouch." What could she say? *Sorry you have an awful boss?*

"Well, what can you do?" he replied. "At least it only happens when they want my dad or my sis—Oh, man." He froze and glanced behind him, knuckles whitening around the empty bowl. "I shouldn't have said that." He leaned down and whispered, "Forget what just happened. Please."

Katira wanted to protest. This wasn't right. But right now, she was stuck here, and no matter how much she hated it, the only way to stay alive was to follow along. She nodded dumbly.

"Thanks. I gotta go." And he was gone again.

Judging by the heavier boots that passed a little later, there was a guard or sailor marching past. Katira started counting the seconds. If she could figure out a routine, she would be able to tell the time. A good bit passed before the next one: one thousand, two hundred fifty-three seconds, to be exact. Divided by sixty seconds per minute, that was right about twenty minutes. She felt hope rise with this small accomplishment and began again. This time, though, she lost count around the seven thousand mark and fell into another fitful sleep.

Katira opened her eyes and groaned. This situation was awful. She could sing, but the way the boy had acted made her think that only human ears could hear her here, no cameras. At least that couldn't be edited, but the fear he had shown was evidence that the ears here would have no pity.

Footsteps came again. She stood up, not needing the wall anymore. All that time pacing, she had gained her sea legs. Her hearing was more sensitive after all the silence, too. There was more than one person. One was leafing through a set of keys. Then came the lock, and the creak of the hinges. Then light.

A soldier shoved the boy with the keys aside. Katira recognized him instantly: Four. She backed towards the wall, but he only threw a bundle of grey cloth at her. "Put this on."

She picked up the smock and waited.

"Do as I say!"

Katira didn't know what to do. "Sir, I—"

Four took a step towards her with a motion as if he were going to put it on her himself.

What could she do? She wasn't wearing a shift beneath her soiled nightdress, and there was no way she was going to change in front of this brute.

Growling, he lunged forwards. Katira darted to the corner but could do nothing other than watch him come closer. The boy jumped then and stuck his bare foot beneath the commander's moving boot, then pulled away just as it landed. Four tripped and fell headlong against the wall. Katira jumped away in time to avoid getting crushed.

He was up again in a flash, whirling around to face the boy, who didn't cower or duck. Four whacked him, hard. He stumbled back across the threshold. The commander marched out behind him.

"Take as much time as you like," he called over his shoulder before slamming the door.

Katira stripped and pulled on the new dress as quickly as she could. She could hear the boy's grunts as Four continued the beating.

She pushed open the door, not caring how furiously Four glared at her when it hit him. "I'm finished."

He took her shoulder again and propelled her onwards. She risked a glance back to see the boy. He was picking himself up off the floor, wiping the blood from his mouth. His eyes caught hers. He nodded to her, as respectfully as if he had just taken a beating for a princess, then turned and limped away down the hall. Katira's eyes welled up. She didn't even know his name.

7

They went up a flight of stairs, opened a hatch and climbed out onto the deck. "Where are we going?" Katira ventured.

No answer. She figured as much. She blinked in the harsh sunlight radiating off the waves, but once her eyes adjusted—land! This wasn't Canada, though. This looked like something off a movie, with a castle peeking over the forest in the distance. Then someone interrupted her line of sight. A tall, dark figure wearing a thin gold crown.

Katira dropped to her knees on the wooden floor of the deck before she was shoved there. Not daring to look up, she remained where she was even after Four straightened.

Prince Adhemar spoke. "What did she choose?"

"Your Highness, I was about to lay the matter before her."

Katira opened her mouth to ask what the matter was, but no sound came out.

"Then the pleasure shall be all mine," the prince said.

There were doubtful ideas of whether Prince Adhemar actually knew what pleasure was, but when Katira finally lifted her eyes to his, she knew the answer. Watching others suffer was his idea of pleasure. That had been the only reason he had always been silent, and it was the only reason he was speaking now.

"Should you not thank me, my dear?"

Katira felt as though he were pouring ice through her veins. He wanted her to thank him for saving her life after he was the one to commit the crime she was being blamed for?

"Well?"

"My gratitude could never measure up to yer kindness, Yer Highness," she replied.

His eyes glinted. He knew exactly what she meant, but her words had been chosen so carefully that there was nothing he could blame her for here. Katira risked a glance to the side and seen Four's lip twitch. She looked down at the planks. He also was not stupid. She would have to be more careful.

"Well, we shall see if I cannot make you further indebted to me." Prince Adhemar waited till she made eye contact with him again. "I shall let you decide your own fate."

She knew she was supposed to respond, but she was not in the mood to humour his royal wishes.

He went on. "You have a few options. You may live on the streets of Larte and beg for every meal, in which case you would most likely starve… Or you may live in the woods and try to forage for roots and herbs to eat, although that would most likely end with you being something else's dinner." His thin lips curved now, knowing that the girl's skin would crawl with his next words. "If you wish to earn a living, though, I am sure there are taverns that would hire you for more than your pretty face. A virgin, right? The first night always earns a pretty penny, though practice can make a girl quite popular."

Katira was frozen in place. Everything else was swaying back and forth, though; then the floorboards rushed up to meet her face.

Prince Adhemar sneered as Four pulled her up again, to her feet this time. "They would expect you to be able to stand. Well? Those are your options."

Her tongue felt thick and swollen all the way down her throat. "Yer generosity leaves me at a loss for words, Yer Highness," she managed.

"If you are willing to accept yet another one of my favours, though," he continued in a mocking tone, "You will allow me to introduce you to what they call a king here in Biatre. The work would be similar to what you have done till now, and it would still give you a chance to become famous."

"Yer Highness is too kind," Katira said. Her lips were trembling. She wished she could have been defiant, to clench her jaw and refuse his "kindness", to make her own way in this foreign country. But she wasn't that strong. She only had one choice. "I will accept yer favour."

He smiled again. "Shame, really. The tavern owners are getting the short end of this deal. Perhaps I would have become a customer." His smile vanished. "Four, I am heading straight to the palace. You know your mission. Seventeen, over here."

"Aye, your Highness."

They headed to the gangplank. Looking down, all Katira saw was chaos. Seventeen pushed her towards the dock and through the tumult. People were shouting, pushing, and shoving to get through. Everyone here was taller, broader, and louder than she was, and there were so many different people.

A fisherman brushed past her, singing about beating his fellows to the tavern. A woman was bartering loudly for the price of a good sized bass. A young man ducked around her with his pole and a short line of fish hanging over his shoulder. In two more steps they passed another fisherman with a black cloth wrapped around his head, who was yelling at a boy for dropping his end of the net after nearly getting trampled by a soldier. A group of children in dirty clothes dodged around them, shrieking in laugher, playing tag throughout the crowd.

"Do you mind?" The prince sniffed haughtily, pulling his cape tighter about himself as if it were protection from the filth.

"Make way!" Seventeen hollered. He had been too focussed on losing his prisoner (who was more likely to faint again than to run away), to see the predicament his prince was in. "His Royal Highness Prince Adhemar is coming through!"

His words worked like magic. They always did. The crowd separated in front of them and bowed, not quite in unison, but pretty close. Even the children ceased their playing to stare at the distinguished person.

Prince Adhemar made a motion with his hand, and the disembarking soldiers formed a marching position around him. His royal personage was now concealed from view, and people went back to their business, or so it sounded over the boots. Katira was in the middle of a contingent of soldiers again, the second time in two days. Who would have thought? Quiet Katy, nobody's friend, neither trouble maker nor teacher's pet, had gotten into enough trouble to have been sent, guarded, to another country with a life sentence on her head.

Using a group of soldiers was very helpful in getting through thick crowds. The whole mass of people at the docks had been very willing to get out of the way, and the commoners, as the prince called them, would fall over backwards to avoid getting trampled. Katira could see enough through her row of guards to tell her that these people feared the Taklin soldiers.

"Are you nervous?" The voice tickled her ear.

Katira jumped. Prince Adhemar was now walking alongside Seventeen and herself instead of hiding behind them.

"Merely speechless from Yer Highness' concern." *In other words, why would you care?*

"It seems like a delicate situation, serving the young king whose parents you killed."

Her head jerked up and she sent a single flaming missile through her eyes into his.

"Oh. That was anger. Let me warn you against that if you wish to opt for self-preservation. I am sure that King Derek would love to get his hands around the neck of the one who sped up his coronation." He dropped behind them again, satisfied that he had made Katira's predicament as bad as possible.

He had.

8

Katira was tired. Physically, she was sore—especially her neck muscles, pulled tight from the near strangulation. She was bruised all over. The restless sleep aboard ship hadn't helped matters. Her head throbbed endlessly, probably from hitting it one too many times, as well as the way it was running. Nothing made sense. And that verse would not leave her alone! *All things work together for good* played in her mind over and over, mixing with her other problems and like them, would not go away.

It was a good half hour before they reached the drawbridge. Seventeen shouted up to the gatekeeper, chains clanked, and the wooden walkway eased its way down, then plunked into place. They marched across.

"Well, God," Katira whispered, "If You're there, I sure could use some help right now." Of course, there was no reason for Him to help her, but a shred of hope was better than no hope at all.

The walkway opened into a beautiful entry garden, well tended but less ornate and showy than the Taklin castle in Canada. Most of the guards had dropped back, leaving just Katira, Seventeen, and Prince Adhemar to go forwards. They turned a corner, and Seventeen let go of his prisoner's arm before King Derek came into view.

The first thing Katira noticed was the hot pain barely contained in his ice-blue eyes. His black hair brushed his cloak of the same colour, which in turn brushed the ground. He was shrouded in the shade of mourning.

"Prince Adhemar, what a pleasant surprise," the king said, bowing slightly once he reached them. His lips pressed into a smile for the sake of etiquette, but nothing more. "I had no idea you had followed the messengers." His eyes darted over Seventeen and Katira, then back at the prince.

"I hope we did not disturb you," Adhemar said loftily, condescending so far as to pretend to bow in return.

King Derek replied with distracted politeness. "Your presence has never been construed to be a disturbance. Taroki, show them to their rooms."

The manservant behind him started forwards, but the visitor held up his hand.

"The maiden is not here to intrude upon your graciousness."

The king looked at Katira again, this time actually seeing her, it seemed. "I shall at least get the castle physician to look at the cut on your forehead, Miss. Pardon me for not noticing."

"That will also not be necessary," Prince Adhemar contradicted again. "She merely tripped on her way into the ship."

Katira kept her head lowered, agreeing.

"In fact, she is the sole reason I came."

She refused to look up, but she could almost feel the king cocking an eyebrow. "And why is that?"

"You see, she had… oh, how shall we say this. She entangled herself in… a situation. She pleaded to me and was willing to serve as an indentured maid."

Katira blushed, heat flooding her face. Prince Adhemar made her sound like a thief, or a murderer, or a harlot! Her head spun more.

"Ah."

"The problem is, between my parents, my sister, and everyone they employ, we have quite the full household. So I brought her here as a gift to you. Perhaps she could even bring you comfort in your sorrow."

Katira inwardly fumed. Her heart pounded, from anger or terror, she wasn't sure. They were both gripping their bony hands around her throat. This *was* a fate worse than death.

Then the king replied, and he sounded hesitant. "How… thoughtful of you. I would be willing to offer her a job here in my castle."

"Her time of service was counted as thirty years."

"Thank you. This is a great courtesy." His words were clipped and short, and Katira wondered if she did not appear fit for service. In a way, that did not sound too bad. "Taroki, show Prince Adhemar to the royal guest suite. I believe Nelda is just inside, cleaning something. Tell her to come and take this maid under her wing."

Taroki led the prince away, and Seventeen went back, probably to join his fellow soldiers, wherever they were staying. It was an awkward moment. The blush on Katira's cheeks remained there, burning her skin. She could feel the king's eyes on her but dared not look up to meet them.

"My mother would say that God never created people to be bought and sold like cattle," King Derek stated, "or gifted, or used. You will do honest work, and you will earn a wage."

By the time Katira looked up, all she could see was his black cape swirling around the corner. Relief flooded her; she wasn't going to be taken advantage of. He seemed so reasonable. Perhaps he would understand if she told him the truth! Or maybe the only reason he was being nice was in memory of his parents and he would hate her for using it to her advantage. She could have prevented his parent's death and didn't. No, he would never understand.

She glanced around. Everything looked so genuine, not the replication that was Taklin. But it made sense. This was the genuine article, just like the king's mother and father were genuinely dead. His mother... his mother believed in God? What could it mean?

Her eyes caught on a young woman coming her direction. She looked a bit older than herself, and had a kind smile. She came to a stop in front of Katira and motioned her left hand in a wave.

Katira stared at the woman. This was her first chance for an almost normal conversation, and her brain didn't know where to begin.

The woman went on. She touched her throat with an apologetic smile, then motioned to her ears, grinned broader, and nodded.

"You can't speak, but you can hear?" Katira ventured. This was the most unorthodox introduction she had ever had.

She nodded, then looked closer at the new girl. Her fingers twitched. She spelled out, "Hello."

Something cleared in Katira's brain. "Sign language. Yes, I can read that!"

The woman's face lit up. "Nelda."

"I'm Katira."

"It's been so long," Nelda signed. She wiped a tear away, but it was replaced and ran down to her beaming smile. "I'm so happy."

Katira could feel her own eyes brimming. If Nelda knew sign language and no one else here did, that meant she wasn't from here. She had been one of Vivian's actors too! "All this time, you've been here... and no one could understand you?" She threw herself into Nelda's arms. They squeezed each other. Nelda had finally received a fellow sufferer, and Katira had found one piece of solidarity in the shifting ground of her life. They suited each other perfectly.

"Nelda!" The sharp reprimand came from the direction of the castle. They jumped, but Nelda kept one arm around Katira as she turned to face the woman in the doorway.

"The new girl," The woman eyed her. "If ye be such a milksop," she announced, "I'll have no trouble throwing ye back on the street ye came from. Can ye work?"

"Aye, ma'am," Katira replied, applying the accent she had learned in Taklin.

"What 'ave ye done?"

"Kitchen work, mostly. Some cleaning."

"Well. We'll see if ye're of any use to me."

Two years later

9

"They did what?" King Derek abandoned his throne. His fists clenched and the blood pounded in his ears. The roomful of peasants waiting to speak with him silenced at once. His advisor took a step forward.

The general stood one step below, helmet in hand. "Burned it to the ground, Sire."

"Were there any survivors? Witnesses?"

"One man was mounted and rode here to tell us. He heard horses, then everything burst into flames."

"Send out a search party. A mounted force is difficult to conceal."

"I can have two hundred men, mounted, armed, and on their way within the hour to go and search the surrounding area."

"Do it immediately. Cover ground as quickly as possible. Search a hundred-mile radius around Ferbundi."

The general nodded. "Yes, Sire."

"Where is the man who got here?"

"He already started back, Sire. He refused to sit still and said we could catch up."

"Then do that, General."

"Aye, Sire." He bowed and marched out.

King Derek started after him as something plucked at his elbow from behind. He glanced back at his advisor, Taroki, but caught the eye of the first man in line. "People of Biatre," he announced. "I apologize, but I will gladly hear out your grievances another day. At the moment, I must go. Good day."

The crowd murmured as they filtered back outside. King Derek exited the room from the opposite end.

The king walked quickly, long strides, slightly hunched. He took the steps two at a time. The guard at the end flung open the door, and he stepped into the stables.

"Jonathan, fetch me Greenheel."

Two grooms in tunics and aprons were brushing down one of the other horses, but Jonathan turned and bowed quickly, then called, "Nick, bring him out."

Nick appeared, holding Greenheel's bridle, at the door of a stall two down from where they were standing. The horse clopped along behind him, fully tacked.

King Derek took the reins from the young groomsman and leaped astride the horse.

"General came storming through here, figured you wouldn't be far behind," explained Jonathan.

Derek looked down at the men. Jonathan had his thick fists planted on his belt, feet apart. Ronald was bowing now; of course, he hadn't heard him come in. And Nick was grinning proudly, arms crossed. They had done their job well and were proud of it. "Thank you, men." He galloped off.

The proposed force was already waiting just outside Larte's limits. Nearly all the men in the city, whether bakers, smiths, or tailors, were trained one month out of three for moments like this. Now they sat astride their horses, maneuvering around each other to get in place while the general shouted orders. Derek cantered around the group to get to the general.

"—straight to Ferbundi!" his voice was booming. Motioning with his spear, he continued, "From there, wheel spoke formation!" He paused to take a breath as King Derek's horse came to stand next to his. "Did you want to address them, Sire?"

"Yes, but once you are done, General."

"I will give directions to your group leader. Keep your eyes on him at all times!" He lowered his spear and nodded to his king. The faintest amount of rustling occurred as the men glanced down to the pads on their shoulders, subconsciously checking their colours.

"Thank you, General." Then the king raised his arm, and only the inevitable noise of horses in tackle remained. "Soldiers of Biatre!" he shouted. "We will not tolerate this terror upon our people! Go out with the flag of Biatre as your emblem. Fight for the safety of the ones you love!" A cheer rose from the ranks: the determined shout of two hundred men with families back home. Men who were willing to give their time, their energy, and possibly their lives. King Derek felt a rush of pride in his people as they rode past him, following the general towards the mountains.

The last row of soldiers galloped by, and the wind chasing the army faded with them. Derek touched Greenheel's reins to turn him and watch the departure. The horse obeyed, but snorted and stamped his hoof, tugging at the bridle.

"I know, Greenheel," Derek said, as the whirling dust vanished on the horizon as well. "I know." They turned around and headed back to the castle.

He wished he could have done more. His brother would have done more. He had been great with the sword and would have led the men on that search. Or at the very least, would have given a more inspirational speech to the men that went... He would have made a great king.

As Derek rode, he saw his reflection in a puddle before the ripples from Greenheel's hooves warped the image completely. With black hair and white-blue eyes, he looked just like him. But he could never be Prince Charles. Like the warped reflection, Derek knew he couldn't compare. He was just the little brother that had killed him.

He reached the castle, returned his horse, and tried to relax in a parlour. No chairs were comfortable. They weren't his.

The brooding fire needed more fuel, but he was content to watch it die out. Spring was nearly over, but even though the castle was always colder than outside, he didn't mind the chill seeping into his bones. Surely it was more comfortable than being burned alive in bed. Who would have done such a thing? Who could have? There were no people missing from Larte, he hadn't heard any reports of such from the port, and surely no Ferbundians would burn down their own town.

But, as Taroki had reminded him, there was nothing he could do about it that had not been done already. Now he had a different issue: the Taklin royalty was paying him a visit. Their timing could not have been worse, but they were notorious for that. The last time they had visited, it had been right after his parent's deaths, two years ago. The time he should have been allotted for mourning had been bombarded with gifts and well-wishes. Now, when he was concerned with the safety of his people, King Rosseen was bringing his daughter, Pricilla, to meet him. He did not need this distraction.

10

Katira hurried away from the kitchen building and ducked underneath the wash lines zigzagged between the kitchen eaves and the castle wall. The stone floor was covered in puddles from dripping laundry, soaking the hem of her skirt. She tried to lift it, but her arms were loaded with the three full kitchen wastebaskets. The outer wall of the castle, the one she was headed to, had window access to the moat. This was the garbage disposal.

She clambered onto the overturned crate, then the barrel, and dumped one of her loads. Down for the next, and up again. Twice. She used to hate this job, but—she put the last wastebasket down and paused to take in the view. On this side of the castle there were no roads or houses, only training grounds, then the royal forest. The trees always looked so wild in their shape but so resolute in their steadfastness, and she loved them. It was almost quiet enough that she could hear the leaves rustling. There was such peace in the sound.

Two years had passed since this had been her home. Off the streets, but confined inside the castle, always working. What else was there to do? As of yet, no one had any idea that their beloved king and queen had been murdered at her hand. It hadn't been her fault, but—*Stop right there,* Katira reminded herself. That train of thought was stuck on a circle track. It didn't help anything.

She turned, jumped down, and headed back across the laundress's domain to the kitchen. The building was a sturdy structure on this side of the work yard. In the middle were the laundry area and gardens. The far end hosted the king's personal stables. The work yard took up the entire back half of the castle, simply walled in to make it look larger. The royal quarters towered up two more stories on the front half.

The noise grew loud again as she drew near the kitchen. As she reached the doorway, Bridget bounded out and nearly ran her over.

The girl's bright blue eyes twinkled as she threw a grin over her shoulder and headed to the garden while her friend stepped over the threshold. Steam hit her in the face, smelling of soup and soap.

The overseer caught Katira as she slid an empty wastebasket under the table. "Kati, help Nelda with the dishes."

"Yes ma'am." Katira grabbed a towel.

"Thomas, yer bread is riz'n enough. Bake it. Benjamin! Ye'd better be started on that fowl." Oregga was nervous about the company they were getting, and all the staff knew it. "Ach, the time. His Majesty'll be wanting his tea. Bridget! Right, in the garden. Kati, put that towel away. Fill the teapot, the kettle's boiling. Use the yeller china. Git!"

Katira left the dry dishes in a stack and hurried to obey. She had never served the king in person before, but what did that matter. She had been here for two years and knew almost everything there was to know about serving. The tea set was on a tray in the back of the cupboard. She unloaded everything but one cup and saucer. Hot water was ladled into the tea pot, three of Thomas' scones were selected, and it all was arranged on the tray. Then she headed out the door.

There were multiple tripping opportunities on the short walk between the kitchen door and castle servants' entrance, but she avoided them all. This was going well… too well. What had she forgotten?

She stopped short halfway up the stairs. She didn't know where the king was! There was no way she could turn in the narrow staircase without either raising the tea above her head or dumping it, which would both end the same way. On she went. Besides, if she even went back to ask, Oregga would scold her and send someone else. That was not a bad idea—she shook her head. "Nonsense," she whispered. She was a normal servant. It didn't matter.

He was done seeing people this time of day, so he was probably in a parlour. The west side was where the most light would be right now, and the large window would afford him a view of the approaching road. That was where he would be.

Every step she took echoed. At the last turn, she could see the door of the room standing half open, with a guard stationed on either side. Even through their visors, Katira could sense them watching her suspiciously. Pretty Bridget was the one who usually delivered room service, probably charming the guards with her smiling chatter as she sidled past them. Katira glanced at them while gently pushing the door farther open with her foot and walked through as quietly as she could. She put the tray down on a small table near the door, then lifted the whole thing and brought it to the king's side. He was sitting hunched in his chair with his head in his hand, staring into the dying fire. The silence seemed awkward. Was she supposed to say something? Or would it be improper?

She opened her mouth and took in a breath, then said in her most docile voice, "Yer tea, Yer Majesty." He didn't look up. Katira bit her tongue and gazed at the floor. "Would ye like anything else?"

He finally lifted his head. "Sorry, what did you say?"

Katira, not sure what to do, glanced up at him. His eyes, at first unfocused, connected with hers. She ducked her head. The first rule anyone learned in serving royalty was that you never looked into a royal's eyes. She knew that. "May I do anything else for ye, Yer Majesty?" She grasped at the first possibility, trying to prove that she knew what she was doing. "Perhaps rebuild the fire?"

He shook his head and returned to the mesmerizing embers. "The fire is fine, thank you."

The white cap Katira was wearing almost fell off, she so hurriedly curtsied and left the room. As soon as she was around the corner, she shook her head vehemently and the cap went flying. She quickly retrieved it and pinned her long braid back up inside it.

She felt immensely foolish. Why did the king make her feel so nervous? Could it be the trivial fact that he had the most stunning, white-blue eyes she had ever seen? She had seen her share of handsome men, so why this one should be different made no sense.

The stairwell wasn't short enough for her to get out of before reality caught up to her. No, that wasn't why she was nervous around him. It had been the depth in those eyes that had pricked her. No matter how hard she tried to hide it, she was scared that he would somehow find out that she had had a hand in murdering his parents. Again, it hadn't been her fault, she had been framed! Maybe it would be better to just be out with it and tell him the truth? But then he would ask why she had waited so long. He would think her an assassin living in his castle, trying to get close to him, waiting to play her next move. The longer she waited, the worse it would be. To stay silent was torment, but it looked like the only option if she planned on keeping her head on her shoulders.

All things work together for good. That verse repeated itself in her brain again. "Where's the good here?" she hissed at the door, then flung it open. If she sat in the mire of her guilt so long, they would all be able to smell it on her. She needed to get back to work.

II

"Kati! Did ye deliver the tea, or drop it on yer way?" Oregga dumped ingredients into a bowl, not waiting for an answer. "All that's left is the flour." She left to oversee the rest of the kitchen.

Once the dessert dough was kneaded, there were vegetables to cut. All of these jobs were normal, but today there was a far vaster array: multiple courses of different breads and meats, with lots of fresh produce from all over the kingdom. Even the cheese course had more than the usual four varieties. Katira knew better than to sample the delicacies, but they looked so good... Chef Thomas saved her from temptation by whisking the bowls away to arrange little portions onto individual saucers. He lined up the dishes in order of service, saving the last few plates behind for items that were still in the oven. Katira went to the sink, where Bridget was not.

"Did ye hear, Kati?" A voice overcame the racket next to Katira's ear. She jumped, almost dropping the pan she was drying.

"Bridget! Do ye plan on stoppin' my heart?" She had come to share more gossip, no doubt.

"I will try, my friend." Bridget plunked one hand into the dishwater and used the other one to fan her face while she spoke in what was supposed to be a whisper. "I saw it with my own two eyes. Ronald smiled at Nelda! Sasha was facin' the other way, and she told me that Nelda smiled back! Our Nelda! Can ye believe that?"

"Yes, Bridget, I can." Katira began filling the pan with the rest of the clean dishes. The younger girl could be fun, but she was so hyper, so dramatic... and so romantic. She was hopeless.

"Oh, Kati, ye're no fun." Oregga turned in their direction, and Bridget diligently resumed washing. Katira took her pan of dishes to the cupboard to put them away. Bridget turned to Nelda herself, who was turning the spit of a game fowl a yard away, and resumed, "I'm so glad ye're more kind than yon dish-dryer. Ye listen so well and never reprimand me for talkin'—"

"If only ye'd have been the mute one," interrupted Oregga. "Some days I think I may have it arranged!"

Bridget went on, undeterred this time. "And I think one day others will come to realize how wonderful ye are for listenin', Nelda. And how wonderfully perfect ye are for Ronald. If ye could teach him those finger-words of yers, it wouldn't matter that he can't hear. Why, I'll wager that before his month is up, he'll have asked ye to climb the mountain with him! Ah! Is that a blush?"

Katira heard the end of this speech as she came to get a second load of dishes. "Bridget, she's standing in front of a fire. Keep washing."

Oregga came by with a new set of tasks, and Katira was happy to lose herself in them. Kitchen work was perfect for that.

"Everythin's prepped, go set the table."

"Colour?" asked Katira. She had learned a while ago that colours mattered a lot to Oregga. Something to do with setting the mood.

"Red. Benjamin! They arrived an hour ago and will be coming to supper before another quarter. Your course should be ready!"

Katira ducked out of Thomas' way, who was muttering something about mint springs and could he find nobody to run out to the garden for him and a chef of French descent deserved a dedicated assistant! She suppressed a grin, then opened the door to the silverware closet. She stood on tiptoe to get the basket with the red ribbon. It slipped out of her hands but she managed to catch it before it crashed into the ground. She glanced over her shoulder. Of course Oregga had seen that.

"I'll get those, Kati," Bridget chirped, giving her a gentle shove out of the way. While Katira selected the silverware she wanted from the basket, Bridget reached up and easily took down three chalices. Then she took the basket and set it back, gave another grin, and bustled away.

Katira heard her name called the instant she entered the kitchen again.

"Kati, table's set?"

"Aye, ma'am."

"Nelda, are ye done?" Without waiting for a response, Oregga pointed to where the beautiful array of dishes was lined up in order of service. "Ye're both goin' to have to transport the dishes to the dinin' hall tonight. No speakin', no trippin', y'hear?"

"Aye, ma'am."

12

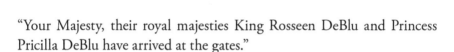

"Your Majesty, their royal majesties King Rosseen DeBlu and Princess Pricilla DeBlu have arrived at the gates."

Derek stood, taking a deep breath. "Escort them to their rooms, Taroki, and ensure all their wants are seen to. Invite them to dinner tonight in an hour hence. I will formally meet them there, in order that we may all make as favourable an impression upon each other as we possibly may." The advisor bowed and left. Derek walked to one end of the room, then the other. This was the first time he would meet the princess, and the first time he had ever formally hosted guests alone.

"Your Majesty, you must stop pacing if you wish to be presentable in time for this evening."

Derek sighed and stood still while his valet handed him the outfit appropriate for the occasion. The stack was thick.

When all that could be done had been, Derek dismissed his valet and waited a few more minutes, savouring the silence. There was not going to be much more of that, he knew.

He pushed open the door and went to meet the future.

When he reached the doorway to the dining hall, Taroki was standing ready. Derek took his place beside him, and he whispered, "Your Majesty?"

The king turned about to face the grand stairway he had just descended. "Yes, Taroki?"

"May I suggest you employ your greatest reserve of wisdom?"

King Derek looked at his advisor. "Taroki, are you hinting that Her Highness is not a wise choice?"

Taroki looked him straight in the eyes. "This is a very important decision you will make tonight."

"I am aware."

"And you will be hard pushed to accept."

"I am prepared to push back."

"There will be two of them and only one of you," Taroki insisted. "There will be no one to stand with you if you refuse."

"Would you sit at my table to support me and my decisions?" Derek would have willingly ordered another place set.

"Of course not, Sire. Your visitors seem like the type who would be insulted by having to sit down with anyone less than nobility. I simply want you to hold your own."

"I shall have to manage. I will need to be polite, of course; there is no need to start a war. Our army is not large enough for such a confrontation."

"Do you believe war is at stake?"

"I do not know what to believe, Taroki, but I am suspicious."

"That is good. Remember, you are choosing a queen, not merely a wife." He turned back to face the stairs.

"My thanks, Taroki. I shall keep that in mind."

Then the royal party arrived at the top of the stairs. As this was a private dinner, they were not announced, but it was obvious who they were.

Instantly, Derek was stunned. All the women he had ever seen vanished from his memory.

King Rosseen came first, a fat man wearing far too many jewels over his layers of clothing. But behind him, not walking but floating down the steps, was the famed princess of Taklin.

She was more beautiful than any rumour or report could have expressed. Her long dress was a sparking midnight blue, accentuating her curves as she swayed down the stairs. Her hair was in shades of spun gold, falling in waves and curls about her porcelain face. Watching the steps in front of her—for she was not being led—she daintily stepped with jewelled slippers peeking out the bottom of her gown. Once she reached the bottom, she stood beside her father, who was making the customary greetings to his fellow king.

"I apologize that my wife and son could not come as well; but it is my great delight to finally introduce my lovely daughter to you," he began concluding, "My dear Pricilla."

King Derek, who had only barely glanced at the king, willingly turned back to his daughter. He dropped to one knee and kissed the gloved hand she held out to him. "Princess, it is a pleasure to finally make your acquaintance."

"Charmed, I'm sure," her pink lips responded. Knowing she had his full attention, she lifted her eyes to his, blinking slowly with long lashes to suggest she really was charmed.

The young king suddenly realized that he was still on the floor. He stood up hastily as Taroki opened the door to the dining hall, then proceeded to pull out three chairs. "Have a seat, Princess. And you as well, King Rosseen." Again, the old man received only a moment's notice. "I must say, travelling does not take its toll on you, Princess. You look lovely."

She sat down slowly and arranged her skirt over her knees. "Thank you, Derek."

The manservants returned, each with one hand bearing a dish, the other tucked behind their backs. They laid the beautifully plated food down in unison. The chefs were on point tonight. He glanced at the princess, but she was eyeing the closed door next to where the manservants were posted. She looked displeased with something.

"What is the matter, Princess?"

Her expression did not change, and she did not look at him. "I don't want to be rude, but are all your servants that impertinent?"

"Impertinent? No, not that I have ever noticed, but I do not pay them much mind. What do you mean?"

"Well, there were a bunch of girls behind the door, all crowded together, staring at me."

"They were probably bringing up the dishes, and I cannot blame them for staring. Not only are you royalty, Princess, but you are beautiful."

She blushed and ducked her head. "Thank you, Derek. I suppose I am not used to strangers."

He turned to his plate and speared one of the apple slices. The drizzled topping was sweet and mixed well with the tart flavour of the fruit. The princess sighed with delight as she took a bite of her own.

"This is amazing. And I must ask, are these roses on the plates all hand painted? They must have cost a fortune! The details are so exact, the red so bright."

"They have been in the family long before I was," Derek replied, smiling. "I am not aware of who crafted them, but my mother—" he drew in a sharp breath and let it out quietly. "She painted a set nearly like it, only with grey-blue petals, and darker leaves."

"That is incredible. It must take a lot of patience to make something so delicate."

"Do you paint, Princess?"

She shook her head. "Not like this."

Their dishes were only empty for a moment before Taroki and the two other servants whisked them away, replacing them with small plates of salad. Derek noticed that the princess was toying with her utensil. Did she not like the leaves? The dressing? But then he noticed—she was pushing away the pieces of chicken and bacon that had been scattered overtop. Did she not like the meat? He had not wanted to offend her. Perhaps he should apologize? But perhaps she would be offended if he pointed it out. He turned to her father, who was chewing a large mouthful over his empty plate. Derek looked down at his own, untouched, and took a forkful. It was excellent, at least according to Biatre's standards. He swallowed.

"Were the seas kind to you on your journey?"

King Rosseen nodded. "Very smooth sailing, very smooth. Almost forgot we were on a ship at all!"

"You must have an excellent shipwright."

"Oh, yes. Very good at his job."

"Do you enjoy being on the waters?"

"It's bright, but the trip isn't very long." Bread was served, and he eagerly took a large bite, then continued. "At least we keep moving. Tried to go fishing once, but as soon as the boat stopped, the way those waves rocked, I was feeding the fish."

Derek nodded politely, imagining the look his mother would give if he were to talk about such a thing at the table, especially with his mouth full, and the lecture his father would give about using etiquette when dining with guests. It was obvious now that Rosseen's greeting speech was just that: a speech. He did not seem especially intelligent. He turned back to the princess.

13

"Atila, are you sure you'll be all right?" The lack of windows in the damp cement walls kept him from seeing the face of the woman in front of him.

"I'll be fine, Lato. You know we can't all go, and Rati—" she motioned to a lump in the corner. "There's no way he can run like this."

Lato nodded. This had all been discussed before.

Footsteps sounded outside the door, and the bolt slid in the lock. Atila ran and knelt at Rati's side as planned, and Lato plastered himself to the wall beside the door. A soldier with the number Twenty-Three on his breastplate entered the cell, holding their rations. Before he could close the door, Atila rounded on him.

"I've had it!" she yelled, stomping. "You guys are practically starving us, we hadn't seen the sunlight in days, and you beat us every chance you get. I refuse to be treated like an animal any longer!" The temptation to glance at Lato was almost overpowering, but she kept her stare on the annoyed guard. He sneered at her defiance and dropped the containers he held to the ground. The clay bowls shattered, the precious gruel and water spilling out on the dirty floor. Atila dashed towards the guard's boots and tried desperately to scoop the water back into one of the shards. He laughed and took a step forwards to splat his boot into the mess of gruel, catching one of her left fingers.

"Ow!"

"It's only been two days. And I'm not bringing more, either," he informed her. "So, when your pals get thirsty, guess whose fault it will be." He shifted his weight so that his boot ground over her finger. The pathetic girl whimpered.

"Please, stop. And he'll die if we don't get enough water!" Atila's eyes burned, wanting to produce tears, but she was too dehydrated.

"He'll die anyways," Twenty-Three replied. "You all will!" He looked around the cell to include all three in his threat—but there was only the one man curled in the corner and the girl whining in front of him. Too late, he realized it had been a trick. The door was still open behind him and the other man was nowhere to be seen. He reached for his radio to alert the others. Atila jumped up at him and jabbed her fingers at his eyes. Twenty-Three howled and brought both hands up to his face. She grabbed the radio off his shoulder, breaking the connecting wires to the transmitter on his belt. She threw it to the ground. The thin metal case cracked along the seam. The torn wires sparked as they came into contact with the water, and Atila almost allowed herself a grin. That had worked exactly according to plan.

Twenty-Three turned and hollered as he dashed out the door, one hand still over his eyes. "Hey! Escaped prisoner! Man the guns! Reinforce patrol! Activate the fences!" His orders were accentuated with more colourful words while he fumbled to lock the stubborn door behind him.

Atila turned back to Rati, who had lain perfectly still through the whole escapade. Kneeling at his side, she wiped his damp brow with her dirty sleeve, then, grimacing at the pain shooting up her finger, untied the makeshift bandage around his stomach. The ugly wound glared up at her.

"Well played," the injured man mumbled. "Quite the acting skills. Almost as good as me."

"Thanks." She tore off another strip of her leggings and folded it underneath the bands of his shredded tunic. The wound had scabbed over but was still very tender. It had been only slightly cleaned with more than they had been able to spare of their drinking supply. "How does it feel?"

"Like I got stabbed with a sword." His voice was quiet, his breathing quick and shallow. She knew he despised the weakness he felt. "Did he get away?"

"I think s—" The cell vibrated slightly with a growing noise. Atila went to the door and leaned her ear against the crack. "A lot of troops. I think they've got their Spider, too," she reported. "That means he got out before they turned on the fence." She returned to Rati and re-tied his

46

bandage, then used the knife from her boot to cut off another section of her legging and wrapped it around her little finger. "Can you tie it?"

"Tight?"

"Yup." She gritted her teeth, but the finger felt better now that it was supported. She folded her hands together and lifted her face to the ceiling. "God, we're in Your hands," she prayed. "Please—" her eyes popped open as another few sets of boots pounded outside. The bolt was removed again, and the door swung open. Four was back, along with Seventeen. She jumped away, but a gloved hand grabbed a fistful of her short hair. She kicked and thrashed. Four's fist smashed into the side of her face. Their anger wasn't pacified by the cry torn from her mouth.

"Where is he going?" Four released her hair and shook her by the shoulders.

Atila licked the blood off her lip but didn't say a word as the tangy taste of iron filled her mouth. Four shoved her against the cement wall. After securing her hands to the shackles attached there, they stood in front of her. She knew what was coming. Dread filled her being. She couldn't stop the long chains from rattling.

Four stared her down. "Now, what do you say? Where did he go?"

She gritted her teeth. He nodded at Seventeen, who pushed a button on the back of his glove, and searing pain flowed through her body from her wrists. Her knees buckled. She slid to the floor, jerking against her arms. It must have only lasted a second, but where is time when agony is concerned?

When it stopped, she gasped for breath. They asked her again, and still she did not answer. The second time was worse. Sparks flashed in her darkened vision and the strength left her. "He's... headed... east," she moaned. Behind her, Rati let out a groan. "Now leave me alone!" she shouted. "Haven't you done enough?"

Electricity enveloped her body again, but this time a merciful blackness received her.

14

Lato's heart pounded. He had his back against the building across from the prison and could still see the inside of the cell. Four was crushing Atila's finger. She was doing her best to keep him occupied. Anger roiled inside him, but this was the only way he could help.

A guard patrolled the alley next to him. He needed to get past him before Twenty-Three turned around and seen him. Then Atila actually hit Twenty-Three—in the face, no less—who yelped and stumbled out the door toward Lato. He flinched, but Twenty-Three had his hand over his eyes. He hollered something, and finally the alley guard ran past Lato and towards the cell. Lato dashed toward the fence.

He slipped his right leg between two wires in the fence and swung the rest of his body through. He was shaking with adrenaline, but then he heard a sound that made him freeze. The wires were crackling with electricity. Here he was, one foot on each side—a leg trapped between the wires—and the fence was on! Lato gritted his teeth, steadied himself, and jumped away from the fence, pulling his leg behind him. His foot brushed the wire and he fell heavily to the ground. The crippling agony only lasted a moment, though, and he pushed to his feet. He took a few unsteady steps. By the time his balance was restored, he was running. His breathing was loud. He could not hear the commotion from the camp behind him. He glanced around. There were no trees large enough for proper cover, only clumps of tall grass and scraggly bushes.

Used to being in shape, Lato hated the weakness that soon overtook his legs and arms. He ducked behind a thorn bush and calmed himself. There were sounds of men marching, mixed with the whirring and clanking of the Spider. His heart pounded. Their plan had been that Atila would keep them distracted as long she could, but then make sure that when they left, it would be in the wrong direction. Still, pain was a great motivator, and the soldiers knew that.

"Oh God, please help her. Please help all of us."

Once he was recovered enough, he began working his way farther. None of the plants were taller than him, but if he crouched, they provided sufficient cover. The sun sank the rest of the way into the horizon. The way was becoming increasingly difficult to see. To go on in the dark would be hazardous, and he would make better time if he saved his energy for daylight.

Lato chose a sprawling bush with the thickest foliage he could find. He crawled into it, facing away from the camp. The noise had all but faded.

Sleep refused to come. He leaned his head back and looked up at the stars that were starting to come out. He had missed seeing the open sky almost as much as Atila had.

Was she all right? How far had she gone to convince the soldiers that they had gotten the truth from her? What would they do to her when they realized it was all a hoax? What would they do to Rati? He was already wounded, and once another's life was in jeopardy, Atila would tell the truth. Lato needed to be as far away as possible before that happened. He opened his mouth to whisper another prayer when he noticed a gleam of light in the east. The moon was rising! Lato smiled and sent up a prayer of thanks instead of petition.

He waited till the whole glowing orb had risen above the horizon. It was only a little over half full, but the sky was clear. It was bright enough.

Rising was difficult; his muscles were already stiff from sudden use after their stay in the cell. He stood up anyways. A furry little something scurried away from his feet. A hyena barked in the distance. The night creatures would no doubt be afraid of a human, and he was used to these sounds—though he had never been alone with them before.

Lato, Atila, and Rati had made quite the trio. The army had not expected the three to be such skilled warriors. They had had the advantage of surprise as well as weapons that Master Blackwell had created, but numbers had overwhelmed them, and they had been imprisoned.

15

The cots were not quite big enough for two. This was not usually an issue, as most servants went to their own homes overnight. With the visiting royalty, however, there was much more to do, and that meant more servants were staying the night. Bridget had pinched Katira twice for tossing before falling asleep despite it. They were all exhausted; still she could not sleep. The look in the princess' eyes when she seen them behind the door… Bridget had just wanted an innocent peek at the beautiful princess. Katira had known better than to look too, but she had, and she was certain Pricilla had recognized her. Would she mention her? Even a word to the king could spoil the anonymity she had worked so hard to attain.

All things work together for good. Those words from Miss Eillah's poster ran through Katira's head again. They were still confusing, but now they sounded like an invitation. How much she wished it were true.

Katira slid from underneath the blankets. Bridget did not move. Stealthily, Katira slipped past the cots, one at a time. Nelda sighed and shifted, but she seemed fast asleep. She knew she could pay dearly for this venture if she were caught.

There were no guards patrolling the servant's section here, and she hadn't seen many scenes filmed at night, except in that one corner: that dark, secluded, perfect-for-flirting corner between the guards' wing and the servants' quarters. Katira crawled along the opposite wall, knowing that corner was probably monitored full time. All these secret dramas between servants were not secrets to anyone who had access to the internet.

But that was why she was leaving. She crept along down the hallway and out the door to the work yard, then turned left, towards the stables. She figured, remembering a horse theft once, that the camera on the stalls was monitored, but that was not where she was headed. Right inside the door was the tackle room. Several hooks held horse blankets for winter and towels for rubdowns. She reached for the nearest one. A horse snorted. Katira jumped. She waited to compose her breathing and try to calm her heart rate, then put the blanket around her shoulders and exited as quickly as possible.

She tiptoed between the garden rows, staying out of sight from the soldier that was guarding the exit to the grounds. Her heart pounded in her ears. Every little cricket chirp made her flinch.

Finally, Katira got to the window that she had dumped the garbage from earlier. She glanced back over her shoulder for probably the twentieth time, then stepped onto the crate, then the barrel. Another glance. Onto the windowsill.

The ledge was thick enough for her to sit on and wide enough to swing her feet around to the outside. She shoved the corners of the stiff blanket into her mouth. It tasted like sweaty horse, but she needed something to cover her nightdress with, so she clamped her teeth firmly.

Katira couldn't believe she was doing this, but it was too late to waver now. She twisted a bit more and scooted off the edge. Hanging by her hands, she flailed her legs to find one of the exposed tree roots she had seen earlier. It took a few perilous seconds. One bare foot caught a surface. It was thin but not too slippery. She gripped the ledge tightly until her other foot found another one of the roots. She let go. Her body dropped to a crouch so that she could balance with her hands as well.

It was too dark to see the water beneath, but the sound of it rushing reminded Katira that it was still there and very willing to swallow her. The rainy season was over long enough that the level in the moat was down. Usually some farmers opened channels from other streams to feed more water into the moat during the summer, but they hadn't yet. Katira was surprised that these roots hadn't been seen by anyone else.

She got to the other side of the moat without any mishaps. The roots held firm, a testament to the tree she crawled out beside. She dashed across the open area towards the woods as the moon came out from behind the clouds and she realized her head was exposed. Her hair had been loosed from its usual braid before going to bed, and certainly it was catching the moonlight and making her visible. She released her jaw but didn't grab both ends in time. A corner landed on the ground in front of her. The grass was wet with dew and she was running too fast to stop. The stiff blanket skidded forwards. She landed on top of it with a grunt but jumped up, tugged the blanket from underneath her feet, and pulled it over her head as fast as she could. Her heart had doubled its pace again, but she dared not resume her speed. If a guard had seen her, she would be caught no matter how fast she ran. If one hadn't, all she could do was keep it that way.

16

The night air floating in through the window was cool and sweet compared with the thick, warm air in Derek's bedroom. Someone had built the afternoon's embers into a blazing fire while King Derek had been in the dining hall with… the princess. He leaned against the window frame. The stars were twinkling brightly in the cloudless sky, like her eyes this evening. Perhaps tomorrow night he should take her up the tower, to the roof, to see the stars—but—why would he? He didn't even know if she would like that kind of thing. Come to think about it, he couldn't remember what exactly they had talked about during the whole meal. He did know that the topic of the marriage alliance had not been raised.

But how should he be allowed to think of such things as stars when there was a band of riders setting fire to innocent people's homes? Such a vile act proved what this group was capable of, and surely it wouldn't end there. Why were they doing this? Was there a rebellion rising? In the two years of his reign, had he already lost the people's loyalty?

Something moved out on the training grounds behind the castle, where the stables let out before the fenced woods. Derek blinked and looked again. A small figure stood up from the ground, all in white, with long hair glistening in the moonlight. Then the apparition bent over and disappeared? No, if he looked closely, he could still see it, shrouded in a dark cloak.

This new curiosity seemed to lighten the burden of his current problems. Perhaps a little problem, one he could solve, would be helpful to his current mental state. How hard would it be to follow this sneak into the familiar woods and apprehend it?

17

Her breaths were hard to keep quiet. She kept on till she reached the trees, then allowed herself to relax slightly. The trees rustled overhead in a slight breeze. The sound was soothing. Beads of moonlight dripped between the leaves and fell to the ground, where they splashed and disappeared. For a moment Katira forgot why she had come, and a song floated to the surface of her distressed mind.

> *"My rest is away on the hills*
> *My sleep is chasing the moon*
> *My dreams dance under the stars*
> *While I am left alone..."*

Then the words died away. She had not come out here to be alone. Away from people, yes, but not alone. This was something she had wanted to do for a while already.

Katira glanced around. Ahead was a little clearing where the moon shone unhindered. She made her way there and sat down, facing away from the direction she had come. She slipped the blanket off her head, then her shoulders, and arranged it around her. The early summer night was not chilly enough to need it. She bowed her head with her hands in her lap. Tears began to slip down her cheeks, and she allowed them. Finally, she was in a place where she didn't need to act. She could simply... be. She took a deep breath.

"God," she whispered. "If You're there. Miss Eillah said You would hear those who call out to You. Well, I need You. Really badly." Katira heaved a sigh. "That poster, the one on Miss Eillah's wall, will not get out of my head. She said that You loved us, that You would chase after us, and maybe that's what this is.

"It said that all things work together for good. For those that love You and are called according to Your purpose. God, if You love me, then I guess I had better love You back. I don't know if I can help your purpose, God, but I'm willing to try. I am such a wretch on my own.

"I guess if You are there, that would make sense why King Derek was so nice when Prince Adhemar brought me here, and why I found Nelda, and met Bridget. But God, there is so much more bad than good.

"This whole world is such a mess. Almost everything I do is being watched, edited, and broadcasted. No one else here even suspects it. They all just live their lives, not knowing that binge-watchers everywhere are eating it up like a soap opera! Even if I tried to explain it, no one here would understand me, but the cameras would catch it, and surely someone would come to remove me. They'd probably kill me!

"So, God, I don't know what to do. I—" Katira's words choked in her throat. A branch had snapped. Her heart stopped. For a horrible second, nothing moved. Icicles prickled through her veins. Then her brain kicked into gear and she bolted.

18

Mason Blackwell sat up straight in bed. That was a knock, but he hadn't heard the pattern. He waited. There it was again. One, two, pause, three. He rushed to the door and opened it.

"Lato!" The young man's blue eyes were bloodshot, his cheeks sallow, his face and exposed arms bruised. "Come in, come in." He ushered him inside, shut the door, and led him through the trap door into the basement. Lato collapsed into a chair while Mason filled the kettle and hung it in the fireplace. He knelt beside the ashes and stirred them, adding more wood. "What happened?"

"Atila has too much compassion, Master Blackwell."

Mason sensed that his safe little world had shifted, but he kept his hands steady with the knife as he cut thick slices of cheese and bread. He handed the plate to Lato.

He wolfed a few bites down. "She spoke to an old woman in the marketplace, about—" he swallowed. "About God."

"And Taklin heard."

"Yes; how did you know?"

"I knew this day was coming." Mason shook his head. "But we are not ready."

Lato looked up with a glint in his eye. "That woman died, Master Blackwell. She was ready."

Yes, God did have His own ideas about timing. And there was no going back now. But first things first. He took the kettle off the fire with a pair of tongs, then poured two cups of tea. "You need to sleep."

"I know. But I've got to get Atila and Rati out of there. They've probably been tortured to tell where I was headed, and I don't know if they were able to…"

"Withstand?"

"I was thinking survive."

"They are both strong in their resolve, and those guards will not kill them if there is any hope of making them recant."

"Now that I got away, though, the soldiers will be harder on them. Rati was injured in the fight, and Atila is, well, a woman among men."

Mason pressed his lips together. "She is in God's hands. They both are." He motioned to the cots in the back of the room. "He is most likely going to work through you and I, though, so I suggest you get some rest before whatever happens next."

Lato obeyed and was snoring the instant his head hit the pillow. Mason swallowed his own tea and set the cup down. He had work to do.

He went out the back door. There, behind several tall trees, was his balloon prototype. By the light of the rising sun, he loaded the tray beneath the balloon's opening with torches. He hurried back inside to get a stick of fire. This would have only taken a short time in Canada, but all his tinkering here would never amount the advances in technology there—except in one thing. But Lato was without his staff, so that weapon must have been lost.

The flames took quickly, and as the balloon filled with the warm air, he cut the restraints holding it upright, leaving only the anchor. The sun climbed higher. How long would it take for the Taklin soldiers to realize it had been a trick? He began to load a corner of the basket with more torches: sticks of dry hardwood, wrapped with hide strips and soaked in oil he had harvested from puddles in the swamp. They would need food too, and on second thought, extra clothing. Lato had mentioned injuries, so they would need some linens for bandaging.

He was loading the sacks of provisions into the basket when the sound of mounted troops became audible. Lato came dashing from the house, and Mason had to laugh.

"Right on time."

Lato shook his head and grinned as he followed him into the basket. Mason leaned over the side. The rope tying them down was pulled taut. He sliced through easily, and they were off.

They crested the tree line. The wind caught them, going east for once, which meant a storm was coming. Mason didn't mind. At least they were going the right direction. He looked down at the soldiers who had forced entry to the house, but none thought to look up.

"Thank God the wind is going the right direction," he remarked.

Lato nodded. "Do you have any weapons on here?'

"A few knives. Did you all lose your staves?"

"Yes, about that! Were they supposed to—do—like that?"

"I take it they worked, then?"

"It was like a magnificent shield around us."

"Perfect!"

"We raised them to fight, and then it did—that. We had no idea what was going on."

"They weren't finished yet, but you needed to have something on you, just in case."

"How did they work?"

"Well, that might be a long story…"

19

Twenty-Three positioned himself in front of Atila before Seventeen pressed the button to release the locks on her shackles. She gasped as her arms dropped to her sides, the stiff muscles protesting against gravity. Twenty-Three didn't help matters as he quickly locked her hands together in a new pair. The metal chafed against the electrical burns on her wrists, but she couldn't resist a smirk. They were treating her like a wild animal, and she could take a compliment. Twenty-Three glared at her insolent expression, then shoved her back while ducking out the door. It slammed shut, and the bolt clanged.

Now unmounted from the wall, she went to see how Rati was doing. They had both remained quiet since Lato escaped. She wanted to check his bandage, but her chains were too short to untie it. "How are you feeling?" she asked instead, settling herself beside him.

"I'll be healthy as you in a couple days," Rati answered, his voice sardonic.

"What do you mean?" Atila asked sharply. "You need to rest and heal before you try to get your strength back up."

"Don't kid yourself." Rati placed a hand on Atila's arm. "Their queen is coming. Her plans involve both of us resting—in the ground somewhere."

"Lato escaped, Rati." Atila's chains jangled as she stood up and began pacing. "We can't give up. Not until we meet God himself."

"That's what I'm afraid of."

Later that morning, the door opened again. "On your feet!" Four held the door open, flanked by several under his command. "Let's go. Her Majesty has arrived and will see you now."

Atila stood, rolling her shoulders. "Must I wear my decorative bracelets for the occasion?" She cocked an eyebrow. "You wouldn't want your queen to think that you can't control me without chains, do you?"

Twenty-Three glanced nervously at Four, who smirked. "On the contrary, I think Her Majesty would like to see that we use the resources she has made available to our advantage."

She shrugged and walked towards them. "It was worth a shot."

Four's shoulders barred the door. "Her Majesty wants to see all of you."

"But Rati can't move. In his condition, it could rip the wound back open."

"Oh, he's coming. But she wants to see *all* of you." Seventeen came into view. "I challenge you to deny us information again."

"Challenge accepted." Atila raised her chin.

"I'll let you two refuse her in person, then." Four motioned towards Rati. The other soldiers entered the cell, heading for the man in the corner. Atila darted toward Rati but one of the soldiers spilt and intercepted her.

Rati clenched his jaw and watched the soldiers come. All three soldiers had to help in getting him to his feet. He let them do all the work. Even when they reached a standing position, he let his gaze wander, then slumped against Fourteen. The soldier stumbled while the other two recovered their hold on the injured man.

"You can't possibly expect him to walk like this." Atila hated how fragile Rati looked. The soldiers thought they could hurt him however they liked, then expect him to function without warning? "Let me help him."

"Absolutely not!" Four declared.

"Why not?" Twenty-Three asked, slacking his hold on her chain. "It might work faster than this." He motioned to Rati, who flopped between the guards as they tried to hold him up and push him forwards. They could not do both at the same time. Four released his annoyance by glaring at Twenty-Three for questioning a superior. The soldier immediately agreed with him, though there was a touch of sarcasm in his tone. "You're right, Commander. She'd probably hoist him on her back and run."

"She'd run straight into the fence, the way her friend did." Four watched her reaction. "You didn't think he got away, did you?"

She knew he had gotten away, otherwise the guards would have been gloating about it. On the contrary, all of them seemed jumpy, and

Twenty-Three was downright funny. That is, if she could think about things like that when they were probably going to get executed. No, first tortured. Then executed.

"Men! Stop wasting my time. Just grab a limb, each of you, and drag him out."

The guards let their cargo slump between them. Two and Six each grabbed a foot while Fourteen took the arms. Rati let loose a groan this time. Atila twisted over her shoulder to watch as he was carried behind her. He didn't even try to hold his head up.

They were led through the camp and toward the fence. Seventeen used his fancy glove to activate the panel beside the only gate. For a brief moment, they were out of the gates, out of the shadows—but they were hustled into the next building so quickly, she could hardly glimpse the sky.

20

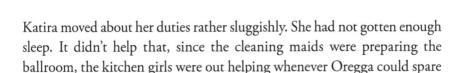

Katira moved about her duties rather sluggishly. She had not gotten enough sleep. It didn't help that, since the cleaning maids were preparing the ballroom, the kitchen girls were out helping whenever Oregga could spare them. Even the rag she was using to clean the hallway candelabra felt heavy.

She did not remember much from the night before. After hearing someone behind her, she had run like a frighted deer through the woods. Two words had been shouted: "Wait. Stop!" Then a loud crack had sounded, and the chasing footsteps had stopped.

Curiosity had almost made Katira turn around to see who it was. The male voice had not been the voice of a stranger. But the animal instinct of fear had driven her on, on, back to the castle. The water level in the moat had risen and was splashing over the roots, making them extremely slippery, but she had gripped them with all her might and had made it across. She had no idea how she had managed to get back up through the window, but it didn't matter now. All that mattered was who had seen her. Why had he sounded familiar? And why had he seen her? Was it someone from Biatre who had seen her sneaking out and decided to follow? Or, more likely, was it someone from Taklin, sent to spy on her in person?

"Kati!"

She jumped. Bridget was standing there.

"Are ye even listenin' to me?" Her hands were on her hips as she shook her red curls exasperatedly.

"What were ye sayin'?" Katira asked. She hadn't heard a word.

"Ugh. 'Tis no use to repeat it now, ye would still be deaf to it. What's the matter?"

"I've a lot on my mind, 'tis all." Katira resumed wiping. The dust was difficult to get out of the intricate carvings.

"Who is it?" Bridget asked, a grin blooming over her face. "Come now, do tell!"

Katira couldn't help the smile that creased her lips as she shook her head. "Oh, Bridget, if ye only knew there are more important things in life than handsome groomsmen!"

She gasped. "Ye're calling them handsome now?"

"I was repeatin' yer own words to make a point: a point that ye obviously missed."

"Oh, Kati, ye know I don't understand yer big words. They make no effect on me." She spun around, laughing. "I'll get us fresh water, then we must talk more of these things."

Now it was Katira's turn to roll her eyes while the younger girl skipped down the hall. "Bridget, if ye only knew…" she whispered to a candle as she put it back in place, then moved on to the next one. What would Bridget do if she knew? If, right now, Katira were to tell her all, what would her response be? The thought almost made her laugh aloud at the last night's events. The girl would probably be speechless for the first time in her life.

Footsteps sounded from up the hall. Katira glanced up, expecting another servant to bustle past, but instead it was the king of Biatre! Her brain instantly clicked as it matched the voice from last night to the man walking toward her. Her heart skidded and her knees went shaky. She continued to clean, but it was impossible now: underneath the crown, beneath the black hair, was a large bruise. Right on the forehead. The same type of bruise that she imagined would come from running into a low branch in the woods while chasing after a suspicious person at night.

"Does it look that bad?"

Katira's heart wanted to give up. This was crazy. She turned around and curtsied. "What are ye referrin' to, Yer Majesty?" She refused to make eye contact but knew that he was scrutinizing her.

"My shoes."

Her mind was now completely off balance. "What?"

"I am sorry, I was merely being sarcastic. The nasty mark on my forehead. Do you think the princess will find me horribly repugnant?"

King Derek being like this—almost speaking to her like an equal—made Katira feel either like a complete fool or rather significant. He was joking with her! Using sarcasm! Her brain was all tangled up, but after he put all this effort into making conversation, he deserved an honest response. She took a second to compose herself, then said, "I have heard, Yer Majesty, that wounds can actually increase attraction, depending on how they are gained." She could not keep her smile completely hidden. Was she going mad?

He took a moment to respond. "I suppose so. Thank you. A woman's perspective on these things is very appreciated."

Bridget bounded back into the hallway, carrying her bucket of clean water. She pulled up short, blue eyes wide, then dropped into a curtsy. She sidled up to Katira and began to work diligently on the light fixture, rubbing vigorously over the same area as if there were some difficult spot there. Katira risked a glance up at the king. He had a half smile on his face as he watched Bridget scrub the imaginary spot. Then he looked at her again, and Katira seen a flash. It was as if his eyes elicited a white beam that arrested her own if she dared make eye contact. Then he was gone, down the hallway.

"Kati, is that it?" Bridget had stopped working now and an impish grin slit her face, revealing unashamed crooked teeth.

Katira dipped her rag in the bucket, wrung it out, and moved to the next candelabrum. She began to wipe it down, one golden arm at a time, then glanced over to Bridget. It was unusual for her to stay silent for long. "Is what it?"

Bridget began to hop up and down. "It's the king, isn't it!"

"What is?"

"Ugh! The one ye've been moonin' over all day!"

Katira dropped her rag into the bucket. "Listen to me, Bridget. Not everything is about romance! Maybe I had a crazy uncle who I recently realized looked like King Derek, okay? Stop trying to turn everything into a love story!"

Bridget's mischievous smile fell from her face. Tears welled up in her eyes, and she ran from the room.

A hint of annoyance flitted across Katira's emotions but was quickly replaced by regret. Why did she do that? The cameras would have picked it up. Miss Director would register it as being defensive and would love to try to turn it into a love triangle. *Who would the king choose? The lowly servant girl with a secretive past or the beautiful princess with a peace treaty?*

She splashed her hand into the bucket and wrung out her rag as tight as it would go, then viciously cleaned the candelabrum arms one by one. It looked like she would be finishing these alone.

Alone… loneliness… not alone… God. Great. She had just been such a brat. Why would He help her now?

21

Derek continued down the hall, heading to the garden, where Taroki was probably having his breakfast. Any servant could have been sent to get him, but Derek needed to get moving. Fresh air would probably be good for him, too. His head still ached. The bruise was quite obvious, judging by the reactions he had gotten. Gerald had not believed his story of a nightmare that ended with hitting him falling out of bed and hitting his head on the side table. The servant girl hadn't asked, but she had been confused, to be certain.

He exited the main castle and entered the courtyard. He turned a corner. There was Taroki, framed by flowers, sitting at a small table with his breakfast. He looked up and stopped mid-sip of his tea.

"I would say good morning, Taroki, but I fear it is not entirely true."

"Sire!" Taroki's mouth was open, eyebrows furrowed in concern. It was the same face he had made the time a younger Derek had fallen out of a tree while supposed to be doing his lessons. He placed his cup and saucer back on the table. "What happened to you?"

"Which story would you like? The truth I am not so sure of, or the story I will need to tell the princess?"

"Both, if you please, Sire."

Derek motioned to the food. "Please, continue eating. I did not mean to disturb you."

Taroki obediently resumed.

"Last night, there was a girl on the training grounds."

"A girl?"

"Yes. I thought her perhaps a servant turned spy, so I followed her."

"By yourself."

"Yes. She was small and could have done no harm to me."

"Had you been discovered, it could have been enough to drive away Her Highness the Princess."

Derek frowned. "Taroki, I have avoided scandal these two-and-twenty years. I will keep that reputation."

"I am sure, Sire. Proceed."

"I attempted to follow her through the woods, but she was as elusive as a ghost. Then she began to sing."

Taroki watched the expression on his king's face. It was distant as he recalled the memory of the night before, beholding another figure entirely than that of his princess.

"Then she began to speak, or rather murmur, or mumble, but there was no one else there. I got nearly close enough glimpse her face. Then I stepped on a branch, and she froze. For an instant, I thought for certain that time had stopped." The memory held Derek in its trance. "Then she jumped up and ran away."

"Where did she go?"

"I am not sure exactly. All I know is that she was a good deal shorter than I, and managed to duck under a horizontal tree trunk faster than I could."

"That is where the chase ended?"

"Yes."

"But she did not come back to injure you."

"I don't believe so." The thought sobered him. "It would have been easy enough, though, had she intended harm."

Taroki drained the last of his tea and stacked his dishes together. "So either there is a non-violent, female spy who likes to sing while running loose in the woods at night, or Your Majesty's imagination needs a new outlet."

King Derek shook his head, a wry grin visible for a moment. "I am not sure, Taroki. But see to it that extra guards are put on tonight. And warn them to be vigilant."

"Yes, Sire. Another thing…"

"What is it?"

"I believe we need to find a way of covering your... blemish... before your princess awakes."

"Ah, yes, I did sleep rather late. Is she not up already?"

"Neither of them are. In fact, one of the maids that Her Highness brought along was downstairs as I came through. She was getting hot water, I believe, and said they would likely sleep for quite a while yet."

"Then we have some time to conceal the proof of my adventures. But how?"

"I shall go see what I can find." Taroki bowed and headed back to the castle.

Derek followed him inside, but found himself wandering aimlessly after being left alone. The passages were silent, but he liked them better than the large rooms that always felt empty. These instead were filled with painted eyes that watched him in the light of the windows. He studied a few of the portraits: grandfathers and great-grandfathers, gazing sternly as something just beyond the artist. They all appeared so regal, so confident. Derek wondered if they had always been like that. Of course, he knew better, but the way they looked, one would have thought they were born to carry a kingdom on their backs.

22

Queen Vivian straightened the crown on her head, enjoying the feel of its weight. The two remaining prisoners—the injured one and the girl—were being brought into a newly erected building, outfitted with the extra cameras she had brought along. The soldiers had destroyed most of theirs in the burning of that little village.

She would be doing their interrogation herself. Hopefully Miss Director would be able to use some of the footage. Maybe they could pin the fire on them! The other prisoner escaping certainly made them look more suspicious. If only he hadn't managed to do so where it wasn't monitored. It would have made a great scene.

But there was a greater problem. These three had spoken of God. The mere thought was enough to rise her hackles. When she and her brother had first discovered Biatre while cruising on her private yacht, she had been delighted at their welcome. The island was amazing. It had stayed frozen in the medieval ages, but there was no mention of any deity. Finally, there was a civilization who did not depend on divine powers. It was refreshing, really; but more than that, it was perfect.

They had managed to pass as visiting royalty: she, with her hair freshly styled and her favourite cover-up dress over her swimsuit, was obviously a queen, and her brother, wearing only cut-off jean shorts, a servant. He had protested, but what else could they do without spoiling the illusion?

She had secretly texted her husband that if he or the kids needed to reach her, they could text his brother in law, whose phone was on mute. She then video-called her favourite producer and hid her phone behind one of the portraits in the throne room. The few hours of footage they had gotten were incredible. These people were actually stuck in the past, and she could document it—turn it into a reality show, with no one the wiser. It had been perfect.

But now these prisoners could ruin it all.

Two soldiers came to get her for the grand entrance. There was Four, her commander, and Seventeen, the technology expert. They walked in front of her as she swept into the interrogation room.

The two prisoners were shackled to their chairs, facing away from the door. She rounded them slowly, her dramatically layered skirts billowing around her, taking her time to examine them. The girl held her head up, but the injured one sat slumped in his chair. She took a glance at their faces, then turned to Four. "So, these are the ones that have such a reputation? I must say, I'm unimpressed."

Four took it as an insult. His force had suffered several injuries during the capture of the three young people. "We have weakened them, Your Majesty. They are not nearly as strong as they were before."

She tilted her head. "And yet one got away."

"He tried, Your Majesty."

Ah. So this was the angle they were taking. "Hmm. Now, get the injured fellow out of here. I want to speak with the woman."

Twenty-Three and Thirty-Seven picked up the chair he was chained to and placed it down outside the door. The prisoner remained entirely unresponsive. She could not tell if he was conscious or not. The soldiers returned.

"Now you may leave as well." The other soldiers were out looking for the one who got away, and it would not do to have an empty camp. Besides, interrogations were much more compelling with the fewest possible present.

Four looked surprised and unwilling, but it was Twenty-Three who spoke up. "Your Majesty, are you sure you want to be alone with her? She can be dangerous."

"I thought you had weakened them."

"They are weak, but not broken."

Four tried to mend the situation. "We reserved that pleasure for you, Your Majesty."

"Thank you. I most appreciate it. Now, leave me." She motioned them away, and they all turned to go. "Oh, and... Four," she called, with a touch of high and mighty condescension, "Please guard well. I don't want another one getting tangled in the fence."

He could not leave fast enough. She loved being the one who signed his paycheques.

"Oh, men," she sighed. "So useful, and yet so stupid."

The prisoner—Atila, her name was—shifted in her seat. She was on edge. Perfect.

"I'm sure you know the feeling," she continued, walking around her. "But they do have a way of getting things accomplished, and a few of them are quite nice to look at too. I'm sure you've noticed." She could see that Atila's resistance was fading to boredom. But she would be thinking that this vain rabbit trail was the queen's usual train of thought. This meant that she would be more susceptible to anything Vivian announced. She needed to believe her friend was dead. "It was a shame to see that other fellow lying by the fence. He looked like a really handy one."

Her head jerked. She wouldn't make eye contact, but she was listening.

"His face was all twisted, though, so he wasn't very handsome. But I guess anyone looks like that when they've been left hanging on a fence with electricity flowing through them. A shame, really, because his hair looked nice, and he had a good amount of muscle even after those soldiers decided to starve you all."

Atila sat silently, and at first Vivian wasn't sure if she was buying it. Then she took a shaky breath. "I want his body back." Her voice was rough and scratchy.

"Trust me, dear, you don't want him now." She toyed with her bracelets, jangling them back and forth.

"Lato deserves a proper burial."

Oh, yes... the body. "I'm afraid that I was disturbed by the sight, and ordered the soldiers to have him incinerated."

Atila pressed her trembling lips together. "Then, could I at least... see the spot where he fell?"

Vivian had been working on her sympathetic expression, though it didn't matter much, because Atila wouldn't look at her. "Isn't it hard enough to know that he is dead?"

"I want to—to touch the ground that held him during his last moments. I want to envy the place that heard his final words."

Pathetic. This was going to be easier than she had expected. The girl was perfectly heartbroken, and she knew how to capitalize on it. "Of course, my dear. But you must understand that a soldier, as inept as he may be, must go with us. I can't have you running off."

Atila's chin lifted, and the defiant expression returned with a spark. "And you think that a soldier, inept as he may be, would be able to stop me if I tried?"

The queen stiffened. The prisoner had called her bluff. If she were to insist that a soldier were to come along, it would invalidate all her previous claims. Atila would no longer believe her friend was dead. "Good point, my dear. Let's go together, shall we? Four! Get in here and free her from her seat."

23

The bruise on Derek's face was masked by a concoction of items that came, from all places, the kitchen. Oregga had mixed a paste from oil, flour, and ground spices, then massaged it into his tender brow. The pain had been worth it. He no longer looked like a schoolboy who had gotten into a scuffle.

He reached the large staircase when he met King Rosseen coming out of his rooms.

"Good morning, my fellow king!" the fat man shouted. "What's for breakfast?"

"I am sure something delicious," replied Derek with a fake smile.

With the amount the man had eaten the night before, there was no way he was hungry now. He still seemed eager to get to the dining room, though, passing Derek on the way down; then he turned and looked back. "What are you waiting for?"

"Would not the fair princess like to join us as well?"

"Pricilla? She never eats this early. Come!"

Derek followed begrudgingly. He took the steps down one by one, glancing up at the large picture hung on the wall across: a portrait of his parents, newly crowned and married. They too had come to the throne early.

He entered the dining room. Rosseen was already sitting in the place he had been given the previous evening. Once Derek joined him, Taroki walked out from the hidden door with the two other manservants behind him. The third in line stopped when he seen that the princess was not there and made a hasty retreat.

Once the meal was over, the two kings—one very happy with a full stomach, the other rather sick—walked together down the hallway.

"So, what do you usually occupy yourself with, Derek?" King Rosseen reached up to throw an arm over his host's shoulders. "Surely in such a peaceful little kingdom, there is not much to worry about."

"In the mornings, I usually train with my guard," King Derek replied. "Even though our contact with others is limited, one never knows what the future holds. And it is wise to keep a trained force nearby at all times to deal with lawbreakers."

"Ha! Lawbreakers! Where?"

Something in Rosseen's tone rubbed Derek the wrong way. He decided to not mention the attack on Ferbundi. "Though we cannot always see them, Rosseen, they always exist. Would you care to join me for some sport?"

"No, I will leave that to the young and energetic," he replied, patting Derek's shoulder.

Derek was relieved when he seen Taroki standing at the end of the hall. He ducked out of the awkward embrace and gave orders for Taroki to arrange for a comfortable seat to be erected for the visiting royalty. Taroki nodded and hurried off, and they continued their walk.

They reached the back door of the castle. A guard standing there saluted and opened it, revealing the training ground already filled with a hundred soldiers marching in neat form. To the side was a little area adorned with two soft chairs and small waiting tables.

"Now, if you don't mind, Rosseen, I must change my attire but shall return swiftly. Have a seat. The servants can bring you any refreshments you desire." He didn't like leaving him alone. It made him nervous. The little eyes watching him from behind the fat cheeks weren't evil. They were just beastly, lacking mental or moral restraint, like a man who knew no boundaries on what he should or shouldn't have.

King Derek had to admit, though, that surely Rosseen had no idea what an inconvenience he was being. There was no way for him to know that there had been an attack on Ferbundi.

"His kingdom must be small or well managed by another," he explained as Gerald helped him change. "There is no way that this man, as concerned as he is with himself, is ruling other people and they have not rebelled against him." Gerald simply nodded and agreed until his king was prepared for his exercise.

Derek exited and nearly bumped into Pricilla herself. "Princess!" he exclaimed. It was obvious what had taken her so long: she was stunning. The rose-coloured dress she was wearing fit her exactly. A delicate necklace hung around her collarbone, matching both the dress and her perfect lips. Her eyes—were looking right at him. Sparkling. Blue. Like the ocean right after sunrise.

Her lips curved as she looked him up and down as well. "Good morning, Your Majesty." She curtsied.

"Oh, please, call me 'Derek', Princess."

"Then good morning, Derek."

The king opened his mouth to reply but halted for a moment, bracing himself against stuttering. She spoke first.

"Where are you off to, dressed this way?" She was looking him over again, taking in his loose white tunic, tan breeches, and the sword at his side.

"I was going to—to ask you if you would like to watch this morning's exercises. I am afraid there is no—not much to entertain a lady. Anymore, that is."

"I suppose there hasn't been much need for it since the passing of your mother." She gazed into his eyes. "I am sorry for what happened. It was all so sudden; first your brother, then your parents a few years later, and you, so young, to take on such a huge responsibility."

Derek tried not to let his face show the impact her words made. Not a day went by when he did not think of them, but it was always inside his head, where no unsympathetic soul could intrude. To have someone else say it, like a simple, solid fact, was like prying a festering wound open farther. But the way she said it seemed like she was actually sorry for him. The way she was looking at him…

Her eyes widened. "I should not have brought it up. I beg your pardon, Derek." She looked at him with watery eyes, then blinked quickly, as if embarrassed. Moving closer and taking his arm, the princess tilted her head up towards him and allowed a smile to grow again. "I would love to watch your exercises this morning."

The guard was in good performance. They went though a series of drills, then full-fledged combat exercises. King Derek found himself torn between dramatics and distraction. He frowned every time he realized it. Why? But then the princess would catch his eyes, and she would smile, or raise her glass to him, and he was lost again.

"Princess, I do hope you are enjoying yourself," King Derek said as he walked arm in arm with Pricilla a few hours later. The garden was lovely, and the blooming flowers hopefully masked the scent of the powder Oregga had re-applied for him.

"As it so happens, I am, though I am accustomed to a little more entertainment."

He chuckled at her audacity.

She smiled back at him. "But I cannot blame you for that. I do appreciate your time and company, for I am sure they are dearly bought."

"This morning, I had messengers go out to tell the folk that they would have to operate peaceably among themselves for the day; my visitors were of such high importance that I could not spend my time judging their grievances today."

"That was so thoughtful of you."

Derek changed the subject. "Tell me, princess, are you fond of dancing?"

Her eyes lit up. "Oh, yes. I consider it one of life's chiefest joys."

"Would you then consider an invitation to our ball this evening?"

She opened her mouth, then dimmed. He was confused.

"Who will be attending?" she asked. When he didn't respond immediately, she explained, "I haven't seen anyone else of importance here. I know there is no other royalty, but no nobility, no gentry? Are there perhaps dukes, or mayors of other villages travelling here for tonight?"

"No..." Derek trailed off, entirely surprised at the direction this conversation was going.

"Wait." Pricilla stopped walking, pulling Derek to a halt as well. "Will the peasants be attending?"

"No. Yes!" Derek stammered. "But they are good folk: well mannered, decent. Is there a problem, Princess?"

"It's... it's just that I've never attended a ball with commoners," she explained lamely.

"Why not?" The king could feel himself growing defensive. This was a practise his parents had held for as long as he could remember. "Every month we hold a feast for those who served the month before, and their spouses and any older children. This means that everyone who will come tonight will have been in the castle, one out of three months, nearly their whole lives. They know proper etiquette, and don't you agree that even royalty must stay on good terms with their subjects? Besides, they are people too, who enjoy a good evening." He hoped she would at least try to see his point of view.

"I don't know, Derek." She bit her lip and looked at him again with bewildered eyes. "Would you mind terribly if I went to my room? I've a sudden headache. Hopefully it will be over in time for the ball."

"I hope so too, Princess." Derek knew she was using this as an excuse to get away and think. "I'll escort you to your rooms."

24

Queen Vivian led her prisoner out the door. They walked past her injured friend, who barely acknowledged them. She wondered if he could even walk. Would Atila try to run without him? The other one had taken his chance. She stopped by Seventeen.

"Give me the control to the cuffs, then run ahead and put my cameras on the fence."

"These are battery-powered. The current isn't as strong as the wall-mounted set."

"It will have to do. Hand it over."

He obeyed, unstrapped the buttons from his glove, handed it to her, then hurried into the building to get the cameras. She glanced back at Atila, who had her head tilted towards the sunshine, soaking it in. She looked almost peaceful… till she opened her eyes again. Vivian turned to hide a smile as she continued. She seen Seventeen scurrying away from a section in the fence and decided that it was good enough. She stopped, holding out her hand. "Here is the humble place that holds the sacred memory of your friend," she announced solemnly.

The girl stared a long moment, uncomprehensive, then her dry eyes widened, she shuddered, and collapsed to the ground. "Why?" she screamed, her voice hoarse. "Why Lato? Why did you take him, God? I needed him!" She sat on the hard ground, shaking as she sobbed.

Nodding with success, Queen Vivian relaxed. This was working exactly as she had hoped: Atila believed Lato was dead. She was heartbroken, vulnerable, and beginning to doubt the entity she had believed in so strongly before. All of this was in Her Majesty's favour. Soon, this God would be forgotten again, and all would be as it was before: in the profit margin. She sighed with satisfaction, then drew her eyebrows together in kind sorrow as she placed a hand on the girl's shoulder. "My dear, it will weaken you to weep this long. You should compose yourself before one of the men sees you like this."

"They are no men," Atila retorted, her voice hiccupping. "They are beasts! How else do you explain this cruelty?"

"I am sorry I was not here," the queen responded gently. "I must admit that I have pressing business in Taklin that I should not have left, but when I learned what had happened here, the king himself could not keep me away. I wanted to meet you, for I admire your courage—to fight so valiantly against the men that oppressed you. Your boys were said to be fairly good fighters too, but I am sure they would not have been so successful without you. Why, you have survived longer than both of them! Now please, dear, dry your tears before the soldiers come to check on us."

"What do you mean, survived longer?" Atila glared at the ground. "Lato died for a cause he believed in, but I remain with a chance to deny it. And Rati is not dying. And why should I care if the soldiers see me like this?"

Her statements were delivered in rapid succession. *The ploy worked too well,* Vivian thought. *Now the girl can't think straight.* She would give her something else to think about.

"Well, a man is nothing without a woman. I'm sure that I could work out a deal with one of the soldiers—the commander, perhaps—and you could have all the freedom and power you desire. Simply by letting him have your hand. It wouldn't be that hard, would it?"

"The price my hand comes at is too high for even the commander to pay."

Her defiance was great, her wording impeccable! Seventeen had better have turned the cameras on—this scene was too great to miss.

"Not only freedom and power, but luxury, wealth, and connections… your own mansion and servants, access to my court—what more could any beautiful young woman want? Once you get what he can offer, dispose of him and live however you like."

79

Still sitting on the ground, Atila shook her head, but her voice wavered. "Nothing comes at such an easy price."

It was time to put her cards on the table. "What I am offering you is far greater, and cheaper, than what your God has offered you."

Atila shook her head again, but this time it was firm. "My God has offered me eternal rewards: something you never could. You know, Jesus died for your penalty too. He is willing to forgive you, and that is worth so much more than power."

Was she serious? Vivian's lip curled. "I don't need forgiveness from someone who doesn't exist. I'd much rather have power now." The button was easy to press. The girl crumpled in on herself and shook. Vivian released the button, and she lay still. She wondered how strong the current actually was. Then the girl stood up.

Atila stared at the queen, and Vivian felt her confidence crumble as the prisoner straightened. Her eyes were dry, and all pretence was gone. "I gave you the option. You made your choice."

Vivian fumbled with the glove, but Atila moved like a cat. Vivian tumbled to the ground, cursing dramatic petticoats and fabulous high heels all the way down. The wind left her body, and she vaguely felt something happening to her wrists.

When her eyes allowed colour to seep into the sky again, she knew it was too late. Her wrists were chained with Atila's shackles, and she was gone with the remote.

Then a shadow seeped over the blue and white of the sky. She struggled to sit up. Was that a hot air balloon?!

25

Rati sat in the sunshine, probably more physically comfortable and mentally aggravated than he had been all week. The soldiers nearby were ignoring him, nervously watching the building where Atila and Queen Vivian had disappeared. Oh, if only he had his full strength. It would be so easy. That is, unless there were other men in the camp that were not out searching for Lato. As it was, he would wind up in chains again, with a bigger wound than the one he had now.

What could he do? He looked around as if trying to see an idea somewhere. Lato was probably in the balloon that just crested the edge of the camp. Atila was probably challenging the queen. Wait—balloon?

"When I was sinking down, sinking down,"

Rati began under his breath. He didn't know a lot of songs, but it was something. Twenty-three glanced his way.

"When I was sinking down, beneath God's righteous frown,"

He continued louder.

"Christ laid aside his crown—"

Four backhanded him across the face. Rati whipped his head back and stared at the soldier.

"For my soul."

He felt a grin creep up as he defied the commander, only increasing his volume.

"To God and to the Lamb, I will sing, I will sing.
To God and to the Lamb, who is the great I AM.
While millions join the theme, I will sing."

Seventeen and Thirty-Seven were watching him now too. The balloon got closer, but no one was watching the skies. They were staring at the prisoner gone mad.

"And when from death I'm free, I'll sing on, I'll sing on."

He was almost shouting the lyrics now.

"And when from death I'm free, I'll sing God's love for me.
"For all eternity, I'll sing on!"

He ended on a triumphant note as the middle of a long rope was flung out of the balloon overhead. The U-shaped noose tripped Thirty-Seven and Thirteen. Lato came repelling down from one end.

26

As soon as he was on the ground, Lato threw a punch at Four's face, then withdrew his knife and sliced off a section of the rope. He lassoed Seventeen and Thirty-Seven, tying them together. He threw their trussed bodies against Twenty-Three, who yelped while being crushed to the ground. Where was Four?

Lato spun around. The door was closing. He grabbed for Seventeen's glove, punching the buttons on it. A muffled sound came from behind the door and it stopped halfway. Lato yanked it open. Rati, hands released, had fallen to the floor. Four's hands were returning from the place his radio should have been. He levelled a punch at Lato's gut, followed by another one to his cheek. Lato grunted and stumbled back but then Four tripped. Lato rolled, using the momentum to launch himself back to his feet. Four hit the cement floor. He immediately tried to rise but Lato brought the chair down on his skull. Rati clambered up from under Four's legs, grabbing Lato for support as they ran from the building.

"Come on!" Lato shouted, grabbing for the dangling end of the rope. The balloon was well past them now, and the wind was picking up. "Rati, let's go!" He began climbing up hand over hand.

Rati had the rope in his hands, stumbling along, but Twenty-Three tripped him from behind. He landed hard.

Lato heard the commotion and dropped himself back down as the basket swung wildly overhead at some sort of impact.

"Sorry," Rati groaned, getting up again. Lato caught him with one arm, locking wrists, and the rope with the other hand. A torch flew past

Rati's ear. A yell sounded from behind them. Lato gripped the rope as tightly as he could. He couldn't climb one-handed, but maybe he could just hold on…

The balloon slowed dramatically and lowered almost to the ground. They tumbled headfirst into the basket. Master Blackwell was there, loading more torches onto a rack beneath the inflated sail. Atila! She didn't even glance his way as she tied down the ends of two large slits in the balloon. It sealed the hot air in again. They slowly started to rise.

Twenty-Three's grunting was replaced by the click of a gun.

"Don't shoot!" demanded Seventeen. "The queen wants them alive!"

Atila settled down more comfortably. "Hallelujah."

Master Blackwell and Rati joined her on the floor responding with, "Amen."

Lato remained on his knees to peek over the basket's rim. The Spider and most of the soldiers were out, ironically hunting him down elsewhere, but Twenty-Three must have freed the other two soldiers. Seventeen had his radio in hand, shouting as they ran. Four was nowhere to be seen. The three soldiers chasing them on foot would not be able to keep up. So, until they ran out of fuel, they could relax.

Lato turned to Atila. "One word," he said, as if scolding her. "One word. How?"

She shrugged, though clearly pleased with herself. "I grabbed the controller from the queen." She held up her burned but free wrists. "I gave my shackles to her and threw the controller over the fence. Then I chased you guys, climbed up the ladder on the side of the building, ran across the roof, and jumped into the basket."

Master Blackwell tried to frown. "And then you cut a hole in my balloon and let all the hot air out."

"Only some. And I fixed it." She motioned to the sail flap that she had tied back. "See? And we couldn't have picked you guys up unless I hadn't." She leaned back against the basket wall, a smug smile on her face.

"How are your feet, Atila?"

She looked quizzically at Mason. "My feet are fine, why?"

He motioned at her burned wrists. "You were electrocuted, right?"

"Yeah, that word sounds familiar."

"Good. If your feet are fine, that means the electricity didn't have to exit your body as forcefully. Remember those iron strips I put in the soles of your boots? They let it pass right through you."

"Oh wow. That's neat."

He read her expression. "I take it that it still hurt. I am sorry; my improvisations here aren't their best. I brought along some bandages, though, so I can wrap up your wrists, and Rati, what happened to your stomach? Oh. I'll do that first. I've got an extra tunic in here, too."

27

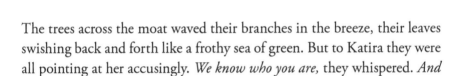

The trees across the moat waved their branches in the breeze, their leaves swishing back and forth like a frothy sea of green. But to Katira they were all pointing at her accusingly. *We know who you are,* they whispered. *And we both know who followed you. Now it's only a question of when he finds out.*

"It's always been that question," Katira reminded the wind as she dumped the contents of her cleaning water into the river below. She hopped off the barrel and crate to the dirt floor of the work yard, heading back to the kitchen. The door opened before she reached it and Bridget came out.

"Hello, Kati," she said rather coldly, then passed by her.

"Bridget!" she called after her. "Wait."

She turned, drilling Katira with a hard stare. Her words had a bitter tone. "Of course I am mad at ye, Kati. Don't worry about it. Everyone knows how short-tempered I am. I'll get over it. Until then, leave me be." Bridget headed towards the garden.

"No." Katira stepped in front of the younger girl and put her hands up on her shoulders, looking straight into her eyes. "Bridget, I was wrong, and I'm sorry. I don't want to wait until you get over it. It was my fault, and I want to make it right."

Bridget's eyes suddenly went shiny, and she blinked away the tears that threatened to spill out. Katira dropped her hands, wondering if now the girl would expect endless patience for her foolishness.

"Why are ye so good to me, Kati?"

"What do ye mean?"

"No one else would have said that. Why are ye different?"

Katira ducked her head. "I don't—I don't—" but she did know. She was trying to please God. But the cameras had audio receptors. "I'll have to tell you later."

Bridget grabbed her hand. "Let's get to the garden before Oregga see us standin' out here. I'm supposed to get green onions and celery and thyme for the stew tonight. Benjamin is tryin' somethin' new again."

The matron who tended the herb harden with her daughters looked tired, as usual, but when Bridget told her what they had come for, their hands worked skillfully. Katira helped, but Bridget was busy smiling and waving at Nick, one of the groomsmen, until their aprons were filled with the greens. They hurried back to the kitchen.

"Dump those over there with Benjamin's group," Oregga directed.

The rest of the morning was spent in preparing for the ball. They needed to feed the regular crowd of two hundred—the soldiers and servants on duty, hence the stew—but today they also had to prepare for the averaged five hundred guests.

Thomas and Benjamin were not pleased. They were of French decent and enjoyed creating delicacies in small serving sizes. These nights, though, they had to please a crowd.

Women from the village whose men were currently on duty were called in to help, so the normally spacious kitchen and work yard were full. The laundry cauldrons were replaced by cooking pots, and all the counters inside were surrounded by women cutting, slicing, and chopping all manner of fruits, vegetables, meats, and cheeses. Katira enjoyed these days. She thrived in the hectic energy.

"Nancy, if ye cut the pepper around the neck, ye can pull out the whole pith with all the seeds at once. Kati!" Oregga gratefully spotted her second favourite runner. "Go ask Thomas if the bread is ris'n yet."

"Yes ma'am." Katira turned in that direction, but pulled up short to avoid a collision.

A girl held out a bowl of chopped radishes. "Where do these go?"

"In that corner." Katira pointed. "Benjamin will tell ye." She circled another cluster of women to get to Thomas, but as she passed, one of them stepped back and knocked her directly into the chef. The lump of dough he was kneading fell off the table, but Katira grabbed it before it could touch the floor and handed it back.

"Sorry, lass," the woman said, then turned back to her onions, raising her apron to wipe the tears from her face.

Katira handed the dough back to a flustered Thomas. "Is it ris'n yet?"

"Does it look like it's ris'n?"

"Oregga wants it to be."

"It'll be soon enough."

Katira managed the treacherous trip back, but Oregga was no longer there. She followed the sound of a sharp scolding to find the supervisor outside by a cauldron of heating water. Apparently the three women washing dishes were not doing it well enough. She approached her from behind but was intercepted by a stable boy.

"Could ye point me to the woodpile?"

"Aye, it's just outside the gate, across the bridge, there." She pointed to a guard standing near the stables. "He'll show you."

The mood in the work yard only intensified as the day progressed. Everything was crazy while being perfectly organized, and Katira loved it. She felt purposeful.

28

As it turned out, King Derek could have spared some time for his people during the afternoon after all. King Rosseen was napping, claiming that watching such a young, energetic man had worn him out, and Princess Pricilla was in her room with her "headache". Nevertheless, he would take advantage of this time to himself.

He walked down the hall to the library: the centre section of one of the towers, devoted entirely to books. His mother's favourites were kept in her private collection, but the collection of knowledge kept here was more suited to what he was looking for.

Derek craned his neck backwards to look up. There were two stories of bookshelves filled with the annals of history, agriculture, strategy, maps, transportation, wildlife, astronomy, and nearly every other topic under the sun. He knew what he was looking for, but he didn't know where to start.

A cough caught his attention. An older man with spectacles was bowing from behind a desk covered in parchments, inkwells, and quills. "Your Majesty, welcome to the library. Is there any way I may be of service to you?"

"Thank you, sir. Could you direct me to the histories of our interactions with the royalty of Taklin? Or any other literature pertaining to their ways and customs?"

"Of course. Right this way, Your Majesty." He led King Derek to a section with several volumes stacked together, each one with a year embossed on the spine. "I believe we have only been in contact with them for the last two generations, starting with year 357. Then again in 358,

360, 363 and 365." He began pulling out the tomes as he named them. "Do you want 368 as well? When they invited your parents instead of coming to visit?"

"Yes, thank you." Derek took the volumes from him and headed to a private desk in the back.

An hour later, Derek still had not found much that was particularly interesting in the annals. The ball that he was holding later today was the first that any from Taklin had attended here; they were used to fancy dinners, guided tours, and private parties while visiting. Perhaps she simply was not prepared for the idea. It did not seem this was the custom in Taklin at all: they were used to guests of the nobler sort. This annoyed Derek. How could the princess be so sweet one moment and the next be turning up her nose at those he associated with?

An idea sparked in Derek's head. "Taroki?"

His advisor looked up from the opposite side of the desk, shutting book 358. "Yes, Sire?"

"Could you send for that maid, the one who came from Taklin some years ago? Perhaps she could shed some light on this matter."

"Of course, Sire."

"Oh, and send a message to Princess Pricilla with one of the other maids. Ask if her headache is any better, and if there is anything we can provide for her."

"Yes, Sire."

Shelves divided the private study area from the rest of the library, but Derek didn't use the solitude to study any further. Instead, he watched the spot where Taroki had disappeared from, mentally listing his questions, hoping that she would be able to answer a few of them.

She wasn't dimwitted. He had only seen those brown eyes a few times before, but they had had so much life in them. She seemed like one who observed everything in the world around her, and once she was certain, she would contribute. But if she was so clever, why was she a kitchen maid? Perhaps this interview would settle that question as well.

29

Katira was heading back from another trip to the garden when she noticed the strange commotion. The king's advisor was walking towards the kitchen. The people in his immediate vicinity stopped in their tracks, unsure of whether to ask him what he wanted, or bow, or ignore him and work very hard. She had to smile when she seen Ned and Nick, who were obviously trying to do all three at once. Katira watched him glance over the crowd when his eyes snagged hers. He changed his direction, and Katira's heart fell. She could feel the blood draining from her face. Her hands began to shake, threatening to drop the corners of her apron and deliver the fresh basil leaves to the dirt floor.

"Are you the maid from Taklin?"

"Aye, sir."

"Then come with me."

Katira looked down at her apron full of leaves, but the ever helpful Bridget was by her side in an instant. She and Sasha emptied Katira's load and she was left with no excuse.

Taroki headed up the servant's staircase into the castle.

The king figured out who was in the woods. I'm going to be tried for trespassing. I'll look like a spy. I'll be tortured for information.

Katira's heart hammered. Taroki took a few turns she had never seen before, but the wall ahead was now curved. That could only mean he was taking her to the tower.

Her memories went deeper, filling her heart with ice and despair.

Pricilla told King Derek who killed his parents. Rosseen seconded her story. I'm going to be killed. It's over.

Taroki opened the door and ushered her in. It was not a torture chamber. Instead, there were books... books, hundreds, thousands, of books. For a moment, Katira's situation faded in the awe of so many stories, the work of so many hands. Then confusion swept back in. Why was she wanted here? He led her around a bookshelf, and there, behind a simple wooden desk, sat the king himself.

She curtsied. Waited. Kept her head down. Opened her mouth.

"How can I serve ye, Yer Majesty?"

"I am looking for information. Please, take a seat... What is your name, Miss?"

This is a strange place for an interrogation.

"My name is Katira, Yer Majesty."

"Miss Katira, you served in the Taklin castle, if my memory serves me correctly. In that time, did you personally serve the royalty there?"

Only once. I personally handed your parents the poison that sent them to their graves.

"Not often, Yer Majesty. I worked mostly in the kitchens, as I do here."

"Did you ever come in contact with Princess Pricilla?"

Wait... Pricilla? Is that what all this is about?

"Never in personal contact, Yer Majesty."

"But I am sure servants talk; is there anything you could tell me about her personality?"

How much dared she tell him? If he was already decided and she told him the truth, he could accuse her of trying to ruin the princess. But if he was already decided, why would he have asked her?

The person he seemed to be deserved the truth. She took a deep breath, lifting her head so that her words would be clear. "She is very beautiful."

"I know this, I can see it. But what are her interests, her motivations? What can I do to entertain her while she is here?"

"You do not understand. Her interest is beauty. Her motivation is to not ever lose it. To entertain her, you need only gaze."

King Derek frowned, and his voice sharpened. "You do realize that your words could be viewed as disrespect and therefore treason, correct?"

"I do." The fact that he was still listening said something, though. It said that there was a chance he believed her. She could not let that slip. "Your Majesty, what could I gain by insulting the princess? Only a noose. There is no motivation for me to say this unless it was the truth, and in your favour to be aware of."

The king leaned back in his chair. "Good point, and well made," he said, surprising her. "I will take it into consideration. Tell me, do all the servants in Taklin speak so eloquently?"

Not only was the king ignorant of her past, but he believed her statement... and was that a compliment? She smiled and ducked her head. "Only those who wish to, but most do not know the difference between eloquence and bein' longwinded."

He smiled too, then returned to the main subject. "What does she think of her subordinates?"

"They are just that: subordinates. She is not accustomed to think of anyone as her equal."

"What does she think of religion?"

"She does not care for it. Her mother strongly believes it is a waste of time."

"Curious."

Indeed.

"Does she read a great deal?"

"Not much, from what I remember."

"What about hunting?"

She is so vegan I don't think she would even pet an animal.

"There is a reason she does not eat meat."

"Horseback riding?"

"She is terrified of the beasts."

"Viewing a play?"

"If the theme is romantic."

"Music?"

"If she is the one singing."

"Dancing?"

"That she enjoys."

He ran out of questions. It was probably a lot to take in.

"Miss Katira, if you don't mind me asking, why do you look so perplexed?"

Katira looked up without meaning to. "I do not intend to disrespect you, Your Majesty, but why are you asking me?"

His eyes were the colour of ice, but they were not cold. They were confused. Had no one ever asked him about his motivations before? Or did he not know them himself?

Katira asked the question that had plagued her since he began his. "Would she not be better able to inform you, not to mention that you would get to know her, rather than only what she likes? Then she could get to know you in return, and so build a relationship?"

"I did not want to look the fool by suggesting anything she did not fancy," King Derek admitted, leaning forwards. "Also... now, you are under royal secrecy here, but... I find it difficult to speak with her face to face. She is simply so..."

30

"Beautiful?"

"Yes!" he agreed, then startled. The girl was leaning slightly forward, gazing at him with a sparkle in her deep brown eyes, and he realized that he was confiding in her. "That is all for now," he said in a much colder tone. "Thank you, Miss. You may go."

Her eyes showed a flicker of disappointment before she looked down again. She stood from her seat and curtsied. "I hope I was of service to ye, Yer Majesty." Then she left.

A cough sounded from his right. "Sire?"

"Yes, Taroki?"

The advisor moved to take his seat again. "What are you going to do with this information?"

Derek adjusted his quill so that it was perfectly straight alongside the neat stack of empty note paper. "I don't know. Firstly, is she a trustworthy source? Did you hear her accent change?"

"Now that you mention it, I believe I did. Her voice became more smooth and sweet when she was using 'eloquence', as you so bluntly put it."

"I was merely trying to startle the truth from her. Is that wrong?"

"Perhaps not, but you did induce her to be quite comfortable, then sent her away suddenly."

To hear Taroki put it like this made it sound like he had used the girl. He opened his mouth to respond in defence of himself but thought—perhaps he was right. Why had he told her about the way he felt around the princess? He adjusted the quill again.

"Sire, if you don't mind me asking, why do you look so perplexed?"

Derek jerked his head up. The wrinkles around Taroki's grey eyes had deepened. "Are you mocking me?"

"Of course not, Sire. But, if we conclude that she was startled enough to speak the truth, what do you think of her insights on the princess?"

"To go by what she said, the princess I am nearly betrothed to is naught but a perfect example of vanity!"

Taroki's voice quieted. "And do you have any evidence to the contrary?"

He thought about the question. "Nothing tangible, no."

"Sire, I have a suggestion."

"I am eager to hear it."

"I believe that this maid, Katira, was telling the truth. She was willing to risk her neck for it, which means she could be a useful asset."

"But—"

"Sire, I believe you should put her in a place together with the princess. We shall see if she continues her ideas when both parties are present."

"That has sense to it, Taroki. But they are not equals; she would not be able to express herself while, for example, serving tea."

"Sire, is not the ball tonight?"

"Aye, Taroki. But I cannot use ask her to come out of rotation. It would be unfair and show a marked preference."

"I do not believe she is in the rotation, Sire."

That was true. Actually, she probably hadn't ever left the castle, or even had a day off. She had been brought as a slave, which meant she had no family in the rotation who would be invited to the balls. He had never though of that before—the girl was alone here. Prince Adhemar had brought her as a 'gift' right after the king and queen of Biatre died overseas, his warped mind proving itself in his twisted generosity. The girl had blushed furiously in humiliation, but after the prince left, he had assured her that she was to be treated decently. Then he had forgotten her until today.

"You could claim that she has served well and is now to be integrated into the system of honour that is granted to any who serve in Biatre."

Derek nodded. "Aye, that is perfect, Taroki. She seemed quite capable with handling herself in conversation, and this is the only event where she could be considered near a rival to the princess. It will be a perfect scenario."

"Sire?"

"What is it, Taroki?"

"Sire… what will she wear?"

He hadn't thought of this. Of course, she would have nothing fitting the occasion. "Mother always had those women help her. Hire them for the evening but keep them in the servants' quarters. I do not want to see them."

"As you wish, Sire." Taroki bowed and left to make the necessary arrangements. King Derek rose to his feet, inserted his books back into their places, and exited the library. The afternoon was waning, and the ball approached. Gerald was ready for him when he got back to his quarters and began the tedious process of sprucing him up for the evening ahead.

31

The afternoon drifted on, as did the balloon. The scenery was beautiful: the grassland was getting rockier, the bushes turning into trees. Master Blackwell put the last few torches into the tray, glanced at the soldiers below who were falling behind, then gazed out at the horizon before turning back to the interior of the basket. He chuckled. The three had fallen asleep on the small floor, piled on top of each other in the cramped space. He poked Lato, who was at the bottom of the pile, with his boot, and waited for them to stir.

"Take a look at these mountains."

"They're beautiful," Atila remarked, yawning, combing through her short, messy auburn hair with her fingers.

Her graceful movements were not lost on Lato, who stared for a moment before turning to the mountain range as well. He cleared his throat. "Are we going to make it over?"

Master Blackwell shook his head at the two young people with their backs toward him: warriors, the rest of the kingdom would consider them. They were so young for this burden. "I added the remainder of the fuel I brought from home. It will get us over the peak, or rather between the two of them, depending on the wind. The reverb should keep us from crashing into them."

"Then what?" Rati looked up at them from his spot on the floor.

Atila and Lato glanced at each other, then turned to their leader. "He's right, Master Blackwell," Lato agreed. "We've been so focussed on getting out of the prison that we never thought about…"

"We didn't expect to get out of there," Atila explained. "Do we go live in a forest somewhere, or what?"

"They would eventually find us," said Rati. "There is nowhere we could hide forever. And what about that army? They weren't just here for us, were they? I mean, they did burn down an entire village."

Lato nodded. "The people of Biatre are in danger." The soldiers had turned back but were still a threat. "We need to warn them."

Mason agreed, solemnly. "We need to tell the king."

"What are we all telling him?" Atila asked.

"What do you mean?"

"Well, we're telling him about Ferbundi. And the Taklin army. But are we telling him about us?"

Rati frowned, seeing her point. "Because it was our fault."

Lato disagreed. "They could have said that to throw us off."

"But why would they imprison us then?"

"I don't know."

"My point is, if Taklin is attacking Biatre, they have the right to know why."

Mason nodded. He liked these kinds of discussions, where they had to figure things out for themselves. Then his eyes popped back into focus. "Children! The mountain!"

Lato and Atila whirled around while Rati strained to see from where he sat.

"We're going to crash!" Lato turned urgently, grabbed a sack of supplies from the floor and tied its straps around his waist.

"Master Blackwell, you said the wind reverberation from the mountain would keep us from hitting it!" Rati exclaimed. "So what's the matter?"

"It's gotten too strong. It'll hurl us into the rocks before we can change direction. We might have to abandon balloon." He took a coil of rope from the floor and fastened into the side of the basket, then handed the rest to Lato. "Lasso one of the trees!"

The wind was much louder now and seemed intent on smashing them into the mountain face.

Lato tied a noose and flung it out, but the wind threw it off course. He tried again, and again, but it refused to catch. Atila fastened another sack of supplies to her own waist while Mason helped Rati stand up.

Atila's eye caught Lato wrapping the rope around his hands. "Bad idea!" she hollered above the gale. He glanced at her and their gazes clashed as he jumped over the side.

"What are you doing?" Rati yelled, but Atila had already tied the last rope to the opposite side of the basket. She gritted her teeth. Stupid or not, he wasn't doing it alone.

The trees rushed up to meet her as she plummeted downwards. The rope pulled taut to where she had wrapped it around her wrists, jerking her spine, then a thud knocked the air from her lungs.

32

Lato knotted the end of his rope around a large nearby trunk. It had been a long piece, and he was grateful. Soon it would pull short and snap, though; all it would do was slow the balloon down for a bit. Then a crash sounded in the trees ahead—Atila? She had followed him! He dashed towards the sound, and it continued. She was being dragged through the trees. Was her length not long enough to reach the ground? Lato flew ahead and climbed up the limbs of a sturdy oak while she tumbled along. He braced his left leg against a branch and planted his right foot on a lower one, leaning that leg on the trunk behind him. As his own rope pulled to its end, Atila hurtled at him. Her body slammed into his. He grabbed the rope above her hands and held on while the balloon fought. Why wasn't she scrambling to get her footing? Then his own rope snapped, and in the second before this one was pulled along again, he grabbed the knife from his belt and slashed it. He had just severed the last link they had to the balloon—but that didn't scare him as much as watching Atila tumble to the ground below.

33

She had had been recorded. The realization hit Katira as she was going down the stairs. Oh, great. Now what? The king had been right. Her words could easily be interpreted as treason. Would they expose her now? Or let her suffer for drama's sake? Why not kill her and let it be done and over with! She didn't want to die, but maybe it would be preferable to the wait.

And the king had mentioned religion. Queen Vivian hated any mention of God. *Castles in Time* had always been anti-theistic. What would happen now?

The sunshine outside seemed too bright, the bustle too loud, to be real. Had the last half hour been simply a bizarre daydream?

Bridget bounded up to Katira the instant she seen her. "What was that about?"

Katira should have known better than to hope it had all been a nightmare, or that at least it was a secret. Everyone had seen her leave with the king's advisor, and everyone would want to know what happened.

"Ye know that I came here from Taklin. His Majesty the King wanted more information about the princess."

"Ye got to speak with him?" Bridget looked nearly ready to burst.

"Aye, and he seems to be mortal like the rest of us."

"Aye, but a mortal with a crown!"

Katira laughed and brushed past her on the way back into the kitchen. "Ye're hopeless, girl!"

Two more hours passed in the wonderful frenzy of the kitchen. Then a finger poked Katira's waist. She jumped and whirled around. "Bridget! I told ye not to—" she cut off short. Bridget was there, dancing on her toes, but Oregga was behind her, arms folded. "Aye, ma'am?"

"The king issued a new tradition today."

"Oh?"

"Those who do not have a family to attend the ball with will be allowed to attend every third one, startin' today, in rotation with the others."

"Ye mean..." Katira grabbed onto the counter behind her to keep from falling.

"Ye're goin' to the ball tonight!"

What could she say to this? It was an entirely unexpected turn of events. She wasn't prepared, she had never been to an official ball before, and... "What do I wear?"

Oregga scowled. "Ye're goin' to go?"

"Would it not be rude to refuse?"

"I suppose. Just be back in the kitchen by midday tomorrow, y'hear?"

This made her smile. Oregga was going to miss her. "Thank ye, ma'am. But wait—" another thought occurred to her. "What about Nelda? Is she goin' too?"

"We were just goin' to ask 'er."

"But—"

"Kati, quit yer stalling if ye want to go. There are some ladies here to help ye get ready. Don't keep them waitin'."

Katira turned obediently and headed towards the servants' quarters. This really felt like a dream, but it was far more pleasant than any she had ever had. She was going to the ball? There were ladies here to help her get ready?

The usually drab apartment was unrecognizable now. At least three of the beds were covered in tulle. Two more of the beds were occupied by women. One was surrounded by shears and thread, the other with palettes. A third was poking metal rods in the fire.

All three women looked up when Katira entered.

"Let me measure, then ye go wash while I adjust the dress," she first woman said. She cut lengths of string around Katira's body, humming to herself while her long fingers worked. "I'll have to shorten the hemline. Tighten the waist, too."

The bath was a room that Katira usually only got to use every couple days but she loved it. Hot water had already been poured for her... this was so strange. After scrubbing all the kitchen smells off, she washed out her hair and would have soaked for a minute had not the voice of one of the women warned her that she was about to come in and help. She jumped out and pulled on a slip, then was surrounded.

"The hair definitely needs to be trimmed."

"She has such nice eyebrows!"

"Too bad her ears aren't pierced."

"The colours will go so nicely."

Katira watched the three women in amusement. The last time she had been fussed over like this was when she had made the worst decision of her life. Hopefully, that wasn't the case again.

"Shai, ye need to get that hair out of her face so I can work with it," one woman finally said.

Shai ushered Katira over to the fire, where several metal rods were now on the hearth. She took a pair of shears and asked, "Ye don't mind, lass?"

"I suppose not, but please leave it long enough to go into a braid afterwards."

Shai seemed disappointed, but she went to work. Snippets of hair fell till the floor around Katira was covered in chunks of brown locks. A while ago it would have made her sad, but this past week had been so chock-full of surprises that now she was waiting to see where else it took her. Then Shai picked up one of the metal rods.

"What're ye doing?"

"Curlin' yer hair. Ye know, I'm a hairdresser from town. Ye've naught to fear from me." She set about to prove her words. Soon Katira's face was surrounded by ringlets, with a pile of them on top of her head.

Then Brielle painted her face, and Jeanette buttoned her up in a gown. One of them produced a hand mirror, and Katira gasped when she saw herself. The elaborate hairdo framed a beautiful face, albeit not one she recognized, with defined eyebrows and long lashes and darkened lips. The dress was a rich chocolate brown. The skirt was full, the tulle ruched and bunched with matching silk flowers tucked into the folds. There were no sleeves, and Katira felt self-conscious over her bare shoulders and collarbone. The bodice was tight around her waist, stitched with tiny seed pearls, and came up high enough to satisfy her propriety. To be completely honest, she was stunning.

"Thank you," she managed.

Shai, Brielle, and Jeanette all smiled back. "It's been a while since we've all gotten to work together, ye know," Shai said.

"We used to work for the queen," Brielle explained, "But not since—well, ye know. Now we all have our little shops up town. 'Tis not the worst thing, but when the king asked if we'd like to do a work on a girl in his service, we couldn't say no!"

"Did the king say why he extended this courtesy?"

"Nay. But ye will be late! Hurry along, child."

"Yes, but what about Nelda?"

They looked at each other. "I only brought the one gown," Jeanette said.

Then the door flung open. "Nelda's not—Oh! Kati! Ye are beautiful! Oh, my, ye have worked wonders on my dear friend! Kati, this is lovely! I wish I had a dress like this."

Katira laughed. "Is Nelda coming?"

"Nay, she has"—Bridget swooned—"a previous engagement. I was goin' to tell ye earlier, but I was busy. Ronald asked her to walk with him later, so Oregga let her go early."

"Oh." All three women went back to their own piles of supplies.

"Aye, but it does not matter much, for after they have climbed the mountain, he will take her to the balls with him and she need not go by herself."

"How are ye so sure they will climb the mountain?"

"Kati, why must ye be so dimwitted about such things? Of course they will, and probably soon, too. But now. I came to tell ye. And ye look lovely. Tis a shame that ye did not get to go with next month's group, for that is when my family will attend. Now go, have fun, and meet some handsome young men!"

34

"I cannot believe they did that." Rati shook his head in frustration and sighed.

The balloon rounded another corner between the mountains, now going slow enough to avoid the gigantic rocks. The wind bouncing off the slopes kept them moving forward through the pass.

"But of course they would. Of course they did."

"That they succeeded in slowing us down enough to make it through is more surprising than the fact that they both jumped off to try," Mason said. "I did not think it could be done—" he cut off as there was a close call with a large rock formation jutting out nearby, but they swirled past it, and he relaxed again. "Safely, that is."

"That is the issue. Whether it was done safely or not, we don't know!" Rati got to his knees, slowly so as not to tip the basket or hurt himself more. He peered downwards but could see nothing amidst the trees and rocks that filled the pass. "What if Lato and Atila are both dead down there? We need to get off this balloon!"

"I've already removed the torches," continued the rational voice. "That will let us down gently. If I open Atila's flap, we will crash into the mountains for sure. That is what Lato and Atila were trying to avoid."

"I know." Rati slumped against the basket wall, rocking it. "What can we do till we land? I've done enough quiet contemplation in that cell to last me a long time."

"I suppose it depends on what you were contemplating. Did you ever just think about the goodness of God?"

"Of course, but I have to admit, I couldn't really see it there. Why did He let us get captured? All we were trying to do is help an old woman, and He let us get captured for it?"

"God didn't let—"

"If God didn't let us get captured, then what happened? We weren't exactly on a picnic. This gash in my stomach isn't from a trip on a walk. Isn't God in control?"

"Of course He is."

"Then where was he when I was bleeding on a cement floor?"

Mason gazed at his distraught pupil, the narrowed brown eyes demanding, nay, daring him to give an answer. He turned away to look at the majestic scenery. The wind blew gently between them. Finally, he opened his mouth. "Someone had to make those mountains."

Rati looked out at the view himself. He wanted to believe it—he had thought he did. But now nothing was making sense.

"You are worried about Lato and Atila," the older man continued. "The emotions we feel could not have come out of thin air. Those were created, just as we were. The Creator gave us the same compassion He has for us."

"Then why does evil exist?" Rati challenged. "Why does God have to make Himself so hard to find?"

"Evil exists because God gave all of us a choice. He didn't make us as machines, to follow His every whim. Yes, we can handle life better if we do, but from a choice of love and devotion, not force. And we can decide to refuse that." Mason turned towards his pupil again. "Also, God is not hard to find. You simply have to look for him."

35

The world was a blur. A rather pleasant blur, with spots and swirls of bright colours. Rich greens and browns were all around. Above were speckles of blue. Beautiful blue, that blinked and was gone, covered by green, then peeked out again. Atila knew this was a dream. It was too wonderful to exist.

A dark something appeared that refused to blend with the liveliness around it. Whatever it was, it was blocking her view, and it was very annoying. She lifted her head to shift her position and see better. Or tried, rather. Her head wouldn't move. She attempted opening her mouth to say something, but it wasn't working either.

"Atila! Can you hear me?"

How did this person know her name? And why was he—for it was a he—holding her head down? He was pressing way too hard, it hurt!

She tried again. "Let go of me," she groaned.

"Shh. Lie still. Don't move."

"I said let me go." Her own voice was so quiet.

"I'm not even touching you, Atila. You had a little fall; you're going to be fine."

How did he not understand? "You're hurting me."

"Atila."

Something warm and heavy landed on her shoulder: his hand, she guessed. The pressure in her head was different. Her next breath almost choked her from the water flung in her face. She snorted and coughed, tried to sit up but failed. The swirls disappeared, leaving an unfamiliar forest around her and Lato in front of her—"Lato?"

He looked relieved. "Yes."

Atila relaxed her tense muscles, trying to ease the throbbing that was taking them over. The water trickled down the side of her face and into her hair. "What happened?"

"You jumped out of a balloon," Lato explained wryly, untying the length of rope from her hands.

She gasped when he moved the finger Four had stepped on. "Of course I did."

"Yes, but you didn't trust yourself to hang on, so you tied up your hands. The knot was too short for you to reach the ground. You hit a branch."

"Only one?"

"Well, a couple. Then I cut your rope, and you fell. The balloon escaped too."

Yes, that was what had happened. "Did they make it through?"

"I think so, but I'm not sure." Lato tied the water bottle shut and tucked it back in the sack on his belt. "We'll have to go check the mountain face to find out, and it'll be a way to go yet."

"I can walk."

He put his hand on her shoulder again, stopping her from trying to get up. "Wait a little longer and rest, then we'll go."

She submitted, and every part of her body thanked her for it. The ground actually seemed quite comfortable.

36

Lato resisted the urge to lie down beside her. He had napped enough on the balloon, and they were not safe. Twenty-Three, Seventeen, and Thirty-Seven might have given up the chase, but they were probably only waiting for their Spider, horses, and reinforcements to get back. They knew which direction the balloon went; soon the whole mountain would be crawling with soldiers. But they were not going to get anywhere while Atila was in this shape. It was better to wait a while, then move faster.

Leaves rustled beside him and he jerked his head around. It was only a squirrel darting from one hiding place to another.

"Lato?"

He jumped, then chided himself again. "Yes?"

"Will you let me get up now?"

"I suppose." He held out a hand, and she took it. She groaned but was standing in a few seconds. "How do you feel?"

She rotated her joints and stretched. "Like I escaped a prison, jumped from a balloon, swung from a rope, slammed into a tree, and crashed to the ground. After getting whatever-Master-Blackwell-called-it the day before."

"Electrocuted?"

"Yeah." She grimaced as she inspected her wrists, the bandages Master Blackwell had put on completely shredded.

Lato hadn't noticed his own hands until now. His wrists were fine, but his palms were rope-burnt and bleeding. He shook them out and rejoined, "Funny—I'd be worried if you felt any different."

Atila turned in a circle, looking around at the trees that closed them in. "Which direction is the mountain face?"

"Uphill," he replied, leading the way.

37

The balloon jolted as it scraped against the ground. Still caught in the wind, the sail kept going and pulled the basket along for a while before tipping it. Rati and Master Blackwell were dumped onto the hard ground. They watched it meander farther and farther away, till the branches of a tree arrested it. The sail slowly sank as the last bit of hot air reached regular temperature.

"That was a little more exciting than I had planned for my test flight to be," remarked Mason. He stood up and gathered the supplies from where they were scattered. Only two skin water bottles and the already opened sack of food were left.

"Well, if Lato and Atila are alive, they certainly won't be going hungry," Rati said as he hauled himself upwards. Mason immediately offered a hand of help, but Rati brushed it away. He grimaced fiercely, but not a sound escaped his clenched jaw as he stood. After a few steadying breaths, he stilled his wavering body and lifted his eyes again. "Which way now, Master Blackwell? If Lato and Atila are fine, we waste time going back; but if they are injured and we go on, it could be their death."

"The wind no longer pushes us along; we must choose our own path now," he replied. "What do you think, Rati?"

"I want to go back and help them. Not that I am much use right now, but I could be, if…" he trailed off, not wanting to think of the shape they would have to be in to need his help.

"What about our purpose then? The king needs to know what is happening to his country."

A scowl grew on the young man's brow. "How would he accept messengers that would abandon their closest friends?"

"How about a greater love, for the unaware? I pray that Lato and Atila are all right, but if they are not, they could not better die than in the hands of God and return to their Creator."

Rati could not believe his ears. "You would leave them behind? Do you want to leave me here too, then, so you can make better time on your way to the king?"

"I cannot help them. They are far enough away that, if they sustained life-threatening injuries, they would be dead by the time I got there. If they are alive, they can fend for themselves better than three of myself could.

"But I can help you. Come with me, and we will begin the journey as a twosome. With God's blessing, we will end it as a foursome."

Rati took a deep breath and exhaled it all at once. "No."

This time it was Mason who was astonished. "What did you say?"

"I am sorry, but I will not follow you on this path, Master." Rati stared back at him. His loyalties were being torn in two separate directions, and both choices seemed logical in this scenario. Was there a right path?

Mason shook his head. "I should have brought four sacks." He wrapped a few pieces of bread and dried meat into a handkerchief, then stuffed it into one of his pockets. Handing the rest of the sack and the skin bottle of water to Rati, he said, "God keep you safe."

Rati nodded. "Thank you, Master." He turned and limped towards the mountains.

The old man watched him go with a mixture of pride and sadness. It was incredible how much the children—no, they were not children anymore, even though he liked to think of them as such—how they had grown in character as well as body.

"God keep you safe," he repeated.

He began walking west, towards Larte, allowing his memory to distract him. It was more than ten years now since he had lost his wife and stepdaughter. The loneliness had tortured him, every night bringing their sweet faces to the forefront of his mind, reminding him how much he missed them. Then one day while in the Ferbundi marketplace, he had caught a boy stealing apples.

It was a scrawny little boy who upended the table, grabbed a fruit, and dashed before the shopkeeper could catch him. Mason, in the right place at the right time, grabbed him by the scruff of his shirt. It tore, but he grabbed the boy's arm. He glared up at him and aimed a kick at his foot. Mason held on till the shopkeeper came around her stand and took hold of his other arm. She began scolding, but Mason shushed her. He thanked her for helping him and how much did the apples cost? She answered. He asked her if the coin he had on him would do. She exclaimed that yes, it would do very well, for half a sack, if he wanted. The boy quit struggling when Mason told him the apples were his. He let him go.

"Would you like a job?"

The boy's head raised slightly, his protective grip on the bag loosening. "Doin' what?"

"I need someone to take care of my orchard while I am busy. How old are you?"

"Ten." The shoulders went back, knees adjusted to stand rather than flee.

"And what is your name?"

"Lato."

And so, he had a companion. With proper food and attention, Lato grew like a weed. When he wasn't tinkering, Mason taught him about God, how to read and write, and, as a precaution, how to fight.

It was three years later when they found a girl. She was bruised and facing off with a larger, well dressed boy who held a piece of bread above her head. She made a move to grab the food with her left hand, but he moved so that she missed. Then she brought up her right fist against his nose. He howled and dropped the bread. She picked it up, and he kneed her in the head. She fell back, still clutching the bread.

Before Mason could intervene, Lato ran past him and tackled the boy to the ground. They rolled in the dusty road, growling, punching, and grappling for advantage. It took Mason and the nearby tanner a struggle to separate the two. He scolded both. Lato folded his arms defiantly, but the other boy only pouted. His father came out of the tailor's shop then, and Mason braced himself for the parental rage to come, but the man just motioned for his son to follow him and strode away without a word. Lato then defended himself and his actions while he and Mason chased the girl, who had dashed down an alley. They cornered her.

"What did ye do that for?" she asked, spitting blood from a previous hit onto the road. "Now he thinks I can't defend myself."

"You didn't want *him* to beat you up, did you?" Lato asked, wiping his own blood off his forehead.

"He'll just pick on me later again." She shrugged, still holding her piece of bread in her fist. "Thanks, but I gotta go. Don't need no charity."

"But—" Lato looked up at Mason, who nodded with a bemused smile. "Do you... need a home?"

Again, the little street urchin was suspicious, but they brought her home with them, and soon Atila was part of them.

Rati came nearly two years after that. Lato and Atila found him in a ditch, more malnourished than they had ever been. They pleaded with Mason to take him home with them, and he relented. It meant a bigger orchard, he said, and they were all right with that.

He enjoyed teaching them. They had days working in the orchard, days bent over books, and days training with makeshift weapons of his own designs. Who knew when Vivian's regime would go too far? No one knew like he what she was capable of. But those types of regimes always fell, and a few extra warriors could make the difference. They would be ready when that day came, he promised himself.

Now they would be put to the test.

38

"Thank you, God, that Jeanette gave me flats instead of heels," Katira muttered quietly as she approached the line of guests entering the ballroom. They made way for her, and she inserted herself into the flow of well-dressed people. There were so many faces she had never seen before! All her life in Biatre had been spent behind the stone walls of the castle. There were so many friendly smiles to return and greetings to reply.

Then she reached the doors. Every family walked in together, stood at the balcony as they were announced, and then made their way down the stairs. Katira would be walking in alone. The footman asked her for her name, and for a moment she considered giving an alias. Of course it would be useless. Everyone she had to fear knew who she was. She gave her name and stepped out as it was announced.

"Miss Katira of Biatre!"

This could all be a setup for the most dramatic revealing possible. She might as well go as regal and unforgettable as possible. She waited for a moment at the balcony, summoning every idea of grace while taking in the ballroom.

It was huge. She had never been in it before, not even to clean. And it held so many people. More than she had ever known her whole life, even in the orphanage. *If only they could see me now,* she thought, then realized, *they do.* She felt the smile slip from her face as she took another glance around. There was the open area meant for dancing, now full of people mingling and watching the new arrivals. There was the servants' entrance where Bridget was disappearing into after replenishing a dish in the array of food. And there, yes, there were curtained alcoves where she could hide in once she tired of the unaccustomed enjoyment, or simply to avoid making a fool of herself in front of the cameras. But she had to get down there first.

Katira started down the marble steps. Another step. Another step. She could not trip. And she didn't!

Folk were getting in line for the treat-loaded tables now, but there was no way Katira could eat. Musicians were in a corner, some playing softly while others tuned their instruments. Music was something she had not heard since before Biatre, and to hear it again… the sounds drew her toward that corner. A pianist was dancing his fingers up and down the keys while a flutist swayed to the piercing tones of her instrument. The melodies had not been written for each other—Katira could tell that they were both in different time and keys—but somehow, they complimented each other, taking turns rising and falling, weaving in and out. It was beautiful.

"Excuse me, Miss?"

Katira whirled around, her skirt taking its own time to follow the movement. There was a tall young man there, looking quite sharp in his military uniform, with blond hair neatly combed. He looked her over once but met her eyes again, smiling. He seemed quite friendly. "Yes, sir?"

He bowed. "Might I have your first dance?"

"Of… of course ye may, sir."

He immediately moved closer and took her gloved hand, kissing it. "I shall be honoured to have such a beautiful lady grace my rude hand. Say, shall we sit together till the music begins?" He began to guide her to one of the shaded alcoves along the wall.

Katira's heart thudded once. Enough to let her know that something wasn't right. She stopped. "If ye don't mind, sir, I enjoy watching the musicians from here."

"But the view will be much better from a cushioned seat," he insisted. She tugged her hand, which he had not let go, to test the waters, but he held firm while advancing to the curtained bench. "Ye will not deny me the pleasure of gettin' to know ye better, will ye, Miss?"

"I am sorry. It's simply—this is my first time at a ball. I'd like to meet others as well."

His expression fell. "I see how it is. I am the one to be sorry, Miss. There are many finer than I to pass your evening with."

"No, sir, it's not like that. I suppose it is only until the first dance, and there will be many."

"Wonderful!" He proceeded to lead her on.

Katira glanced over her shoulder once. There was no one nearby but the distracted musicians. She had watched enough drama to know what went on behind curtains in ballrooms, but perhaps this man was merely being friendly. Hopefully so.

39

The ballroom was not extremely crowded, but it certainly felt like it when one was hemmed in on three sides by jovial villagers and the other side by a fat king.

"A fine night for a party, Derek! These tidbits are delicious, and the wine magnificent! And say, these commoners of yours clean up nicely, do they not? I said to my dear Vivian before I left that…" and so he continued. Was the fellow really dimwitted enough to not know how annoying he was?

"Rosseen, did the princess inform you if she was well enough to attend this evening?"

"No, she didn't. She has a mind of her own. Mind you, it's a good mind, but she is like her mother. She doesn't usually miss a chance to dance, though…"

At the top of the stairs, people were still coming in. Family after family, soldiers and servants with their spouses and older children, dressed in their finest, smiling brightly, streamed in and swept down the stairs. Then a pause happened, and a single figure came to stand at the railing. It took a few moments for Derek to recognize who it was.

"My dear King Rosseen, if the food is so good, I suggest you have your fill before it is gone," he muttered by way of excuse while starting in the direction of the landing. When he got there she was gone. Now he hoped the princess would arrive so he could see both women together. If he could not go to Ferbundi and solve matters there, he would solve problems of his own here. Now, where had she gone? There was quite a crowd around the tables, King Rosseen included. He would look elsewhere first.

The dance floor was quite empty except for those just arriving. Only one young man was walking away from the food. It was a young soldier, who would no doubt be interested in a woman he had not seen before. King Derek followed him, and there she was.

The color brown had always struck him as drab before, but the gown on the young woman was fabulous. It fit her perfectly and set off her glossy curled hair. She was facing away from the crowd, swaying slightly to the musicians' opening pieces. The officer approached her.

"Your Majesty!"

Derek turned to see one of his personal guards from last month standing before him with a lovely woman on each side. The one was older and obviously his wife, but the younger was suppressing a smile and turning a bright pink. "Officer Warren. How do you do on such a fine night?"

"Wonderfully, Your Majesty. My wife and I would like to introduce to you our youngest daughter, Marita."

"How do you do, Your Majesty?" she asked, curtsying.

"It is a pleasure to meet you, Marita." He bowed over her hand and kissed it. Her perfume was very sweet. "I hope you enjoy the ball tonight, and many more to come." He bowed to her mother. "Lady Warren." The ladies curtsied again and walked away, but the father stepped forwards and began to speak in a quieter tone.

"I know you have a princess visiting, Your Majesty, but if you were to consider one of your own people, they way your father did, Marita would make a fine wife."

"Of that I am sure. And I hope for all your sakes that she will be swept off her feet tonight by a man who will be as good a husband to her as she a wife to him. You had best go watch her and see that the man suits your approval, Officer Warren." That sufficed. The man walked away, and King Derek set his sights on whom he had come after.

The young officer was leading her towards a seating area along the wall. She motioned to the musicians, but he insisted on leading her away.

"Yer Majesty!" Another voice interrupted him.

"Good evening, Officer Shaphan."

"If ye tire of dancin' with the beautiful princess later, I'd be willin' to take her off yer hands."

Derek smirked. "Aye, if she will take the likes of you."

Shaphan laughed too, then headed to the tables with the rest of the crowds.

He was out of the stream of new arrivals now, and there they were. The girl glanced over her shoulder towards the crowd, and Derek instinctively understood the look. He caught up to the pair.

"Officer Glen."

They turned, breaking the hold he had on her hand. Officer Glen dropped into a bow, then saluted. She curtsied.

"Miss Katira."

"Good evening, Yer Majesty," the officer replied.

"I see you are quite pleasantly engaged. Would you mind terribly much if I steal her from you?"

Officer Glen did not look too pleased, but he couldn't exactly refuse his king. "Of course not, for ye, Yer Majesty." He bowed again and left.

Now how was he supposed to begin a conversation with the lovely young woman in front of him? *Hello. Are you lying to me?* That was out of the question.

40

Katira wasn't sure if she was allowed to speak first, but she did anyways. "Your Majesty, you just drove away my first dance."

"Would you mind terribly if I provided a substitute?"

Her hand flew to her mouth. A warning flashed through her brain—something Brielle had said about touching her face making her look nervous—but as quickly it was gone. The king of Biatre, the ruler of the country she had been exiled to in shame? The son of the couple who had received their fatal draft from her naive hands? The person who had chased her, unknowingly, though the woods last night? The man who had the most invigorating, ice-blue eyes she had ever seen?

He was asking her to dance?

"I would be honoured, Your Majesty." She couldn't quite decide where the words came from, and her rustic accent was harder to hold onto when she was dressed so well. Anxiety began to well up inside her. But there was something in his presence that made her want to be bold, for once in her life: to refuse to bow to Vivian, and enjoy where she was, in spite of it all.

"Thank you, miss." King Derek turned to face the musicians. "It seems the princess has fallen too far ill to join us tonight, and as I was prepared to dance the whole evening, I needed to find a worthy companion."

"Is that a compliment, Your Majesty?"

"It may have been meant to be. Why did you feel the need to ask?"

Katira was also watching the musicians, but she caught the shrewd glance sent her way. He didn't seem annoyed, but interested. She plunged

121

ahead. "From what you said, I am a replacement for one worthier. I do not disagree; however, that might not be the best way to gain a lady's favour."

A smirk crossed his lips. She had never seen him smile before. "Perhaps I am not trying to win the lady's favour."

"Well said," she conceded, smiling too as their eyes met again, "But then why, pray tell, did you ask her to dance?"

He took a breath and opened his mouth, but no words came out. Instead, he laughed! Only a short chuckle, but it was genuine.

Blushing, Katira turned back to the musicians. Why did his happiness effect her so much? She tried to compose herself. The musicians were fascinating again. A violinist was checking his strings, swiping his bow across a few times to add to the noise, while the director fiddled with his papers and fussed over how they were supposed to sit.

"I sometimes wonder if they actually know what they are doing," the king said. Katira looked at him. A strand of his black hair fell forward when he shook his head. "I wonder if they are just making it up as they go along, and can get away with it because we don't know any better."

"I don't think musicians are the only ones who do that," she responded, understanding the switch from gaiety to seriousness. "But then they play."

"They prove themselves."

"Exactly."

"At least they get time to practice beforehand."

Katira wanted to ask him what he had meant by that, but then the music stopped. The director called out the first waltz, and everyone lined up on the floor. She was opposite the king.

The first notes sounded: a piano prelude. Then the violin swooped in, and the dance began. The partners stepped toward each other, arms extended, then met and spun. King Derek's hands were firm and steady as he held her waist and led her through the dance. She tripped once, but he caught her so fluidly it felt like part of the choreography.

"Sorry. It has been a while." They separated, barely holding gloved hands, then he pulled her back near to him.

"On the contrary, you dance quite well."

She smiled while leaning back gracefully, then spun closer again. "Thank you, Your Majesty."

41

Katira was wittier than anyone he had met in a while, but not in an uppity way; she was intriguing and, quite honestly, fun. She was quite a good dancer. Perhaps a bit out of practice, but she knew the steps, and more importantly, she followed his lead. He smiled. He hadn't been this lighthearted since... since his brother died. But he wouldn't think about that right now. He didn't need to.

Her smile mirrored his own face. She was enjoying this too. He opened his mouth to ask her where she had learned, then stopped short. Everything in the ballroom vanished, leaving him staring. He could no longer hear the music.

Princess Pricilla stood at the balcony, waiting for the crowd to notice her. And notice her he did. She was impossible to miss.

Her white dress dipped low, loose curls falling on the exposed skin. She walked down the stairs. Slowly. Every step rang through the ballroom. As she reached the last step, she flipped the hair out of her face, lifting her eyes to his. They were bright with daring.

A tug on his hand startled him out of his reverie. The servant girl was removing her small hand from his. This was ridiculous. Obviously, the princess deserved every attention worthy of her rank, but she had been late. Miss Katira deserved the rest of the dance he had asked her for. It was a matter of honour. He fully intended to finish what he had started.

She smiled, rather forced but almost... sympathetic? then shrugged and melted into the mass of people. She was gone.

The princess approached, and he bowed. She dipped into a deep curtsy, and her lips spread into a coquettish gaze that made him feel that they two were alone in the room. He took her hand, the musicians started up again, and they danced.

42

Katira wandered for a bit, replying to greetings. She felt a bit out of place; there was no one here with a dress as formal as hers excepting the princess. Everyone seemed willing to give her attention. This was so different than Katira's usual life that she wasn't quite sure how to handle it all. She headed to the tables.

Heaping a plate with dried fruit, cheese, and tarts, Katira planned her course. The alcove near the musicians was still empty, from what she could see, so she made a beeline towards it. Past the tables again. Through the admiring crowd. Around the dance floor.

Then music. The noise of the people was drowned out from here. The curtains would conceal her from any glance in the direction, so she could watch to her heart's content.

Her dress would easily crumple, so she sat very carefully. And she couldn't lean back on the cushions all the way: she didn't want to wreck her hair. But now to the food. It was simply transcending. Servants didn't get dessert on duty, which for her, had been the last two years.

Which brought her to the train of thought that had been wanting attention all evening. Why had the king sent her a personal invitation? Perhaps his interview earlier had brought her to his attentions, and he was being generous and thoughtful to a misplaced servant girl. He had then made sure that she would not be embarrassed by hiring his own mother's former maids. That, too, could be explained away as a courtesy to someone who wouldn't have anything to wear. He also came and spoke with her. Maybe she was different enough to be interesting, or he was just confirming suspicions against her. But then he danced with her! To be fair, he did literally drop her when he seen the princess.

Katira could see the pair spinning on the dance floor. They were truly a beautiful match. She was a gorgeous vision in white and gold against the handsome king in his formal black suit. The scene sent a shaft of pain through her. Why? Maybe it was because she knew she could never hold a man captive the way the princess could. People had told her that she was pretty, but she wasn't stunning like the princess, or even vivacious and fun like Bridget.

The king… was he really entranced? He was concentrating, to be sure, but was he happy? It didn't look like it.

Wishful thinking. Entirely. She needed to distract herself. Tarts were so good. And the marzipan…

"Excuse me, Miss?"

Katira jumped. It was the young man from before, holding two mugs of what must have been ale. "Officer Glen, correct?"

His polite smile widened. "Aye, Miss."

"And why do ye not have a parter?" Katira asked lightly.

"I pleaded for a break."

"The ladies wouldn't leave ye alone, would they?"

He cocked an eyebrow, smirking. "Could ye blame them?"

She dropped her coquetry, opting for honesty instead. "I suppose I don't know many to compare ye too."

Officer Glen took a seat at her side and offered her a mug. She took a sip and wanted to spit it back, but concealed her expression. Acting was what kept her alive.

"His Majesty the King called you Takira?"

"Close. My name is Katira."

"Ahh. Miss Katira," he pronounced, letting the name roll off his tongue. The he furrowed his brows in mock thought while gazing at her. "Now, I cannot remember ever seein' ye before. The king did ask ye to dance, so are ye, perchance, one of the party from Taklin?"

"Nay, I am not."

"That is a relief."

"Why?"

"Because ye would be leaving with them."

"Oh. I see."

The silence was awkward. He asked, "I still have never seen ye before, and I know I would have remembered seein' a damsel so beautiful. Where are ye from?"

Katira's voice faltered. She lifted her full mug and attempted another sip. This was flattery—she knew it—but what harm could it do? "I was from Taklin originally, but was brought here about two years ago."

"Brought?"

She had never had to tell her story aloud before. "I am a servant here in the castle. I was wrongfully accused of a crime in Taklin and sentenced to live as a servant for years to come." The revived memory, with a listener, brought her hidden shame and anger closer to the surface. "They brought me here as a present to the king, like an animal."

"That must have been awful for ye." He leaned towards her. "Such a traumatic experience."

"It was. I—" Katira realized that he was no longer meeting her eyes. He was watching her lips. She laughed and stood up quickly. "But it doesn't really matter anymore. I'd like another tart. Shall we go back to the tables?"

He stood up too. "I am afraid the servants have already removed them, Miss Katira."

"Shame." What was she to do now? There was no way she was going to stay in a dark recess with the man any longer, whether he was nice or not. It simply was not a good idea.

The musicians helped her once again by starting another tune. "I believe I still owe ye a dance, sir. Might I be allowed to pay my debt?"

"I would be honoured, Miss Katira."

43

This dance was not at all like the first one. Officer Glen was a fine dancer, to be sure, but he was much more familiar in the way he held her. When he pulled her in close as the dance required, something caused her to inwardly shrink away from him. Had it not been for Prince Adhemar, she would have been flattered by his advances, but her naivety had been robbed of her. Throughout the moves, all she could see in Officer Glen's smiling face was the one of that prince, haughty and proud and wicked. Her acting skills were not enough to keep her from stumbling. She apologized anyways.

"My first dance was not enough to brush the dust off my lessons, I suppose."

"Do not worry. I shall see to the remedy, if ye so desire."

"Ye're very kind. I fear I am an incompatible partner."

"Nonsense, my dear. Ye are a lovely partner."

His words were too sweet. Genuine meaning was lacking; they were fake.

The dance ended, and he began to lead her back to the seat they had come from. "Pray tell, where did you learn to dance? I don't suppose they let anyone besides royalty dance in Taklin."

"On the contrary, they enjoy dancing with a crowd, albeit a trained one." Katira slowed beside him. "It is rather warm. If you don't mind, I'd prefer to not go near the curtains. They will be smothering."

"I agree. There's a balcony here." He changed course. "If ye danced for the Taklin royalty, am I correct in assuming you served there as well?"

"That's true." They reached the balcony and stepped out. The breeze was cool and smelt of rain, but some glittering stars were visible peeking through the dark clouds. "This is beautiful."

"Astoundingly beautiful, Miss Katira."

Something in his tone of voice made her look his way. He was gazing at her lips again.

"I am glad Taklin sent ye here, for ye are not worthy of them," he said, his voice deeper than before. His head leaned towards hers, and his hand went from her arm to sliding down her back, drawing her closer.

Oh no. Oh, no. What do I do?

Katira slammed her head forwards, catching his jaw with her forehead. This loosened his grip. She turned. He grabbed for her wrist, but the balcony was small and she was already inside the ballroom. Where could she go? Somehow, she remembered not to run through the middle of the dance and hurried towards the stairs. Her dress wouldn't fit through the servant's entrance.

"Please, Miss Katira," he called from behind. His stride was far quicker than hers, but really, almost everyone's was. "I didn't mean to offend you. I was blinded by your charms. I only meant to—"

She didn't stop. His voice was drowned out by the rustling of her skirts as she gathered them up in armfuls. She ran up the steps. The guard at the top looked at her quizzically, but opened the doors. Katira escaped down the hall. The doors shut behind her.

The corridor was quiet and dimly lit. She let down her dress and walked on, slowly, catching her breath. Where was she to go now? She was surprised to find that she didn't want to change and go back to the familiar bustle of the kitchen, even if it was reasonable. The thought of meandering through the moonlit woods in the ballgown flitted through her mind, but that was asking for trouble.

Katira blinked. Her aimless wandering had taken her to the opposite end of the castle. In front of her was the curved wall of the library. What a strange bit of the afternoon had been passed there! She had seen the king, and spoken with him, three times that day alone. He had been quite friendly to her. But tonight, he asked her to dance. How did that suit appearances? Was he apologizing for his sudden coldness before? Was he being the gentleman? Or was she simply the most royally dressed person until the princess walked in, when he seemed to forget her existence? But the look he had given when she backed away... had he been sorry?

A guard was eyeing at her strangely. Katira gave a little smile and nod, and moved on. The poor fellow had simply been confused. One minute the princess wasn't there, the next she was, and she was dazzling. If even Katira could tell it, who knew what that image did to a man. Almost anywhere in the modern world, lewdness was normalcy, but this king had probably never seen that far down a woman's gown before. He was bound to be rather flabbergasted. The thought made Katira uncomfortable. Miss Eillah had once said something about how much more special a secret was if it was kept only between two, or something like that. Either way, it was terribly chaste and awfully romantic at the same time. How did that work?

Katira ended up back in the servants' quarters. She undressed, laid the finery carefully on an unused bed, and sat down on the floor. She leaned her head against the straw mattress, gazing in the direction of the empty hearth. It was dark, but she didn't mind. Her head was filled with lively recollections, and she was trying to decide how to impart them to Bridget. The girl thrived on such stories.

Should she tell her about Officer Glen? A shudder went through her at the memory. Of course she would tell her about it. Perhaps it would make Bridget think more seriously about the perils of handsome men. Katira shook her head, trying to stop the memories from surfacing. But it was never any use. They came anyways, burned in her mind and determined to show themselves.

Prince Adhemar was always a part of the dance classes. He was a fine dancer, one of the best. He and his sister made a fantastic couple on the ballroom floor, surrounded by circles of spinning servants, but they rarely danced together in practice. She liked to dance with the muscular guardsmen, and he was always eager to help with the new girls. He enjoyed being so close to them, whispering awful things in the most silken of tones, casting wicked sparks with his dark eyes while he flawlessly led them through the motions.

Another face appeared in her memory, as clear as a flashback in the TV show.

Elisa.

The maid who refused to dance with him.

The victim who was beaten to death.

The girl who breathed her last in agony while the world watched and thought it all drama.

"Kati? Why are ye back here already? The ball's barely begun!"

Katira half stood, jerking around at the voice, but couldn't see who carried the bright spot that must have been a candle. Her eyes were brim full. She swiped at the tears with the back of her hand, but more came and spilled over. She crumpled back down to the floor.

"Kati! Oh, Kati." Bridget knelt beside her and wrapped her arms around her. Katira gripped her friend and held on tight while the sobs came. She let them have their sway, let them rip out of her body, let them choke her.

44

They danced to several more songs before the princess decided it was time for a break. Derek led her to a seat, then ventured to where only one table was set up now. He glanced around. Everyone seemed quite happy, most likely from the alcohol. He took the two nicer chalices that had been set aside for him and started back.

Katira was nowhere to be seen. Where was she? Certainly not gone already. She had taken the next dance with Officer Glen, then disappeared; they were probably somewhere in a corner together. King Derek was annoyed by that. He had asked her here so that he could see the two women in each other's company, but she had run off the moment the princess arrived. Now his plan was foiled. There would be no better opportunity.

"Derek, what is the matter? You look worried." Princess Pricilla stood up. A touch of bitterness entered her voice. "Is that father of mine making a fool of himself again?"

"Of course not, Princess. He seems to have made many friends." He handed her one chalice, and they sat.

She took a deep draft. "I can hear the tone of your voice. You are annoyed by him." Her mouth formed a little pout.

That much was true. He couldn't disagree with the princess. But nor could he agree with her, for that would be to disrespect his fellow king.

"It's all right, I know how you feel. I knew I should have come here alone. It would have been so much easier." She took another sip. "So much more enjoyable."

She was leaning much closer to him now, bending in such a way that the front of her gown—he needed to change the topic. Now, before he did something he would regret. His mind raced.

"I was hoping to introduce you to a girl tonight, one whom I believe you might know."

It worked. She sat back, the siren song in her eyes effectively extinguished.

"Who?"

"Her name is Katira. Your brother brought her here as a gift after my parents' passing in the way of courtesy during my grief. She seems to be quite intelligent and must have been one of your best."

"Oh... her." Pricilla's lip turned up in a sneer. "Yes, she was intelligent, but rather smart-mouthed and flirtatious. We had hoped sending her here would help the poor girl as well as you. She needed to get away from whatever was influencing her."

"Really? I do recall your bother saying something of that sort, but I have never seen nor heard tell of it. She has always been respectable." His brain immediately contrasted the way they had danced—Katira had been happy, gentle, and willing to be led. The princess had danced with a haughty perfection, demanding his entire attention.

"I really do hope that is the case, but I don't know if I could be so sure. I had hoped..." Pricilla gave a disappointed sigh. "Didn't you see her leave the ballroom?"

"No, I did not. Why, pray tell?"

"Just after she left you in the middle of a dance, I seen her pair with a soldier, or officer, or whatever you call them. A fellow in a uniform, anyways. A little afterwards, I seen her running, quite forgetting decorum, leading him across the ballroom and up the stairs towards the door. I haven't seen either of them since."

"Oh. I—" he was disappointed for some reason. "That is a shame."

"Why? Why would you bother with a servant girl when I'm right here? You're not—" She gasped and covered her mouth with one hand. It was almost the same look Katira had given him when he had asked her to dance, but the princess' eyes were filling with tears. "She's not your—"

"What? Of course not! Princess, I simply wondered if she would like to see a familiar face after these years; if you might like to strike up an acquaintance with her again."

"Please, Derek, she's worse than a commoner! She's a servant!" She shook her head, frowning in disbelief and frustration.

"I'm sorry that our views on commoners are so different." Derek put just a touch of ice in his voice.

Pricilla's watery blue eyes opened wide. "I didn't mean it like that, Derek. I just—my family is not like you. We keep to ourselves. Servants get uppity and high-minded if you treat them like equals, and then you can't control them."

"Service with respect is always better than service with fear."

She stayed silent for a moment, her pout fading as she gazed at him. "Wow," she breathed.

"Pardon me, Princess?"

"I wish my mother thought like that. It sounds so nice. And, Derek, I am trying. I came to the ball tonight, did I not?"

"Aye, you did."

"And if you wish for me to meet this girl, I will do it." The princess nodded resolutely. "You are too good. But I will try to be like you."

"Thank you, Princess," Derek said sincerely. "But—" he shifted uncomfortably at her opinion of him. "Much as I would like to be, I am afraid that I am not the perfect example of goodness to follow."

"If you are not, then who is?"

"I—I don't know." She looked so sincere that he dared to continue. "Sometimes I wonder if being good is different for different people. But if there is a standard, who put it in place, and what right did that person have?"

Pricilla was lost. "Umm... yeah. I don't know."

He had been wrong. Instead of understanding, she made him feel ridiculous for thinking such things. He forced a laugh. "I am sorry, Princess. My mind like to go on these rants sometimes."

"Of course. Now, Derek... another dance?"

45

"It's all right now," Bridget crooned, stroking the back of her friend's head. "It's all right."

The sobs began to let up. She was far away from Prince Adhemar and anyone like him. She was safe now. She had a friend. She was safe.

"What happened, Kati?"

Katira extracted herself from Bridget's arms and attempted to regain her composure. "I must have fallen asleep and had a nightmare," she said lamely.

"Now, Kati, how stupid do ye think I be?" Bridget looked her straight in the face, seeming older than her fifteen years. "What happened?"

She took a deep breath, sorting through her memories carefully. "For the first time in my life, I know what it is like to want a kiss," she admitted. "But then I was almost kissed by the wrong man, and now..." she shuddered and pulled her knees to her chest, wrapping her arms around them. "The mere thought disgusts me."

"Kati..."

"Not that it really matters, I'll probably never marry anyways."

"Now, why not?"

"Bridget, I'm different. I'm not like ye. I live here. I have no real life. I'm stuck."

"I'm sure if ye'd ask the king, he'd let ye fully out into the system with the rest of us. He invited ye to the ball, did he not?"

"But what would I do out there? I have no family, no connections. What I have earned would not be enough to buy my own house. The only place that would take me is the tavern, and God forbid that!"

Bridget frowned and looked at Katira strangely. "Why? Who is God?"

She almost chuckled in spite of herself. *Screw the cameras.* "Ye do not mind if we change our topic from handsome men to history?"

The girl wrinkled her nose. "History?"

"A lot of people say it's just a story." Katira related the tale Miss Eillah had told her: how a good God had created a perfect world. To do anything wrong, like falsehood, murder, or rape, would earn the penalty of death, but it seemed this was all that humanity did. Then he would punish them, and they would come running to him for forgiveness. This did not work. The fine needed to be paid. So he killed his own son.

Then came a twist—the son rose from the dead afterwards. He proclaimed that death had no hold on those who had never sinned. Now anyone who asked for forgiveness was offered it, because the fine was paid, but they would also defeat death in the end, and live in a beautiful eternity.

Bridget's eyes were wide. "And ye believe this, Kati?"

"Well, I would like to… but I don't know."

"What do ye mean? It's crazy, but it's a good kind of crazy, methinks."

"Aye…"

"What does that mean, aye? Seems to me either ye do or ye don't."

"I like to think that it could be real. The idea of a God who loves us is comforting, but he certainly doesn't seem to be doing a lot right now."

"Seems to me He's done enough. And I've done bad things, too, Kati," she went on, sobering. "I don't know how I knew that they were bad, but somehow I do. And if He's goin' to forgive me, I'm goin' to take it. God?" She looked up at the ceiling. "If Ye're still handin' out forgiveness, I'd like some. And Kati wants some too, so save some for her till she asks, please, Sir."

Katira stared at Bridget.

"What? Did I say something wrong?"

"I don't know… Ye're goin' to believe in God just because of a story?"

"Kati, it's the closest thing I've some across to truth, ever. What else am I goin' to believe? We didn't all pop out of nowhere."

"I suppose not, but—"

Then a few other women entered the room, bringing a flurry of noise with them.

"I can't wait to get to bed."

"Another night from home, but it'll do."

"That'll be one mess to clean up tomorrow."

"Aye, but I ain't worryin' about it tonight."

Then one spotted Kati and Bridget on the floor.

Bridget jumped up. "Kati told me a story about—"

The woman cut her off. "How's our party girl?"

Katira stood up and shrugged her shoulders, swallowing. "It was much grander than I expected," she answered, pulling off the shoes. The women laughed while Bridget helped her move the dress to a chair, then they hopped into bed in their chemises.

"Thank ye, Kati," Bridget whispered. Then the candle was blown out.

46

At first Derek was concerned that the princess would want to stay in the ballroom after everyone had left, to dance slower, by themselves, without music, and to create the most romantic situation possible. But his "rant" seemed to have had a strange effect on her; no more would she sit and talk seriously. She was willing to meet the people he introduced her to, she danced whenever there was music, emptied a few chalices, laughed, giggled, and rattled on about nonsense. She left as soon as the ballroom began to empty, smiling over her shoulder, flouncing away. King Rosseen had been borne to his room some time earlier, completely drunk. Derek shook his head in disgust and found a wall to lean against. He was exhausted.

"Yer Majesty!"

Oh, lovely. A moment's reprieve, if you don't mind. "Officer—Glen?"

"That exquisite princess escaped your grasp?"

"Aye, she fled like a swan with the first chilled breeze of autumn. Where is your maiden?"

Glen laughed. "Which one?"

"The one you did manage to steal from me."

"I am aware that ye are a king, Yer Majesty, but ye can't hold both at the same time."

He was drunk too. Derek frowned. "That is not what I meant, Officer."

"Spirited wench, that one." Glen laughed again, then joined some other officers on their way out the door.

The ballroom was a mess. Usually this was a civilized gathering, but tonight—was everyone having fun? Was this what having fun looked like? If so, he would much rather go back to being stiff and formal and reasonable.

King Derek turned to leave the room. The ribbon Gerald had used to tie his hair had long since been loose, and pieces of it were falling over his forehead. One fell in front of his eye. He blinked and brushed is away, swiping the heavy crown off at the same time. His advisor was waiting for him at the door, looking tired.

"Were you able to determine which of the women you can trust?"

"As always, straight to the point, Taroki. And no. I scared away both of them."

"How, sire?"

"By mentioning the other in her presence."

"So there must be bad history between the two of them."

"Which leaves us to the same conjecturing as before."

"Surely you have learned something that we can work with, Sire."

He turned the crown over in his hands. "I am too tired to deal with it tonight, Taroki. Good night."

"Sire?"

He could not hide the edge in his voice. "What is it, Taroki?"

"The king and princess are leaving tomorrow."

Strange. "Were they not supposed to be here a fortnight? The princess talked of plans tomorrow."

"There must have been a change, or so King Rosseen's head servant had me believe a few minutes ago."

"Well, I must say I am glad of it."

A gasp came from the shadows behind the open ballroom door. Both men whirled about, and Derek's hand flew to the hilt of his gilded sword.

Princess Pricilla stepped out into the light.

"Princess, I was not aware you were there. I should have offered you an escort to your rooms."

"Why?" So you could discuss your hatred of me behind my back?" Tears spilled down her face as she walked closer.

Derek gritted his teeth. "Those were not my words."

"Oh? Then explain to me what you said. You can't trust me. You are glad to have me gone. What else am I supposed to think, Derek?"

"Princess, let me explain."

"Go right ahead and try."

"Did you expect me to love you at first sight?"

"Why not?"

Derek ran a hand through his hair. How was he supposed to explain this? He put his crown back on his head. "Princess, I invited you here to meet you. Not to marry you."

"All marriages start with a meeting."

"But not all meetings end in marriage."

"But ours could have! You are a king. I am a princess. You are respected. I am admired. You are handsome. Everyone calls me beautiful. There are no obstacles. Why not?"

Because you are frustrating, selfish, and awful queen material. He could not be so blunt. "Because I do not love you."

She stared at him, her face contorted in hurt. Then in one swift, desperate movement, she grabbed the lapels of his jacket and pressed her lips against his.

Derek was frozen for a moment. Spikes of electricity flowed from his mouth throughout his body. No one need know. What had they been arguing about anyways?

Then his mind kicked in and overpowered his body. He pushed her away. She stood there, waiting for him to say something. Taroki watched, dumbfounded.

King Derek turned on his heel and stomped off.

47

Pricilla sighed as one of her maids loosed the strings of her dress. "Set up a call with Mom," she demanded. A maid brought a laptop to the dressing table and opened a video chat link. Within a few seconds, Queen Vivian was on the line.

"Mom, I—Ouch!" She slapped at the hand of the maid who was trying to undo her hair. "Don't pull it all out! Mom, I'm done. This dude is so boring. He's not even a good kisser."

"Pricilla, this is amazing drama. Even Miss Director is all excited about it. Do you know how mad and confused King Derek is right now? He probably can't decide whether to exile or marry you."

"Ugh. Imprison me, more like it. Did you catch what he was talking about today, about "someone who could define good" and all that stuff? Seriously, I just wanted to throw up. I'm not going to marry him, Mom."

"Of course not, dear; you'd bring him to the top of the mountain and leave him there. It'd be fantastic. You could pretend to die and make it a whole tragedy, or break his heart in the cruellest way possible. Any way you wanted, really."

"All I want is to go home. My feet hurt from dancing in those stupid gorgeous shoes. I have a headache from listening to screechy violins all night. I'm tired of wearing a gown all day."

"Pricilla—"

"A couple hours on set, no problem. But playing princess all day is exhausting. And everything smells weird! I just want to go home and wear hoodies and watch movies and go to clubs where they have real music."

"And I suppose you won't even stick it out to the end of the week?"

"No."

"Fine. Let your father know. I've got a bit of drama elsewhere, anyways. There's these three young people who escaped the secret camp, and they want to go warn the king. We might even get a real battle out of it!"

"Mom, I don't care."

"They're good fighters with lots of spunk, too. The only problem is that they keep talking about—"

Pricilla slammed the laptop shut. "I don't care, Mom. Now, would you hurry up with my hair? I'm tired."

48

"The way that fire dances, it's almost like it knows how happy we are to have it," remarked Atila, turning the spit. The rabbit they had managed to catch was slowly roasting to a dark, crusty brown over the flickering flames.

Lato stacked the dry brushwood he had gathered nearby, then plunked himself down beside her. "Fire doesn't have feelings, Atila."

She rolled her eyes, then grinned. "I'm soliloquizing."

"Sure, whatever. But as long as we're talking about non-living things having feelings, I hope that rabbit feels like he owes me. After all that running and chasing I did, not to mention the excellent knife throw that finally got him, he had better taste good." Lato cocked an eyebrow. "Don't you think?"

"Whatever I think, he looks like he feels the same way," said Atila, then lifted the spit off the fire. The meat smelled amazing, and paired with bread from one of the packs, it made an excellent meal.

Lato dropped the last bone to the little pile he had made. He wiped his mouth with his hand and sighed. "That was so good."

"Amen!" Atila agreed. "Now we'd better get some rest before dawn."

"I don't trust those soldiers retreating. We ought to take turns sleeping."

"Alright. I'll take first watch."

"I got it; you sleep."

"Fine." She was grateful. She put the water bottle back in the sack and threw a few more sticks into the fire, then lay down. Her arms would have to do for a pillow tonight. The owls were sounding a lullaby. The clouds thickened overhead, disguising the smoke. It didn't smell like rain yet though.

Her mind refused to allow her body to rest. Her muscles stiffened slowly, and her finger throbbed. She loosened the bandage to allow it to swell properly, then tried to relax again. Every move Lato made beside her was a reminder of a hundred more things that had happened all in one day. She let her eyes open. Lato was… taking off his boot? Maybe she was dreaming. She let her eyes fall shut again, but it was no use.

"Lato?"

49

"What is it?"

"I can't sleep."

"Hm."

"We escaped."

"Mm hm."

"We did it."

"Not yet." Lato got up and walked around the fire, but nothing was to be seen after the firelight ended and the darkness began. Silence pervaded. He sat back down, picked up Atila's rope and looped it neatly, then again. He probably should have waited to eat his share of dinner until it was his turn to sleep. Exhaustion and a full stomach were a perfect defence against staying awake.

"I still can't sleep."

Lato took out his knife and shaved a strip of bark off a stick. "Hm."

"What was in your boot?"

Lato held up a sheet of folded paper. "Master Blackwell must have stuck it in there while I was sleeping at home."

She propped herself up on her elbow. "What does it say?"

"*The Lord is my shepherd.*"

"Master Blackwell's favourite." She smiled. "Read the rest of it."

"*I shall not want. He maketh me to lie down in green pastures: He leadeth me beside the still waters. He restoreth my soul: He leadeth me in the paths of righteousness for His name's sake.*"

"Man, that sounds nice. Keep going."

"That's it."

"What?" Atila sat up the rest of the way.

He turned it around to show her. The rest of the page was blank.

"Why would he do that? It's the best part!" She frowned and thought for a bit. "Maybe it's to prove something."

He frowned too. "What?"

She pushed her point. "Can you say it off by heart?"

"Maybe… I don't know. This is one that he drilled us on, but I'm more familiar with the Gospels than the Psalms."

"*Yea, though I walk*—" she looked pointedly at him, and he joined in. "*Through the valley of the shadow of death*," Atila grinned as they continued. "*I will fear no evil; for Thou art with me; Thy rod and Thy staff they comfort me…*" They both trailed off.

"What comes next?"

He shrugged.

"I think it was something about eating while your enemies were around you… just, that you were safe, even on the battlefield, that kind of thing." She contemplated for a bit. "Oh! The end was *Surely goodness and mercy shall follow me all the days of my life; and I will dwell in the house of the Lord forever!*"

"If that can't put you to sleep, what will? I mean, there's not anything much more comforting than that."

"I think you're right."

50

Walking actually helped ease the ache. Rati was amazed at how much some exercise, proper rest, and food had improved his state. Along with that, he had not been injured as much as he had led the guards to believe. It had been in their best interest to appear as weak as possible to make those brutes underestimate them. Running with Lato to the balloon had been hard though; he had lain perfectly prone for two days before that. *That.*

That had been crazy! How had it all worked out? There was definitely something beyond on-the-run luck planning and luck—something, Rati had to admit to himself, something rather divine. But there was something inside him that argued against that reasoning. Look at where he was now!

Rati plowed through the undergrowth. The sun was sinking, and the trees around him were absorbing the last rays. The terrain was becoming rockier and steeper. He flung his hands out in front of himself as he hurtled to the ground. His boot had caught in a small bush wrapped around a stubborn rock. He groaned. Rolling onto his back reminded him that no matter how well he felt, injuries still took their time to heal. He sat up, crawled to his boot, and pulled it from the tangle of vines and bushes.

Bending over to pull his boot back on was harder than getting it. His stomach hurt. He was tired. Why was he like this anyway? Why was he the one wounded and alone? Of course he wouldn't wish it on Lato or Atila, but why had they been attacked in the first place? For telling an old woman about God? Wouldn't he be pleased by that? Couldn't he defend himself?

These thoughts felt like blasphemy. Sure, when the kindly man welcomed him to his home after Lato and Atila pulled him from a ditch, he was willing to accept anything to be loved and cared for. When Master Blackwell told him of a good God, a Creator, a Saviour, Rati had accepted it. After all, how else could he explain the good fortune of being found by them? He had thanked God for that day. But now he wondered if it would have been better to starve then instead of dying like this.

He stood up again and looked around in the darkness. The clouds, bright and puffy during the day, covered the whole sky now, blocking out the moon and stars. The wind breathed past him, bringing with it a spattering of rain. He threw out his hands. "Where are you now, God? Now when I need you?"

No one answered. The wind brought more rain, and Rati shook his head in disgust. Then it parted the clouds. A single moonbeam shone through. It illuminated the area the way lightning does: it made the trees look sharp enough to cut a finger on. It even made the rocky outcropping of a slope, invisible before, look like a shelter from the rain. Rati started toward it, but the clouds covered the moon again.

51

How dare she? Derek tossed in his bed, unable to fall asleep. The princess had hung on him all evening, complained whenever something did not suit her whim, required his every thought. Then, when he should have been alone, he had been merely truthful. No, it was not flattering to her, but whose fault was that? She had flirted with him all night. Not only had her dress dipped in the front, far past propriety, but at their dance's first spin he had been astonished to find that there were slits up her skirt. Her legs were exposed while she twirled. She must have seen that he noticed—he had been quite concerned about the state of her clothing—for then she shot him a seductive smirk to let him know that it was intentional. He could not deny that he had wanted her.

But the face of his mother kept flitting through his mind, the quotes she used to instruct him and his brother with from her ancient book of… proverbs, she called them. And somehow the face of a servant girl haunted him too.

Derek rolled out of bed and went over to the window. The lawn was empty tonight. The wind was louder than it had been last night. It felt good on his forehead. The slight lump there was going down, but he would still have to have it powdered tomorrow. A drizzle moistened his face. He closed his eyes and let it soak him, dripping off his hair and running down his cheeks. In the wind that rushed towards him, fresh from the mountains, he could almost hear his mother's voice echoing.

"Keep thee from the evil woman, from the flattery of a strange woman. Lust not after her beauty in thine heart; neither let her take thee with her eyelids."

A sad smile formed on his lips. His mother had loved those books. He and Charles had always assured her that they would not be so foolish. Of course, that had been rather easy, with very few girls ever to be seen except at the balls, and there they had been chaperoned. In fact, he had not noticed girls much until recently. Two women had intruded on his peace: the beautiful, haughty princess, and the pretty, intelligent servant girl.

Had Charles had someone in mind for his queen? It probably would have been a quiet girl, very sensible and supportive. Where was she now? Never having been acknowledged, she had probably mourned alone and moved on. Derek had been surrounded by every comfort imaginable, but he had not been able to put it behind him. How does one forget the murder of one's own brother? Or rather, how does one forget the murder one's self committed?

Treaties and business as usual had bored everyone for the day. Tea time was nearly come, only to bring with it more formalities, and Derek's neck was itching terribly just above his tunic. He could only imagine what his brother was going through beside him. Being the topic of conversation between four very important adults was never exactly relaxing.

The king and queen were still as regal as their fame had upheld them to be throughout the country—they could even look regal while declining an offer that could well open avenue to war.

"King Rosseen, there is no need to put such things in place now. The children are young—"

"But they will not always be. My daughter is already acclaimed as a beauty, and that will only increase. With my son in line for my own throne, her position is perfect. There is nothing to prevent their happiness in such a union! So why not?" King Rosseen waved his hands in agitation as he argued his point. Derek wondered if his heavy rings would eventually fly off his fat fingers if he continued to gesture so wildly.

"While the points you make are valid, they will still be there when the children are older." King Willhem replied calmly. His face was set, and there was no changing his decision.

"But her hand may not!"

"With the relationship we have now, is a marriage alliance really necessary? Are our lands not at peace without signing away our children's choices in the lives they will live?"

"*Of course they are.*" Everyone in the room knew it was, at best, a very temporary truth. "*Of course.*"

"*Very well then,*" said King Willhem, with a tiny hint of relief in his voice. "*With that settled, we would like to show some hospitality, at least. Would you like some entertainment after tea? We have excellent players, if there is any act you would like to see performed.*"

"*Oh, that would be lovely. I do adore a good play,*" Queen Vivian said. "*Do they know Macbeth?*"

"*Of course, that is a classic.*" Queen Marielle responded. "*Do you enjoy much Shakespeare?*"

Queen Vivian explained casually, "*Most of his plays are too sentimental for me, but Macbeth has some excellent battle scenes. Rapier skills are adamant to increase... fascination.*" Derek thought that was an interesting statement. He knew there were some fights in that play, but they were not the focal point. Still, if action was what these royals wanted...

"*Your Majesties, if you wish to witness good swordplay, our players are not what you are looking for,*" Charles interceded. This was looking more interesting by the minute.

Derek tried to focus on the water streaming down his face, but the cool breeze reminded him of his old tower room. He had moved there after Charles died, welcoming the discomfort. There he could awake screaming from his nightmares in solitude.

52

The dreams always began the same way. He was walking down a long grey hallway with a door at the end. He stepped through. It shut behind him. The room was empty, so he proceeded to the door at the other end of the room. It was identical. Then came another one, but this one was not empty. His free will was abandoned as his feet led him inside.

Everyone was laughing. The kings and queens accepted the cool drinks and fanning services the servants offered. Derek's loose tunic was much more comfortable than the stiff one he had been wearing before. He was still wearing his high laced boots—his mother refused to let him fight bare footed. He placed his formal crown on the waiting pillow that a servant held out to him.

The door behind him slowly closed.

"You know, where we come from, it is an honour to win with the crown on one's head," Queen Vivian said, sitting down beside Queen Marielle. Her full skirt poofed out around her.

"You heard her, boys," Queen Marielle said, turning from her chafing 'friend' to smile at her sons. "Why don't you wear your crowns?"

Both boys shrugged. They exchanged cocky grins while taking their crowns back, then made their way to the middle of the marked circle.

Another door opened. He went forwards.

"Maybe I should just beat you," Derek suggested quietly, smirking. "I'm sure they don't want their beautiful daughter to marry someone as lousy with the sword as you."

"Hey, that's a good idea," Charles agreed, also whispering. "Except then they would just have her assassinate me and marry you afterwards."

"Good point." Derek raised his blade. "Since we can't fight to lose then, I guess we'll be just forced—"

"To fight to the death and uphold our honour," Charles proclaimed, then lowered his voice again, "And that way she can only kill one of us."

They both laughed. Charles' voice, finished transitioning, was way deeper than Derek's. He ran a hand through his thick black hair while Derek rolled his eyes.

He glanced back. Water started bubbling underneath the shut door behind him.

The fight started well enough. They were both used to each other's strengths and weaknesses, so there was no circling and careful prodding. They 'went it lively' right away, but the fight escalated more, the way it always did. Charles sliced his blade downwards, so Derek parried to the left and thrust. Their audience gasped, but Charles had been expecting the move and was able to recover in time to follow his sword out of the way. Derek was overextended, but pulled back on his thrust and turned the momentum sideways. Charles swung his blade and pushed his brother's away to the right. They exchanged blow after blow, evading and advancing with skill.

The clashes echoed in Derek's subconscious, bouncing off the walls. He passed an additional door, which slammed behind him. It too echoed. He walked quicker as the memories flashed past him, images he could never forget. He ran. The doors slammed, but nothing could stop the water that gurgled around them.

The spark of red staining the tip of his blade.

Slam.

Charles' eyes widening.

Slam.

His hand shaking away the drips.

Slam.

The reassuring grin.

Slam.

That grin fading.

Slam.

The pair of familiar white-blue eyes rolling up.

Slam.

Charles' sword falling from his hand.

Slam.

Charles lying on his back.

Slam.

Mother's gasp.

Slam.

The crown of a prince rolling away on the hardened ground.

Slam.

The last door closed behind him.

He splashed to the ground beside his brother, falling hard on his knees. "Charles!" he screamed, over and over. "Charles!" Walls rose from the ground *around him. Ghosts of his mother and father swirled around him, saying it was going to be all right. The walls grew together over his head, enclosing him. The ghosts vanished. He looked back to the body at his knees, but it had vanished. He couldn't see it anywhere. He dashed around the chamber as it shrank about him. A door appeared, only to slam shut in front of him this time. This one held back the water, and it rose past his knees, then his belt, then his shoulders. It covered his head and he swam upwards, but the water had reached the ceiling.*

There was nowhere to go.

The memories were so mixed with his nightmares that he could barely tell them apart, but the one truth remained: his brother was dead.

Dr. Hiem had suspected poison, but there was no proof. And who would it have been? It didn't really matter now. The villain had never done more. It had been Derek who cut him, so the blame might as well sit right where it did: on his own two shoulders.

A shudder slipped down his backbone. The night had turned chilly. He mechanically closed the shutters and walked back to bed, wiping the water off his face. His problems were leaving tomorrow, he reminded himself—but they weren't. Only one was. In two days he would hear the first word back from the men who had gone to investigate the fire in Ferbundi. Perhaps it was the same villain who had poisoned his blade, who had bided his time before causing chaos again. He still did not know who the suspicious girl in the forest last night had been. Perhaps it was a servant girl. Perhaps Katira would have an idea.

53

"What are ye saying, Miss?" The elderly woman's grip tightened. Atila knelt on the road beside her in the fading light. "That there be a God, I am sure right well, now ye put it like that. But He loves me?"

"Yes, Ma'am, and He offers us rest after this life."

"But I don't deserve it. Ye might, pretty young thing, probably ne'er done a wicked thing in yer life. But not me."

Atila laughed wryly. "You're not saying that you've forgotten me, have you? I used to end up in all kinds of trouble. And Lato used to steal the apples from your stand all the time."

"Oh, yes, that quick boy child. But I been worse."

"That doesn't matter. No one deserves it, but forgiveness is forgiveness, and God gives it freely. His Son paid the penalty for us."

"Ach, child, ye give me joy. The last joy, methinks, I can have in this mortal world."

"The greatest, yes, but surely not the last. Lato or Rati will be back with the doctor soon."

"'Tis no use, child." She smiled faintly, then faded away before the brimming eyes of the girl.

Atila laid the damp hand down. Her tears spilled out and mixed with the dust she was kneeling in. A few villagers on their way home looked at her strangely for a bit, then glanced away, far too busy to ask why a girl was weeping over an old woman beside the road. They hadn't seen the mounted soldier that had knocked her down.

Rati ran up then. "I can't find the doctor," he panted, then stopped short. The urgency drained from his muscles.

"'Tis no use," Atila murmured as she turned to him with a half smile. "She doesn't need one anymore."

"Oh." His shoulders sagged. He had assumed it would come to this, but still, the news was like a kick to the back of the knees. "Well, we could at least take her out of the road." He bent to grasp the frail shoulders, but stopped when he heard a scream behind him. The horrid sound of flames eating thatch came next, then as he and Atila turned, startled, the entire roof of a house near one gate was licked and consumed by flames. The horse galloping towards them carried a rider that no longer held his torch, though many behind him did.

Lato was running in front of the herd, flames leaping from house to house after him. "Run!" he yelled. They jumped up and grabbed their staves, entirely confused but for one thing—if they didn't move, it would cost them their lives. Dashing through the streets, taking every twist and turn they could, they tried to get out of the town, but it seemed to have become a giant maze. The mounted soldiers behind them were confounded by the corners, but the speed their horses had on straight paths was enough to even the odds. More and more houses were set aflame. The air was thick with smoke and screams of the waking victims.

Finally the three made it to Ferbundi's gate and burst out of the flaming village. Lato ducked right. Atila and Rati followed suit. The horses galloped right past them into the darkness. One soldier was more cautious, though, and had been riding more slowly; he saw them beside the gate. There was no way his troop would hear his cry for them to turn back, so he turned alone to face them. There was a number on his breastplate: the number Fifteen.

The beast of a horse would have trampled Rati but he jabbed his staff into the horse's eye. It reared. He ducked to avoid the flailing hooves. The rider was bucked off the saddle and landed hard on the ground. Finishing its dreadful whinny, the horse shook its great head, then took off after its comrades.

Lato covered Fifteen immediately and held him to the ground with a knife to his throat. "Why are you chasing us?" he demanded.

"It doesn't matter," Atila interrupted. "We need to help those people!" She started back towards the gate.

Rati blocked her. "There's nothing we can do now. It would be suicide to go back in there," he said firmly. Atila glared at him, then hung her head and covered her ears. The sound was horrible.

157

The soldier, having recovered his breath, responded now. "I'd suggest you put that knife back where it came from, or you'll end up doing something you'll regret."

"I'd be happy to oblige," Lato replied through gritted teeth, not moving his weapon, "As soon as you tell me why you were burning that village after us."

Fifteen clenched his jaw.

"Why?" Lato demanded again. "If we had done something wrong, you could have arrested and tried us legally. What reason could you possibly have to set innocent people's homes on fire to catch us?" He nicked the exposed throat. The man arched his neck away, but Lato followed him with the knife.

"I was not one with a torch," he spat out. It wasn't enough for Lato, who gave him another encouraging scratch. "We weren't chasing you."

"Oh really? It sure seemed like you were."

"Lato—" Rati broke in. "Won't the other soldiers notice when that horse joins them riderless?"

"Soon," he answered.

"Am I the only on hearing that? We've got to go!"

The thunder of the re-approaching horses was becoming audible, and louder by the second, but Lato was entirely focused on his prisoner.

"If I'm going to die, I'm going to fight first. If I'm going to fight, I'd like to know why! Especially if I'm going to die fighting!!" These words were hollered into the prone man's face.

"We weren't chasing you. We were chasing the girl. You can save yourself," he said.

"That's ridiculous." Lato adjusted his knee on the man's chest.

He grunted. "She spoke… of God," he admitted. Lato pulled back on the knife, startled.

The horses halted abruptly, only a few paces away, in a cloud of dust. It settled to show more numbered soldiers dismounting. All of them looked eager to snuff out the challenge. The soldier under Lato's knee twisted suddenly, tripping him, and rolled out of reach. He stood and drew his sword.

All of them charged at once. Lato, Atila, and Rati backed against each other and raised their staves—then everything disappeared. They froze in place, holding their staves above their heads, scared to move. A rippling sphere surrounded them.

"What happened?" Atila demanded, her tears dried by surprise, her body rigid.

"Can they see us?" Lato asked.

Rati stood silent for a bit. "I think," he said, arms beginning to shake with excitement, "Master Blackwell succeeded with his magnetic shield!"

"And he hid it in our staves?" Atila asked.

"How do we get out?" Lato asked. "What's holding it in place? Can we move?"

"No!"

They both snapped their heads toward Rati.

"It's got to be the way we're holding the staves," he explained. "The instant we move, it goes down."

They stood there for another minute, catching their breath.

Atila had been too horrified with the burning village to hear what had gone on with the soldier on the ground, but now it plucked at her curiosity. "Lato, what did he say to you?"

"They were chasing... you," he said, still utterly confused.

"Me? Why?"

"He said it was because you spoke of God."

"Why would that—wait, how did they hear me?"

"They weren't Biatrean soldiers. Taklin hears everything," Rati reminded her. "Master Blackwell thinks they have the whole castle rigged with cameras—those little eye devices."

"I never believed him," Lato admitted.

"If they really have that technology, then I guess it would be no big deal to have them in Ferbundi too."

"It's another thing to add to our list of what to tell the king."

Another minute passed.

"Any strategies?" Lato asked.

"The longer we wait, the better the chance that we can catch them off guard," Rati suggested.

"But then we'll be tired," Atila countered. "They'll probably set up camp around us, so no quiet escape."

Lato nodded. "We might as well fight."

"On three then?"

"One. Two. Three."

The lowered their staves.

The strange shield disappeared, or rather, everything else appeared again. For a moment there was complete silence. Soldiers stared at them, holding blunted swords with edges dripping molten steel. Half-burned arrows lay around the ring where the shield had been. Several soldiers lay prone on their backs, smoke rising from their corpses.

Lato yelled and dove into the fray, Atila and Rati right behind him. If they could fight their way out... but it was all they could do to stay alive.

Rati deflected a thrust downward, ducked a swing to the head, parried another thrust upward and jabbed ahead. It was difficult to aim for the blunt sides of their weapons, but Rati soon adjusted to the adrenaline that rushed through his veins. One man fell, another followed. Lato was doing even better than he was, and Atila was doing really well too. Master Blackwell must have known this was coming, *Rati thought.* He must have known the name of God was this dangerous. But why?

Then everything happened at once. One soldier cut across from an awkward angle, and the blade cut into his weapon, breaking it in half. Sparks flew as the metal stem inside snapped. He reared to swing the shorter piece again anyways, but another soldier thrust his sword into the fray—and directly into Rati's unprotected abdomen.

Rati screamed, doubling over in agony. His eyes flew open. Sweat dripped down his forehead, mixing with the rain that was blowing into the little cave he had found. Well, if there was anyone nearby, he had just alerted them to his whereabouts.

54

He shook his head to clear it, then tucked his knees tighter in the little space. Pulling down his hood, he allowed his memory to take over again.

Lato and Atila tried to cover him, but it was no use, and now they were distracted. In a matter of seconds their hands were bound behind them in metal shackles. Rati had been pulled to his feet, eliciting more cries of pain, and shackled too. The command to march was given.

Every step sent anther spasm of pain through his nerves. He only took three before his body crumpled. Boots landed beside him. A kick to the ribs followed.

"Get up!" the soldier snarled.

Rati clawed his fingernails into the dirt, gasping for breath, but he could not obey.

"I didn't ask, weakling." The boot loomed in the air to kick again.

Twenty-Seven shoved the attacker aside. "What part of 'take them alive' do you not understand?"

"He needed a lesson," protested the kicker.

"Get back in line, Ninety-One!"

He grumbled as he obeyed. Another soldier, Four, stalked over.

"What's this?"

Twenty-Seven turned to face him head-on. "A minor disturbance, Commander."

Four turned back to the pathetic form in front of him. "Twenty-Three!" He barked. "Get over here. Dismount. Get this deadweight on there."

Being moved onto the beast's back was only more misery, and Rati found it hard to think about anything other than the pain. Everything faded to black.

Rati lifted his head. Enough self-pitying recollections. The rain had turned to a light drizzle now, and it was no longer as dark as it had been. He could see the outline of the trees in the mist. Stretching his legs, he was again surprised at how well he felt. He was not as tired and sore as he had expected to be. He felt for the sack lying beside him. Reaching his hand in was a wonderful feeling.

He ate a piece of bread and a strip of dried meat, then downed half the water. Revived fully, Rati stretched out his limbs again, then took a deep breath and stood up. A moist wind was hailing the light—the sun was still on the other side of the rock—and it felt good. He tied the sack to his belt and walked into the middle of the little clearing to get his bearings. The mountain jutted quite directly before him; the little cave he had slept in looked like a crack in the toe of a giant. He started forwards.

55

When dawn finally came to the castle, it was only a lighter shade of grey than the night had been. Derek got out of bed the moment the changing of the grey took place and rang for Gerald. The poor fellow had a difficult time, but eventually it was good enough for him to leave. Derek headed to his office and rang for Taroki.

"Good morrow, Sire."

Derek nodded in return.

"You did not sleep well."

"Do I look like I slept well, Taroki?"

"Yes, and it also looks like your bruise has disappeared. But I know Gerald better than to trust your appearance. What is on your mind, Sire?"

"Where do I start?" He ran a hand through his hair, wanting to rip it all out. "What makes the princess think she deserves me? Which villain set Ferbundi on fire? Who was the girl in the forest two nights since? How did Charles die? And why does Miss Katira not leave my mind?"

Taroki waited to make sure he was finished. "That is an impressive list of questions, Sire."

"Thank you. I spent all night arranging them for you." Derek could not bite back the sarcasm.

"Now, what order should they go in?"

"Pardon me?"

"Which is the most urgent?"

"Ferbundi, of course. But I cannot do anything about it from here till my men come back."

"All right. Ceas worrying about it if you can do nothing. What is next?"

"I suppose the trespasser in the forest."

"Have you not already had the forest searched?"

"Aye, I sent Officer Kendrick to gather some men and search immediately upon my return."

"And there was no result?"

"None."

"So either she is long gone and has done no harm, or she was a ghost of your imagination. Irrelevant either way. Next?"

"The princess, I suppose." And angry flush reddened the king's face. "What am I to do with her?"

"As she is leaving today, I do not believe you need to concern yourself with her."

"Which leaves me with the old question of Charles' death."

Taroki sighed. "We have been over this a hundred times, Sire. Other than a poisoned blade, he shouldn't have died, and there is no idea of who could have poisoned it. I am afraid that your question will never be answered. And"—he held up his hand to stop Derek from interrupting— "Since no one else has ever gotten hurt, it is not urgent."

"So you are saying there is nothing for me to worry about. Consequently, nothing to do or be needed for."

"Did you not have another question, Sire?"

Derek's forehead creased. "Did I?"

"Something about Miss Katira, I believe."

"Oh." Had he said that aloud? Of all the unfortunate things to have said... But why not? The only women he spoke to were his officers' wives and daughters, and that was always small talk. He was entitled to have... what would he call her? Another advisor? A confidante? A friend?

Taroki coughed. "Whatever it was, Sire, she is not going anywhere, which means that this matter is not urgent either. I believe that King Rosseen and Princess Pricilla were planning on leaving quite early this morning. You ought to have breakfast, then see them off. After that, I am sure the people will have questions for you."

King Derek did as his advisor suggested. The only thing he learned from Rosseen during breakfast was that leaving, it seemed, was Pricilla's idea. No surprise there, he thought. *Either she   :ven up or has been properly embarrassed.*

They met in front of the grand doorway.

"Farewell, Derek. I hope we meet again soon," she whispered, as demurely as possible.

"Farewell, Princess." He omitted the wish to reunite, for he refused to lie.

Her smile twisted with a pang of bitterness. She turned, straightened herself, and marched out the door. A whole entourage of maids and manservants carrying trunks followed her. King Rosseen waved, and headed out the door as well.

56

As the morning grew on, it got warmer. The sun peeked over the mountain and evaporated the mist. The rocky terrain was beautifully dangerous. A small stream had eaten a fissure in the rock, and it sent out tributary branches across Rati's path. The depth of those chasms promised a bloody end on the rocks below. He had to watch out for them between the scraggly brush. His abdomen preferred the cautious steps, anyway.

The direction itself was fairly easy to follow; it was like walking along the seam of the two mountains. The ascent slowed while the mountains grew on either side, enclosing him in a ravine.

It was silent here except for the birds flitting about overhead. It had been a while since he had been completely by himself, and it took his mind a little while to adjust. Once it did, though, the silence was peaceful. Ideas were readily available. Sense was easily found. He plodded on.

These mountains were not large. They were just large enough, he realized, to cause them a lot of worry and danger. Even a little thing, or a little person, could do so mu—Rati grabbed for a nearby branch as his feet flew out from under him. He caught it and held on as his feet dangled below in one of the empty river gouges in the rock. The strain pulled on his wound, threatening to tear the skin apart again. He kicked, flailing wildly, trying to catch his feet on the edge, but he had fallen in frontwards. The wall was behind him, and he could not get enough leverage to push himself out. He could not turn around. His hands began to sweat. He slipped down the branch, stripping it of its leaves.

He looked down. This one didn't look as deep as some of the others, but it was still quite a fall to be unprepared for. "Hey!" he shouted. "Hey!" He held on a bit longer, holding his breath. There was no answer. He let go.

The landing was hard. It jarred all his bones. His feet were bent forward in the water, the heels jammed into the base of the crack. He braced himself between the walls and lifted one foot. The ankle protested, but he wedged the toes into the crack instead. He repeated the process with the other foot and was able to stand.

The chasm was about twice as deep as he was tall. The walls were not jagged enough to climb out, and no convenient roots grew into this one like he had seen in others he had passed. He glanced to his left. The chasm got narrow, but not shallower. He tiptoed to his right. It grew deeper, and the trickle of water grew. There was a river that he could hear now, running down the main shaft that this path branched into.

Once he got to the juncture, he saw that it was here he had seen the roots before. They were hanging into the water from both sides, from every nearby tree. *Perfect.* He leaned out and grabbed a handful. Tugging on them, he decided they would be sturdy enough to hold his weight. He swung out on them and braced his feet against the slope. Climbing strained his stomach, but it was either this or starve. Or drown. That was an option too.

About halfway up, he stopped short. Were those footsteps? They were hard, like boots on the rock, and there were two different rhythms. He climbed again, but slower and quieter. Perhaps the guards had resumed their chase again. Whoever it was, they were passing very close. He paused again.

"I was sure I heard something," came a voice as the boots passed overhead. His eyes widened.

"Atila! I'm right—" then one of the roots in his right hand snapped. The rest followed, and his left arm, already shaking with strain, gave way. He plunged into the river.

"Rati?" Lato dashed to the brink. "Rati!" Are you all right?"

"I'm fine," he laughed. "Quite refreshed, actually." He looked up at the faces of his two friends peering down while he sat in the shallow river. "Man, am I glad to see you guys!"

167

Atila lowered a rope to him. Rati knotted it around his chest and held on. "Ready."

With Lato and Atila pulling on one end and Rati climbing on the other, he was out in less than a minute. They collapsed on the ground and breathed hard.

All three sat up at the same time. They looked from one to another, and huge grins burst on their faces. Atila leapt onto him and squeezed him like a snake with its prey. Lato followed, and Rati returned the fierceness of the hugs, laughing out loud. "Man, am I glad to see you guys!"

57

Mason trudged along. Countless steps he had taken, and countless more were sure to follow. He had slept in the cover of a tree during the rain the night before, or at least pretended to sleep. Even this tramping along in damp clothing was preferable to that.

The meadow he was walking through so urgently this morning would have been nice for a stroll with his wife and daughter. Oh, how he missed them. His sweet Nancy, his little Betta. And to think that—no. But he remembered all too well. *The house he had built for them, under a bluff beside the ocean, turned into a pile of smouldering ashes. His girls nowhere to be found. The crackling of the dying embers still ringing in his ears.*

Startling out of his reverie, Mason turned to the side. He wasn't imagining that sound, but it wasn't a fire; it was... He groaned. "Why does what I create always come back to haunt me?"

The trees beyond the meadow parted to show a fantastic mechanism: a metal spider. It had eight multi-jointed legs, currently half retracted. It was running on the wheels below the belly of the machine. Soldiers dressed in Taklin grey marched alongside. The soldier in the front was surprised by a man not cowering in fear of the metallic beast; instead, striding purposely towards it.

"Who are you? Why are you here?" the lead soldier demanded.

"Is a man not allowed to roam the fields of his country?" returned Mason.

"A man should stay in his own fields," retorted the soldier as the ensemble came ever closer.

"What about a man who invented the beast that follows at your bidding?"

The soldier raised an eyebrow. He was not impressed, but he was interested; or at the very least, amused. "Oh, really?"

"Indeed." And he walked right up to the machine, ducked the arm that he knew was going to swing out in his direction (he had noticed the man at the top was ready with the levers), and pushed his palm against a nearly invisible indentation in the belly of the beast. It groaned, and despite the alarm of the lever man, it retracted the wheels and legs completely. Mason smiled as the body came to rest on the ground. "Mason Blackwell, at your service."

The soldier tipped his head. "Commander Twenty-Seven," he said curtly.

Mason couldn't have imagined better luck—or providence, rather. "Hove you any relation to Soldier Fifty-Two?"

The soldier looked at Mason Blackwell again. "Commander Fifty-Two is my father," he replied, bewildered.

Chuckling, the older man gazed at the young commander. "You have your father's spirit, lad, and if I dare say, the looks he was so proud of."

"Oh?" The word was uttered without a sense of warming to his familiarity. "If we are that alike, why don't you compare us in person?"

A stately grey-headed man emerged from the ranks. The lines on his face were stretched thin, but his step was firm. Proceeding towards the strange parley in front of the retinue, his sharp eyes took in the scenario—and froze on the face of the wrongdoer. He halted. "Blackwell?"

Mason's grin stretched across his face. The two of them had shared many a conversation while training in Queen Vivian's army. "Pierre!"

The young commander looked back and forth. "Father, you know this man?" he finally asked.

"Yes, I do," he said, coming forwards again while his expression changed from disbelief to happiness. "Oh, yes, I do!" The untied friends shared a manly embrace.

"So, *Commander* Gustav Pierre?"

"Commander Fifty-Two, now," he replied. "The queen decided her army would fight better for her cause if they could not fight for the glory of their own names, so we are all numbers. But that happened while you were still with us, right?"

"Oh, yes; I had forgotten."

"Deserter, you." Commander Fifty-Two turned to his son. "We have extra supplies and were up since early this morning. What say you to a break, Commander Twenty-Seven?"

"Aye, sir." He turned and began shouting orders for the men to rest easy and get the food out. Soon they were all seated, eating the plain soldiers' fare. Once they finished, the men stretched out under what shade they could find to take advantage of the respite.

"You must have found yourself a woman too, Pierre?"

"That I did, Blackwell, and she's waiting at home to scold me for my career choice again once this term's up. How's your... Nancy, right?"

Sadness crept into Mason's eyes' and his smile turned bittersweet. "She passed on."

The older commander was willing to wait for details, but his son, in a tone that still tired to sound stiff and professional, asked, "What happened?"

"I came home from the market in Ferbundi to find the cottage in embers."

Pierre leaned forwards. "The little girl, too?"

"Yes."

"I'm sorry."

Mason nodded. "Thank you, Pierre."

Silence pervaded for a bit. Commander Fifty-Two's face darkened. "Why, Blackwell?"

"Why what?"

"Why did you have to go and get yourself all tangled up in all this?"

"What are you talking about? I've stayed out of Vivian's way; I came upon you by accident."

Pierre shook his head, his features settling low. "You haven't. Those kids you adopted. You told them about Christianity?"

"About God, yes."

"And you know she hates him."

"So? They haven't told anyone—except the old lady, and she died after getting—" everything caught up to him: the fire in Ferbundi, the imprisonment of his adopted children. By these men. By his friend. In the blink of an eye, Commander Twenty-Seven had a pistol to his head.

"There is so much more going on here than what you see, Blackwell." He gave a mirthless laugh. "More than what anybody here sees. But everyone else sees it, and that's what matters."

"Pierre, are you serious?"

"I've enjoyed this, and I hope you won't take too much offence, but I'm going to have to take you into custody."

58

"So, Master Blackwell left us to fend for ourselves?" asked Lato, stuffing a piece of bread into his mouth. "I would not have expected that."

"I didn't either," said Rati. He frowned at his own piece. "I was hoping that if I turned around, he would too, but..." He didn't finish.

Atila tied the half-empty sack back to her belt. "He must think there is a lot more at stake than us."

"This is so strange," said Lato. "I feel like we set something huge in motion, but now we're on our own."

"I know what you mean," Atila rejoined. "The way he raised us... this seems so out of character. Did we fail him somehow, and now he is just going on by himself?"

Rati shook his head. "No matter how I wrack my brain, I keep coming up with those same conclusions."

All three continued in their own thoughts well into the afternoon, broken only by the sound of their footsteps changing. The click of their boots on the rocky ground slowly gave way to the softer rustling of summer grass. The mountain path had dissolved into the surrounding woodlands again while the sun led the march to the west.

Atila stumbled on a rock in front of a little creek. Her arms flailed wildly, but she jumped across before ending up with a bath the way Rati had.

"Pay attention!" Lato scolded.

She shrugged. "It's so beautiful here. It's easy to get distracted."

He looked her way and nodded. It was nice, with the trees overhead, the grass underfoot, the birds singing all around.

"Isn't God just amazing?"

"Yeah, He sure is."

"I was especially thinking about the fact that He is in control. Even though He lets us do our own things and suffer our own consequences, He can always work His own will through it."

"You're talking about Master Blackwell, aren't you?" Rati asked. "You're forgiving him, even though he abandoned us, because you believe a greater good will come out of it."

"Yes," she said. "Does that make sense?"

"If you believe it, who am I to stand in your way?"

Atila was a little surprised at his tone of voice. Of course, it might have been because he had just walked into a thorn bush. She stomped on the branch that was clinging to his pant leg while he pulled it free. His boot came off, and she handed it to him. He pulled it on. They resumed walking.

59

Taroki had been right about the people. They were lined up by the time the gates were opened. Some were teachers, headed to the library for study. Some were the servants that did not sleep in the castle. Come afternoon, though, a new line was there, and they all came with problems.

King Derek sat on his throne at the far end of the room. Guards let the first man forward, and he bowed.

"What is your name?" Derek asked.

"My name is Finley, Yer Majesty."

"What can I do for you, Finley?"

"Yer Majesty, I have a young daughter. She is near death with a disease that none of our physicians can heal. Ye know what it is like to lose someone ye love."

"Aye. What would you have me do?"

"I need your permission, and perhaps supplies to last the voyage. Me and several of my crew would be willing to sail to Taklin. They are far more advanced than we, and surely that pertains to medicine as well."

"We have attempted to reach Taklin before, Finley. But the rocks, and the storms... none of those ships have ever come back."

"But they have been able to reach us. They must know a channel."

"Are you proposing to follow them?"

"Exactly, Yer Majesty."

"Do you have a vessel built to withstand such travel?"

"Only my fishing boat, Yer Majesty."

"I am afraid I cannot let you go, Finley."

"But my daughter—"

"Would you rather leave the rest of your family without a provider?"

The man looked like he wanted to argue, but he shook his head, agreeing. Of course he seen how foolish and futile the attempt would be. He had probably come simply to have tried.

Another man approached the throne and bowed.

"Good afternoon to you, sir."

"Good afternoon, Yer Majesty. Are ye perhaps in need of a new pair of boots? I have recently come into possession of the family cobbler's shop, and take great pride in our work. We would be honoured if ye would like a pair."

"I believe I would."

The man whipped a roll of twine from his pocket and immediately knelt down to measure the king's feet, cutting the string off at appropriate lengths and holding them between his fingers.

"And how much do you charge?"

"For Yer Majesty, nothin' at all."

"Are you sure?"

"Of course, of course. Whenever someone asks where you got the fine boots from, ye just tell 'em "Tyson's" and I'll be as good as paid."

"I will do that, Tyson. Thank you."

He grinned, bowed again, and walked out the door.

A woman approached next. "Yer Majesty." She curtsied.

"State your name and case, please, Madam."

"My name is Margaret, and I want ye to arrest my husband."

"And what, pray tell, is the reason for so strong a suit?"

"He's a drunk. He's off near every night to the tavern. I want ye to close it down and arrest 'em all!"

"Madam Margaret—"

"Ye need to make the drink illegal and put all 'em unashamed girls where no one can see 'em!"

"Madam—"

"I tell ye, its takin' over the society, Yer Majesty." Margaret waggled her finger, determined for her speech to have an effect.

Derek waited for a moment to make sure she was finished, then tried again. "Madam Margaret, I am afraid there is nothing I can do."

"Ye're going to let all of 'em get away with ruinin' folk's lives?"

"If I were to make it illegal, Madam, they would do it anyways. I can do nothing about where the problem lies."

"Hmph! Imagine that!" She stalked out.

King Derek looked at Taroki, who only shrugged and shook his head.

The rest of the afternoon was filled with property settling, a business transaction gone wrong, the legal declaration of a couple who had climbed the mountain, and more of the same. Finally, the last issue was settled, and Derek retired to the west parlour. Before his tea was brought, Taroki came rushing in.

"Sire! Escapees from the Ferbundi fire have arrived!"

Derek jumped from his chair. "There are more? How did they manage to get here so quickly?"

"The people had started walking already. When your men met them, a few turned back to escort them the rest of the way."

"Great. Where are they?"

"We had them escorted to the guest rooms immediately. A servant was dispatched to get victuals."

"That is perfect, Taroki. Thank you."

60

Katira handed the box up to her friend, who was precariously balanced atop a ladder. "Be careful with those, Bridget."

"Why? I'm not afeared to die, anymore," she proclaimed, lifting the box above her head.

"Aye, but perhaps ye should be afeared of breakin' those dishes."

"I suppose." Bridget pushed the box onto the shelf, then jumped off the ladder. They walked back into the kitchen. Oregga was standing still, her hands on her hips, looking for once like she did not know what to do. The kitchen seemed empty without the extra help for the ball. Only one unfamiliar man came around the doorway—one of the serving men.

"Ah, Sebastian. Were ye not sent home yet?"

"Ma'am, the survivors from Ferbundi have arrived."

"They'll need victuals." She thought for a moment, muttering to herself. "The last preserves went into the tarts last night. Thomas! Put the almonds away, ye can make marzipan later. We need more pancakes. Benjamin, ye can help him." Despite the chef's protests, she went on firing orders. "Bridget, Nelda, clean the serving trays first. Kati, put the big kettle on—How many people are there, Sebastian?"

"I do not know, ma'am. Frederick—" He glanced over his shoulder. "Ahh. Here."

"There are four, Ma'am, and they will need more than pancakes."

"I am well aware, Fred," Oregga snapped. "But they will have to make do till supper. Now, come help."

They all did as they were told. Within a quarter of an hour, there were several plates and cups stacked onto one tray, pots of tea on another, and the third was heaping with dishes of pancakes.

"Kati, ye'll have to carry. Bridget's in the garden again." Oregga handed the tray of pancakes to her. "Don't trip."

They set off outside, then up the narrow staircase. Katira watched her step carefully, working hard to keep up with Sebastian and Frederick and their heavy loads. They didn't speak to her, just kept going through hallways and doors. She nearly bumped into them when they stopped abruptly in front of the king and his advisor. The strangeness of the situation, even though she was just a servant, hit her immediately. Maybe it was just the fact that they were all taller than she. Either way, it was awkward, and she wanted to leave, but what choice did she have?

They walked into the room, where a young man and woman were sitting on the edge of the high bed. They slid to their feet and paid obeisance as soon as the door swung open. Sebastian set the table and Frederick poured the tea while the king made inquiries as to their comfort. Was he not going to ask them about the fire? Katira looked at the couple and caught the girl's eye. She seemed to gain confidence from her, somehow, and took a deep breath.

"It was not an accident."

6I

Derek turned to her in surprise. "How so?"

"We have discussed it, Yer Majesty: the speed everything caught fire. A stray spark would not have done that, especially because we just finished the rains of spring. There were multiple houses ignited, and purposely."

Her statement was well thought out and logical. "Thank you. I shall take that into consideration. Is there anything else I can do to make your stay here more comfortable?"

"No, Yer Majesty, this is fine," the man replied. "But where are we to go?"

"Have you any relatives or friends here?"

"No; they were all... in Ferbundi."

The king thought fast. "After tonight, I will provide lodging at an inn, here in the city, until you can find a means of supporting yourselves."

"Thank ye, Yer Majesty."

"One question, though: where were you when the fires broke out?"

At this, the young couple blushed. She began to play with her fingers while he shuffled his feet. Finally the man looked up and said, "We were out watching the stars, Yer Majesty."

"Ahh." It had not been dark enough for stars yet when the fires broke out, but he would let that pass. Obviously, this couple had not climbed the mountain yet, which was why they were so bashful. He considered offering a second room but decided against it. They would want to be close to each other after the rest of their world had burned. All romantics aside, they would not have noticed many details. "Did you hear the troop of horses that the others reported?"

"Aye, Yer Majesty. We did not see it, but the sound was what made us start back to Ferbundi, only to see it go up in flames."

"Thank you. We will catch those who did this. Until then, good day." The young couple bowed, and King Derek left the room.

When the guard opened the next door, they were greeted immediately by a desperate-looking middle aged man.

"Have ye found them?" he demanded. His eyes were wild, framed by deep bags, his face and arms scorched, his hair a tangled mess.

Derek took a step back in spite of himself. "Not yet," he conceded. He needed to sound more confident.

The man stepped back, upset. "Why not?"

"The first men that returned from the mission were with you, but I have no doubt more will return with news in no more than two days. In the meantime, is there anything you could tell us?"

He began to pace. "I was out watching the sheep. Matthias was sick and stayed home, foolish boy—" he halted, shoved a fist against his mouth and scowled fiercely. "The sheep all twitched their ears toward town, then I heard the noise too." He resumed his pacing. "Like far-away thunder. I jumped onto Whitefoot and rode towards it. Then the whole village lit up like Moriah's cooking fire. Little Rose was learning to cook, too. She always loved to help, always got in the way—" here he stopped again, grinding his teeth. "Then the thunder vanished. When I got too close, Whitefoot reared and dumped me. I tried to run into the flames, I did. I could hear them. Screaming. For me. I tried to run in, again, and again, but the smoke was too much. Billy and Lena pulled me away later, they said. I don't remember. Then I rode for help. Is that enough for ye?"

"Did you see anything else, anything that could help us identify them?"

"I would've told ye if I had. I was on the north side of the walls. I couldn't see either gate. What was I supposed to see?"

"That is not what I meant—"

"Those villains killed my family!" A dish clattered behind Derek as the man grabbed him by the shoulders. "Do ye know what that is like?"

Derek felt something snap inside him. "Yes, I do!" he retaliated. "And I know what it is like to blame myself every waking moment for their murders!" The room echoed his words as he strove to conceal the pain

181

inside again. The man let him go. He drew a shaky breath and attempted to speak with more composure. "That is why you can be sure, sir, that I am doing the best I can, and will do all I can to see that at least one of us gets justice." His cape swished as he turned and strode out of the room, entourage behind. Once the door was shut, Taroki turned to him. Derek held his hand up to silence the words before they could exit his throat. "I know what you are going to say, Taroki. I don't want to hear it."

62

Katira couldn't help it. In that moment, she had seen how truly broken King Derek was; how much damage had been done to this man in the name of drama. "Yer Majesty?" she ventured.

"What?" he snapped.

She refused to back down. "Ye did the right thing."

He looked at her again. His ice-blue eyes held a hint of regret amidst the pain. "What?"

"Ye showed him that that you felt his grief and frustration, but you hold the power to do something about it. That comforted him."

He stared hard at her, his expression changing to... wonder? She dropped her eyes, mentally kicking herself. She had dropped her accent, after talking to him, after looking at him. Did she want Vivian to kill her? She needed to be more careful!

"Thank you."

She held her breath till he turned to the next door, then breathed out. The door stuck, and the moment dragged on. She could feel the other men watching her in surprise. The door finally gave, and she walked past them, following Derek into the room.

A dirty little girl with a tattered dress stared at her, then at the king, then at her again. She seemed frightened and out of place. Katira smiled at her while the king approached.

"Hello. My name is Derek. What's yours?"

The girl appraised him carefully, crossing her little arms. A determined look grew on her face and she stuck out her chin. "I ain't scrubbing yer floors. I didn't ask to be 'ere. If ye'll just let me go, I'll do fine on my own."

The king seemed surprised. "You are here as a guest, child. I would not make you work."

"S'pose I'm too young to work 'ere anyways. Ye ain't sendin' me to no tavern, neither."

The mention of a tavern reminded Katira instantly of Prince Adhemar, and she interrupted. "Of course not." She laid the tray she was holding onto the table and knelt to the girl's height, taking her hands. "Ye are not goin' to a tavern, even if ye wanted to."

Her squinted eyes relaxed slightly at this. "Then why did ye bring me here?"

"Well..." She pretended to think hard. "I had some extra pancakes and needed someone to eat them for me."

"Pancakes? Really?"

Katira felt a pang of hurt at how excited this little girl was for food. When was the last time she had eaten? But no proud little soul likes to be pitied, so she laughed instead. "Yes, and if ye hurry and eat them now, they might still be warm." The girl wasted no time in filling her mouth, swallowing faster than Katira would have thought possible. Katira pulled up a chair opposite her and laughed again. "If ye keep eating that fast, ye will choke."

She looked up, as if she had forgotten that Katira was there. A dribble of syrup was rolling down her chin. A stray strand of hair stuck to it. Katira quickly wiped it away and tucked the hair behind her ear. The girl shied from her touch, but looked at her with that curiosity in her eyes again. Before she could put more food in her mouth, Katira spoke again.

"What's yer name?"

"Gina." She inhaled another piece of pancake.

"My name is Kati."

"Are ye 'is servant?" Gina motioned to King Derek, who was watching the proceedings. Katira had felt his eyes on her and knew she was acting out of place. It didn't seem like he minded, but it wouldn't have mattered anyways. She was going to make Gina feel comfortable and safe. "Aye, I work for His Majesty."

184

"I don't work fer no one. They were all mean—'cept a few."

"Ye mean the other people from Ferbundi?"

"Yeah."

"I'm sorry, Gina."

She looked up from her plate. "What fer?"

"The fire."

"Ye didn't set it, did ye?"

"Nay, but I am sorry for ye. Yer family, yer home."

"Oh. Then ye don't need to be. I ain't got neither."

"What do ye mean?"

"I ain't never had any." She scraped her plate clean. "Why're ye askin'?"

"Well, that's what people do when they want to be friends. They ask questions to get to know them."

"Oh."

"Are ye still hungry?"

"Aye!"

"Do ye think ye can wait till suppertime?"

"What can I do till then? It's dull in here." She stole a look at the king to see if he heard her complaining.

"I don't know..." Katira turned toward him too.

63

No doubt Katira wanted to spend more time with the little girl; he had seen the instant tenderness in her face when she approached her, insisting that she would be safe here.

"Miss Katira, you stay here. Sebastian and Frederick, you may go, and Taroki and I shall leave also. Supper shall be brought up when it is ready."

A gentle smile spread over her lips. "Thank you."

"If you please, though, a word?" He motioned for her to come near the door. She stood and obeyed, curtsying when she reached him. "Would you be able to ask her about the fire, if she saw anything?" He smiled wryly. "I have the feeling that the general himself couldn't drag it out of her, but you might."

"I will do my best, Yer Majesty."

"I know. Thank you." The words left his mouth before he knew he had spoken them. He knew that she would; he had faith in her, somehow. But to speak that aloud? And on such little ground? Her own resolve slipped at his confidence, and she accidentally glanced up. He saw the warmth in her brown eyes upon being trusted. Then he left, for he could do no more than hinder.

It was too late now for tea if he planned on having supper, so Derek went into the library to peruse the history of Biatre's interactions with Taklin. Most of it he had skimmed over before, but this time he read them more closely. There were some interesting things to be found.

Firstly, it seemed Katira had been the first maid to be *officially* "gifted" to Biatre. A bystander had reported that they seen the mute girl unloaded from a Taklin ship a few days before she applied to work at the castle; it had been recorded but disregarded since there was no way to find out the truth. Now, though, it looked very suspicious.

Secondly, there was an account of a man, a Mason Blackwell, who had come with the first two of Taklin's visits. He was reported to have remained in Biatre, and to have climbed the mountain with a young widow from the port. That was curious.

Thirdly, Taklin had always been the one to initiate visits. Biatre had never gotten a ship through the rocks. Once, when Taklin invited King Willhem and Queen Marielle to visit, they had sent a ship for them. The pass was a secret, since the royal couple had never come back.

This led to another thing that Derek had mulled over countless nights: every member of his family had died while visiting with Taklin royalty.

Derek didn't throw the book down, but he wanted to. He had killed Charles. He might have thought about the risk before playing so recklessly.

Further study was useless. Taroki was waiting in the hall when he stepped out of the library.

64

"Well, Gina, what would you like to do?"

"I ain't ever been in a castle before. Can we explore?"

She smiled. "Of course we can."

They walked down the long hallway, discussing how uncomfortable the ancient royals looked in all their stiff finery. Katira had never taken time to look at these portraits before. There had been whole episodes on them; about the differences in reigning techniques, the passage of the bloodline, and even how fashion changed throughout history. At the end of the hallway, though, was one she had never seen before. It was King Derek, facing the artist as he was sworn in as king. He was kneeling on the dais while Taroki placed the crown on his head. Though his head was bowed, his eyes were raised, and the artist had captured them perfectly: the warmth of pain, love, and resolve encased in an icy blue. The gold frame held an inscription which said, "To forever serve, guide, and defend my people: the people of Biatre."

"Kati! Are ye goin' to show me the rest of the castle, or look at that portrait all day?"

Katira jumped at the little girl's reproach. "I'm sorry, Gina. Of course. Let's keep going." She led her charge through a few more hallways to the door leading to the ballroom. This wing of the castle was only used once a month for the balls, so surely they wouldn't be disturbing anyone. As she had suspected, there were no guards by the double doors. "Cover yer eyes," she told Gina.

"Last time I did that, I got knocked down."

"I promise I will not knock ye down."

Gina eyed her suspiciously. "Would ye swear to it?"

Katira knelt in front of the little girl again, looking her straight in the eyes. "No, I will not."

"And why not?"

"Because I believe in keeping my word. I will not knock ye down. If ye don't want to, though, ye don't have to." She stood back up and walked to the doors. They were heavy, but with a lot of grunting, they opened. She turned back to Gina. She was covering her eyes with her little hands. Katira smiled. "Now, Gina, I will put my hand on yer shoulder and lead ye forwards. Keep yer eyes closed." She led her out to the top of the stairs. "Ye may look now."

Gina's face brightened with surprise and delight. All the vast room was visible from this vantage point. They were high above the floor that now, without gowns and suits filling it, showed a beautiful mosaic pattern. All the curtains had been washed and put back up, the floor was clean, and it all smelt wonderful.

"Would ye like to play hide and seek?" Katira suggested.

"What's that?"

"We, ye count to twenty while closin' yer eyes, and I hide. Then ye must come find me."

"Ye do a lot with me closin' my eyes," Gina protested.

"If ye'd rather keep explorin', that's fine."

"Well... I can only count to ten."

"Oh. Ye could count very slowly, then. Perhaps I could teach ye more later?"

"I would like that," Gina admitted. "But now, go hide." She covered her eyes.

Katira tiptoed down the steps as quickly as she could. She looked around her but could not decide which alcove to hide in. She glanced up at Gina and saw her turning. She ducked into the nearest space. It was the little balcony Officer Glen had taken her to last night. She could feel the memory reeling over her, but she consciously pushed it away. She was not going to let that man ruin her life. He certainly was not worth spoiling a perfectly good game of hide and seek over.

From a gap in the curtains, she could watch Gina run around the floor, peeking around cushions, stooping behind chairs, and flinging aside hangings. Finally, she gave up, walked to the centre of the room and stamped her little foot.

"It's not fair! Kati, I can't find ye."

Katira laughed, giving away her position. "Ye give up so soon?"

65

Derek asked Taroki to find him when supper was ready; he needed to walk for a bit. His feet led him to the ballroom. The doors were left open, and he could hear voices inside. He stepped into the room just in time to see little Gina, far below, throw aside the curtain to the balcony. Katira was behind it. She jumped out and began to tickle her. Gina shrieked and giggled. He leaned against the balustrade. It had been a long time since he had heard the sound of childish laughter and watched a motherly woman play so carefree with her charge.

Footsteps sounded in the corridor behind him. Derek ducked behind a tapestry before he could be discovered. Taroki entered and looked about, no doubt expecting to find his king here but only seeing the maid and the little girl. "Excuse me, Miss, but the suppers are being delivered." He left the room.

Katira and Gina walked out of his line of sight and came up the stairs. Gina was chattering about the height of the chandeliers and asking how they lit them and imagining what they would have for supper. When they passed the slit in the tapestry he was standing behind, he felt the need to divert his eyes for fear Katira might feel him staring, but she did not look up. She was far too busy gazing at the little girl whose hand she held gently in her own.

He waited till he could no longer hear them in the hall, then extracted himself from the tapestry and went in search of Taroki. When he found him, the older man's face was drawn and creased. Derek could feel himself slip back into the role of a king.

"What is it, Taroki?"

"Sire, a messenger from the search party we sent has returned."

"What does he have to say? Is he still here?"

"No, Sire, he left immediately. He was merely here to inform us that they have found the tracks of a large group of horses. Half of the contingent split to follow the trail."

"Which direction?"

"Leaving Ferbundi's west gate, going southeast."

"But there are no settlements south of Ferbundi. Could someone else have found the pass through the rocks to Biatre and is now wreaking havoc by way of introducing themselves?"

"We have never had any visitors but Taklin."

Derek narrowed his eyes.

"Who have always been on friendly terms," Taroki added quickly.

"Be that as it may, I would not put it entirely out of their doing. Also, they could have passed the information on, accidentally or not—even though they never would tell *us* the way out."

"It is a possibility, Sire."

Derek's stomach growled. He could smell the food from where he stood now, but he turned around. "You may eat now, Taroki. I am going to see if Miss Katira has learned anything from the little girl."

66

When they got back to Gina's room, they didn't have to wrestle with the sticky door. Not only was it already open, but supper was laid out, and Bridget was pouring hot water into a tub in the corner.

"Would ye like to wash before ye eat?" Katira asked her charge.

"Why?"

"Well, to be clean. It is much more comfortable to relax and enjoy yer food when ye are tidy and fresh."

"All right… but ye must stand in the other corner, and not look."

Katira nodded, managing to keep a straight face at the little girl's firm command in exchange for cleanliness. She walked to a corner and stood facing the wall. "I shall not stir."

For a moment there was silence as Gina stood still; the corner Katira was standing in was not the one she had pointed at. Then her footsteps sounded towards the tub, and splashing ensued. Katira breathed an inward sigh of relief that she had not put up a fuss. Her facial expression, however, she kept carefully schooled in naivety. Perhaps Vivian would think that she had forgotten about the camera in this corner and that she was blocking it by accident. Perhaps.

Bridget walked up beside her, also facing the wall. "Ye'd never guess what Sasha seen yesterday, Kati."

Katira's eyes threatened to roll while a smile tugged at her mouth. "Do I want to know?"

"King Derek kissed the princess!"

"What?" The word had very little volume, even after the effort it took to create and expel. She could feel her smile drop. It snagged her heart, filtered to her toes, and oozed out through the soles of her shoes.

"She was passin' by the ballroom door, when everyone was leavin', cleanin' up a few things before bed, and she seen it! Said it was passion if she ever saw any, and she has two sisters and a brother that've already climbed the mountain, so she should know. Can ye believe it?"

A response was expected now, and she did her best, mechanically speaking while imagining the fun Miss Director was having behind the camera. "Of course. What could be more natural?"

"Ugh, Kati, ye're no fun." Bridget spun on her heel and left the room.

"Ye can look now, Kati. I'm all done."

Katira turned around. Gina had scrubbed herself surprisingly well, and had dressed in the nightgown laid out for her. "Are ye ready to eat?"

"Aye!"

She wolfed down her supper as if she had not had a stack of pancakes only an hour ago. Once she was polishing off her plate, Katira decided it was time to ask the question.

"Gina, did ye see anythin' happen the night of the fire?"

"I see lots of things. Why?"

"If ye tell us what ye know, we can catch the people that set it."

"I seen a bunch of men on 'orses, carryin' torches. They was the ones who burned it all."

"Did ye see anything else? Why would they set a whole village on fire?" The second question was more of a hypothetical one, but Gina answered both.

"They was chasing these other people, three of 'em. I was sneakin' 'round Madam Frenney's fruit stand, 'cause she don't like me, and I didn't want 'er to see me. She comes out just then, and I duck under the table. A man comes up on his 'orse to talk to Madam Frenney, and the 'orse rears, and it kicks 'er, right in the 'ead! The man rides away, and this big girl comes and talks to the old lady, but she don't get up. One man comes and says something, then another one comes down Main, runnin' and shoutin' somethin' awful. And right behind 'im's a whole 'erd of those soldiers."

"Soldiers?"

"Aye, they looked it. All was carryin' swords and they was on big 'orses, too. They chased 'em, and set their torches to everythin' they passed. One even set fire to Madam Frenney's stall, right above me! I get out after they pass and run down the street by Ollie's place, and get out through the hole in the fence there. Then…" The excitement faded from Gina's storytelling as she mumbled the ending. "Then it all burned." Her lower lip trembled; her big eyes filled with tears.

Katira got up from her chair and went to the little girl, wrapping her arms around her. "It's all right, Gina. Ye're safe here." Gina began to sob, so Katira picked her up and carried her to the bed. She sat on the side and rocked her back and forth. Katira had not held a small child in a long time. It brought her back to her days in the orphanage, where she had sometimes helped with the babies. She had missed the feeling of a little body in her arms, the shared warmth, the peace seeping from herself into the troubled little mind and making all things right.

After a few minutes, Gina quieted, and Katira whispered to her again, "It will be all right." She wiped away the last tears and tucked her into bed, bestowing a kiss on her forehead. "I'll see ye in the morning, Gina. Sleep well."

Katira tiptoed out of the room and shut the door quietly behind her. She turned to walk down the hall and there was the king! Her feet betrayed her and she tumbled forwards. All was lost. All pride, all dignity, all composure. It was all lost.

But she did not hit the floor. Strong arms caught her.

King Derek put her back on her feet.

She gasped, mortified. "I am so sorry, Yer Majesty."

67

Derek chuckled, which silenced her instantly. "It is all right, Miss Katira," he said.

She gave a curtsy to regain her composure, then stood quietly, waiting for him to speak.

He cleared his throat. "Did you learn anything about the fire?"

She nodded. "Aye, I did. She seen a group of mounted men in armour chase—"

"Please, Miss Katira." He interrupted her. She was speaking to the floor again. "Pardon me for interrupting you, but please look me in the eyes. I am finding it very difficult to concentrate."

Her head tilted up, brown eyes fastening onto his. Why was she being shy now? She had been perfectly eloquent in the library and at the ball. She had even stood up to him before when even Taroki was afraid to. Now she was acting like a servant again. Even though that was technically what she was, she was his informant now, nearly his equal.

"Thank you. Now, what were you saying?"

68

Katira felt that now, she could not concentrate. His ice-blue eyes were intently studying hers, waiting for her explanation. "She seen a group of mounted men, on horses. She said that they were soldiers, that they were carrying swords." *Stupid stupid stupid! Wow, they were mounted on horses? Or soldiers with swords? Really?* She took a deep breath. "First one soldier came and spoke to a fruit seller. His horse spooked and kicked her, then he left. A girl found the fruit seller, knelt down and spoke to her, and two men came. One was followed by the soldiers, who gave chase and set the village on fire behind them. Gina escaped through a hole in the fence."

Derek nodded. "How big of a group? Did they have any symbol on their armour? Which direction did they come from?"

"I do not know, Yer Majesty."

He ran a hand through his hair, exasperated. "And the child is sleeping already, no doubt. Why did you not ask her?"

Katira could feel ire rising in her. Gina was only a little girl, and she was traumatized, and she was tired! She frowned. "Well, pardon me, Your Majesty, but I've never conducted an interrogation before!" Her anger dropped as her stomach plummeted. She dragged her hands from where they covered her mouth to straight at her sides, standing rigid. Had she just raised her voice to the king?

His tone matched hers. "Why are you so scared of me? I can barely get you to say an honest word, and then you cower!"

The moment hung in the air. The change in topic had given her whiplash, so she just answered his question, speaking to his shoes. "In Taklin, they would've had me whipped for that."

Suddenly her hand was encased in his. "I would never do that."

She raised her eyes and searched his, wanting to believe, but shaking her head. "How do I know? What could make you different?" She pulled her hand back to herself and walked away. He did not call after her. She was grateful, for she knew she would have turned back.

The kitchen was usually perfect to distract one's self with, but now even the bustle could not clear her head. Her mind spun.

The king had kissed the princess. Really, what could be more natural? Just because she had seen little affection on the king's side didn't mean it didn't exist. But when she had been helping with the survivors, her mind had immediately jumped to being a help to him, standing by his side, being his queen… she had immediately killed that idea and reminded herself of her situation, but apparently it was not completely dead. When Bridget said that he had ki—she shook her head and worked faster. He had every right to do as he pleased. He had every right to kiss whomever he wanted, and if it affected her, it was her own fault.

Why was it affecting her? She groaned inwardly. Vivian and Miss Director were getting their drama! It was the only reason Pricilla had come, to be sure; Katira knew that there was no way the pampered "princess" would consent to leave behind the amenities of the modern life to play queen in a real life movie set for the rest of her years.

No, no one would choose this life willingly. If they were forced, though… would they eventually want to stay? There was something to be said for this way of living; it was so much more real, genuine, purposeful.

Except for being filmed.

That fact doused Katira's thoughts the same way she doused the fires with leftover dishwater before she left the kitchen.

69

What could make you different?

When she tugged her hand out of his, he let her go. He wanted to call her back, but there was nothing to say. Her question echoed in his mind as she disappeared around the corner. What could make him different? Everyone tried to be good, and most people thought they were. His conversation with the princess came back to him. *Is there a standard?*

A cough sounded behind him. "Sire, if you do not eat soon, your food will be cold." It was Taroki.

"I am afraid I don't much care."

"You must keep up your strength. There will be more news tomorrow."

Derek nodded and followed his advisor to his room. When his parents were still living, they would have guests often, and dinners were a jovial event. There was always much conversation and laughter around the long table, especially before Charles—

The king now took his meal in his own quarters.

Sleep was not an option. The world was too full of turmoil. How could he sleep when his people had been so violated, and were so at risk even now? Rationality told Derek that he couldn't do anything about it right now, so he ought to get some rest. But just when he had convinced himself and began to relax, accusations rose up in him for his apathy. But what was there to be done?

He opened the door to broaden his pacing. The library had no new answers, so his feet took him to the gardens. From there he walked through the servant's work yard, past the guard, and over the bridge to the back lawn. His bodyguards followed him this time, to protect him from any young ladies singing in the woods. He gave a little chuckle at that thought. It seemed so long ago.

Who could it have been? Like the first time, he felt the problem should be a sufficient distraction from his current issues. These woods stretched nearly to the mountain, but a large section was fenced in for royal use. Since no one could have gotten over it, the girl must have come from the palace. It was the night before the princess and her father arrived, so it was no one they had brought along. Only a few of the castle servants stayed overnight, since most of them had homes nearby, except Katira—of course! The young lady sitting in the moonlight, whispering her indecipherable sorrows to the wind, had had long, dark hair that was still crimped from being in a braid. He had not seen her face, but when she had run away, he had seen her height: barely up to his shoulders. Short enough to duck under a branch that he had not.

He had solved the mystery! Miss Katira had been out here that night. She had been the one singing, the one who had haunted his dreams... Why had she been out here? Was she a spy? She certainly was a most peculiar mix of bold and terrified, and her accent was continually fluctuating between rustic and refined.

Derek turned around and headed back into the castle. The guard that night had not seen anyone, which meant she had gone without permission. How could she have gotten out? Perhaps he would ask her that. In the morning.

70

"Kati, could ye tell me more about the God ye say ye don't believe in?" Bridget whispered, snuggling deeper into her covers, her face peering out at Katira in the darkness.

"I don't know what to tell ye."

"Surely there must be somethin' else that ye remember. I was thinkin': it's all well and good to know that there's something beautiful after death, but what about right now? Does God say somethin' about that?"

"I don't know." Katira realized that whenever she thought about God, she only thought of what he could do for her now, in her current situation. If he had provided eternity, then did any of this matter? Still, Bridget had a point. "Actually, there was this one poster in Miss Eillah's room—"

"Who's Eillah?"

"Oh, sorry. She was a mentor at my orphanage, before I worked at the Taklin castle. Anyways, she had this poster that said everything works out for good, to anyone who loves God, or something like that."

"Everything?"

"She said it might not look like good always, but it was always coming. Even if it was only after death, it was always worth waitin' for."

"I like that. And why don't ye believe it, Kati?"

"Just because ye like it doesn't mean it's real. And I don't know." Katira shrugged underneath her covers. "It just seems the good never happens."

The answer was simple enough for Bridget. "That's prob'ly 'cause ye're not dead yet."

"Maybe so."

"And what happens to the people who don't love Him?"

"Miss Eillah said there's this place called hell, with everlasting fire."

Bridget sat up straight in bed. "Kati!"

"Girls," Oregga's voice intoned. "Git ye some sleep now. I won't be goin' easy on ye tomorrow if ye stay up late tonight."

Katira stayed quiet for a while, appreciating the break in conversation, but it still demanded an answer. "I don't know, Bridget. What if it's not real, and ye spend yer whole life chasin' after a fairy tale?"

"So what?"

Beds creaked as a few women rolled over, disturbed by them again. Bridget whispered, "I'd rather be safe than sorry, Kati. And I'd rather have some hope than none at all."

Those words gave Katira a lot to stew over.

71

Nelda closed her eyes, trying to sleep, but she knew the summons would come, and it did. Her hand vibrated. She made sure the blanket was over her head, then drew it out. One of Pricilla's servants had brought her a new phone, and she was not skilled in its use yet, but sadly, texting was easy enough.

Miss Director: Do you have it on you?

Her hands shook of their own accord.

Nelda: Yes.

Miss Director: Use it.

She didn't respond. She could hear Bridget and Katira whispering again. Why wouldn't Katira keep her mouth shut? Nelda hadn't been allowed to warn her about how dangerous it was to talk about God here. But surely she knew! Why was she blabbing about Him now? She clenched the phone in her fist, wondering if she could break it if she squeezed it hard enough. She pushed the lone button and it turned on. *Oh, snap.* There was a text there from three minutes ago. Miss Director knew she was hesitating. It was a silhouetted picture of someone in the moonlight climbing the rigging of an old-fashioned ship, with a simple caption beneath it.

Miss Director: We wouldn't want him to fall from there, would we?

Nelda: No!

But just as she sent it, another text came through. This one was a video. She pressed play.

The figure was called down from where he was. Or rather, he must have been called, because there was no volume on her phone. But he looked around, then started to descend. Nelda gasped and shoved a fist into her mouth. Her eyes misted immediately and she rubbed the heels of her palm into them, wanting to see as clearly as possible. He landed on the deck and turned to face whoever was recording him. It had been a long time since she had seen him. He wasn't a scared nine-year-old anymore. He was tall, suntanned, and muscular, the soft edges of boyhood on his face nearly worn away. "Samuel," she whispered. Another man came into the picture and grabbed his arm, injecting him with a syringe before he could resist. She bit her lip till she tasted blood. This always happened. He stiffened and followed the man below deck, where they bound him in a chair. His face contorted in fear as the man drew back his fist and drove it into his gut. The man struck again and again until Samuel's mouth was open in a cry of pain. There were tears on his cheeks. The video ended.

Nelda: Stop! I'll do it!

Miss Director: Of course you will. You should know by now.

Nelda: When?

Miss Director: Within the hour.

Nelda shoved the phone under her pillow again, grabbing fistfuls of her sheets and squeezing them until her white knuckles screamed for relief. She welcomed the pain. She pinched her arms, bit her tongue, and writhed in agony. Why did she have to do this? And yet the look on her brother's face—she would do anything for him. She had to do this.

Katira and Bridget finally quieted, and Nelda slipped out from her covers. She shivered from the change in temperature, but more from the cacophony of emotions running through her: hatred for herself, love for her brother, pity for herself, and love for Katira. The memory of their first meeting in Biatre was still fresh in her memory, revived every time she used sign language to communicate with the other servants. Katira had taught the hand letters to everyone working in the kitchen. Nelda had been so grateful. Pretending to be a mute was much easier when there was another way to communicate. She didn't know why that had been one of Miss Director's demands. She didn't know why Miss Director even gave her demands. But she knew that she had to fulfil those demands if she wanted to keep her little brother safe.

She had gotten the syringe from under her mattress and rounded the corner of Katira's bed when she heard a muffled vibration. She stood still, her heart pounding. It was repeated. She tiptoed back to her bed, crept under the covers, and withdrew the phone.

Miss Director: Not Katira! Bridget!

Nelda: Ok.

She responded right away, but her heart plummeted even further. Yes, Katira was her best friend, but she should have known better. Why would Miss Director want Bridget? An innocent fifteen-year-old who had absolutely nothing to do with anything? It made Nelda sick, but there was nothing she could she do. She got out of bed again, gripping the syringe in her fist. She hated Taklin and would willingly have inserted this syringe into Miss Director's heart instead of into the freckled elbow lying atop the pile of blankets.

Her own blankets twisted and tangled, but when morning came, Nelda was the last to get out of bed—or rather, the second last.

"Bridget!" Katira was shaking the girl beneath the covers. "The sun is up already! Oregga will have yer head if ye're not up in another minute. Bridget!"

Nelda could not pull her eyes away as Katira yanked off the blanket. Katira gasped, and Nelda couldn't hide her own horror. Blood was in a pool on Bridget's pillow, sticking to her mouth and nose. She was lying on her side, whiter than the sheets, curled in a ball. Her eyes were wide and red.

Nelda felt herself getting lightheaded just as Katira crumpled to the ground. Someone caught her, and Nelda steadied herself on the bedpost. Skirts rustled as the women surrounded the bed, blocking the sight. Then a strangled scream split the air. One woman had rolled the suffering girl onto her back. Katira stood up next to her, visibly trembling, and fought her way back to the bedside. A few women were cleaning away the blood while Oregga directed something about cold water. Katira reached for Bridget's hand, and Nelda forced herself to stroke it. It was sweaty and limp.

Bridget's wide blue eyes found Katira's face and focused on it while tears flowed down the tracks on her cheeks. She took a deep breath. Her pupils rolled back in her head, but they returned. "Kati..."

"Shh, it's all right, Bridget. Hush. I'm right here," Katira whispered.

"He's... waiting... for me... aye?"

Nelda flinched. Miss Director would not like this, but what more could she do?

"Who, Bridget? Who's waiting for ye?"

"God... I hear..."

"No, Bridget, ye don't hear anything," Katira persisted. "Ye're going to be fine."

"I... hear..." Her eyes rolled upwards again. They didn't come back down.

"Bridget? Bridget!" Katira shook the hand she was holding, but it was unresponsive. "No!" she screamed. One of the women took her from behind while Nelda numbly pried the living fingers from the dead ones. "No!" She kicked and thrashed. Nelda helped hold her back while she continued to scream. "Bridget!"

Nelda's hate transformed to utter loathing as she remembered the text she had come back to after the dreadful deed. She lowered her head to Katira's ear. "Quite the acting skills, Katherine." The girl froze in her grip, and she continued. "Especially when it's your fault she's dead."

Katira felt limp and senseless on the floor. Nelda slumped beside her, crushed with grief—and the thought that those words should have been meant for herself.

72

Derek was up early again, sleep being elusive as if afraid that he would forget his discovery. After a few hours of candlelit reading through papers and documents concerning building regulations and tax margins on this year's harvest, he was relived to hear a knock at the door.

"Good morning, Taroki."

"Good morning, Sire. Did you sleep well?"

"Not a whit. Who proposed this increase on the wheat tax?"

"That was Datio, I believe."

"And what does he hope to gain by it?"

"Most likely that in collecting more for you, Sire, more might accidentally fall into his own wagon."

"As I thought. I do not believe the increase will be necessary." Derek wrote a few lines on the paper, then picked up another. "Now, what is this business about another tavern?"

"It appears that Harique does not think two is enough. He wants to buy Morton's boarding house, but Morton will not hear of it, even after the ridiculously high price he was offered."

"And why is this my concern?"

"Because Harique believes his wealth should hold some standing of importance."

"I shall have to let him know otherwise. Was there anything else that requires my immediate attention?"

"Not presently, provided you have gone through all those parchments."

"I have. Now, Taroki, I have deduced something that eases my mind at least a little. The girl in the woods was Miss Katira!"

Surprise was evident on his advisor's face. "How do you know this?"

"Her height. I heard her sing, you recall, and it was not a young girl's voice, but she was quite short."

"And one cannot climb the wall."

"Exactly, do you see?"

"Perhaps."

"Now I must somehow get her to reveal it. A well-placed question of her whereabouts that night, or an excuse for her to sing—"

"Is that wise?"

"If you have a better course of action, please do share it."

"What I meant, sir, was this: is it wide for you to question her? If you are sure it is she, are you in any danger? Perhaps she simply wanted a moment alone. Everything she has done till now seems to prove her loyalty and sincerity."

"That is what worries me, Taroki. The first time I ever heard her speak was a few days ago, just before Rosseen and Pricilla came to visit, and now it seems that she is everywhere."

"At your request, Sire."

That was true. "But the way she acts; it is not like a servant. Not to mention her accent continually oscillates. And I caught the way the princess glared at her a few times. There is history there."

"That is true, Sire. But please do use caution. She could prove a useful asset."

"The last time I thought that, I ended up doing all the talking. There is something about her, Taroki, that I do not trust."

"Are you sure you would not like me to question her, Sire?"

"Thank you, Taroki, but I shall. Do ask the kitchen staff to have her send up my breakfast. I will stew over the predicament till then."

"Aye, Sire. I shall call for it now."

Derek had barely arranged the papers on his desk back into their appropriate stacks before Taroki was back. His eyebrows were knit in concern and his mouth held a note of urgency.

"Sire, you will have to wait to break your fast a while longer."

"Training begins in an hour. What is the reason?"

"The girl who usually brings your food—Bridget—is dead, Sire."

"What? How?"

"Oregga believes it must have been something she ate, though no one else has any symptoms. It has the look of poisoning."

A sick feeling began to crawl up Derek's stomach as Taroki described how the girl had been found in the morning, drowning in her own blood and vomit. Bridget was always so cheerful, her red curls escaping her cap as she bounced lightly through the door with his tray. Surely she would come in a few minutes, like she always did; but no. Derek had lost someone too many times to be tricked by the instinctive denial. This was real. He picked up his crown and placed it on his head.

"Has her family been contacted?"

"Aye, Sire. They want to bury the body as soon as possible in the case that the poison might spread."

The body. The words seemed so calloused and cold. "Send word to the guard. Their king will not be training with them today. They are to go on as normal. Have a message run down to Cally's for a casket, and one to Maurice's for flowers."

"Aye, Sire."

Taroki left to carry out his orders. Derek sat down, his knees suddenly weak, the crown heavy. Bridget had brought joy while she was here, but now she was gone, and what had she accomplished? The smiles she had incited would be forgotten in a few years. Poisoned. Who could poison such a pretty, happy girl? Who would possibly... no, it could not be Katira. Could it? He had no reason to mistrust anyone else.

73

Having heard that his suspect had fainted, the king decided to forgo his questioning till later. He accompanied the group of servants with the casket to the cemetery, where they met with her family.

Bridget had been the youngest of her siblings. There were several of her little nieces and nephews crowding around to get a look at the casket, then shrinking back as soon as they caught sight of it. Derek said a few words to her parents about her cheerfulness and hard work. They nodded and tried to smile through their tears.

He watched as they all paid their last respects, then left the graveyard. Some wailed and howled; the little ones watched with huge, startled eyes; the older ones shook their heads and wiped away silent tears with calloused fingers. They all looked so... hopeless.

Taroki greeted Derek as he entered the castle. As soon as the guards left him at the door, he said quietly, "Sire, there is someone you must attend to."

The gates had not been opened to visitors yet. "Who?"

Footsteps rounded the corner ahead, and a little girl came streaking around the corner. "There ye are!"

"Miss Gina, did I not tell you to stay put?" Taroki scolded.

"I don't wanna go back to bed. Where's Kati?"

"She is ill. King Derek is going to speak with her, and perhaps you may see her afterwards."

The little girl insisted on following them to the door of the maids' sleeping quarters. Derek knocked. Nelda opened the door, and he entered. The room seemed of damp linen, blood, and sweat.

His eyes caught Katira instantly. She was leaning back, her hair messily splayed across the pillows. Her face was mottled with red. Her puffed eyelids tried to open as she took a breath, but then they slammed shut and her chest shuddered beneath the blankets. Either she was sincerely grieving, or she was an incredible actress.

Before he could reach the bed, though, Gina dashed past him. Taroki gave a muffled exclamation from behind the door. Gina ran to the bedside and immediately demanded why she had not come to play with her.

Katira responded to the little girl's impertinence with a faint smile that nearly won her redemption. *But first things first.* He scolded Gina and sent her to a corner.

What he was going to say, he had not planned enough. "Miss Katira, I would like to say that I am sorry for your loss. The other servants say you two were quite close."

Katira nodded, a fresh tear running down the tracks on her cheek. She looked absolutely miserable.

A pang struck his own heart, and he could not refrain from saying, "I know this is what everybody says, but it will get better. The world does not stop turning, and in a while, you will be glad it didn't."

74

The words penetrated Katira, filtering through her sluggish mind, waking it up. A rogue thought took that moment to flee its confines and escape. "Have you reached that point yet?"

"I—" he sighed. "I like to think so sometimes. But there are days... well, I am sure you know."

"Actually, I don't. I never cared much for anyone before, and now, I wish I hadn't." It seemed that other ideas were following the first villain. "You know, she died thinking that God was going to take her to heaven. But is that even real? There is no proof for any of those ideas. There are so many different religions, too. How could I know that—" her voice caught in a sob. "I want to see her again."

Nelda sat down on the bed and wrapped her arms around her. They leaned into each other until the sobs ran dry.

"I do not know about other religions, and Biatre has never acknowledged God before, but my mother had a few books about Him," Derek offered. "I will send them over, and you may read them if you like while you rest. You do not need to work until you can get your strength up again. Nelda, could you get one of the other girls to play with Miss Gina, please? Have them take her out to the gardens." He left the room.

Nelda did as she was told, then came back to Katira. "Eat," she signed.

"I'm not hungry."

"Need anything?"

Katira shook her head, shoving away the covers. "I'll get dressed and come to the kitchen."

"No."

"What else have I got to do? I'll go crazy."

"Read."

"Right." She let her protesting head fall back onto the pillows. "Thank ye, Nelda."

She nodded sadly and left the room. Katira marvelled at how calm she was. No doubt tonight, when all the women were no longer occupied, it would be a noisier affair.

Bridget was so young. She had never climbed the mountain and had children, which Katira knew she had looked forward to, after a seasonable time of flirting, of course. Now she would never get to.

75

Did you learn anything to aid you in your suspicions, Sire?" Taroki asked once they were nearly at the other end of the castle.

"No. I did not even think to ask."

"Where are you going now?"

"To get some books from my mother's study. I believe they might comfort Miss Katira."

"A moment ago, you were considering that she had been the one to kill Bridget!"

"And I am not sure yet!" Derek stopped at the door to his parents' rooms. "But—I do not know. Perhaps what is in those books could help her. My mother clung to those books when Charles—died. Or perhaps they could open up avenues of conversation that could trick her into revealing herself. Did you know, Taroki, that this is the first time she has said something honest, without her accent, where she did not try to cover it up or apologize?"

Taroki eyed him warily for several breaths. "I fear, Sire, that Miss Katira is succeeding where Princess Pricilla failed."

Derek did not know how to respond to that, or even what to think. He walked through the room, glanced back to ensure Taroki was not looking, pushed back the tapestry, and opened the secret door. The hallway was narrow and he had to feel his way through the blackness. The wall gave a turn into the little room. He found the fireplace, then took the little pieces of flint and steel from his pocket and lit a small fire in the grate.

The flickering light mixed with the scent of old pages transported him back eighteen years.

"Shh! You don't want to get caught, do you?"

Derek clapped his hand over his mouth and shook his head.

"If you make any more noise, we're going back to bed."

Derek nodded, eyes wide. He followed his older brother down the dimly lit passageway. Charles reached the end and eased the door inwards, then pulled back the curtain just a hair. Warm light spilled in, and they could see the shelved walls of the small room covered in books. The gilt lettering on the spines gleamed in the firelight.

In the overstuffed armchair sat a woman. She had her bare feet over one side and her hair let down around her face like a cloud. Her dress was white— it was her nightgown—and her tiara was on the nearby table, crowning a stack of books waiting to be read. Everything about her was laughing in the face of decorum as she relaxed, quietly reading to herself.

"Intreat me not to leave thee, or to return from following after thee: for whither thou goest, I will go; and where thou lodgest, I will lodge: thy people shall be my people, and thy God my God—"

Just then the curtain on the other side of the room was drawn aside and in walked the king. Derek and Charles nearly fell over each other in their rush to move so he wouldn't see them.

The queen looked up and smiled, reading the last line a little louder. "Where thou diest, will I die, and there will I be buried. The Lord do so to me, and more also, if ought but death part thee and me."

"When the servants said they couldn't find you anywhere, I knew this would be where you were." He let the curtain fall behind him.

"You know me well." She smiled and swung her feet over the lean to the floor, then stood, leaving the book behind her.

"I also know that you should be waiting in bed for me by now." Her husband's brow creased, and he rubbed his forehead. "This is far too late to be up if you want to be coherent during the daytime."

"I know, dear. I'll simply hold onto your arm and let you do the talking." She raised her crown from the stack of books and placed it on her head. He reached out and pulled her to himself.

"Doesn't that sound like a model queen." He kissed her, and she melted into him. Just then, giggles erupted from the curtain the boys were hiding behind. The pair pulled apart, then turned toward the curtain, eyebrows raised. "Boys?"

Charles was immediately scolding his little brother. "They wouldn't have even noticed us!"

Derek frowned in defence. "You were laughing too!"

"Boys." The tone in the king's voice was enough to draw their attention back to him.

"Yes, Father?" They were guilty, and they knew it.

"You know what we said about using these tunnels, boys. They are for escape purposes. If we use them too often, the servants will figure them out."

"Yes, Father. We just wanted to listen to Mother read. We like that story," Charles explained, his six-year-old wisdom setting it all straight.

"Well, I suppose we'll have to finish the story, then, won't we?" King Willhem sat down on the floor in front of the fireplace, and the boys eagerly climbed into his lap. Queen Marielle smiled at them. She sat down in her chair and read aloud until Derek and Charles fell asleep.

Everything was covered in dust now. Derek picked through some of the books on the table, swiping the covers to read them. One was a pretty little book that had probably belonged to an elegant lady on the ship that had crashed when Biatre was founded. Katira would like that one. There were two others, just below it, that would interest her as well. These had the inscription of belonging to a priest, or holy man, who had died within months of the new colony. He picked them up, doused the fire, and exited the little room.

Derek passed the books off to the first cleaning maid he seen, then went on about his business. He was too late for training, but there were always more people to see, meetings to preside, gifts to accept, and disputes to settle. Taroki had left for his half-day, but he would manage fine.

76

Atila stopped in her tracks. She hissed for silence, then dove headfirst into the nearest bush. Following her example, Lato and Rati ducked into hiding as well. They laid low among the bottom branches and made sure that the leaves closed again over their heads. The sound of an engine rumbled through the woods.

They scrambled to get out of the way. The noise crunched closer and closer, but not very quickly. Once it was visible through the woods, they could see that there were ranks of Taklin soldiers surrounding the Spider. They were marching in impressive order in the uneven terrain. Not a single soldier even looked to the right or the left. It took a while for the entire convoy to pass.

"So they got through the mountains." Lato crawled out of his bush. "They didn't look like a search party, though."

Rati agreed, unconsciously brushing the tender spot on his stomach. "They looked more like an army."

"I still want to know how they found us out, though. I wonder if there is such a thing as the cameras. The old lady certainly didn't tell anyone—" Lato cut off as he felt Atila's glare into the side of his head. "Listen, I don't know her name, and she couldn't have told anyone, right?"

"I just wish we didn't have to refer to her as 'the old lady'. It sounds so rude." She kicked at the grass.

"That's what you're harping on? Come on, we have bigger problems."

"And we might encounter more old ladies dying on the side of the street, so we'll need to tell them apart. Let's call her Bertha."

"Bertha?"

"Yup."

Of course Atila would take personal offence to this. Lato exhaled. "Fine. So, we know that *Bertha* didn't tell anyone, and none of the soldiers were there when you were talking to her, right?"

"The first ones I seen were the ones chasing you." She shuddered. "I wonder what happened in Ferbundi. Do you think any villagers got out in time?"

"Maybe a few, but I doubt it." Rati's words sounded dull as they fell to the ground.

Without noticing, Atila's pace slowed. The thought of all those homes, where families had thought they were sleeping safely, burning to the ground—all those terrified children, frantic parents, powerless elders...

"Guys!" Lato asserted. "This is why we're going to the king, remember?"

"I thought we were going to tell him about God," Rati remarked almost sarcastically.

"It's kind of the same thing," he explained. "Fifteen said they were after you, Atila, because of what you said. Maybe Master Blackwell was right about the cameras. Vivian doesn't want God involved. If we tell the king, he can order all the cameras found and removed, right? Then we can tell anyone about God, the way it should be."

"You're right, Lato." Atila's steps quickened again.

"Let's run?"

Without responding, Atila took off in the lead, but Lato and Rati were not far behind.

77

There were three books on the bedside table beside the untouched bowl of stew. Katira reached for the top one, brushed off the dust, and opened its yellowed pages. She lifted it to her nose and took a deep breath. She sighed. It had been a while since she had read anything.

The cover was a rose colour with the name "Ruth" written across it in gilt lettering. She had never heard Miss Eillah talk about Ruth before. She opened the book, its pages crackling and the ink in the looping cursive faded, but still very legible.

The story was a romance. The tale was lovely, but what Katira was interested in the most was that, in the beginning of the story, God's people disobeyed Him, so He sent a famine on their land. In the end, when the repentant Naomi and loyal Ruth returned, the people had also changed their ways, and the land had been restored. *So God punished those who went against him, but he forgave them when they turned back to him,* she realized. Even Ruth, who had been an outsider, was accepted. *Whether God accepted people was dependant on their state of heart; he would take anyone.*

The end result was very satisfying. Katira felt as though, if God were real, Bridget was in good hands.

Bridget.

Guilt smacked Katira on the side of her head, sending her tumbling. How could she be enjoying a book, curling deeper into her bedding, sighing in satisfaction, when Bridget was dead?

Facts were facts. The only difference was what one did with them. Katira sat up straighter, wiped the tears away, and picked up the next book. This one was inscribed as "The Gospel of Mark". She started in and was oblivious to the world for a while longer. It was the story Miss Eillah told most often, the one about God's Son, Jesus. He taught huge crowds of people how to live better, healed their sick, and told them little stories. Some rulers got jealous and had him killed, but He rose—from the dead— after three days in the tomb, then went back to His Father with a promise to return. It was a fascinating story, to be sure, but was it more than that?

Katira could feel herself wearying of sitting in one place for so long. Helping out in the kitchen would at least give her purpose. She pulled her body out of bed and changed into her day dress, but that was all the energy she had. Back into bed she climbed, and reached wearily for the last book.

It was entitled "The Epistle to the Hebrews". The brown leather cracked as she opened it to thick pages filled with a firm, clear script. Some sections were underlined. All the letters began to look the same. She gathered vague notions, but no words would stick.

She lifted her head and rested her eyes, rolled her neck, and tried to calm her brain. There were several little sections with different topics, but they all seemed to be focussing on one point: that the Son of God was better. When she opened her eyes, she seen that the fire had dwindled to a pile of coals. She slipped out of bed and put a few more pieces of wood on it, then went back to her bed to grab her blanket. Curled up on the floor in front of a fire felt strange after two years with only one evening off. She opened the book.

The first words to greet her eyes startled Katira. *How shall we escape, if we neglect so great a salvation.* The phrase struck a chord in her heart, and she winced, then shook herself. "It could all be fairy tales," she whispered to herself. "There's no need to get scared of a few words on a page." She shut the book to prove it to herself and leaned against the bed behind her, closing her eyes. Her head still felt thick from crying before, and her eyes were exhausted. But those words… how could words come to life like that? It was the same way the words on Miss Eillah's poster had impacted her. Ringing through her head, demanding her to listen… but it was the same thing whenever she heard a catchy song. Those could always be lost by distraction, by singing another tune. Miss Director liked when she sang, and it might be a good idea since she had done nothing all day long but cry and sleep and read.

Various tunes flitted through her head, but they all had to do with mourning. She wanted distraction. A fixed rhyme and lively tune were just the thing.

"Down in the forest and over a brook
I chased a little fairy
It flew on glittered wings of finest glass
And sang along before me
It led me to a ballroom full of folk
All of her own shining kind
I wanted to join in the dance and fun
But they disappeared in time.
I wandered around in search of a sprite
Or elf, or moonbeam, or flower
I sought for one who could prove me not mad
But none were in the bower.
Well tricked, hard played, I hunted all in vain—"

Her voice faltered. A lump rose in her throat. In her mind, that little fairy had taken on curly red hair and freckles. *She wore a little apron, a bright smile, and blue eyes that were sparkling mischievously as she peeked from behind a tree, but by the time Katira reached it, the fairy was nowhere to be seen. She turned about it twice, then climbed up into the branches. The fairy had to be here. Why would she have disappeared? Didn't she want to be found? Isn't that why she was so happy? The branch snapped. She fell down, through the branches, and grunted as she landed on the rock hard ground. It hurt. It burned! The grass her foot had landed in burst into flames—*

Katira jerked her foot back as her eyes flew open. She was sprawled on the floor of the sleeping quarters. Gingerly, she reached for her foot and found no damage. She had merely touched the warm hearth. It had all been a nightmare. All a nightmare. She schooled her breathing and wiped away the tears that were searing her swollen cheeks again. "So much for distraction." She hauled herself up to her feet and headed back to bed. She pulled the covers up, not bothering to undress, hoping for sweet respite from the turmoil of reality.

78

"Running through the woods has got to be one of the best feelings," Atila said as they crested another hill. The setting sun lay in the west. Everything was golden while she rested her hands on her knees, catching her breath.

"Nothing like it." Lato was panting too.

They had run as much as Rati could keep up with. He was spent, but this was a marvellous vantage point. He stretched up to see the distance ahead. "There it is!"

All three stood still, gazing at the sparkling river that encircled the castle. Lato nudged Atila with his shoulder. "Yes, I know, it's beautiful," he said.

"I hope it's as beautiful up close. What's the matter, Rati?"

He was staring solemnly at the city. "What now?"

Lato looked like a wave had asked his permission before splashing him. "What do you mean?"

Tracing the branches in the road ahead with his eyes, Rati said, "Our path isn't laid out for us anymore."

Atila looked at him seriously. "What we set out to do still needs to be done. We need to speak to the king."

"Master Blackwell has probably already told the king. There's nothing for us to do."

"What about the army we seen?"

"Taklin burned Ferbundi. It was an obvious act of war. Master Blackwell will figure it out, and he's proven his capability in decision making."

"You know he—"

"I've had enough of this," Lato snapped. The sharp tone startled them both into silence. "No matter what he did. We all make mistakes. But he was the one who taught us how to forgive those mistakes, and I know he's forgiven plenty of mine."

"And God has forgiven all of ours," Atila agreed. "No matter if Master Blackwell leaving us was right or not, we owe it to God to forgive him."

Rati nodded. "I know; I know." He started walking down the hill. "Forget I said anything."

Lato and Atila shared a troubled glance. "What's up with him?" she asked.

"I don't know," he said, frowning, then went after Rati. Atila followed, and they set off toward Larte: the capital city of Biatre.

"Careful, Atila, or you'll fall over backwards."

She laughed, twirling in the street as she looked around. "This place is so much bigger than Ferbundi. It's incredible; but the sky is so much harder to see."

"The sky isn't why we're here. It'll wait. Now, pay attention so we don't lose you."

"Ugh. Lato, why did Master Blackwell have to choose you?" She swatted him on the back of the head.

He chuckled. "Someone had to look after you."

"Guys," Rati interrupted. "I think we turn here."

They turned and walked on. Smells of home-cooked food filtered through the shuttered windows and tantalized them, but it was counteracted by the scent of dog waste and old vegetables. The homes gradually faded to shops and storefronts with wooden signs advertising all types of wares. There was a cobbler, a baker, a tailor, and an apothecary all in that one street. Atila was glad the shutters were closed, otherwise there was a good chance that she might have been distracted.

"You folks lookin' for a place to stay?"

They turned to see an innkeeper standing in his doorway, framed by the warm light spilling out. Lato took a step forward. "Actually, sir, could you tell us when the king takes visitors?"

"Sorry lad, he's all done for today. Tomorrow afternoon, he'll be open again like normal. He's prob'ly still awake, though who knows what he does in that palace all by himself when he's done workin'. You could always go ask."

"What—just walk up to the gate?"

"Aye, lassie. It ain't that hard."

"Thank you, sir." The trio left him and walked down the street in the dusk. The castle they approached only had light coming from a few windows, but they marched on. There were two guards standing in front of the drawbridge gate.

"Who goes?" one asked.

"Three travellers, sir. We come with news from Ferbundi."

The spokesman nodded and led them across the drawbridge. The door to the castle opened smoothly, proof of its frequent use. The only weapons they had to lay aside were the daggers Master Blackwell had supplied them with. One guard was told to start a fire in the hall, and a servant was dispatched to find the king.

The room was a large one. Tall windows showed the blackness of the sky outside and the twinkling of windows below. As the fire caught and grew, it illuminated the room to show portraits—not just of former rulers, but of farms and houses and fields and people, common people. They were not all professionally done, either. Some were quite rustic and obviously done by children. A smile grew on Atila's face as she caught sight of one painting after another, but she dared not go and look at them closer. This place was designed to look welcoming, that much was certain, but it was still large and imposing. She stayed close by Lato and Rati.

79

Derek took off his crown and laid it on the table. He finished his supper while going over the day's events in his head, mentally replaying everything that had happened and thinking about how he could have done better. Bridget's family deserved a gift; perhaps a food basket. Her death needed to be investigated. If Katira had been the one—it sounded so preposterous, but she was the only suspect, so he had to consider it—then she had somehow acquired this poison somewhere. He put down the words *question apothecary*. Doris should recall selling such a dangerous substance.

Taroki's words from before repeated in his mind: that Katira was succeeding where Pricilla had failed. In what? Seducing him?

"Sire, there are visitors here."

"Who would come at this time?"

"Three young people. They say they come from Ferbundi."

Derek jumped up, putting his crown back on. "Send them into the throne room. Wake Captains Hemminway, Fide, and Gresham. I will be there in a minute."

It was a very interesting trio that greeted him. They all wore light tunics, trousers, and high boots, and looked rather dirty. The brown, blue, and green eyes all eyed him with distrust.

80

A young man walked in, dressed in a fine suit and wearing a gold crown. Lato felt his back stiffen, but he forced himself to bow beside the other two. He stood straight first and noticed that the king was watching Atila.

"What's your problem?" he asked, the words coming out before he meant them to.

The king looked startled at the direct address. "Pardon me?"

"Perhaps he thought I was pretty," Atila cut in saucily, tossing her head.

Lato felt the jab. He refused to look at her and stared hard at the king, who looked uncomfortable.

"I am sorry," he apologized. "I simply noticed she did not curtsy."

Atila blushed, and Rati picked up on Lato's defensiveness. "So?"

The king held up his hands. "I did not say that she should have. It was a rogue thought that entered my mind. No warrior should curtsy, but female warriors are uncommon here. I did not mean any offence. Now please, Taroki said you had news about the fire?"

The three relaxed somewhat, and Lato took the position of narrator. "It was the Taklin army."

"Oh?"

"They chased us through the streets, setting fire as they went."

"Why were they chasing you?"

"We are not certain, but we believe it was because we were telling the people about God."

The king took a step backwards. "Why? What would this 'God' have to do with that?"

"Not 'this' God," Atila answered. The flame in her heart whenever she spoke of Him kindled brighter, and she could feel it sparking in her eyes as she specified, "God. *The* God. The one who created the heavens and the earth and everyone and everything in it."

"But no one believes it. Why would they have taken such drastic measures to extinguish the theory?"

"Where are the others?" Rati asked, interrupting. "Shouldn't we be informing the general and a council or something? You obviously don't trust us."

"Be that as it may, I need as much information about this as possible and will decide afterward what to believe. My general is in Ferbundi at the moment with a large group of soldiers, but servants have been sent to awake my captains, who should be on their way to the meeting hall. We ought to meet them there."

A short walk down the hall was a long room with a huge table surrounded by sturdy chairs. The king motioned them to sit. The door opened again. Three men marched in and towards the king. They bowed in unison. All of them looked like they had prepared hastily for this meeting, with messy hair and tunics slightly askew. Their faces, though, looked concerned and grave as they saluted.

"Stand easy. Give introduction," the king commanded.

"Captain Gresham."

"Captain Hemminway."

"Captain Fide."

"Take your seats. And you three?"

"I'm Lato, this is Atila, and that's Rati."

The king began the official interrogation. "Did you live in the village?"

"No. We lived in a cottage nearer the ocean, grew rare fruits in an orchard, and sold them in the village."

"Just the three of you? Are you siblings?"

Lato shook his head. "Not biologically. Master Blackwell adopted us when we were children."

The king leaned forwards, moving on to what mattered. "And why were you in the village this day? What exactly happened?"

They could not have had a more rapt audience. The king and his captains sat spellbound.

81

Lato began a tale to which Derek had never heard the like. They had come across an old woman dying the street. Atila had told her the story about "God", and a few minutes later, they had been chased out by horses and fire.

The story lined up with what Katira said that the little girl had seen. Also, if anything was to be gathered by body language, these three had not been the ones who set it.

But the story went on: how after a battle with a seemingly magical shield in the mix, they had been captured and brought to a prison of wonders. There had been fetters with the capability of burning a victim from the inside; devices that transmitted voices from one to the other, despite great distance; a fence that possessed the same power as the fetters; and a metal spider with both wheels and legs, that could carry riders and weaponry.

King Derek and his captains sat, stunned to silence. Even when the tale was over, his mind could not process all the curiosities it contained. It did, in all truth, sound like a madman's ravings.

The three stared at him. "Do you believe me?" Lato asked.

"I am not sure." Derek's words were slow. He didn't feel like the ruler of a country.

He turned to the captains. "And what about you?"

"I have never heard of these things before; they are difficult to comprehend. How does this 'electricity' work?" Captain Fide asked.

The self-proclaimed spokesman was nearly pulling out his blond hair. "I don't know how else to explain it." He grabbed Atila's hand. She flinched when he touched her little finger, which Derek now noticed was all black and blue. Lato unwrapped the cloth from around her wrist. "Does this look like a normal burn?" Without waiting for an answer, he turned to his other side. "Rati, take off your tunic."

King Derek stared at the black and red welts that encircled her wrist, then looked at Rati. The young man winced as he pulled away the cloth that stuck to his torso, glued on by crusted blood. A sloppy gash slit across his lean abdomen: an awkward slice that could only have come from battle.

Lato broke the dead air. "Do you believe us now?"

Rati stood in his trousers and glared at them until Atila helped him wrap it back up. Then he pulled his tunic over his head and stood behind his chair.

Derek nodded. "At least to some extent." He turned to his captains. "Captain Hemminway, I want you to take Officers Forrest and Wile, get horses from my stable, and catch up with the general. Give him the update and check out this new lead."

Captain Hemminway saluted and left. Derek gave permission for Fide and Gresham to leave, then called to a maid down the hall. "Show these guests to the empty bedrooms." They all left, leaving him alone.

Smoke swirled in the air, sharp and pungent, before melting away into nothing. Derek watched as the wick faded from red, to white, to grey, then walked on to the next wall sconce, and blew out its candle. Even after the whole room was dark, his mind was no clearer.

82

As soon as she was sure the servant girl was gone, Atila opened her door. Lato and Rati were already waiting for her.

"What do you think?" Lato asked. "I have half a mind to follow that captain and see that he actually goes to Ferbundi, or if they were just bluffing to get rid of us mad folk."

"I'm feeling the same," Atila agreed. "It wouldn't be a good idea though; what would the king think if we disappeared? Then he definitely wouldn't believe us."

Rati nodded. "And did you see the way he looked when we mentioned God? He looked like he'd heard of him before. The captains didn't, though."

"You're right," a voice sounded from behind them.

All three jumped and whipped their heads around. The king was walking towards them.

"I have heard of him before. But why does it matter to the Taklins what we believe in? There is no way it could affect them."

Atila had been thinking the same thing. She locked eyes with Lato, who nodded.

"There is something you are not telling me."

Rati looked furtively over his shoulder. The king unconsciously mimicked the movement. They were the only ones in the hallway. "Do you have a private place to talk? One where—" Rati lowered his voice. "One where visitors have never been?"

"My father always made certain that they never entered his study. We can go there." He led them up a set of stairs and down a few hallways.

"Will it matter?" Atila whispered to Lato. "If the cameras are real, won't they already have heard enough?"

"We should have thought of that before. But at least this way they won't know how much we know and what we plan on doing about it."

The king took a candle from the wall and opened the door next to it. He held it to the kindling already in the fireplace, which caught quickly, then set the candle down on a desk. Lato closed the door behind them.

"What do you all know about Taklin? What are... cameras?"

"I've never seen one, but Master Blackwell spoke of them. He used to live there—well, he said it was only a little part of a bigger country, called Canada—so he knows all about their technology. They are little boxes that can take pictures and record videos."

"Which are..."

"It's like magic eyes and ears," Atila explained. "They can see and hear things and remember them, and if you know how to work one, you can see or hear all it has stored in its memory."

"Alright. You are saying that these magic boxes—cameras—are in my castle?"

"Master Blackwell believed they would be."

"How could they have gotten them here?"

"Through visits, with their servants."

"Why are they spying on us?"

"He said there are devices that let you not only watch what was recorded, but you can transfer it to other devices as well. People keep them in their homes for entertainment."

The king looked incredulous. "And they are watching my castle... for entertainment?"

"That's what Master Blackwell said."

83

Blackwell... why does that name sound so familiar? "Mason Blackwell?"

They looked surprised. "Yes, why?"

The records said that he had come from Taklin, which highly credited their story. Although why would he have waited so long to come out with this information? "Where is he?"

All three looked at each other, then at him.

"He's not here?" Atila asked.

"No, he is not," Derek said, confused by their confusion.

They exploded in a cacophony of sound.

"You haven't seen him at all?"

"We've got to find him. He could be anywhere."

"Anywhere between here and the mountains, unless he came back to look for us."

"We could start by asking around town. Hopefully the tavern's still open. Maybe the inn will be."

Lato turned to Derek. "Can we have our weapons back?"

Derek held up his hand. "After you answer another question." To be entertainment was humiliating and a complete violation of privacy, but—"If what you say is true about these 'cameras' will they harm Biatre?"

"Not any more than they have."

"Unless that's why the army is here," Rati pointed out.

King Derek set his jaw. "Go look for your Master Blackwell. Get four horses from the stables. Then come back here; I need to know everything about this. The army isn't here yet. I've got someone else I can question." He left them to find someone to take them to the stables. There was only one other person in the castle who knew about Taklin: someone who should have been questioned properly, a long time ago.

84

Women's gasps cam from behind the door. King Derek kept pounding till it opened. "I need to speak with Miss Katira."

Some shuffling and whispering occurred, then she appeared around the door. Her dress was crumpled, her feet were bare, and her hair was a tangled mess. Her half-open eyes connected with his, then she stumbled into a sort of curtsy. "Yer Majesty. What can I do for ye?"

He could not let her distract him from what he needed to know. "Follow me."

She did.

He led her to the study he had just left. "Sit."

She did. Her tired brown eyes flickered in the firelight as she waited for him to speak.

He plunged ahead. "You were the girl in the forest. The one who caused my bruise."

"Ye ran into the tree of yer own accord, Yer Majesty."

His carriage of thought lost a wheel at her audacity, and he had to process for a bit. He needed to stay on track.

"What were you doing out there? Relaying information to Taklin?"

"What?" Her eyes widened, the accusation bringing life back into them. "I don't posses the tools—I'm no spy!"

"Aha. But it is possible?"

She looked resignedly at him. "Aye. It is."

Derek clenched his jaw. "Tell me all you know. And please, dispose of the accent. It is entirely useless and very distracting."

"Do you—" Her words were cold with fear. "Do you understand the consequences?"

"Whatever the consequences, this is reality and needs to be dealt with. Are my people and I being spied upon? And watched for entertainment?"

"How did you find out?"

"That is not important. Cease your stalling and tell me."

Katira sighed. "Fine. They have cameras throughout the castle, recording everything. The data gets transferred via satellite signal to the Taklin castle, where it's edited and sent out to television sets across the whole country. It's also posted online for anyone with internet access."

Derek understood enough of the terms to know that Lato's story aligned perfectly. This meant... "They see... everything... that were do here?"

"Anything the editors think is interesting. They like to follow stories, like drama between servants, and important decisions made by royalty. They've also done episodes on fashion, cooking, and such like. Everyone thinks that it's just another reality show; like a play."

So they didn't need spies. They knew everything. No one would willingly live under that scrutiny, would they? He opened his mouth. "Why are you here then?"

"Pardon me?"

He went for the kill. "Did you cause Bridget's death?"

"No!"

"Then if they have all that technology, why would they send you here?"

"I—" she hesitated.

"Tell me," he insisted. There was a missing connection here.

"I was an actor in training, at the Taklin castle. Then they—" She took a deep, shuddering breath. "They poisoned your parents, and I figured out that this wasn't an act: that all this, here in Biatre, was real."

"They poisoned my parents? I knew—" Derek slammed his fist on the table. "I knew something was strange about that. Every time a member of my family died, they were present. Tell me, what about my brother and sister?"

She explained how, when little Tessa had died from some unknown sickness, the avid viewers had mourned for her and only gotten more attached to the show. A year passed, and the insipid people wanted something else to grieve over, so a spy had poisoned the blades used for the fight. Inevitably, one of the brothers died.

He had stared at the inkwell during her statement, but now his gaze wandered around the room, trying to find a grounding point, but his eyes were drawn to the girl sitting in front of him. This answered his initial question. "They sent you here to keep you quiet."

Katira didn't nod or shake her head, but he could see it in the weight that sat behind her eyes.

They did not need to live like this. It was time to do something. Ferbundi needed to be avenged, but the general was going to take care of that. For here, though, "Do you know where the cameras are?"

"Most of them, yes."

"Can we remove them?"

85

That was a bad idea. "I don't know. I've never seen one installed before."

"But we can try." King Derek flung open the door and launched out of the room. "This type of—of indecency—that they would violate so many borders of privacy, and with total deceit—" He whirled around to face Katira, who had followed him out. "Where are they?"

"They've heard you now." She involuntarily glanced up at a corner. "They'll know, and they will retaliate. They have at least one spy in the castle. Bridget wasn't poisoned by a camera."

"All the more reason." He strode two steps toward her and placed his hands on her shoulders, looking down into her face. Her breath hitched at his touch. His ice-blue eyes bored into hers. "Do you want to live in slavery to them or not?"

She set her jaw and released the breath she was holding. "No, I don't. And I'm finished cowering before them."

The king nodded and released her. "Where are the cameras?"

"There's one here." She walked to the wall and pointed up at the corner. The king was tall, but not quite enough to reach it. Katira ran and grabbed a chair from the office. He climbed up and picked at the shiny little thing in the corner with his dagger until it popped out and landed on the floor.

Katira was feeling dramatic. "May I have the honour, Your Majesty?"

He jumped off the chair. "You may."

She would have stomped on it, but she was still barefoot, so she drew the chair towards her and stomped the leg down on it. The camera dashed into a hundred pieces: shards of glass, metal, and technology that had ruined her life.

"I believe that will do," interrupted King Derek.

Abashed, Katira let the chair rest. "I'm sorry, I just—you're right, we should keep going. There are a lot more."

They went down the hallway, looking for the little sparkly pieces hidden in corners and in the folds of tapestries and above doors.

"Is it like this all over the castle?" he asked, replacing a large portrait on the wall.

"Yes. And I believe it might be a good idea to check the tavern and inn, as well."

"If only we could get them all at once. Is there a root to these branches?"

"Oh! Can we get up to the roof?"

The king led the charge to the tower, through the second door, and up the staircase that spiralled around the library.

They emerged to a panoramic view of half of Biatre, bathed in moonlight. The houses of Larte were all scattered about down below, surrounded by acres and acres of silvery woods, bordered by steely mountains on one side and the glittering ocean on the other.

Neither one saw it.

86

It had been years since Derek and Charles had snuck up here against Mother's wishes. It was entirely different now. The clever stone design was nearly hidden by numerous flat, shiny square plates. Each one had a tail that led to a thin tower near the middle.

Katira sat down and scooted to the nearest plate. "Now if I'm correct, they will have thought far enough ahead to replacing them. That means they won't be hardwired on this end." She felt down the wire under the panel, groping for where it connected, then pulled. The wire came out. She held up the free end and smiled. "If we disconnect them all, you have a free kingdom, Your Majesty."

"It shall be done." He did the next one and worked north while she worked south. The planning and technology required for this setup was incredible, but every time he caught himself marvelling over it, he turned it into anger for the way they had used it. He yanked out the last tail and stood to his feet.

"Is that all? They can no longer see us?"

"If I'm right, we cut the power. I don't know how long the batteries will last, but that's it." She tipped her head back, taking a deep breath of the cool night air. "Their reign is over."

He didn't feel her relief. They had only cut off current imposition. "Not quite."

87

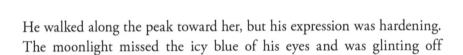

He walked along the peak toward her, but his expression was hardening. The moonlight missed the icy blue of his eyes and was glinting off something else instead: a steely desire for revenge.

She needed to break the spell. "Your Majesty?" she ventured.

King Derek did not seem to hear her. Instead, he was looking down at the streets below. "My people… my family… my self. We have all been wronged by Taklin."

He was going to do something he would regret. "Your Majesty."

His jaw muscles flexed. "We will be rendered justice, if I have to take it myself."

"Derek!"

This startled him from his trance. He stared, and Katira felt beautiful in his eyes, somehow. He took her hand. Chills went up and down her backbone.

"Miss Katira. Do you not also desire justice? They have betrayed you as well." He was not longer talking to her, but rather through her, dropping her hand as his gaze slid back to the horizon. "And they shall pay for it."

Katira did not answer, and he seemed to forget she was there again.

Owls hooted in the distance, the wind rustled the trees down below, a dog barked. King Derek sank to the peak of the roof, bracing his elbows on his knees. He gazed off across the sea. Katira watched him. In this state of mine, he was not safe. She sat down as well but faced the other way.

The night wore on. Hours passed without a single word said. The silence was foreboding, but Katira dared not break it.

88

The full moon grew bright in the sky. They had asked so many people for Master Blackwell, but nobody could help them. The tavern owner hadn't seen anyone of that description during the last two days, the inn master didn't have a single room booked for the night, and every farmer had answered in the negative.

They were tired. Atila sighed as they reached another farm, the farthest one out yet. They marched up to it.

The man opened the door with a scowl. "What could posses ye to come knocking on folk's doors at this time of night?"

Lato repeated the same old story. "I'm sorry, sir, but we're looking for a friend. A man up to my shoulders, short beard, greying hair. Have you seen him?"

"I ain't seen nothin' round these parts. Now git lost so decent people can sleep."

A reedy voice cut from behind him. "Who's at the door, lad?"

"No one, Paw." He closed the door, but it only muffled the conversation.

"Is it them soldiers I done saw?"

"No, Paw, jus' some good-fer-nothin' troublemakers."

"Are ye sure?"

"Course I am. Wouldn't say it if I weren't."

"Ye done been wrong before." Unsteady steps sounded on the wooden floorboards. The door opened, revealing a short man with no teeth left in his smile. "Come in, lads, lassie. Come in."

They obeyed him willingly enough, and he shut the door behind them.

"Now, who be ye lookin' fer?"

Lato repeated himself. The old man looked at them hard, then leaned forwards.

"I'm tellin' ye this 'cause ye seem like good kids, but I done saw soldiers, and a big shiny spider-lookin' thing, marchin'," he waved his left hand, "At the edge of o' my field yesterdee. Asa here don't believe me, but he ain't gone and looked at the awful trail they done made. If ye go there, ye can see it fer yerself. And I can't rightly say, but I'm thinkin' yer grey beard fellow mighta been there with 'em."

Atila wrung the man's hand, ignoring Asa, who was grimacing remarkably in the background. "Thank you, sir." They exited the house, mounted up, and headed in the direction he had waved. It wasn't much of a lead, but it was better than nothing.

The field was a long one, but well tended and neat. They cantered alongside the rows while the moon drifted in and out of clouds. A gentle breeze strayed through the air. Atila stood up in her saddle and whooped, shaking her head, enjoying the way the wind played with her short tresses.

"Are you all right?" Lato asked, concerned for her sanity.

Rati slowed his horse to a walk. "Now they know we're here."

Atila sat back in her saddle. "Oh come on; if they were here yesterday, they won't be anywhere near now. It feels so good to finally have a direction, and to be out of that castle."

Lato chuckled. "What was the matter with the castle?"

"Oh, it was grand and all, but to be inside stone walls all the time wouldn't sit well with me."

"Maybe you'd get used to it."

"No way. Give me prairies and mountains and forests, sun and moon and stars, any day!"

Rati reigned in his horse. "We found it."

They looked down at the trail of broken brush and muddy footprints. The set of tire tracks in the middle was covered by the soldiers that must have walked behind it, but the needle-like imprints of the spider's legs on either side of a fallen tree were still obvious.

"Well, I guess we're following it," Lato stated.

242

"Wait—look at the footprints!" Atila dismounted and led her horse behind her, stooping over the torn pathway. "The Taklin soldiers all wear identical boots. Master Blackwell's would be different."

"If he's with them, he would be in the middle. His tracks won't be there."

89

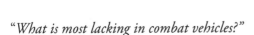

"*What is most lacking in combat vehicles?*"

Commander Seventy-Three paced up and down in front of the rows of uniformed men. These soldiers in training knew that points wouldn't be given for a quick answer, only a correct one; so they stayed silent, glaring straight ahead. He chose one and stopped in front of him.

"*Pierre. What is most lacking in combat vehicles?*"

The young man saluted. "*Speed, sir. History has shown us that the fastest force always wins the battles.*"

"*Does anyone else have an answer?*"

A hand went up.

"*Blackwell?*"

"*Pierre has a point, sir, but the real question is what is slowing the vehicles down. What they need is more maneuverability on the uneven terrain of the battle field.*"

Commander Seventy-Three nodded, surprised, but approving. "*Tonight you will all have homework. Give me a design for a combat vehicle with maneuverability.*"

The hint of a groan went up along the rows.

"*Everyone except Blackwell, three laps around the grounds. Be done before 18:00. Supper does not wait for a slow soldier.*"

Mason broke ranks, ignoring the dirty looks that were being shot his way, and saluted. "*Awaiting instructions, sir.*"

"*I'm willing to bet that with your answer, there was an idea, Blackwell.*"

"*Yes, sir, there was.*"

"And extra time in a quiet office would help it come to light?"

"Most definitely, sir."

Commander Seventy-Three flashed his gloved wrist at the door, which slid open automatically. They walked into the cool hallway. He opened another door and showed Blackwell a small room. The only piece of furniture was a standing desk laden with a computer, stacks of paper, and unopened packs of pencils. He clapped him on the back. "Get to work, Blackwell." He left.

"Why, oh why, did I do that?" Mason muttered to himself as he marched along. "I literally designed my own doom."

"Not doom yet," Pierre remarked, checking the chain from Mason's wrists to the spider in the predawn light. "Just a minor encumbrance. Come up with a dramatic enough sob story for the queen, about how you were so in love, and then the tragedy… she'll gild your cage. You can be an actor instead of a prisoner."

"So it's true then?" Mason asked. "She's got the whole castle rigged by now?"

"Not just the castle." He lowered his voice. "Other places, too. Lots of drama to be found in these little villages."

"It's a violation of privacy!"

Commander Twenty-Seven broke ranks and backhanded him across the face. Mason grunted in surprise, stumbling as the spider pulled him along unmercifully. Pierre—Commander Fifty-Two, rather—opened his mouth, then shut it. He nodded at his son, and then focussed on marching, staring straight ahead. Mason stared at them. He licked the blood off his lip and spat to get rid of the metallic taste.

Then a whirring noise caught his attention. There, on the spider, was a little camera, looking straight at him. He understood. They were all actors.

90

Finally the stars began to flicker and go out. The infinite blackness of the sky faded to shades of lighter grey, and her whole soul yearned for the light. The forest began to show hints of green, and blue filtered into the sky. Other colours followed until it looked like an artist had used every colour in their palette to create as extravagant a masterpiece as possible; then the sun breached the horizon. Katira couldn't help closing her eyes, feeling the warmth soak into her body. *In times like these I could believe anything. That there is a God. That Bridget is somewhere up there, safe and laughing, waiting for me. That there will be a happy ending to all of this.*

When she looked around again, the colours were gone. The sky was a vivid blue, and the sun was completely up. She turned to see the king, still sitting, still staring.

"If you please, Your Majesty, I'll go see about your breakfast."

He made no sign of having heard her, but she left anyways. The tower stairs felt dank and stuffy now as she made her way down to the kitchens. The women eyed her suspiciously, but none of them said a word. Apparently that was Oregga's job.

"Nice to see ye again, Kati. What did the king want last night?"

Katira shrugged as she collected the plates laid out and placed them onto a large tray, along with a pot of tea Nelda handed her, already heated. *This is normal. Act natural.* "He had questions about Taklin."

Oregga raised an eyebrow incredulously. "All night."

"Oh, no! It was nothing like that, I promise, ma'am. Not at all."

"If ye say so, Kati." She sighed and continued her work. "I had thought ye weren't that type."

The tray trembled in Katira's hands at the thought that Oregga had put in her mind. She bit her lip, pushed the door open with her foot (which was still bare), and left the kitchen. She should have cleaned herself up first. Maybe she could find Taroki. Surely he wouldn't mind bringing the king his breakfast.

Taroki was nowhere to be found. She began the ascent up the tower steps, trying to not spill the tea. Looking at the rough cut stone in the walls and the planks beneath her feet brought her memory back to when she was a little girl, when she would pretend to be a princess, locked away from the world, until Prince Charming would come and set her free.

"Look where all that pretending got me," she muttered to herself. The tower caught her voice and amplified it. She instinctively shrunk back—but there were no cameras to be afraid of. Not anymore. She seriously considered yelling, just because she could, but there was the door.

The king was still sitting in the exact spot she had left him. "Your Majesty?" she called as she approached.

He turned at the sound of her voice, which was unexpected. She halted when she seen his eyes, red-rimmed from being up all night, but managed to keep a calm face. She probably looked just as bad, especially with her messy hair and crumpled dress.

"Perhaps they will try to visit and re-connect their wires," he said, as if continuing a conversation. "I will catch them trespassing. After they are imprisoned, I can bring the charge of my family's deaths upon them and watch them squirm. I doubt they will come as an open act of war; that would destroy any future hope of having a show here; but then again, they burned Ferbundi. And once I have them—"

"I've brought your breakfast," Katira interrupted.

He blinked and glanced around as if noticing for the first time that the sun was up, then back at her, and took the tray. "Thank you. You may go now."

Katira knew she should have taken this dismissal as a blessing, that she should be relieved, but something about his tone made her nervous. It seemed the night-long vigil had only heightened his hatred. He was going to do something rash, and if she left, she wouldn't be able to stop it.

Her feet betrayed her by heading off the roof, back down the stairs. She wouldn't be able to stop him; she could only hope that if he brooded long enough, he would realize the foolishness of any action.

91

Lato, Atila, and Rati made camp under a cluster of trees. They spent a few chilly hours there without a fire and were back on their way as soon as it was light enough to see again.

When the sun finally broke the horizon, all three sighed and rolled back their shoulders, allowing the sun to soak into their faces. They rode on for a while longer before a sparkle appeared up ahead. Atila opened her mouth to announce it, but seen both her companions straightening in their saddles. The light was glinting off something in the distance.

All three signalled their horses into gallops. They raced down the beaten path until Rati's horse took a swift leap into the bushes. Atila and Lato followed him, more cautiously.

"What are you doing?" Lato demanded. "You could have broken your neck with a crooked jump like that!"

Rati dismounted and stroked his panting horse. "She just took off. Something must have spooked her."

"She doesn't have any injuries, does she?" Atila approached to check over the animal.

"None that I can see."

"Well, it was about time we got off the path anyways," Lato conceded. "It was probably the light reflecting off the Spider. Let's keep going."

"They stopped." Atila reported from a break in the foliage. "They are all crowded around the spider, facing inwards. We could get pretty close."

"We'll have to leave the horses behind." Rati took the reins and tied them to a nearby tree.

They took off running through the woods, beside the path. Undergrowth always grew thicker next to the open fields, and it provided excellent cover while leaving clear ground for them.

Atila stopped short and ducked. Lato and Rati noticed the guard she had spotted and followed her lead. They dropped to all fours, where the brush was the thickest, and began to crawl.

Nearly all the Taklin soldiers were gathered around the spider. They were being passed something small, which they received, then handed back.

"Those are syringes," Rati whispered. "They're injecting something into their arms."

After each soldier was finished, he would walk back to his place in the perfectly even rows. Once the crowd had thinned enough, they seen a figure not dressed in grey—in fact, he was wearing a tunic similar to their own.

It was Master Blackwell. His figure was slightly bent, as if he was tired—then they injected him as well. He jerked to an upright position and remained there, focussed straight forwards.

"We've got to get him out of there," Lato whispered.

"Atila's the quickest."

Lato nodded at Rati, then fixed on Atila. "Go back and get the horses. Now that we know they've got Master Blackwell, it won't matter if they notice us—as long as they notice you first."

Atila sprinted back to the horses. She untied them, leaped astride her own, then whistled. The other three followed. She slowed as Lato and Rati claimed their horses. "God be with you."

Lato replied, "And with you." Rati stayed silent.

She rode carefully, not wanting to get unhorsed by any low branches. The king had a good stable master, that was certain. The animal was surefooted and fast.

No one even looked her way as she rode beside the army. Atila gripped the reins tightly, summoning her courage and whispering prayers, and rode out in front of them.

There were no shouts. A few cracks of what sounded like thunder exploded, but there were no clouds and no lightning. The soldiers broke into a perfectly coordinated run. She zigzagged across the field, darting into the brush and out again. It wasn't working. Not only were the soldiers incredibly fast and extremely maneuverable, but the Spider was on her tail. She ducked into the woods again and aimed for every branch she could find, hanging out of her saddle to avoid knocking herself out. It still made no difference. The Spider was able to drive on the smooth ground, crawl over rough spots, and crash through anything in its path.

Atila wracked her brain for some ideas. Their formation was still perfect, with Master Blackwell in the middle. She needed to break it up somehow.

"Sorry," she whispered to her horse. She pulled on the reins, forcing it to turn sharply, and kicked her heels into its sides. It bolted straight into the army. Atila pulled her boots from the stirrups and planted them on the saddle. She grabbed the branch above her and jumped. Using the horse's momentum, she flipped herself up into the tree.

The horse neighed frantically below as it reared. Its momentum had carried it into the ranks of the soldiers it was now scattering left and right. It was only a matter of time before—there it was. The Spider spat a projectile with the sound of a small thunderbolt. The horse dropped. Now what? They wouldn't shoot her, would they?

92

Lato watched as the ranks spilt for the Spider. It lumbered toward the tree Atila was in, then reached out two legs, sharp as blades, and hacked at the base of the tree. She inched out on a limb as the tree shuddered. The tree groaned, then tipped. She lost her footing.

She hung there, by one arm, as the tree gained speed on its downward plunge. It crashed to the ground in a terrific smash of branches and chaos.

"Atila!"

Lato plunged madly into the army, knowing Rati would be right behind him. They plowed over the soldiers in their path. They were nearly to the middle. A crack of thunder jerked Lato backwards as his arm exploded with pain. He looked down at the hole in the right sleeve of his tunic, now flooding with sticky red blood. He heard Rati call their master's name. He turned to see him, unhorsed, knife in hand, charging toward the Spider.

Lato was heading for the tree. His horse got shot out from under him. He crawled to his feet and kept going, clutching his arm. Hands grabbed at him, but he broke away. He heard Rati scream. Then everything went empty, except for one motivation: *march.*

March. Forwards. Silent. Untiring. Unfeeling. Unwavering. March.

The thudding of orderly boots was a mind-numbing rhythm, going on and on like drums in a—wait. Like drums. That was a thought. But what about… what had he just been… oh yes, thinking. That was the word.

Like talking to yourself, in your head, where no one could hear. There was a… a feeling! Like relief, like the tiny part of his brain that had broken free was resting after its fight. Lato flinched as the pain in his arm was allowed into his mind as well.

Logic told him he could not look to the side and give away his consciousness. He probed his foggy memory.

Atila had fallen with the tree. Master Blackwell was still chained. Rati. Where was Rati?

Lato moved his eyes without so much as tilting his head. Master Blackwell was beside him, walking in the same mindless state as the rest of the soldiers they were surrounded by.

Whatever was sustaining him was wearing off. Lato's eyelids sank, and he stumbled. The chains jerked his arms. He cried out as pain stabbed through his right arm. The soldier beside him noticed and called for a halt. Lato wanted to sink to the ground. Then a poke entered his left wrist, and he could feel a foreign liquid being injected. "No. Don't! Then I… I can't…"

March. Forwards. Silent.

93

Atila felt like a deer as she ran across the field. If the sun's direction was still faithful, the Taklin soldiers had been marching directly to Larte. She topped another rise and was able to see the city in the distance. This fuelled her, and she ran faster. Her finger throbbed, but she ignored it. Lato and Rati had both been injured after she jumped from the tree. No one had come looking for her, but she assumed the soldiers had taken them captive. There was only one way she could help now.

People jumped out of her way as she dashed through the streets toward the castle.

"Gatekeeper! I need entrance!"

A man poked his head out of the window. "Name and business?"

"Atila. I need to speak with the king. I was here last night."

He opened the gates without any further questions. Atila chose to believe that the king had left instructions for them; hopefully it wasn't this easy for anyone to get into the castle. No one arrived to escort her, so she jogged across the drawbridge and through the door. Where could the king be? She checked the rooms he had met them in last night, but there was no sign of him.

94

"Bridget!" The call echoed through the kitchen.

Nelda's hands froze in her dishwater. Benjamin dropped his spoon into the soup he was stirring. Katira's knife missed the carrot and split her fingertip. Something clattered onto the floor. They all looked at Oregga, who stood still. Ned scrambled to pick up the wood he had dropped, trying to stack it, but it kept falling down and rolling away. No one paid any attention to him.

"Ach, that girl." Oregga massaged her temples, leaning against the nearest counter. She closed her eyes for a moment, then straightened herself. "I'll need to get a new hand in this round. Kati, wrap yer hand and wipe up that blood before it gets all over the vegetables. Thomas, if you keep kneadin' like that, the dough will turn to rubber; it needs to be sticky. Benjamin, fish that spoon out, then slice some of the meat out into a plate and strain it. Alec, get a good slice of the white cheese from the storeroom."

Katira knew that her eyes were not the only ones burning. She wrapped a cloth around her finger and got Nelda to tie it. Neither could look the other in the face. Bridget had been such a spot of sunshine in the kitchen, willing to do anything, with energy to accomplish it all.

"Kati, cut two slices off that loaf and toast them. When Alec gets back with the cheese, arrange everything on the plate with the grey-blue roses, and bring it to the king."

"Aye, ma'am."

Sasha nearly ran into her in the hall. "The fightin' lady from last night is back again, Kati!"

"What lady?"

"The one that was here yesterday, with the two men, all dirty and mussed up. They talked with the king, right before he went to get you. I showed them to their rooms, but Nick says the king let 'em have horses later, and they left." Sasha scurried off to the kitchen to circulate the news.

Katira went on to the tower and almost got knocked over again. She did a double take at the woman. She stood quite a bit taller than Katira, had short hair, and was wearing a stained tunic and trousers. A dagger was tucked in her belt. No doubt this was the "fightin' lady" Sasha was talking about.

"Where is the king?" she demanded.

"Why do you need to know?"

"I have important information I need to give him."

Something in the woman's green eyes was trustworthy. "He's up on the roof," Katira answered. "This way." She walked towards the tower. The woman's quick breathing slowed as she easily kept up.

"Could you not drop the tray and run? This is urgent."

She did the exact opposite. Trustworthy or not, something was going on. "What exactly is so urgent?"

"You wouldn't believe me. Just point the way."

"Try me."

"Fine." The woman planted her hands on her hips. "Taklin is attacking."

Katira did drop the tray.

"Good, now let's run."

They dashed around the halls, taking corners at the highest speed Katira's legs could muster. When she opened the tower door, the woman passed her and started to jog up the steps.

"I'm Atila, by the way."

"My—name is—Katira," she panted back.

"Why were you not surprised about Taklin?"

"I—know—a lot—about—Taklin."

Atila threw open the door and ran out onto the roof, apparently not at all winded. Katira had to stop and lean on the doorframe to catch her breath. It took her a moment to realize the king was lying on his back, his crown caught on the corner of a panel a few feet below his head. Atila reached him, talking, and shook him.

"What are you doing?"

"He won't wake up. Is it his fashion to sleep out on the roof, and in broad daylight?"

"Not usually; he was up all night."

Atila slapped him across the face. "Your kingdom is under attack!" she shouted. When the king still didn't respond, she pried open one of his eyelids.

Katira marched towards her, ignoring the ache in the bottom of her lungs. Atila nodded.

"Sleeping powder."

"What?"

"His pupils are huge. Stay with him. Explain when he wakes up." She straightened and looked around, choosing a new course of action. "Where are the soldiers right now?"

"The training grounds, outside the rear wall by the castle," Katira answered mechanically. Atila ran back through the door and down the stairs.

The clattering footsteps faded away. The door blew shut in the breeze. Katira stood, unsure of what to do; unsure of what had just happened. Taklin was attacking? She looked around the horizon till the mountains came into view. There, through the trees, she caught glimpses of movement. There was a larger thing that was reflecting every bit of sunlight it caught but she couldn't make out what it was. Surely not a war machine.

The thought of what would happen when they arrived made Katira's blood run thin. What could she do? She couldn't fight. There was no one to call for help. The king slept the sleep of the dead as if mocking their inevitable fate.

95

I have to keep going. Rati repeated the mantra over and over. *I have to keep going.* His muscles were cramping in protest, but he kept going, crawling across the open field, pulling his fresh wound open and folding it closed, again and again.

This was going too slowly. Rati forced himself to his feet. He tasted iron in his mouth but just gritted his teeth harder. He took one step, two, three; and tripped on a protruding root. He crashed to the ground. A cry tore from his throat, then gurgled away as sweat dribbled into his eyes.

He could still see the look of immense satisfaction on Four's face, visible atop the spider, as a tiny projectile ripped through his bandage and into the abdomen. Of course the soldier had aimed for the wound already there. Now fresh blood soaked the lower half of his tunic, and his body convulsed in agony.

When he had been hit, Lato had jumped off his horse, but the soldiers had gotten to him first. He had struggled valiantly, but suddenly stiffened and dropped his dagger, then willingly let them chain him beside Master Blackwell, who hadn't even looked their way. Then they had marched away and left him there.

He needed to keep going, but he couldn't. What help could he be anyways? Lato was one of them now, marching with stone-cold eyes alongside Master Blackwell. Atila had fallen with the tree and had not responded to his shouts. Larte and the king there had no idea what was coming. It was hopeless.

Verses that Master Blackwell had made them memorize decided to board his carriage of thought, but he threw them off. He couldn't take passengers that wouldn't pay.

Where was God now? For a while it had seemed that things were getting better. The three of them had been together, with a mission, a purpose. But now: Larte was going to be burned like Ferbundi. The port would be next. Lato and Master Blackwell would help with the carnage, and Atila's body was pinned under the tree. He would be dead soon too.

Darkness clouded the edge of his vision. He tried to keep his eyes open, to focus on the beaten track ahead of him, but it was no use. The thought of dying here, alone, was awful. He had never thought it would come to this.

96

Lato stood as still as the Spider ahead of him. He could not let the soldiers know that their potion had worn off again. Master Blackwell was standing next to him. They were now on the outskirts of Larte. He still had no idea where Rati was.

Then, as if an order had been given that he could not hear, the soldiers cleared out from behind him. Only two stayed behind: Commander Fifty-Two and Commander Twenty-Seven. They were busy pushing some of the many buttons and levers of the control panel in the Spider.

Chains rattled beside him. Grunting accompanied the ruckus, and he dared to focus his eyes and glance at Master Blackwell. He was pulling at his chains for all he was worth, trying to follow the soldiers. Commander Twenty-Seven heard it too and looked down.

"Hey, should I release the old man? He's itching to fight with the boys."

Lato strained to hear the answer.

"No. It's not in his bloodstream fully yet, chances are we'd lose him."

"Should I inject the young one again?"

"No. His chains are secure, and he doesn't need it to march anymore."

The commanders both turned back to their work. Lato felt disgust boiling inside him. He had to get free and stop this. If he could just take over the controls—he began to work on his wrists. Every movement hurt his arm, but it didn't matter. There was a loose link on his chain. If he would just pull hard enough, it would widen enough to slip the other link through. Then he would be free from the Spider and... he didn't know what then. Wrestle with both commanders at once? Sneak up on one and get him down quick enough to deal with the other one? Take over the control panel and hit random buttons? "I'll cross that bridge when I come to it," he muttered through a clenched jaw, straining his muscles against the chain, trying to ignore the spasms shooting up and down his right arm. The metal chafed his wrists, peeling the blisters worn from the sweaty hours of marching.

97

Atila demanded directions from every servant she crossed and was finally directed through the work yard and out the back door of the castle.

A well-dressed older man was sitting at a makeshift table just across the bridge, his hands full of parchments. She decided he must be the one in charge and headed for him.

"Sir."

He looked up with a distracted expression, then quickly frowned. "Who are you? How did you get into the castle?"

"I was here yesterday with two friends. We spoke to the king. Captains Gresham and Fide were there. Hemminway too, but he was sent directly to Ferbundi."

He called them over, and they both affirmed what she said.

"Strange that I had not heard of this. Captain Gresham, why is the king not training with you today?"

"We have not heard from him all morning—"

"I came here from the roof," Atila interrupted. "He was given sleeping powder. Katira is with him and will explain when he wakes."

"Explain what, exactly?"

"Taklin is going to attack."

The man stood up, but still looked calm and calculating. "And why would they do that?"

"I don't know exactly why. They are on their way across the plains, coming from the mountains."

"Captain Gresham, ride out and check this."

"You don't have time! If they even let him turn around, they will be on his heel. You need to get your men armed and lined up for battle!"

"Aye, out of the castle so you can loot it?"

"What? No!"

His gaze had become hard. "Captain Gresham, arrest this woman."

Captain Gresham took hold of Atila's arms before she could jump away. She struggled and managed to kick his feet a few times, but he was wearing boots. Finally she bit his hand. He yelped. She grabbed for her knife and made a slash at him, but Captain Fide grabbed her wrist first, then pried the knife from her fingers. She kicked at him too.

The man watched her coolly. "Would you fight like a wildcat if you were really telling us voracious information? No, no use in stopping now. I am going to see the king." He walked away.

"Now, miss—" Captain Fide began.

"I am no gentle woman, and I will not be holed up in some prison while the city burns around me! Do you care for your own families so little that you would take the risk of being wrong?"

"We will wait till Taroki returns, or the king comes."

"Would it kill you to be ready? Never mind, let me change that. It will kill you if you are not ready!"

"Would you stand still?"

Atila obeyed, and he tied a rope around her wrists, behind her back, then nodded at Captain Gresham, who released her arms.

"Thank you, miss." He then proceeded to give the command of Call To Arms. "This may be a drill."

The men readied their weapons, glancing around confusedly. Then Taroki came spinning around the corner. "They—come!" he panted. "Tower—window. Hundreds."

The men stood stock still for a heartbeat. In that moment, a distant rumbling could be heard. Captain Fide threw his fist in the air.

"To war!"

The aligned ranks turned to a chaos of fury with, at least to Atila's perspective, no order whatsoever. They charged across the bridge and through the gate.

"Hey! You forgot to—Hey!"

No one heard her as they thundered past. Atila yelled at them again to untie her, but they all disappeared, either over ladders against the work yard walls or through the castle. Soon the grounds were empty. Only one noise remained—gasping?

Down on the ground lay Taroki. The man who had once looked so dignified was lying in the dirt, clutching his chest, and wheezing.

"Sir? What's the matter?"

His eyes rolled up to meet hers, but he did not say anything. She knelt to his side. His face glistened with sweat, and he began to shake. Then he vomited.

Atila could feel herself wanting to panic. Battle, she was fine, but sick people? "Okay. He's old, he has pain… he's going to choke." She got on to her feet, then slid one foot under his back and managed to roll him over, but lost her balance and fell flat on her back, smashing her hands. Her broken finger screamed at her. "Oh, why did they have to tie me up!"

"What's the ruckus?" There was a sturdy-looking woman standing in the doorway leading to the work yard. She seen Taroki, hiked up her skirts, and ran towards them.

Atila sat up, then folded her legs underneath her. "I think he strained himself too much. We have to get him inside." She managed to stand up.

"And who are ye?"

"My name's Atila. I'm a friend. Can you untie me?"

"Nay, there's a reason ye be tied, I'm certain." The woman reached for his shoulders and heaved him over.

Two blank eyes stared up at them.

"Oh, gracious." She dropped to her knees and pushed up Taroki's sleeve, placing her fingers on his wrist. She waited, then looked up at Atila. "What happened? Where did the men rush off to?"

"They're off to battle. Now please, untie me. You need to hide, or get ready to fight."

"Battle? With who, Ferbundi's ghosts? There be no one else on all o' Biatre."

Atila groaned. "Why is this so hard for you people to believe? Listen!"

The marching sounds from before had been replaced by a general rumble. Then faint screams filtered from the other side of the castle. The woman's round face went pale.

"Can everyone fight, or do we need to get them into hiding?"

"Everyone can fight, sure. With pots and pans!"

"Now is not the time for sarcasm! If they can't fight, we need to get them out of here!"

The woman snapped out of it. "Aye. Follow me." She led Atila through the work yard and into the kitchen building.

"Oregga?"

"Those o' ye who can fight, git to the front. Everyone else, git to the forest. Larte is under attack."

98

The kitchen erupted into pandemonium. Everyone was running a different direction. Oregga grabbed a knife and sliced through the rope on Atila's wrists, then reached for two cast-iron pans.

"What are you doing?"

"As ye don't have nothin' to fight with, I'd suggest ye take one of these."

Atila accepted it. She had grabbed her dagger, but her staff was long history. "Wait. Can I get a broom instead?" Oregga grabbed one and threw it at her, then they charged out of the kitchen, though the castle, and into the courtyard.

The gate was closed.

"How do I get up there?" Atila demanded. Oregga pointed out the door. She threw it open and took the stairs two at a time. The room at the top was empty aside from the giant wheel used to lift the gates. That fool of a soldier who was supposed to be here had left his post! Atila threw herself against the wheel, braced her feet against the groove in the floor, and pulled with all her might, but it was too heavy. "God, give me strength," she muttered between clenched teeth. Then Oregga breached the stairwell and grabbed a spoke on the other side of the wheel. It groaned but began to move. *Or just a really big woman*, she amended mentally, then banished all thoughts. *Pull.*

99

Katira realized that Derek had fallen over onto the eastern slope of the roof. The Taklin army would only have to look up to see them from where they were. She wrapped her small hands around King Derek's leg and pulled. Grunted, and pulled. He was so heavy. Up, up, over the peak, down the other side. She could not afford to trip on the solar panels. His head dragged behind, and she apologized as his ear scraped against the roof.

Once he was safe, she crawled to one of the chimneys and stationed herself behind it, close enough to the side to peek around. A huge metal spider was stationed by the tree line. The soldiers marched on into the city. A shriek rose into the air, piercing her eardrums. Taklin was going to destroy Larte... they were going to destroy all of Biatre. She ran back to the king. Her fists clenched and unclenched. What could she do?

"Your Majesty, get up. Taklin is attacking! They are going to kill your people. You need to wake up! Derek!" His name left her lips unbidden, but just like last night, it had an effect. His eyelids raised, slowly.

He yawned. "And why would they want to do that?" he murmured before rolling over.

"No. Don't go back to sleep. You need to command your army. Come on!"

It was no use. He was senseless again. His question echoed in her mind. Why would they want to do that?

Vengeance. She had spoiled their big secret.

She should sever have been asked to take those drinks to the king and queen; she should never have been sent to Biatre; she should never have been used so cruelly. She should never have signed up for that acting experience.

Now the film industry was out to get her, and get her it had. She had one choice: to bend her knee, and play their game.

Katira straightened up. She left the king helpless and descended the tower stairs halfway, then took the branching passage into the castle wall.

100

The chain slowly clanked upon itself. Horrible cries were coming up through the windows now. There were cries of relief from the window facing the castle, where a measure of safety was provided in the courtyard. But the window facing the outside brought only cries of pain, cries of anger, and cries that were the last to be uttered. Atila could feel the tears coursing down her cheeks. She needed to keep the gate open.

"I'm 'oldin' it," Oregga grunted. "Get the peg."

Atila let go and looked around. The peg was leaning against the wall. She grabbed it and shoved it through the spokes, jamming the wheel in place. "All good."

Oregga let go of the wheel. Her dress was drenched in sweat. She used her apron to wipe her face, then set off down the passage through the wall.

Atila leaned out the window to the fight. Soldiers of both Biatre and Taklin were locked in fearsome duels all throughout the city. Other civilians, soldiers off duty, had armed themselves with farming implements. Some were set in a line, trying to protect the women and children who were fleeing to the castle. So many were falling to the Taklin swords.

"Shut the gate!" shouted a man below. He was on horseback, and the men were rallying near him. "They're in! Shut the gate!"

Atila reached for the heavy mallet and hoisted it up. The door flew open, crashing into the wall. It was a Taklin solder. Forty-Two. He advanced, sword out, and thrust. Atila parried his sword away with the mallet, but the momentum pulled her along as it flew from her grasp. She ducked the next swing of his blade and threw herself in a roll to where her broom lay. He swung again. She blocked, smacking the flat edge of his sword up, then rammed the butt end into his gut. He showed no pain and swung again—then dropped in a heap at her feet. Oregga stood behind him, triumphantly holding her pan with both hands. Atila used the respite to retrieve the mallet and whack the peg out of place. The chains rattled wildly as the wheel unrolled, then the sound of the gate crashing down outside completed it.

"There be more comin'," Oregga announced.

Atila readied her broom. "From where?"

"Through the wall; they must've gotten across the moat somehow and found the passages." Oregga bent over, gathered up her skirt, and tucked it into her apron strings. "Fast workers, these Taklins. Mayhap ye should find one to climb the mountain with."

It was grim humour, not to be laughed at, but to be shoved in death's face that they were still capable of it.

"Not a chance," she replied, and they took off through the wall passage toward the incoming troops. Atila glanced down through a window to the courtyard to see the frightened group huddling together, pointing at a spot in the wall just ahead. Oregga gave a battle cry and charged forwards, but the leading soldier turned and bolted out an access door into the courtyard. There were more coming.

"I got these. Ye go!" Oregga kept running full force to meet the oncoming invaders.

Atila darted out the access door and chased the man across the courtyard, but he was fast. His sword was out and swinging, at the innocent, the mothers, the children—Atila did not hesitate as she unsheathed her dagger and plunged it into the man's back.

101

Derek blinked. His eyes were bleared and sticky. He was lying down. His head ached. What was that rumble? He crawled along the peak to the front of the castle on all fours. The noise was an awful mix of shouting, clanging, screaming—he reached the edge and looked down.

Larte was under attack.

He sprang to his feet and nearly fell backwards, then dashed to the tower. The steps clattered as he took them two at a time. He only had a light sword on him, but it would have to do.

A soldier in a grey Taklin uniform met him in the hall, weapon ready. Derek drew his own blade and cut the man down in two strokes. Had Taklin already arrived? And he had slept through it?

He burst into the courtyard. The gate was closed, and the grounds were filled with women and children. A shriek split the air on the other side of the group, and a perfect ruckus followed. King Derek was halfway there when he noticed more foreign soldiers coming from the walls around him. He intercepted every one he saw. These soldiers were well trained, but none could match his rage. Two, three, four strokes served to fell each one. On to the next.

How dare they attack my people.

102

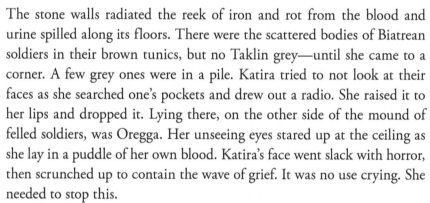

The stone walls radiated the reek of iron and rot from the blood and urine spilled along its floors. There were the scattered bodies of Biatrean soldiers in their brown tunics, but no Taklin grey—until she came to a corner. A few grey ones were in a pile. Katira tried to not look at their faces as she searched one's pockets and drew out a radio. She raised it to her lips and dropped it. Lying there, on the other side of the mound of felled soldiers, was Oregga. Her unseeing eyes stared up at the ceiling as she lay in a puddle of her own blood. Katira's face went slack with horror, then scrunched up to contain the wave of grief. It was no use crying. She needed to stop this.

She grabbed the radio and held in the button. "I'm coming."

The radio crackled in reply. "And who might this be?"

"You know very well who it is. Now stop this. You have who you want." Katira dropped the radio and walked to the gatehouse, guarded only by dead soldiers, and took the steps down from there without stumbling. Soldiers were beginning to retreat; they had gotten the message. She joined them in the exodus out of the castle. Not one of them touched her—in fact, they seemed to be giving her a careful berth.

Once outside the gates, she allowed herself to look around. It was a mistake. There was death everywhere. Just to her left there was a little boy, covered in bruises, crumpled on top of a man with a dagger in his stomach, pleading for him to get up. Tears pooled in her eyes, but she forced them back. She did not have that luxury. She did not have the right.

103

More screams came from the other side of the group. Atila leaped over the writhing bodies on the ground and confronted another soldier. He thrust. She deflected downwards with her broomstick and sliced his throat with her dagger. His head tipped backwards as he toppled over, but there were more coming. Faces blurred together as Atila lashed out at every number she seen. Eighty-Three. Twenty-Four. Eleven. All fell to her righteous wrath.

Only more came, dripping from the doors in the walls like spoiled milk seeping from a broken jar. Then a creaking mixed with the roar of battle and Atila knew the gate was rising. She felled soldier Thirty-Five as a hot blade sliced her arm. Another sword pricked her left shoulder from behind. She was slowing down. More were coming through the gates now.

A whirlwind appeared beside her, wielding a sword. He was shouting violently, cutting down soldiers left and right, fighting like mad. Even without his crown, Atila recognized the king. But there was no such thing as hope. There was only blood, struggle, and death.

Then time slowed. The soldiers not engaged retreated towards the gate. Soldier Sixteen dropped his defence and watched as Atila drove her dagger into his chest. Hot, sticky blood spattered her hand as it bubbled from his wound. She pulled it out and watched the life ebb from his eyes as he crumpled to the ground. His body flailed, trying to crawl toward the opening gate with his fellow soldiers.

The king followed, cutting them down from behind, vengeance in every move. But why were the soldiers leaving? Atila dashed to the nearest wall and entered the passage, running along its now empty lengths to get to the gatehouse again. From the window, she could see a ring of grey forming through the passageways and streets. The Taklin soldiers were regrouping around the Spider.

A crack split through the grey on a street pointing straight from the castle. One figure walked through it alone. Atila squinted. The figure was wearing a servant's dress and had a dark braid hanging down her back. She walked with short, fast steps toward the Spider and the head soldiers waiting there. The circle formed again after she had entered it, sealing off any escape.

104

The soldier Derek was fighting turned and ran. He turned to the next closest, but he retreated as well. The gate was lifted, and all the soldiers were running through it.

He chased them, felling everyone he caught up with. They did not resist. The street was closed with them. He left only dead bodies behind.

Suddenly his sword was blasted from his grip. Soldiers closed in and descended on top of him. He struggled violently, but it was no use. They had him imprisoned. They bound his hands, then tightened loops around his torso. Several soldiers surrounded him, each one holding the end of a rope, making him the centre of a wheel—entirely stuck.

A large metal spider (that matched the description given by Lato) marched in front of the soldiers. They passed out of Larte and through the port streets, then onto the docks. There was a grand ship there. It was not made of wood; it was sleek and shining. They were admitted to it by a wide gangplank.

King Derek was led to the rear of the deck. They tied his ropes to various crates and pipes on board, then left him facing his country.

105

Lato could not help turning his head to watch what was happening. No one was paying attention to him anyways. He vaguely noticed Master Blackwell calming down as well. The sound of carnage faded as the Taklin soldiers, most of them worse for wear, came marching back. They surrounded the Spider like a battered stone wall, then parted. Through the opening came a girl.

She was short, and wearing the same uniform as the maids from the castle. Her face looked set and brittle, like a piece of shattered pottery that was held together only by the glaze.

Commander Twenty-Seven descended from his perch to meet the maid while Commander Fifty-Two pressed buttons that retracted the metal loops the prisoner's chains were strung through. Sixty-One led them through the wall of soldiers and to a tree, flinging a chain around the trunk and locking it through the chains on their cuffs. The regiment left.

"We have to get on that ship."

Lato swung his head to the side. Master Blackwell had a firm glint in his eye.

"They're going to take her to the Taklin castle and probably kill her. But if we get there first—"

"So you're not crazy anymore?"

"No. Those injections have to be taken regularly to have a long-term effect. I faked it for most of the battle. Now, we need to get out of these chains."

Lato leaned back as far as his chains would let him, grasping them both with his left hand, then climbed up the tree trunk with his feet, suspending his entire body weight on the chains. The veins on his left hand popped out, turning purple. His right arm throbbed. The chain gave. Just a bit. He pushed hard against the tree trunk with his legs, and it gave again. He dropped to the ground, still shackled, but now that one loose link he had noticed before had opened a little farther. He worked the next link through the opening and was free!

"Don't bother with mine," Master Blackwell instructed. "You can get me later. You need to get on that ship."

"And do what?"

"You've got to hide until they reach Canada, then speak to a policeman."

"A what man?"

"A policeman; like a peace-keeping soldier. They're not under Vivian's rule. You need to bring them to the castle Taklin while the girl is there. That will prove that what the cameras are showing them is actually real."

"But what about Atila? And Rati, and you? I can't just leave you here."

Master Blackwell set his jaw. "We'll wait. You need to cut off the head of the threat, or it will keep coming back."

Lato nodded.

"Get a uniform from one of the dead soldiers. Then catch up with the others and say that your injury detained you. Do as they do, and no one will notice a thing."

"Anything else?"

"God be with you."

"And with you, Master." He took off in a run towards Larte, the loose chains jangling from his wrists.

Before he passed the first houses, he reached a downed soldier. This one lay on his face, the back of his neck sporting a nasty slice. He was dead, but Lato apologized anyways as he stripped him of his uniform. He picked up the jacket and was about to slip his arm into the sleeve when he noticed a woman in a bloodstained tunic walk around the corner of a far building. She was carrying a child in her arms and leading a group of people. Even from here, he could hear Atila calling everyone to the castle courtyard. She had made it!

Something fell from the jacket pocket. He picked it up. It looked like the piece on Seventeen's glove. He pushed one button, and it did nothing.

He pushed another, and his shackles fell off. He gathered up the uniform and ran back to Master Blackwell.

"What are you doing back here?"

Lato held the device near his wrists, pressed the button, and his chains released as well. "You know what to do. I've got to—" his eyes caught on a spot above Larte.

A cloud of smoke was rising from one of the buildings in the centre.

Lato dropped what he was holding and sprinted back towards the city. Atila was there.

A moaning sounded from the second house he passed. He ran by it, then turned and ran back. The door was hanging crookedly from its hinges. He walked past it, and when his eyes adjusted, he seen a woman draped over a man that lay prone on the floor. Her head jerked up when he entered, eyes wide.

"Don't!" she screamed, shrinking away, both hands over her swollen stomach. "Please."

Lato held up both hands to show they were empty. "I'm not a soldier. I'm here to help." He slowly approached the man on the floor. He was face up, his head lying in a pool of blood. Lato knelt down. The man didn't move, but kept heaving shallow breaths. "Can you hear me?" He didn't respond. "My name is Lato. I'm going to check your head, here…" He continued to speak, gingerly lifting the man's head and feeling his fingers through the matted hair. There was a broken dent in his skull.

He had been hit with a blunt object, probably the pommel of a sword. Lato laid the man's head back down. "Rest easy," he said.

The woman's face crumpled, fresh tears coursing down the tracks on her face. "Please, is there nothing you can do?"

"Nothing for this life." He hated feeling so helpless. "But I can tell you about the next," he said. "The God who created us—"

"What use is a next life?" she demanded. "I need him now."

"If you believe—"

"I don't want to believe anything!" she screamed. "Now get out!"

Lato bowed his head and obeyed. The woman's pitiful cries echoed in his ears. *Will, don't leave me. Will, stay, if you love me. Will, what about the baby?* He dashed the back of his hand across his eyes and made for where the smoke was rising—only now there were two trails in the sky.

106

Atila brushed the sweat from her brow. The late afternoon was warm, and the adrenaline that had raced through her blood during the fighting was now lessened to a slow, dull throb. The little boy's weight was straining her wounded shoulder. He was crying, too, but he hadn't been injured: unlike his mother whose arms, even in death, had refused to let him go. "Come to the castle!" she called over her shoulder again. "There is food and medical assistance there." They were almost there, and she could put this heavy toddler down.

"Fire!"

The lone cry hung in the air for a moment. The crowd behind her picked up on the agitation, then the cry was repeated.

"Fire!"

Everyone began to push and shove. Each was calling out someone's name while frantically running back and forth.

"We've got to get out of the city!" Atila shouted, but no one heard her. She looked up at the sky. She couldn't glimpse the smoke from here, but in a town built so snugly, there was no time to wait. This was Ferbundi happening all over again. The whole town would go up in flames—but this was not like last time. This time she was in the city, and by God, she was going to do something. "Hold on," she instructed the little boy, then flung him around her. His legs settled around her waist and she fastened his chubby arms around her neck, then took off running toward the castle.

Only a few people noticed her enter the gates. The castle servants who had hidden during the attack were distributing food to the injured while others were binding their wounds. It was a giant infirmary.

"Everyone!" Atila shouted. "We need to get out of the city. It's not safe here."

A general ruckus followed. Atila tried to continue, but there was no way they could hear her above the tumult.

"I wonder why?"

"Pr'aps the army is comin' back!"

"I can't walk with this leg."

Atila caught a nearby servant. "Can you lead us through the castle? We need to get out the back. There is a fire in the city."

The girl did not say a word, clutching an armful of linens against her bloody apron. Her eyes were wide as she nodded. They turned to the crowd, which was pure cacophony now.

"What could've happened?"

"Come here. Hold Mama's hand."

"But where's Papa?"

"My arm—"

"Where are we to go?"

Atila sucked in a breath and shrieked at the top of her lungs. The little boy on her back, shocked, stopped whimpering. The crowd fell silent.

"Follow me!"

107

Lato ran through the castle gates. There was a group of survivors hurrying into the castle, and at the top of the steps, was Atila, leading the charge. He was about to chase after them when a hand grasped his forearm. He looked down to see a little hunchbacked figure. "Grandmother, can you tell me where they are going in such a hurry?"

"Through the castle, to the other side. They said there was danger, and now they are all off, and leavin' me behind. Shouldn't they know that I am old? I can't keep up with them! The nerve, to talk about danger, and everybody runs, leavin' poor, helpless me to fend for myself. My wisdom will all die with me, and it will be their loss."

"We couldn't let that happen, now could we, Grandmother?" Lato could feel a smile threatening to show and mock the old lady, in spite of the circumstances. "Here, take my arm, and we shall follow."

She was slow, but he couldn't let that irritate him. The crowd they followed wasn't going much faster, and Atila was heading towards safety along with the rest. When they emerged, he seen her put the little boy down and begin talking to him. She was safe, but there were others who were not. His mind flew back to the young pregnant woman crying over her husband.

The bridge was crowded with folk coming towards the safe area, but here the river was deep, not wide, so he ran and jumped across. He forced his way through the gate into the work yard. His legs were tired, and if he let himself think, the wound in his arm was burning. But he didn't have time for pain. The doorway into the castle was full. He looked around. There, past the stables, was the castle wall, and there were ladders leaned against it. He climbed up, leapt over the moat below, ignored the shock in his ankles, and kept running.

108

Atila pointed at the little boy. "You wait here till I come back, alright?"

He wiped his nose with his dirty sleeve. He mumbled something.

"It's okay. You'll be safe here."

He grabbed at her tunic before she could turn away. His big blue eyes looked up at her through mussed reddish hair. His childish lisp formed the words clearer this time. "Where ye goin'?"

"I'm going to get more people."

"Ye goin' to get Mama?"

Atila didn't know what to say. Tears sprang to her eyes again, but she simply caressed the boy's face. "You wait here for me." She couldn't stay any longer, so she turned and ran. If she looked up now, she could see the smoke rising from beyond the castle.

There were more people in the halls. She shouted directions while working her way against them. These people were all healthy enough to move on their own.

At the entrance of the castle, Atila came across a young mother. Her face was twisted as she limped, clutching a tiny, bloody bundle in one arm and a small child in the other. Two more children clung to her skirts. Atila scooped them up and escorted the group through the castle and to the woods.

She went back for a third trip, and a fourth. The castle courtyard was empty aside from the dead, those nearly so, and the flames breaching the wall. She branched off into passageways inside the castle, calling for survivors. The smoke from the city was billowing through the east windows. She coughed and kept going. Her voice was getting hoarse. Breathing became more difficult.

There was an answering call. Atila shouted again, and again an answer. She followed the shrill little voice and found a door. She grasped the knob, but it was stuck. She jiggled it harder.

"It's stuck!" a little girl said from behind the door.

"Come—on!" Atila choked out between coughs, wrestling with the knob, shaking it back and forth. Smoke was flooding the hallway. She could see the flames in her peripheral vision, but something blocked them. Dark spots appeared, swimming in her vision. She threw herself against the door harder, but it would not give. The smoke was clogging her lungs. She hurled her body against the door again, then slid down to the floor in a crumpled pile.

109

The city was a huge inferno. Lato made a wide circle, praying against all odds that the house on the outskirts would not be engulfed yet. His prayers were answered. The wind was blowing toward the castle, so the entrance to the town was fairly safe for now. He knocked on the open door. The woman looked up. She recognized him, but her expression held only heartbroken grief.

"Tell me," she hiccuped, swallowing, "Tell me he's not dead."

Lato could see from where he was standing that there was no life left in the man prone on the ground. To please the woman, though, he stooped to the ground and felt for a pulse. There was none there. "I'm sorry." It was all he could say.

The woman convulsed with another sob, but it was quiet, exhausted.

"Ma'am, would you come with me?"

A spark of the anger returned. "Let me mourn while I may!"

"There is a fire in the city. I fear it may come here."

One of her hands went instinctively to her stomach, but the other remained on her husband's still chest. "I—I can't leave him."

Lato motioned to his bloodied arm. "I cannot carry him. But you must leave, ma'am. Think of your baby."

Nodding, she looked back down at her love and ran her hand along his jawline. She bent, rather ungracefully with her swollen belly in the way, but pressed her lips to his one last time, then stood up. A sob shuddered through her. Lato put his arm around her shoulders and led her back around the burning city.

They were on the wrong side of the wall. The ladders were only on the inside. They would have to cross the river.

She gripped Lato's arm with her sweaty palm, but he removed it and headed toward the bank. "It's all right. I've got a plan. I'll be right back." He dove into the water as best he could with only one arm above his head. The current was fast but the moat here was narrow. He got to the other side, climbed out, and ran into the woods. He found a fallen branch and picked it up. She was waiting for him on the other side. He held out the branch. "Grab on and walk into the water. I'll pull you through."

She took hold of the branch and Lato prayed that she would be able to hold on. She stepped into the water. The incline was steep, and she lost her footing and splashed all the way in with a little scream. Lato walked backwards, pulling the branch. The water reflected the flames of the burning city, but more red was streaming from around the woman. He hadn't noticed any injury on her; perhaps it was her husband's blood on her clothes that was seeping into the stream. When she bumped into the bank, he dropped the branch and took her hand, hoisting her out of the water. She coughed and panted. She must have swallowed some water. He dropped the stick and would have gone on, but she bent forwards, coughing, then doubled over.

"What is it?" He eased her to the ground.

Her face was pale and her eyes wide. "I—I think—" she gave another strangled gasp. "The baby—"

Lato did his best not to panic, but he wanted to. "Wait here. I will get some of the ladies."

Sweat beaded above her lip. "Hurry—I've never done this before."

"I will. God be with you." He ran. A little farther in the woods was a tree whose branches spanned the wall. He leapt to reach the last one and kicked his legs, swinging his body up onto the branch. His right arm screamed from the exertion, but his terror of the soon-to-be-not-pregnant-anymore woman spurred him on. He stood on the branch and reached the one above it. He shimmied along the branch, using his left arm as much as possible. The blood was dripping down his tunic sleeve again and running down his side. He crossed the wall and dropped to the ground. There was the group of refugees just ahead.

285

He found a middle-aged woman tending to her children. "Ma'am, there is a woman about to have a baby on the other side of this wall. Please, could you go help her?"

"Oh, yes, of course." The woman immediately sat a chubby little girl down on the ground and dispensed instructions to her children. "Quinn, stay here with Heather and Hale. Jenny?"

"Yes, Marie?"

"Come with me. Where is she, lad?"

"Follow me." He boosted them up over the wall, then returned to the group. He scanned them, but no sign of Atila. *Of course not.* He looked back as the castle, whose rearward panes of shattered glass were evidence of the fire raging inside. He shook his head and started toward it just as someone emerged from the smoke cloud billowing over the bridge. Lato rushed to meet them.

A little girl was trotting alongside Captain Gresham, covering her mouth and nose with a cloth, but the woman in his arms hung limp. Lato approached. It was indeed Atila.

"Sir, is she—"

"Still living," he replied gruffly.

Relief flowed through him when he heard that. He accompanied the little group back to the makeshift camp. It irritated him that Atila was being held by another man. Reason tried to tell him that the feeling was irrational, but it remained nonetheless. So what if there was something lodged in his arm? He would have gritted his teeth and borne it, if only he was the one carrying her, the one rescuing her.

They finally reached the safe area. The man laid Atila down. Lato knelt beside her. She was still breathing.

"Got too much smoke. Blood loss from her shoulder. If it's not infected, she'll be fine."

"What can I do for her?"

"Water would do her good, but you look like you need some yourself. What's that on your arm?"

"Never mind that. I'll get the water."

"Nonsense, lad. I know that look. It'll do you no good to go traipsing about in that condition. You've lost enough blood yourself."

"I cannot just sit here!"

"Fine. Come with me, then."

110

Biatre looked so peaceful. All visible solders were on board, and from this distance Derek couldn't see the bodies littering the streets, but he knew they were there.

No. Was that smoke? He stilled and stretched upwards, trying to see where it was coming from. There was a grey haze filtering through the sky above Larte. He watched in horror. More and more dark clouds appeared, billowing over his beloved city. Then flames licked upward from the port buildings as well.

He threw himself against the ropes, trying every direction. "Have you not done enough?" he cried aloud. No one answered. The ropes stayed fast. His fingers writhed, trying to get a grip on the ropes that bound his hands, but it was too tight. One house near the water collapsed in on itself, sending up a shower of sparks. Another followed it. And more.

The soldiers let him stand there till the fires had quit devouring the homes of his people. His castle had belched flames too, but the stones were still standing. Derek wondered if there was anyone still alive who would take refuge in it; but the chances of that were slim. Taklin had done their job well. They had crushed his kingdom. They had crushed him.

He wasn't fighting anymore, even when they took the loops of rope off from around him and brought him below deck. What else was there to fight for?

III

Atila coughed. Water spilled out of her mouth and ran down her cheek. She sat up and tried to wipe it away, then gave an involuntary whimper when her shoulder protested.

"It's all right, Atila."

The worry that had been nagging at the back of her mind was finally allowed recognition at the same time it was given its relief. "Lato?" Her vision was blurry, and she used her right arm to rub her eyes and wipe away the dribbles down her neck. "Why are you always talking to me when I'm on the ground and can't breathe?"

He chuckled. "Why do you always insist on getting into situations that take your breath away?"

He came into focus. Her limited sight was immediately drawn to the brownish patch on his sleeve. "Oh! I forgot you were wounded!"

"He'll be fine," Captain Gresham said. "Nelda!"

The girl who had led them through the castle appeared now.

"Help her." He turned away and dragged Lato with him.

Nelda approached and motioned for Atila to turn around, facing away from the crowd. She revealed a knife and motioned at Atila's shoulder. Atila nodded. Obviously, the girl was a mute.

She removed the tunic sleeve completely and cut it into strips. She dipped a corner of her apron into one of the buckets of water and wiped around the wound. Atila winced, but the cool water calmed her muscles. The cut must not have been too deep. Nelda tied the strips under her arm and around her shoulder, then patted her once it was finished.

A random thought entered her brain. "Where did they get the buckets from?"

Nelda smiled at the absurdity of such a concern and motioned to the trees. Several maples had small buckets hanging from their trunks. They must have been for sap in the spring, and not taken down when the season was over. She smiled and thanked Nelda. "Is there anything I can do?"

She shook her head, then brought her finger up as if she remembered something and darted back toward the crowd.

A growling noise sounded nearby. Atila turned carefully to her right, and there was Lato, lying on the ground, with a branch between his teeth and one in each hand. His face and knuckles were white, all muscles strained. Captain Gresham was kneeling on his chest, holding him down while a little girl dug her finger into the hole in Lato's upper arm.

A young voice exclaimed, and Atila was distracted by the little boy dodging around the people and running to her. He threw his arms around her neck.

"Did you find Mama?"

Atila did not know what to say. She hugged him tightly. "What is your name?"

"Ronnie." He pulled away. "Papa says Ronald."

"Well, Ronnie... Mama couldn't come."

"Why not?"

She couldn't lie to the child. The lump in her throat hurt. "She died."

His blue eyes grew huge and began to swim. "Like Auntie Bridget?"

A hand touched Atila's shoulder gently. She looked up to see Nelda, who nodded sadly. "Yes, Ronnie, like Auntie Bridget."

His lower lip quivered. "So she can't play with me anymore?"

Atila shook her head. Ronnie's little body shook as he buried his head in his hands. She rocked him back and forth, her own tears dripping down onto his curly red hair.

Lato sat down next to the pair and wrapped his uninjured arm around Atila's shoulders. She stopped rocking and leaned into him.

They stayed like that for some time. The bustle of the setup slowed around them, fatal silence replacing the frenzy of survival. All that could be done for the present had been. Everyone was watching the last of the smoke rise from Larte.

Then a strange sound came through the air. At first Atila couldn't place it. It was almost a cry, but it was so thin and fragile—

112

Mason grabbed a handful of his beard and sliced it off as close to his skin as possible. The knife sawed through roughly, but none of the soldiers had been given much time for personal hygiene, so hopefully it would go unnoticed. Once he was satisfied, he got up and ran—or jogged, rather—behind the retreating group of soldiers. He was too old for this.

Some other soldiers joined him, returning from Larte. He made sure to be on the outside of the group, because as soon as they reached the docks, they would be expected to march in file. The magnetic attractions in their bloodstreams from the injections would line them up perfectly. If he was in the middle, he would be crushed and revealed as an imposter.

He boarded the ship without a problem. It took quick thinking to mirror their moves, like the salute he had never seen before. But no one caught on. He followed the soldiers below decks to the armoury, where those who still had swords replaced them, then to the bunking quarters. The sleeping area was one large room, sectioned off only by the rows of narrow bunks. Every bunk was numbered, and he found his. There was no food, which he had been rather hoping for; instead of that comfort there was only strange, forced silence.

113

Katira sat on the hard floor in the darkness. She wondered if they were filming this, and how they were going to account for the bloodshed. Of course, if it was all drama, who would protest to a battle scene? But that was the thing. It wasn't drama. It was cruelty, and she wished she could do something about it. For a moment she had thought she could, but that moment was over. They had won. She was going to be taken to the Taklin set, and probably killed to keep silent. Or who knows, maybe they would start an insane asylum for "retired actors" and record her there too. Either way, they had control of her life.

A click, then a scuffling noise woke her some time later. The light was harsh on her dry, weary eyes as it outlined her cell and the dozen other empty ones. There was a soldier, dragging… the king? She stayed on the floor, motionless. Chances were she was hallucinating. If she wasn't, it was better that Vivian thought she didn't care anymore. The soldier turned off the light and closed the door.

Her chains jangled as she crept to the cold bars. "Your Majesty?"

There was a jerk as if she had startled him. "Don't call me that." His voice sounded like a dull blade scraping across a stone.

She opened her mouth to respond, but then shut it again. The silence stretched on. She waited.

"There is nothing left to be king of." He took a deep breath, then forced the words out between his teeth. "They made me watch it burn. We didn't leave the harbour until all that was left had turned to ash." His cracking voice broke entirely.

Katira exhaled, slumping against the bars. Apparently nothing was too low for Vivian. But she already knew that.

"Did you know this was coming?"

"I did." Her tone was emotionless, fatalistic. "I warned you when I told you about the cameras; but the damage was already done when you asked."

"So... so now what?"

"We go there and die. It will be recorded, and everyone will remark how lifelike the acting was and how amazing the special effects are. Then Vivian and her director will come up with a different show, and we will be forgotten."

"But this is ridiculous. What will they gain from it?"

"Money."

"I mean from killing us. From destroying my people and my land. Why not just cease watching us?"

"To prove a point. Even if we will only realize it while hanging from the gallows."

"Gallows?"

"If they're feeling merciful. Torture makes great drama. They'll probably let us mire in the realization for a while first though."

"And pray tell what point, what realization, might this be?"

"That Vivian always wins."

"That is why they have done all this? To prove a point to a couple of bodies rotting in their graves?"

"I don't understand Queen Vivian, and to be honest, I don't want to."

They both stayed silent for a while after that. There was so much to process, and the thought that it was all futile: that everything that had happened was come to this end... Katira laid down on the hard floor. What use was there, to anything, if this was it? Where was God now?

Her last conversation with Bridget came to mind. Bridget had thought that God's plans were not for the present, but for the future. Maybe God did have a plan in all of this.

114

"The baby!" Lato exclaimed, jumping up. "I completely forgot."

"What baby?" Atila asked.

He was already halfway toward the wall. A few women followed him, one grabbing a bucket of water as she ran.

Lato boosted the women up over the wall. He then paced back and forth until one called up to him.

"Lad! Ye can come now, we need help over."

He wasn't quite sure how he was supposed to climb from here. He leapt for the branch hanging overhead. His left arm responded properly, but it only grasped air.

Captain Gresham seen the situation. "Boost me over, lad." Lato obeyed, kneeling for the man to get on his shoulders, then stood up. He was far heavier than the women had been. They stood there for a minute, then, "Slowly down, now."

His knees were shaking, but he did his best, finally landing back on his knees. Captain Gresham stepped off gently. He was holding a tiny bundle of torn cloth in his leather-clad arms. The women then appeared over the wall, scaling the tree branches more gracefully than Lato had before. Marie took the baby, but its cries only grew louder.

"She needs her mother," one of them remarked.

"Where is the mother?" Lato asked.

The oldest one, last off the tree branch, breathed heavily, supporting her back with both hands. "She didn't make it, lad."

"Oh." Lato followed them back to the group and sat down next to Atila again. He explained what had happened, and Atila breathed out words of sorrow.

"What will they do with the poor thing?"

Lato didn't answer. He and Atila watched as a young woman relinquished the bloody bundle in her arms to accept the fresh little newcomer to her bosom.

"I wonder if that's going to work," Atila remarked.

"Why not?" Lato asked. The baby, underneath a blanket, had ceased to wail.

"I mean relationship-wise," she specified. "I helped her through the castle before. She's heartbroken. With her baby dead, will she be able to love this one? Or will it always remind her of what she lost?"

"Oh. I don't know."

Once the baby was finished nursing, one of the other women offered to take it from her, and she allowed it.

115

Sleep was somewhere far away. Katira didn't know how long the trip was; not that it mattered. But something was different this time. She wasn't alone. This time, as awful as it was, there was someone who shared her fate. This journey need not be passed in silence.

"Your Majesty?"

"I told you—"

"I know;"

"I am simply… plain Derek."

Katira bit her lip. "But I don't know Derek."

He gave an exasperated sigh. "What did you want?"

"Well… what were your plans?"

"Pardon me?"

"For your life. Was there something you wanted to accomplish?"

"What does it matter?"

"For what it's worth, it matters to me. And, I don't know, maybe it would feel good to talk about it?"

"And is there truly no allowance for silence?"

"I have made this journey in silence before, Your"—she corrected herself before he could say anything—"Derek. None of what happened is going to make any more sense, no matter how hard you think about it."

He sighed. "I wanted to find my family's murderers, discover the motive, and avenge them."

She gave a wry laugh. "Well, that's two out of three down."

"I suppose, although this is not exactly how I had imagined it."

"Yeah, I'm guessing the embellished version had a little more guts and glory, and a happier ending?"

"It did."

Derek didn't return the question, but Katira went on as if he had. "I wanted to be a famous actress, and live my own way."

"So you got one out of two."

"I guess so. Everyone with access to the internet knows who I am."

"Inter-net?"

"Sorry, long story. Anyone who watches Biatre."

"They are all content to watch your—our fate?"

"Well, they think it's all just drama."

A moment of silence passed. Katira realized the boat engine could be faintly heard. This time, Taklin had not gone to the trouble of using sails and rowers once in sight of Biatre's shore. There was no charade needed anymore. She shuffled to a lying position and heard the king—Derek— doing the same. It felt so strange to think of him by his first name. She couldn't deny that she rather liked it, but it felt like it was the and of the relationship they had had thus far. The romantic in her wanted to think that this was a new beginning, but—a morbid chuckle escaped her. There was no time for a new beginning, only a very dramatic end.

"What is it?" Derek asked.

"Oh—I'm sorry. It was nothing."

116

The unnatural silence surrounding Mason began to ebb as conversations started up. Little snippets caught his ear.

"Finally."

"Wonder how long it was this time."

"Am I ever sore. We must have been doing a lot of marching."

"Oh, man… you guys, I'm bleeding."

"How did I get these bruises?"

"We're on the ship again. Wonder if we're heading back home?"

"Where's everyone else?"

"Dude, I've got blood on my uniform."

"Does anyone else smell smoke?"

Mason needed a plan. These men were all innocents as far as the fight was concerned, but as soon as they would be injected again, they would be an army ready to kill a traitor without hesitation. He had to do something while they could think. He stood up.

"Gentlemen."

They all turned to face him.

"I am not of your rank, but I am trusting you to not kill me."

Some of the soldiers climbed out of their bunks. The others shifted to face him better. All of them watched in distrustful silence.

"Do you know how long Vivian has controlled you—how long you have been forced to do her bidding? Do you know what you just did?"

One man shook his head. "No."

"You just ransacked Larte and killed countless men, women, and children. Then you burned it. And the port."

Murmuring began.

"What?"

"No way."

"Why?"

Forty-Seven spoke a bit louder, in Mason's direction. "Why would Queen Vivian have us do that? Everyone knows she makes a ton of money off *Castles in Time*. That show would be nothing without Biatre."

"I don't know exactly why. But you've woken up smelling like smoke before; the morning after the capture of the three young warriors. Do you remember?"

There were scattered nods.

"That was the night you burned Ferbundi."

Forty-Seven spoke again. "Do you have a point, or are you just crazy?"

"Here is my point. Mind control is wrong. Every person deserves their own choice."

A young soldier furrowed his brow. "What do you propose we do about it? Rebellion never works." His voice lowered. "Some of us have tried." He cuffed his numbered sleeve to show a scar: electric burn marks, identical to the ones Atila carried on her wrists.

Here was the opening he wanted. "What if I could free you?"

A click sounded. Every head snapped to Twenty-Three, who held a cocked pistol in his hand, aimed at Mason. "Wait till Commander Four finds out about you." He lifted his left hand to his shoulder for the radio strapped there, but Twenty-Five's fist met him first. Twelve knocked the gun from his grasp. Forty-Seven jumped in as well, and soon Twenty-Three was flat on the floor. Forty-Seven picked up the fallen gun and whispered a few choice words in his ear, then waved a hand at the others. They got off him. The suck-up stayed where he was.

"What were you saying?"

"They don't need to know that the serum wore off already. They'll know it should soon, but if they don't inject you before we reach the castle, I'll be able to sneak away."

"Who are you, and why are you doing this?"

Mason knew he didn't have to answer, but these men deserved the truth. "I am Mason Blackwell, creator of the Spider, inventor of the mass control serum, and deserter of Her Majesty Queen Vivian's army. I am now a changed man and believe God created all men to be free."

Forty-Seven's gun arm relaxed. "This is all a ploy, isn't it. To call us out as rebels." Several climbed back into their bunks.

Mason shrugged. "It's your choice. If you do what I say, nothing will happen to you, as long as you obey and march in neat rows like nice little ducks; pretend that you are still under their control. If you don't, they'll just inject you and you'll become a mindless army again. Your choice." He put extra emphasis on the last two words, proving that he was no longer the man who had given their oppressors the tools they used.

There was no resounding cheer or synced nod. Forty-Seven tucked the gun into his uniform. Twenty-Three shakily stood up and retreated to his bunk. A few more sat down. Some were flat on their backs. Mason returned to his bunk as well. He didn't know what they had decided. If even one solider acted out of line, the plan was foiled.

117

Rati screamed as something clawed at his insides. His eyes shot open, but everything was a blur.

"Hold 'im fast."

The words filtered through his ears as meaty hands descended to his shoulders, pressing his back to a hard surface. Someone pinned his arms down. He flailed and kicked, connected with something, but then a heavy someone sat on his legs, crushing them into the floor. The probing into his intestines returned, and he screamed again. Was this hell?

It left. Something cool was applied, but it stung. He arched his back again, trying to get away, but he was stuck. Then a picking sensation flitted across his skin and the blackness finally returned to take him away.

118

The door opened. As one, the men rolled out of their bunks and stood at attention beside them. Commander Seventeen stood in the door, nodded once, and stepped out of the way for Commander Four. He also sized up the waiting soldiers, then started calling numbers.

"Forty-Seven. Thirteen. Twenty-Three. Seventy-One." Three soldiers immediately broke ranks and started forwards. Mason hazarded a glance to his sleeve, where the number was marked. Seventy-One. He suppressed the urge to grit his teeth and roll his eyes, instead falling in line with the others. They saluted. He kept his gaze straight ahead, not making eye contact with Commander Four, and more importantly, Commander Fifty-Two, who also stood there.

"You will come with us to fetch the captives. The rest of you, prepare to surround and escort."

The commanders turned and started down the hallway, leading the assigned soldiers. Mason's brain was whirring. How was he supposed to break away secretively while in the middle of the group?

They entered the cell room. Commander Four gestured, so Mason and Commander Fifty-Two stood by as he and Twenty-Three entered the king's cell. He looked too bewildered to resist. Forty-Seven and Seventeen took the servant girl. Mason wasn't quite sure why they had taken her, but he had been gone a long time; enough time for Vivian to develop a whole new array of devious plots involving countless innocent souls.

The guards with the prisoners exited in front of them, Mason and Commander Fifty-Two following behind. Mason prayed that Pierre would not look at him and recognize the imposter he was. They walked out on deck, were surrounded by soldiers in marvellous formation, and marched down the wide gangplank. His veins pulsed. Now was when he should have been running from the edge of the group, dashing toward the city— but no. He was stuck right in the middle.

They marched straight from the private port into the castle. He noticed the prisoners looking around, and took this time to scrutinize them. The king was a strong young man; one who could have broken away from any smaller amount of guards. But he looked dejected. The fellow didn't have any idea of what was going on. The girl, too, walked ahead of him obediently. He wondered how she had fallen into Vivian's trap.

They deposited them into their new cells and left. Mason followed the others through a few passageways and up one flight of narrow steps. If this castle had stayed the same, they were headed to the mess hall.

119

Queen Vivian leaned back in an office chair vacated by one of the editors. Miss Director sat beside her. They were watching the screens that associated with the cameras in the dungeons. Doubtless there would be some good clips they would be able to recover, but Vivian wanted to give immediate orders about what was absolutely not going to be put in the episode. The servant girl, Katira, had gone off the deep end. Hopefully, this had crushed her, and they would get some good dialogue yet.

Vivian had decided to end the show dramatically before word could spread too far across Biatre; she hated that religion. That God would be against everything she had accomplished. But she sent away the disturbing thoughts. Soon it would all be over, and they would break records when the full-length movie, with never-before-seen footage, came out. It would have a dreadfully tragic end for the servant girl: either she would live out her broken life as a silent servant, or she would die. Hopefully she would sing first. She hadn't sung in a while.

King Derek, not quite life-sized even on the large screen, was discovering the security of his prison. The walls, bricked with stone, were heavily mortared, as was the floor. There were no cracks he could even wedge a finger into. The bars around the cell and in the little tantalizing window were firm. He turned to Katira, who was sitting in a front corner of her cell, head on her knees, as far from the blood stains on the floor as she could get. The slanted sunbeams that braved entrance into such a dreary place gave her a lovely halo. She looked every bit the tragic heroine, and her handsome king was losing his hold on his temporary optimism.

"Is there no hope?"

Ah, such a beautiful line. Katira did not respond. *The words should have an echo.* Vivian whispered this thought to Miss Director, who scribbled it down.

The king sat down heavily, but looked up a minute later. "What were you doing in the forest that night?"

Ahh, yes, an excellent question. Vivian had been wondering that as well. Shame that there were no cameras in the forest. Well, at least this meant it had not been a tryst between them.

Katira was surprised as well by this change of topic. She sat up straighter and answered forthright. "I—I was praying. Trying to."

What? After all this, she was still holding on to that? But she had said to Bridget—Well, it would be death then.

"To God?"

"Yes."

"The same God who is in my mother's books—the books I gave you?"

Ahh yes, the ever elusive books. Her servants had never been able to find them, but they had miraculously reappeared.

"Yes."

"What is it like?"

Why was he buying this?

"To pray?"

"Yes."

"I suppose it is like talking to someone who can understand you. Someone who is great and powerful, but who is willing to listen. Someone who is able to help."

"That is incredible. Wait—if this God exists, then he created everything, right?"

"That is what Miss Eillah always said."

"So then he has a standard of good?"

"Miss Eillah said his standard is perfection, and that the only way to please him is to trust in his son, who is the only one that could reach the standard."

"Do you trust him?"

This was sounding so cliche and religious! Were they serious?

"I don't know."

Good. She had doubt.

"There are only two options: either it is real, and deserves to be believed, or it is all hogwash. It should be easy enough to find out. What did you pray for?"

"Well, I didn't really ask him for anything. I just kind of told him about my predicament here. I wanted him to show me the good in it."

"And has he?"

"So far it's looking like the bad outweighs the good."

A good answer. Very true. It looked like the king was growing tired of the uselessness of this conversation.

"Isn't that the truth."

She rounded on him. "What if He's got a bigger plan? What if this isn't the end?"

Vivian stood up, her chair rolling away behind her. "That's it." She stormed out of the room. It was time for some real drama. She'd had enough of all this wishy-washy nonsense.

120

———◇———

Mason was second last in line. He could duck away—but he wasn't even going to try that. The commanders would shoot him before he got around the corner.

They entered the wide, low-ceilinged room. Servants, who worked in the three month rotation adopted from Biatre, served bowls of thick stew at the long tables. Mason sank his spoon into it, thanking God under his breath. It was not that he was ashamed, he argued to himself, but for the greater good that he did not reveal his alliance here.

Conversation started to flow again as the weary soldiers realized the chance was gone. If they played dumb for too long, the commanders would suspect. So they ate with gusto. Mason appreciated the food but could not enjoy it. He knew that, up above, somewhere, Queen Vivian would soon be presiding over a feast at the expense of others. It angered him, but he clenched his jaw and swallowed.

A bell sounded. The soldiers stood up simultaneously and streamed to the washrooms, stood in the lineups, then headed to the dormitories. Mason finished his timed shower, then loitered in front of one of the urinals as long as he dared. A commander was in the doorway. Waiting for him. He walked to the door, catching the number Fifty-Two before he unfocused his eyes. Would he let him pass?

"Halt."

Mason's heart obeyed before his legs did.

"Not you. You."

Fifty-Two waved Mason on, but detained the man behind him. Mason felt relief wash over him. He slowed to catch the exchange.

"What was in your coat?"

Forty-Seven returned to the laundry bin and dug until he found his number. He removed the gun and handed it over.

"How did you get this?"

"There was a scuffle below deck, sir."

"A scuffle indeed if it caused such a weapon to change hands."

Forty-Seven stood silently.

"You will be punished tomorrow. I have greater things to deal with tonight than soldiers who scuffle. Go on."

They marched away. All the men were in bed when they reached the dormitories. It was exactly the way Mason remembered: rows upon rows of iron beds with thin mattresses, a number stamped on the floor in front of each. He went down the row marked Seventy, one bed in.

A pair of eyes caught his from three rows over. Forty-Seven. He was disappointed, as Mason had expected, but not ready to give up.

He had to do this.

Within a few minutes, the only sound in the room was snoring. It took all Mason had to not join them, but he eased his body up and out of the bed. There was not enough mattress beneath him to squeak. He crept past the rows of exhausted soldiers. All of them slept, but most tossed and turned, grimacing. Mason knew that the memories that escaped them during the day would return at night, when the mind was not so easily fooled. They would have nightmares about the battle for months.

The door into the next room, the clean laundry deposit, would be locked. It was opened by a control panel on the other side. But there was a safety regulated opening on the side that only the commanders knew about; well, the commanders, and the one who installed them. He ran his fingers down the side of the door until he hit the tiny dent at knee level. He poked the remainder of his fingernail into it and twisted. The door grated on its hinges. There was no fire alarm connected to it as there ought to have been. Hopefully the people who monitored the screens were busy editing footage from the battle.

He rifled through the hanging uniforms till he found the number he was looking for: Seventeen. The number belonged to the technologically inclined one who had taken Mason's place. Obviously, he hadn't been smart enough to invent anything new. That was fine with him. He put on the uniform and scanned the sleeve at the panel beside the next door. It opened without question. He walked out.

121

"And how exactly is this not the end?" Derek demanded. "We are going to be killed, Katira."

"Well, what if there were such a thing as life after death?"

"Something your Miss Eillah told you about too, no doubt."

She nodded firmly. "Yes, and it's looking pretty good right now."

"But why would he have you killed first? Why not save you now?"

"I—I don't know." He had called her bluff. "She always said that the bad things that happened in this world were because people had turned away from God, and now we all suffered the consequences; but everyone who trusts in God would be allowed to live forever with him, in a perfect world."

Derek conceded half-heartedly. "That is definitely a nice idea."

"But what if it's—"

The dungeon door flew open, crashing into the stone wall. "Shut up!" screamed an enraged Queen Vivian. She stood there, in all her finery, blazing with anger.

Katira and Derek shot to their feet. The queen turned on Katira without so much as sparing a glance at Derek.

"Your God can't save you now, Katy. You are as good as dead, and you might as well act that way."

"Act..." Katira's mind was racing. "Is that what this is all about?"

Queen Vivian shook with fury and indignation, taking slow, measured steps toward Katira's cell. "I had a perfectly fabulous show at no one's expense except my own."

Katira's voice dropped in her throat, dipping low and dangerously soft. "You don't want me to talk about God."

"Why did you have to mess it up, Katy? Maybe I should have let them hang you that day."

Katira was still looking at her feet as everything fell into place. "You killed Bridget because she believed it."

The queen finally realized that the girl was not listening to her. "What are you blabbering about?" she snapped.

"You destroyed Biatre for revenge."

He lips curved into a smile and she relaxed somewhat, remembering that she was in control here. "Yes, I did. You were always too clever to be a servant. Now, why would I want revenge on an innocent little kingdom that only made me rich?"

"I'm sure you would love to inform us. The villain of the story always loves to gloat."

"I suppose so. After all, the hero of any story is only the villain who wins. Yes, I might just gloat.

"You see, when I found Biatre, I found a gem. It was a beautiful place. When I first met the people, I kept waiting for some reference to a deity, some ritual, or prayers, but none ever came. Even their weddings did not take place in a church, but by symbolically climbing the mountain together!" She sighed at the remembrance of her success. "I discovered a society that functioned perfectly without religion."

"But—"

"Silence." She glared at Katira. "It is not your turn to speak. You, as the prisoner, must wait until the villain is finished gloating, as you put it. Then you may come up with any remark you like to try and shake my confidence.

"But I suppose you know the rest. I planted cameras throughout the castle on my next visit. Then you poisoned King Willhem and Queen Marielle—that's right, Derek—and I had to send you away."

Katira stole a glance at the king, who had gone pale. The queen didn't notice, still monologuing.

"I like to think of you as the villain, Katy. I was gracious; I let you live; but you turned around and ruined my show with those ridiculous stories about your God."

Katira waited to be sure she was finished. "Why do you call them ridiculous when they scare you enough—"

"They do not scare—"

"When they scare you enough that you would destroy an entire kingdom to eradicate it?"

Queen Vivian stood dumbfounded for a moment. "Have you anything else to say?"

"Actually, I do. You tried to extinguish their need for God, but you did not succeed. When you killed Bridget, people mourned because there was no hope. They needed a hope, Vivian. You proved it to me." She took a deep breath. "And I'd rather have some hope than none at all. So no matter what you do to me, I am going to trust God and His plan, and I am going to talk about Him as much as possible. You won't be able to record my execution without letting people know that my story doesn't end here, no matter who the villain is."

122

The queen bridled, then reined her temper back in. Yes, she was furious, but she needed to be dignified. She needed to remember that her anger was backed by power.

"So, you claim to be a Christian, then, Katy? I thought Christians were against things like… murder."

"I am—we are. I did not kill them!"

She had taken the bait. "You brought them poisoned drinks."

"But I was not the one who poisoned the drinks!"

"And what proof do you have?"

"I—I would never do a thing like that."

"Word of mouth. What a paltry attempt. Well, it doesn't matter, Katy. Either way, you're dead." Queen Vivian turned on her heel and strode majestically from the room, the heavy door clanging shut behind her. Once the anger had diminished, excitement set in. This revelation to King Derek would set off a whole new round of fireworks. She picked up her skirts and ran back to the editing room.

123

No guards halted Mason until he was out of the castle, across the drawbridge, in front of the gates. The light of the setting sun reflected off the spears crossed in front of him.

"Business?"

Mason nodded stiffly. "I need to get a few extra wires and adapters for this evening. What Her Majesty has planned with the soldiers is more complex than usual. I need more parts for my transmitter."

"Where's Twenty-Three?"

"Why?"

The suspicion was evident now. "Don't you usually send him?"

Mason used the first excuse that came to mind. "Didn't I say it was complex? Do you think I would trust that dolt with getting these tools? I need what I need."

They didn't seem convinced, and rightfully so. He was talking too much, but he had started it now.

"If he were to bring back the wrong ones, I wouldn't be able to get started until he got back a second time. Her Majesty does not like being kept waiting, and I don't want to take that risk."

The two guards looked at each other. Their injections slowed their thought processes, making sure the idea passed logically. Finally they held out their spears to him. He flashed his sleeved wrists at them, and a small green light flashed at the base of the spearheads. They nodded in unison and let him pass.

Mason walked down the winding road. He could not run, but kept his pace at the alert, steady speed of a soldier. The castle must have disappeared behind the trees. He did not look back.

His favourite hardware store was still open on his left. A restaurant was to his right. There was an open sign flicking on in a bar, an elevator zipping past windows in a seven-story apartment. There was the orphanage Vivian funded, another apartment, a bank, and shopping mall. The city only grew larger. Time was wasting. but they could have sent a drone after him. He had to avoid suspicion as long as possible.

124

Derek turned toward the servant girl in the next cell. She was standing, straight and tall as she could get, fists at her sides.

"I did not kill them."

"You have always had secrets, Miss Katira. I should have been expecting another."

"I was framed."

"If that were true, why did you not tell me?"

"I—I don't know. I was scared!"

"Then why should I trust you now?"

"I didn't do it, Derek." She was trembling. "I swear, I didn't do it."

He couldn't look at her anymore. Queen Vivian's speech revealed that there was something to her story—and Lato's story, too, come to think of it—about the cameras. But either way, Katira had wronged him, and so much of this had been brought on as a direct consequence of her actions.

She had returned to her huddle on the floor, mumbling something; he couldn't distinguish the words. When in the forest, the same sound had been so intriguing; here, it was repellant. She was employing the same tactic she had used when she spoke of her "trust in God" to Queen Vivian: it was the last card she could play. She was trying to gain sympathy, to prove herself. *Which self is it this time?*

"Miss Katira, in the words of our gracious hostess, shut up."

She didn't cower at his words, as he half expected her to, but still obeyed after offering a short explanation. "I am sorry if I disturbed you, Your Majesty, but I was speaking to a higher king."

Her lips continued to move, but no sound came from them. He watched her. She looked to be a cross between desperate and peaceful: a look he had never seen before. But it didn't matter. Soon he wouldn't be able to worry about such things anymore. He imagined the rope that would encircle his neck. Perhaps it would be a tall gallows; there would be a drop, and snap, and all would be over. But perhaps it would be a short fall, and the rope would cinch tighter and tighter while his legs kicked uncontrollably while the airflow to his brain slowly closed off while everyone watched him die.

The door opened, hauling him out of his nightmarish visions with the hardness of reality. The first one, marked Four, greeted them with a sarcastic remark. The words were lost on Derek. All he could think of was how he did not want to die.

He waited in the back of his cell till the door was opened and a few guards had entered. They approached him. He waited till they could nearly touch him, then darted around them. Shouts rose up. Another guard blocked his path and knocked him to the ground with a backhanded slap across the face. He jumped up again. His left hand was captured, so he swung with his right and cracked something, probably a nose. Someone kicked the back of his knee. He stumbled forwards, and a soldier followed him to the ground, sitting on top of him. Derek tried to roll, but others joined the first, crushing his body to the ground till he could no longer breathe. His hands were forced upwards, threatening to tear the muscles in his upper back. Then the weight shifted, the pressure was decreased, but his hands were tied.

The soldiers got up off him. They pulled him to his feet. Blood pulsed through the tenderized side of his face. His whole body throbbed. He felt completely battered.

"What are you doing with him?"

The cry caught his attention. It was Katira. She was being dragged out the far door, fighting to look back at him. He was pushed the opposite direction, back into the castle.

125

The sidewalks were mostly empty, the streetlights gradually brightening as the sunlight vanished. A few red and white decorations were hung already. If Mason had kept up correctly, Canada Day was only a few days away. It was strange to think that though he had been only a little over the water, he had been in an entirely different country, stuck in an entirely different era. This world was so different.

A few people were strolling down the sidewalk: a man in a suit, talking through an earpiece, a tired-looking woman loaded down with plastic grocery bags, a young couple dressed for a night out. They stared when he passed, but said nothing. Then a group of teens in hoodies rounded the corner.

"Hey, can we take a selfie with you?" one girl asked, whipping a black card out of her pocket.

"No; he's old," another one wrinkled her nose, barely glancing up from the glowing card she held in her own hand.

"But he's—" The first girl looked closer. "You're not Seventeen! Wait!"

He kept walking, not daring to look back. He didn't know what a selfie was. The card in her hand was probably a phone; he had seen early designs of the idea. If such technology was readily available to kids like these… the world had changed while he had been gone.

The police station was on his right. He waited for the walk light to change, then crossed the street and opened the door. It was bright in here, even after the lit street, and he blinked. An officer looked up from the desk.

"Can I help you?" she asked. Her hair was pulled back tight under a cap, giving her face a severe expression.

"Yes. I am here to report a case of human trafficking, four confirmed murders, and an unidentified amount of others."

Her eyebrows shot up. "Against whom?"

"Vivian Blackwell DeBlu."

She stared at him.

"Could I speak to the chief, please? I fear there will be an execution later this evening."

"The chief is out; I'm the deputy. Are you talking about the television show?"

"Yes, and no. They are not acting. Someone is going to die tonight."

"I'll need a search warrant."

"Do I need to use a payphone and call nine-one-one so you at least have to check it out? What do you not get about this? You need to storm the place!"

Her jaw flexed. "You had better not be fooling me."

"No. And it's not a trap either. I'll go with you. But we need to hurry."

The moment spent felt like an eternity, but finally she nodded and pressed the button on the intercom. "Jay. Mitchell. Get your men and come to the front." She looked back up at him. "And your name, sir?"

"Mason Blackwell. I'm her brother."

She clicked on a keyboard, frowned at her computer screen, then looked up. "Mason Blackwell was pronounced missing twelve years ago."

"That sounds right."

"Do you have proof of identity?"

"Nothing but my DNA."

A door opened, and about twenty officers entered.

"We have a lead on human trafficking and potential violence at the Taklin castle. Let's go. Blackwell, you're with me."

He followed and was stationed in the back of her car. "No lights or sirens would be a good idea."

She complied again, leading the quiet convoy towards the castle.

126

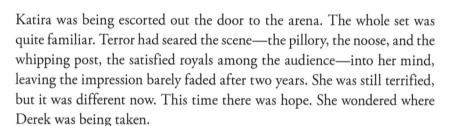

Katira was being escorted out the door to the arena. The whole set was quite familiar. Terror had seared the scene—the pillory, the noose, and the whipping post, the satisfied royals among the audience—into her mind, leaving the impression barely faded after two years. She was still terrified, but it was different now. This time there was hope. She wondered where Derek was being taken.

They walked slowly across the sandy floor to the platform bathed in artificial moonlight. Katira marched straight and tall, planning her words. She could imagine the cameras zooming in on the faces of the audience and herself, and it was easy to envision the faces eagerly watching their screens later, entranced by the spectacle, waiting to see what would happen next. She opened her mouth, then collapsed.

Katira hung from her arms between the guards. The pain had been instant and crippling, but stopped as suddenly as it came. She staggered to her feet. Her mouth felt numb. She had only felt this type of pain once before—as a child who foolishly stuck the end of a fork into a wall outlet. She drew in a breath and tried to form a word, but again was sent tumbling. Her head throbbed, pulsing along with her arm, as the guards pulled her back to her feet again. Seventeen was smirking. He had slipped a cool metal bracelet onto her arm and latched it beneath her sleeve before they exited the dungeons. So this was what it was for.

She was led up onto the scaffold. She did not trip this time, and followed her guards to the other end of the podium. They brought her past the gallows, to stand in full view of the crowd.

127

The soldiers dragged Derek into a room off the main corridor. More soldiers descended and pinned him down in a chair. There was a soldier to each of his wrists, shoulders, and legs, and one holding his head.

Something cold bit the flesh of his arm, where his coat was torn. He stilled enough to watch as a murky liquid was injected into his bloodstream.

"It was a rebel regiment that attacked Biatre," a voice intoned from somewhere, he could not tell. "We rescued you from their ship when they docked. We had to keep you in the dungeon for safety until the last of the rebels were eradicated."

Anyone could have made up that story. To be true, it did line up as a very possible scenario. "But... but what about the cameras?"

"I have never heard of such a thing. What is a camera?"

"It—" Derek tried to remember what he had been told. "It is like a magic eye and ear, with a memory..."

"We do not dabble in magic here. I have never heard of your camera. I doubt such a thing exists. When did you hear of it?"

"I had visitors at my castle. Miss Katira unwittingly backed up the story, and she came from here, so she should know."

"I know whom you speak of. Your visitors, the three warriors, correct? They were the leaders of the rebels. We killed them along with our soldiers who turned against us. As to the servant girl, we have her here in custody. She is being tried for the murders of your family."

"Miss Katira?" Yes, Queen Vivian had mentioned that before. It was remarkable how everything made sense now.

The soldiers let him up. "I am sorry that it took force, Your Majesty," one apologized. Twenty-Seven was cleaning a syringe—what had that been for? His arm itched, and when he looked at it, he could see a pinprick of red on his skin. Four placed his crown on his head.

"I believe they are waiting for you."

King Derek nodded. "Thank you, soldier." The doors were opened, and he stepped out into an arena. His name was being announced. The Taklin royalty were waiting for him, but he ignored them. Distrust, anger, even hatred, built up inside him for the girl standing on the platform. She was the reason everything had come to this. He reached her and did not have to deliberate what he was going to say. The bitterness spilled out though his words of mock pity.

"It is sad, really, to see a girl your age go mad."

Her lips parted, and she flinched, looking hurt, surprised. "What do you mean?"

"You had me convinced that Taklin killed my family, when I had the real culprit right in front of me the whole time."

She retorted, but he didn't hear a word. There was too much he had to say; he wasn't going to let her lie to him again.

"It was a rebel regiment that attacked Biatre. Taklin rescued us from their ship and kept us in the dungeons for safety until the last of the rebels were eradicated. Then they explained your falsehoods. There is no such thing as a camera. You came up with the word, you made up the whole story to try to turn me against them."

"Derek, what are you talking about?"

The sound of his personal name, so informally spoken, on her lips only solidified his acrimony. "You do not deserve to call me by my name." He ignored her protests and walked to where the other royals were waiting for him.

128

Katira scrambled desperately for words that Miss Director would not cipher, words that Derek would believe. "Fine. *Your Majesty.* Don't you remember? We unplugged"—she gritted her teeth and managed to stay standing during the spasm of pain and continued—"the solar panels"—and she was dangling again, breathless. That shock had been stronger than the last ones. Derek had not turned around. He was climbing the steps to the royal box.

"Now, because he has graced us with his royal presence," Queen Vivian continued her welcome, "And because this servant girl has wronged him so fully, we will allow him to choose her method of death: for death she deserves, after taking the lives of so many."

Derek reached the booth and bowed. "You are indeed gracious, Queen Vivian, and I am grateful for the chance to avenge my family. However, the news was cast upon me rather suddenly, and I would like some time to deliberate." Murmurs rose from the crowd. "May I ask that she be put in the pillory until I can decide?"

"Of course, Derek. Would you like suggestions, or do you need some time alone?"

"Alone, please."

The queen assigned a guard to show him to the gardens, then issued a command for the kitchen staff to provide refreshments to the crowd while the servant girl was put into holding.

Twenty-Three lifted the top beam of the pillory, and Seventeen pushed her forwards. He untied her wrists, gripping them firmly, and placed them into the two smaller holes of the wooden contraption. Another hand came down on her head. She willingly bent her neck—fighting was useless and would only injure her further. The wooden beam came down and was latched shut, pinching her braid. The soldiers left.

Katira shifted her feet, trying to find a comfortable position. She sent a whispered thanks to God for allowing her to be so short. Already her neck was cramping, bent forward by the beam and crooked by her braid. Her back was beginning to tense. Her legs tingled, and she swung her knees back and forth to regain circulation, then locked them again.

What was Derek doing? What had they done to him? For a moment she entertained the desperate hope that the man who was plotting her doom was not her king. It was an imposter sent to break her spirit while Derek was still fighting elsewhere… but no. No imposter could have eyes like him—so like the colour of the morning sky, with so much power and passion. No imposter could have had his voice, or the layered bruises on his face. Did he have a plan?

The artificial moon slowly dragged itself across the sky. She could see her shadow inching past the planks by her feet. The crowd was getting restless. She opened her mouth again, and they did not stop her, so she began to hum, then to sing softy to the floorboards.

> *"Pick her some calamint, fresh e'er to be,*
> *Elecampane, to sweeten the air*
> *Mistletoe, for the future so bright*
> *And myrtle, for the young and the fair."*

It was the same song she had sung the night everything changed, and the crowd stilled to catch the wistful tune. Miss Director and Queen Vivian were probably thrilled. It was an excellent way to tie together her character arc.

> *"But pick for me bluebell, to bloom o'er my grave*
> *With laurel, my story to keep*
> *And thyme, to be true, and ne'er forsake*
> *Alas, time 'tis for me to sleep."*

The second verse took on a new meaning as she sang it now. It wasn't a dreamy hopelessness; it was actually the end of her life. It was a goodbye. It was a wish to be remembered.

129

The soldiers standing guard at the open gate fled toward the castle as soon as they rounded the last corner, but the cars screeched to a halt and the officers disembarked.

"Stop!" The deputy shouted. Five pistols were withdrawn and pointed at the soldiers, who obeyed. The officers advanced. One soldier dropped his spear, the other followed. They stood defeated as two officers handcuffed them.

"You'll remember this at the trial, right?" the first one pleaded. The officers, ignoring his words, brought them to a car and placed them inside while reciting their rights.

The deputy looked at Mason and cocked her head. "You first."

He led them into the castle.

There were no more guards in the hallways, nor servants. Everyone must be supplying an audience, Mason thought. He led them halfway through the castle, then up a flight of steps. There was an art gallery here, with tall windows to afford natural light. They overlooked the arena.

"Don't let them see you," he said in a low tone, sidling up to a window. Glancing out, his suspicions were confirmed. There was a large crowd in the arena, looking rather restless, watching someone in the pillory. He looked again. It was the girl. The king was nowhere to be seen.

Across the window from him, the deputy cocked an eyebrow. It all looked like a normal set; very ornate, with cameras hidden, but no acts of outright violence. In fact, there seemed to be not much of anything going on. The crowd murmured, and above it, a voice lilted through. The girl was singing something. Then the sounds drifted away, and everyone continued to wait. Half an hour ticked by. Mason could see the deputy getting impatient. At the same time, though, he knew that this would only solidify in her mind that it was actually happening. Real life couldn't fast forward.

130

The air, even outside in this garden, was not as fresh as it was in Biatre; here it was rather stuffy, and the perfume of the foliage was almost overpowering. The flowers were bright and looked rather artificial. The strangeness of the place was messing with his mind.

Miss Katira denied killing his parents.

Queen Vivian insisted that she did.

Miss Katira had come up with a wild tale, including marvellous technological advances.

Queen Vivian had confirmed it, in the dungeon.

But the soldiers had told him—

A surge of hatred flooded his veins, and for a moment, it didn't make sense. Whatever had happened, whoever had done it, he had been the one wronged. Justice must and would be served.

Reason fought its way in again: the three young warriors had told him the same story that Miss Katira had. He had never seen them before. If they were rebel leaders, they would have had to plan ahead of time. And Katira had not been out of the castle since she had been brought there. Something was not adding up.

He wandered aimlessly around the bushes for some time. Just in case, he pretended to scratch his leg and drew out the knife hidden there, then tucked it into his sleeve and continued to pace. Eventually the guard asked if he had reached a decision.

"We shall see," he responded absentmindedly. "But I am ready to return."

The instant the doors swung open, another rush of indignation swept over him. The sight of the servant girl in the pillory, looking up with such expectancy written over her face, irritated him. After all she had done, she was expecting to receive mercy?

"Well, King Derek," Queen Vivian asked, speaking for all to hear, "What did you decide?"

The hatred pumping through him cinched the verdict. "She has caused me a great deal of pain in the past years. One night of suffering could hardly recompense." His voice was... cruel. The words tasted bitter. He enjoyed them. "Let her be whipped, but not to the death."

The queen smiled in a way that made him hate her as well; but the longer he looked at her and her family, his anger faded noticeably. Curious.

"An excellent decision, Derek. Precisely what I was thinking."

131

Katira could hear her heart pounding in her ears, feel it in her chest. Her breaths came fast. Her knees trembled. The beam above her neck was lifted, and she was pulled from it. Her muscles instantly cramped, and she staggered, but did not fall.

They brought her to the other end of the platform, to the whipping post. She was pressed against it, her arms stretched around it, tied to some point above her head. There was nowhere she could move to. She heard a swish and could imagine a soldier swinging his implement back and forth, preparing to strike. She tensed.

The leather snapped against her back. A scream tore from her mouth. Pain streaked, red hot, across her skin, overtaking her mind. She needed to move, to get away, it was coming again—she pulled at the ropes, but there was nowhere to go.

132

The authentic pain in the girl's cry, the red stream snaking down the torn back of her dress, the smirk on the queen's face, were just what the deputy needed. She flicked her empty hand. Her officers emptied their holsters and rushed for the steps.

133

Katira's scream still rang clear in Derek's ears. He relished it. That sound of agony was in repercussion of everything she had caused him. He glanced back at the queen, and again his anger faded. He heard the swish of another stroke coming, and when he looked back at the cowering servant girl, the surge of animosity returned. Somehow, they were playing him; but as long as he faced Katira, he was free to hate whom he pleased.

The blade in his sleeve slid down to his palm. Katira screamed again. Everyone was diverted. He swivelled around and thrust it directly into the queen.

134

A scream—a gunshot—shouts. The noise confused the grip Katira had on her consciousness. She hung from her ropes, completely helpless.

Hands grasped her shoulders and she shrank away, but when she opened her eyes, it was a woman in a white shirt—not a soldier in a Taklin uniform. *I must be hallucinating.* The woman was dressed as a paramedic.

"I've got you, honey," she said, supporting her. Someone cut her ropes. Her hands dropped, and she collapsed into the woman's arms. "I've got you. Lie down."

They arranged her facedown on a stretcher. She could neither resist nor help. Boots approached, and when the stretcher was lifted, a man's face was level with hers. He asked a question, but the words were all fuzzy.

"Take me away," Katira pleaded. "I'm so tired."

135

Mason followed the police officers back to their cars. Everyone who lived in the castle was under house arrest, but he and Derek were being taken to the police station. Katira and Vivian were being transported to the hospital.

136

The group of survivors had remained stagnant for the whole afternoon and evening. What was there to do? They would have to pick up the pieces of their shattered lives, build a new town, learn how to live with the past: but these all required energy, something which every soul there lacked.

Night fell, as did the dew. They were uncomfortable, but no one complained audibly about such a minor matter. Sporadic weeping marked the chilly hours, and Atila prayed for sunrise to come.

The sky only seemed to darken. The tree branches blocked out any stars there may have been, and no moon was visible. Several times, she fancied the darkness was thinning, but each instance, time proved her wrong and extended the dreariness of her vigil.

A bird began to sing. Atila hailed the first notes with a primal joy. Tomorrow was coming. The green of the trees became visible. More birds joined the chorus. They had survived the night.

Little Ronnie shifted on her lap, then sat up and rubbed his puffy eyes. Chilly morning air replaced his warmth. Atila instinctively pulled him back again. He lay for a few more moments before shifting again.

"I'm hungry," he mumbled.

Atila reached beside her to a patch of greenery, tore off a handful, and offered it to Ronnie. He just looked at her doubtfully. She stuffed it into her own mouth and offered him another handful.

"Ye're eating grass?" he asked.

"It's not grass, it's clover. It tastes way better than grass."

He pinched one stem with his chubby fingers and put it into his mouth.

"And? What do you think?"

"I want food."

Atila smiled and whispered back. "I want real food too, Ronnie, and I think I know where I can get it. But Lato is leaning on me, and I can't get up."

Ronnie seen only one solution. "Push him off."

Atila smirked, put him off her lap, and stood up.

Lato tumbled to the ground, then sat up with a jolt. He looked around and found Atila and her little charge grinning mischievously. He frowned, lying back down. "Don't scare me like that."

"Ronnie and I are going to the garden," she whispered.

"Is it morning already?" He groaned. "I just fell asleep."

"You can stay that way if you want."

He stood up anyways, sighing dramatically. "But you can't go into the castle ruins alone. They could collapse. I'll come with you."

She arched an eyebrow. "Because you can obviously stop a landslide of rock from crushing me."

Lato looked at her for a moment. "For you, I think I'd try."

Her lips parted, and she did not know what to say. Then Ronnie tugged at her tunic.

"Hey! We going? Food?"

"Yes, Ronnie, we're going." They turned and walked towards the blackened castle. The bridge over the moat was history. Lato was preparing to jump the water when Atila picked up Ronnie and handed the little boy to him. She then ran and leaped, landed, and held out her arms. "Throw him." Lato did, then jumped across himself.

The wall around the work yard still stood, and Atila glanced up at the arch warily as they passed beneath. The garden was blackened, but she wasn't looking for what was on top. She got down on her knees by a row of feathery ashes and began to dig in the crumbly soil with her hands. Ronnie followed suit.

Lato looked around. "I'd have thought the garden would be bigger. Didn't he feed his armies?"

"Yeah, that is kind of weird. They must have imported. Maybe this was for his personal use. Aha!" She held up an orange root. "Carrots."

Ronnie looked at it gravely. "Mama had carrots. I helped."

Atila put the carrot down and touched his soft cheek with her dirty hand. "Will you help me, now?"

He nodded and resumed digging. A few drops wet the dirt clods by his feet. Atila pulled a few more carrots from the dirt, unsure what to do. She felt awful for the child. Then she heard a giggle. Ronnie was pointing at a carrot that Lato held. It was two-pointed, giving the impression of legs, and Lato was making it walk towards the pile. Then it jumped violently and landed headfirst on the pile. Ronnie pulled out a carrot of his own and made a grand show of the fact that it was longer than Lato's.

They found onions, potatoes, and radishes too. A nice-sized pile grew with all three of them working. Eventually Lato stood up and announced that he was going to find a pot. Atila dug up a few more potatoes, then rocked back on her heels.

"I think that's good, Ronnie. Thank you."

He looked up and smiled, brushing a lock of hair away from his forehead. His hand left another mark on his smudged face.

"After breakfast, you are going to have to wash up."

"Ye're dirty too."

"I'll have to wash up too. But now let's go see how Lato's doing."

The man in question exited the doorway just then, dragging an iron cauldron with him. "We can put all the roots in here," he said, stopping at the pile. Atila and Ronnie helped load the cauldron. When they went back to the moat, Atila and Ronnie got over the same way they had come, but then there was the matter of the cauldron. Lato balanced it on the edge of the bank and threw the end of the chain to Atila, then jumped across. They each grasped the chain with their good arms, little Ronnie taking the end and grunting valiantly, and pulled it into the water. The iron floated and wanted to drift downstream, but they managed to pull it across.

When they got back to the camp, the others were beginning to stir. Captain Gresham chopped firewood with his sword, which he had marvellously retained, and the older children carried and stacked it. Another man climbed into a tree and hoisted the cauldron to a decent height. Marie took charge of the cooking. Some others went to fetch bowls and utensils.

After everyone had eaten, talk began to spread. What were they going to do now: stay, or leave?

137

Captain Gresham stood up. "Rebuild Larte, raise your hand." He waited a minute, nodding as he mentally counted over the crowd.

Atila leaned to Lato and whispered, "We don't vote, do we?"

"Why not?"

"It's not our home."

"It wasn't, but I think it will be now."

"Oh?"

"At least for a while; they need our help."

She nodded, and they turned back to the captain.

"New town, raise your hand."

Lato looked around. The number was far more, which seemed absurd. He whispered to Atila, "It'd be easier to rebuild Larte. Why do they all want to start over somewhere else?"

"It would be almost as much work to start completely over. Everything in Larte is ash except for the castle. Beside, after all the memories created there, you would be seeing ghosts all the time."

"I guess—"

Atila grabbed his arm, eyes wide and near panic. "Lato!"

The crowd around them hushed at the outburst, but Atila didn't seem to notice.

"Where's Rati?"

"I—I lost him when the soldiers captured me."

They had forgotten completely about him. Lato jumped up, and she followed.

"Wait—what do I do with Ronnie?"

"Ask one of the mothers here."

She turned to the nearest woman. "Marie, could you watch Ronnie, please?"

Marie frowned, looking over her own children. Before she could respond, Captain Gresham interrupted.

"What's this?"

"We have a friend who was probably injured. We need to find him."

"You can't go."

"What! Why not?"

"You have a duty to the rest of us if we want to survive."

"But sir—"

"Do you not think every single person here has someone missing?"

Lato kicked at the ground, grinding his teeth. "Fine."

"Then what do you want us to do?" Atila asked.

"We need to scour the city. There might be more survivors."

Before the sun moved much farther, the people were divided into three groups: the children and appointed caretakers, food providers, and life seekers.

"Corpse hunters," Lato whispered to Atila. She frowned, but they followed Captain Gresham through the castle and split into smaller groups.

Everything had been burned. There were dead bodies, the blackened bones visible, everywhere. They checked every house, stepping over what once were walls, calling out, and scrutinizing every face. There was no one left alive. Few were left recognizable.

"Rati was a good fighter," Atila said as they stepped into another house. "He could have made it. His wound was healing well. But—I heard him scream."

"I did too. He wasn't taken captive." *He must have been too injured to travel,* Lato thought, *so they got rid of him.* But he wrestled that thought into a box and shoved it away into a dark corner of his mind. He could not think like that right now. They needed hope.

Atila must have decided the same thing, because a bit later she asked, "What about Master Blackwell? He was with you."

"I have no idea," Lato said, swinging his head from side to side, nudging the tip of his boot into a pile of ashes and disturbing nothing. "He was going to board the ship."

"What?"

"He was going to masquerade as a Taklin soldier and ride back with them. You know how he always said that Taklin wasn't a country, just a castle, and that Vivian and Rosseen didn't actually rule? He was going to tell the officials there about what was happening; with all the cameras and such, that the attack was real."

"Okay." Atila shrugged. "I hope he comes back soon."

It was a long day. Only one pair of searchers found a man with life in him, but he expired before they could carry him back to the camp. Sunset arrived as the groups straggled back.

Lato and Atila were alone in the work yard, exhausted and depressed, when Atila stopped, holding up a hand. "Do you hear that?"

Lato listened carefully. "No…"

She headed to the well and peered down the shaft. Lato heard it now. That was a yell from the dark, watery depths. It was repeated once more, then it stopped.

"We'll need a rope."

"But where are we going to get one of those?" Atila asked.

"I don't know." He ruffled his short hair, discharging clouds of dust.

Atila waved it away. "What if we got a tree?"

"That wouldn't work to pull up."

"But what if we don't need to pull it up? Just stick the whole thing down there until he can reach it, and hold the top here, and he could climb up."

"I guess we could try it; I'm too tired to think of anything else." Lato had to admit, though, that Atila's plan had merit. They went back to the camp and enlisted the help of Captain Gresham's blade to chop down a tree and trim its branches. They hurtled it across the moat and shoved it down the mouth of the well, shouting instructions to whoever was down there. The top of the tree was flexible enough to have several adults hold onto it. They waited a few minutes, but the tree did not get any heavier. Instead, three more shouts were sent up.

I38

Nelda had been sent to the garden for any more vegetables she could find when she seen the men and women holding the tip of a tree that had been plunged down the well shaft. She walked closer, and above the noise of the would-be rescuers, heard the shouts. She knew that voice. It belonged to—"Ronald!"

Everyone turned to stare at her.

"Nelda? But I though ye were—"

"Oh, screw what you thought, Jonathan! Ronald's down there!" She jumped to the lip of the well. "He's deaf. He can't hear you. I'm going in to get him." Before anyone could protest, down she went.

The stone walls against her shoulders were damp and the freshly cut tree branches were sticky with sap, but these factors made no difference. She climbed down silently, knowing that Ronald wouldn't have recognized her voice even if he could have heard it.

She reached him, chest deep in the chilly water. His face morphed into such an expression of relief that Nelda almost cried. The bucket rope had burned off and fallen to the water, and Ronald had used it to tie himself to a root in the wall. She patted his cold, damp cheek and climbed back up.

"Put the tree down a bit—he can't reach it. And I'll need a knife."

The blond warrior—Lato—handed her his. She stuck it in her apron pocket and went down again. She sawed away at the ropes until the last strand snapped. Ronald flexed his fingers, trying to get the blood moving again, and motioned her to go up first. She obeyed.

Nelda joined the people holding on to the top of the tree. It jerked as Ronald, much heavier than she, climbed up. It slipped. Nelda gasped as splinters were shoved into her palm, but the tree did not go far. Then out climbed Ronald. This time Nelda did cry, and she threw herself at him, flinging her arms around his cold, wet chest. He returned the embrace, closing his eyes against the ravaged work yard. She squeezed him tighter, and they all made it back to camp.

139

There was a good stew waiting for them. Lato and Atila ate their share, then laid to rest with the others.

"We should go look for Rati," Atila said.

"I know," Lato replied. "I can't."

"We'll have to entrust him to God again."

"Yeah. We certainly aren't much to trust in."

Atila wanted to nod, but she was exhausted. They lay there, side by side, too tired to sleep for hours, before it finally caught up with them.

140

The floor was hard. His mouth was dry. His abdomen throbbed.

He pried his eyelids open. There was a wooden ceiling over his head, lit only by the flickers of a flame in the grate next to him. He was lying on the floor of a cottage. The faint smell of dried meat, onions, and garlic that must have been hung somewhere wafted up his nostrils, and his stomach gurgled.

"You're awake."

Rati turned his head to see where the voice had come from. There was a girl, a young woman, rather, sitting in a chair by the fireplace. She gathered the socks on her lap, tucked them all into a bag, then placed it on the floor. She carefully inserted her needle into a spool of thread and set it down as well, then came over to him and knelt down.

"How are you feeling?"

He wasn't able to catch her eye. "I'm not sure. I—I feel like something took a bite out of me from the inside."

She smiled gently. "That's a vivid description. Do you think you could eat anything?"

"Actually, yeah, that would be great." He watched as she stood up and made her way back to the fireplace. She carefully ladled out soup from a cauldron near the fire, then brought the bowl over to him and set it down on the floor.

"If you sit up, I can put some pillows behind you," she offered, placing a cool hand on his bare shoulder.

He tried, but the pain rippled from his insides through his strained muscles, crippling him. He laid his head back down, panting.

"Never mind. Let me raise your head." She tucked a pillow beneath it. "I can try feeding you, if you'd like."

Rati felt rather awkward, but there was no way he could feed himself, and he could only remember one time in his life he had ever been so hungry. "If you would, that'd be great. I'm sorry to be such a burden."

"Oh, it's no great trouble." She smiled again, still not meeting his eyes. "I'll do my best to not burn you, though I shall make no promises."

"To get food, I think I'd trust just about anyone to feed me, now."

"You don't understand. I'm not used to explaining this, but... I cannot see."

"Oh."

"Actually, I can wake my mother. She can help you."

"No; I'm sorry. If she's sleeping, don't wake her."

"Then you don't mind if I touch your face?"

Rati cracked a smile. "I get food out of the deal, right?"

She placed her left hand beside his mouth, her thumb against the edge of his lips, then used the other hand to scoop up a spoonful of soup and bring it to him. His heart was pounding for some reason. He swallowed, then choked.

"Oh! I'm sorry!" She wiped his mouth and chin with the edge of her apron.

"No; that was my fault." They tried again, and from then on it worked quite well. He felt like a child but downed the whole bowl. She took her hand away. His skin felt cold where it had been.

"You must wait till morning for more."

Rati protested, but she continued in a calm voice.

"Mother said that when you awoke, you'd only get the one bowlful. It wouldn't do to overload your system all at once."

He harrumphed.

She placed the bowl and spoon gently down on a nearby table. "My name is Regina."

"I'm Rati."

"Are you comfortable? Could you rest?"

"I think I'm as comfortable as I can get."

"I'm sorry we didn't put you in a bed. Mother insisted we not move you more than we had to when the wound was so fresh." She sat down on her chair again. "If you don't mind me asking, what happened?"

Rati wasn't sure where to start.

"Stones don't usually get lodged deep in people's midsections, Rati. Not around here, anyway."

"We—two friends and I—were looking for our master. A crazy old man told us he had been taken by Taklin soldiers, the same ones who burned Ferbundi—" He sat up, or tried to. His stomach spasmed and he could feel the soup threatening to return. He swallowed the bile, glancing at the darkened windows. "The sun is set?" he demanded. "How long have I been asleep?"

"Hush." She frowned. "That's right, lie back down. You'll bleed through your bandages. There. Marcus, my brother, found you yesterday afternoon. This is your second night here."

"I need to know what happened."

"If you stop straining yourself."

"Fine. I've got my head on the pillow. I'm calm. Tell me what happened."

She waited a moment, then sighed. "They said Larte went up in smoke a few hours before they dragged you in."

"Are there any survivors?"

"I don't know."

141

Lato and Atila must not have made it on time. Were they even still alive? He had to go look for them.

"No."

"I have to!"

"You're not going anywhere."

Rati would have crossed his arms if it weren't for the pain he knew it would cause. He laid there in silence for a while, then realized he hadn't stated his intention aloud. "How could you tell?"

"Sight is not the only sense. I can feel when people get agitated."

Her calm demeanour softened his restlessness. He had never thought of sensing someone else's feelings when he could just look at them. "I'm still mad at you, but that's pretty cool. Sorry for keeping you up. You can go to bed, if you like. I probably couldn't get far if I tried."

She stood up, but only to find her chair and sit back down again, picking up her spool of thread. "I'm usually up all night anyways."

Rati carefully shifted his position so he wouldn't have to turn his head as far to watch her. "Why?"

"The daylight doesn't help me. I can get lost in the fields if I'm not holding on to somebody, and working in the kitchen with others is very confusing. So I sleep during the daytime."

"Wow." He couldn't imagine what that would be like.

"So," she shrugged, selecting a sock and feeling around the hole, "If you want to talk, feel free. Assuming you don't want to go back to sleep, that is."

"I think I've had enough sleep for a while. But if you don't mind me asking… Have you always been blind?"

She turned her head in his direction, then back at the needle she was pulling through and shook her head. "No. Would you like to hear the story?"

"Sure." Rati prepared himself to be regaled. He was interested, of course, but he was used to Atila's stories, and those tended to get rather longwinded.

"Now, Mother says that I must have suffered head trauma from a fall, and Father says it's all hogwash, but I guess I'll let you decide for yourself." Regina knotted off the sock and began another. "Our family took a trip to the mountains after planting two years ago. We had a picnic on one of the lesser peaks. I brought along a book and was reading it while Father napped, then went for a walk. Mother stayed behind with Timae, Rose had fallen asleep, and the other boys were off adventuring somewhere. Then I turned a bend and nearly bumped into a man."

Had it been Atila telling the story, Rati would have raised an eyebrow and teased her. Now he just listened curiously.

"He was wearing a strange grey uniform with the number Four on his chest."

"What!?"

"It sounds strange, I know—"

"No, it's not that. Four is the one who injured me!"

Her eyebrows lowered and her lips parted. "Who is he? Does he just go around injuring people?"

"He's a soldier from Taklin, one of the army who attacked Larte yesterday. The same ones who burned Ferbundi a week ago."

"Oh my goodness."

"He blinded you?"

"It was strange, because at first he didn't seem violent. He said hello and asked if I would walk with him, but I deferred. I lied and told him that I was waiting for my family who had fallen behind. He nodded most graciously, then motioned to the book bag I was carrying and asked if I read a lot, and what I was reading now. My family does not read much, and it was the book Genesis. He asked what it was about. I said it was about the God who had created the world."

"Did you say God?"

"Yes, why?"

"Oh, nothing. Continue."

"He asked if I believed it. I said that I couldn't see why not. Then he hit me over the head."

"And that's how you became blind?"

"All I can see are shadows. The pressure in my head has lessened, but it is still there. That's one reason I don't mind being up at night; it's much quieter."

"Isn't it lonely?"

Her mouth relaxed and her eyebrows drew closer. "Yes. But my family isn't quiet, and my head aches when they all talk at once. I cannot bear it for long."

"That is too bad."

"But I can do nothing about it."

She put the last sock onto the neat pile she had created, drew out a brown garment Rati recognized as his trousers, and began to mend one of the holes in the knees. He automatically glanced down at the sheet that covered him.

"Thank you. They've needed that for a while."

"What?" Then a blush crossed Regina's face as she realized what she was holding. "Oh. You're welcome."

An awkward silence ensued, broken only by crackling of the fire. Rati thought over her story. It was almost too remarkable to be true, and yet it made perfect sense. "Do you still have the book?"

"Yes, I do. Can you read?"

"I can."

She stood up and ran her fingers over the spines of the few books on the mantle.

"Why didn't he just take the book if they didn't want it on screen?" Rati mused.

"What do you mean?"

He hadn't realized she could hear him. "I meant, he only attacked you after you expressed faith in what the book said. Why didn't he take the book?"

"I have thought of that." She handed him book bound in soft, worn leather. "But then I would have proof that I had been attacked."

"Ahh."

She took her seat again and resumed her mending, then her hands stilled. "Would you mind reading it to me?"

"The whole thing?"

"No; just the first chapter, if you want. It's been so long since I could read it."

Rati cleared his throat and opened it to the first page. "In the beginning…" These were the same words Master Blackwell always used. "God created the heavens and the earth."

142

(intro theme)

Host:

Hello, and welcome back to YCN—Your Canadian News. (pause for effect) *Castles in Time*. My, what a shock this has been for all of us. To think that the characters we all loved so much were innocently living their own lives while we watched through hidden lenses... it gave a new meaning to the term 'guilty pleasure'. The final trials found their verdict last week, and the show is finally over. But I know what you're all thinking: What's the whole story? We have some never-before-seen interview footage. I'll hand you over to one earlier this week with the accused's brother.

(cut to int. L4261, 1:31—4:22)

Mason Blackwell:

It all started thirteen years ago. Vivian and I were on her yacht. I had come up with a few new ideas, and I wanted to run them past her. She loved my inventions, and always thought I would be famous for them one day.

Lucy Cunningham, Interviewer:

What type of invention were you debuting this particular day, out on the water?

Mason Blackwell:

I'd rather not say.

Lucy Cunningham, Interviewer:
Alright. Well, I suppose it's not that important. It was on this trip that you discovered the island of Biatre?

Mason Blackwell:
Yes. We both fell in love with the place at once. She saw the potential, and I saw the people.

Lucy Cunningham, Interviewer:
Is it true that you married a local?

Mason Blackwell:
Yes. She was a young widow. Her little daughter ran out to me in the street and—she hugged my leg. She—giggled. She was the sweetest little thing, all blonde curls and dimpled rosy cheeks. Nancy came out of the tailor's shop, taking the pins out of her mouth, apologizing as she tried to pry little Betta's arms away. While Vivian met with King Willhem and Queen Marielle, I had dinner with my future wife and daughter.

Lucy Cunningham, Interviewer:
How sweet.

Mason Blackwell:
When Vivian decided to leave, I went with her, but I promised to come back. Little did I know that Vivian also planned another visit—soon. I tried to talk her out of it, but there was no changing her mind, and I was so set on seeing Nancy again, that I didn't even think to go and tell the authorities. As soon as I got there again, my Nancy and I climbed the mountain together. Then I traded off a few things I had brought—spices and such like—and bought us a little cottage outside Ferbundi. I had also brought seeds for fruit that I had not seen there on my previous visit, and we planted an orchard.

Lucy Cunningham, Interviewer:
How long did you live there before the fire?

Mason Blackwell:
A little over a year. I came home from selling produce in Ferbundi to find... ashes.

Lucy Cunningham, Interviewer:
How tragic. What did you do?

Mason Blackwell:
The usual. I threw stuff around, yelled at God for a while, before coming around.

Lucy Cunningham, Interviewer:
Now, faith in God seems to have been a pivotal point in the bringing down of this reality empire. Did you learn it from the locals?

Mason Blackwell:
No, I had become a Christian a few months before we discovered Biatre. I brought a Bible with me, and Nancy decided to believe too, but when the cottage burned, so did the book.

Lucy Cunningham, Interviewer:
You seemed to have retained a lot of information to pass on.

Mason Blackwell:
Yes, I have excellent retention.

Lucy Cunningham, Interviewer:
How long was it before you decided to adopt?

Mason Blackwell:
About two and a half years. Well, I didn't really decide. I came across a boy stealing apples, and he managed to awaken my compassion and steal that, too. Then there was the girl fighting for food, and the younger boy starving beside the road. We became each other's family.

Lucy Cunningham, Interviewer:
The footage from the night Ferbundi burned—those three used what appeared to be a force field of sorts. You created it?

Mason Blackwell:
Yes. And no, I will not be sharing those blueprints. I have signed a legal agreement to stop tinkering.

Lucy Cunningham, Interviewer:
I see. After it went down, though, they showed some remarkably good fighting skills. I presume you taught them that, too?

Mason Blackwell:
Yes, I did. I knew that if Vivian's show took off, it would eventually lead to violence. I wanted them to be prepared.

Lucy Cunningham, Interviewer:
Very wise, especially looking at the current circumstances. Do you think they are still alive?

Mason Blackwell:
I'd like to be finished, please.

Interviewer:
I understand, and thank you for your time.

(cut to host)

143

Host:

There you have the origin story of *Castles in Time*—a show all of us took for fake reality when it was, actually, reality! A lot of us are kicking ourselves for not figuring this out earlier. But maybe it's a good thing that we didn't know; otherwise we could have ended up like so many of the actors—for instance, Gustav Pierre, better known as Commander Fifty-Two! He was not willing to speak with us, but we got a few words from Samuel Pierre, one of his three children.

(cut to int. S443, 12:04—13:29)

Susan Hastings, Interviewer:
So, Samuel, how long were you on that ship?

Samuel Pierre:
I wasn't just a ship boy, I did all sorts of other odd jobs on land. I wasn't old enough to be a soldier, and Vivian already had enough donkey boys in her castle. But I started working for her when I was nine years old.

Susan Hastings, Interviewer:
Was it hard to see your father and older brother on the ship occasionally and not go talk to them?

Samuel Pierre:

Micheal worked with me until he got old enough to join Dad on the force, so that made the transition easier, but yeah, it was hard.

Susan Hastings, Interviewer:
Now, you are probably best known for that stunt you pulled two years ago.

Samuel Pierre:
Oh, where I took that beating for Katherine? Yeah, I guess that was pretty noble of me.

Susan Hastings, Interviewer:
What provoked you to do it?

Samuel Pierre:
I'm not sure; Commander Four was always pretty mean. He's getting what he deserved, and I'm glad of it. But when I seen him threatening a girl less than half his size, I just couldn't stand it. I knew I had to do something.

Susan Hastings, Interviewer:
From what has all come to light, it seems that it was not your first or your last beating. How did you not become bitter towards your family, since it was because of their failure to cooperate?

Samuel Pierre:
In the beginning, I was pretty confused, but me and Micheal figured it out. It was all Vivian's doing. I just felt sorry for my them. As to the beatings, I don't remember most of them. I was always injected so I would show more fear and pain than I was actually in—and so I couldn't fight back. I do have some pretty sick scars now, though. You wanna see?

Susan Hastings, Interviewer:
And you are quite muscular, too, I see.

Samuel Pierre:
Yup, one of the benefits of slave labour. Just kidding. Anyways, are we finished here? Mom's waiting for me.

Susan Hastings, Interviewer:
One last question, please. Your mother lived here in Canada, correct? Why did she not report anything to the police?

Samuel Pierre:
Actually, she thought me, Micheal, and Nelda died in a car crash. She never found out we were alive because she's got this eye problem—I forget what it's called—and she can't watch TV. We were homeschooled and didn't get out much, so no one else knew us or told her. We cool?

Susan Hastings, Interviewer:
Thank you for your time.

(cut to host)

Host:
Incredible insight on what it was like to be one of Vivian De Blu's puppets. Now, I know you aren't watching just to see Samuel Pierre's tanned abs. That was just a bonus. Here's some more meat, from one of the show's stars: Katherine Shultz, better known to us as Katira! This was all she had to share with us, but boy, is it deep.

(cut to int. T361, 0:07—0:23)

Katherine Schultz:
I acted to stay alive. Everything I did had to be thought out, and like they said, I was good at it. Now... I'm not sure how I can be myself again. I don't even know who "myself" is.

(cut to host)

Host:
She offered no other remark, even when questioned about King Derek and what was between them. The show hinted at some romantic tension, but now we're not quite sure what to believe. King Derek himself refused to give any private remarks, so the only information we have on him is from during his trial, which you can watch full-length on our website, and

ad-free if you have our app. Oh, but he did get his revenge. Vivian DeBlu died that night from the wound he gave her, and most *Castles in Time* fanatics say she deserved it. Was King Derek the right one to dole out the punishment? There are disagreements there, but the jury has decided to honour his plea of insanity, especially considering the effect of the MC-42 serum that was in his bloodstream during the incident. We did get a few words with Vivian DeBlu's daughter, Pricilla DeBlu.

(cut to int. T363, 0:03—0:08)

Pricilla DeBlu:
This is such a mess. All Mom wanted was to be rich. I was part of her plans, you know. I didn't want to help her, I didn't want to carouse with the guards, I didn't want to go to Biatre, I didn't want to be such a snob to Derek—but whatever. Leave me alone.

(cut to host)

Host:
A very sad state of affairs for the poor girl. She will be getting counselling. On another note, thought, Vivian DeBlu's husband, Rosseen DeBlu, and her director, name unknown, have disappeared. All surrounding counties are on high alert, and the authorities have said that they are confident in their capture. Her son, Adhemar DeBlu, hung himself, but there again, many believe that justice has prevailed. Now all that remains to be done is to clean up the effects of the injustice.

(cue theme, end broadcast)

144

Derek mechanically took the plastic dish out of the microwave and dropped it onto the table, then dropped himself onto a chair. It was hard to believe that only a few months ago, he had been a king, with servants to bring him epicurean food at every meal while he kept the peace, organized people, settled debates, gave licenses, and practiced swordplay. Then… his mind finished the story, as it always insisted on doing.

He had taken vengeance on his enemy on soil that was not his own, but was not faced with any charges, considering the circumstances.

He had gone back to Biatre with the aid of the good people of Canada, who had offered supplies and help to rebuild. The only help his people had wanted was food, and that was easily supplied by Vivian's wealth.

The general and his men returned from Ferbundi. They were devastated, but Derek was glad they had been gone. No force could have defeated the Taklin army.

Derek had abdicated his throne, and the general won the election. He then returned to Canada to seek a new life. Everything was different now.

He picked at the food. *Maybe I should learn to cook for myself,* he thought. *Almost anything would be better than these frozen packages.*

Someone knocked on the door. Strange. He wasn't expecting anyone. He went to the door and looked through the peephole, then stepped back. She knocked again. He reached for the bolt and slid it.

It was Katira. Her hair was hanging free instead of being tied into a braid. She was wearing a pink and grey knitted sweater with jeans instead of her maid's dress and apron. But it was Katira.

She stood there for a moment, lips parted.

He remembered the manners of the day. "Come in."

"Thank you."

The door closed on its own.

"I would curtsy, but—" Katira waved a hand at her jeans, then grimaced. "I'm sorry, that was awkward. I just—we never got to say goodbye."

"No, we didn't." Derek did not know what to do. "Is this goodbye?"

"I wanted to thank you first."

"What for?"

"For being so kind to me. I thought Adhemar was going to sell me as a whore, but you gave me a place and occupation and always treated me with respect. For that, yes. I do thank you."

Derek could feel his eyebrows contracting. He gave his tongue a hard bite. "I had you whipped, Katira."

She looked down at the floor, then back up at him. He saw no bitterness in those brown eyes. "You know what happened."

"They only influenced me, not controlled me. I—" he broke off and ran a hand through his cropped hair, trying to disentangle his memory and prove himself innocent. He failed.

Katira reached for his hands and led him to the couch, turned off the television, and sat down opposite him. "Tell me."

She had always been easy to talk to, but these words—they hurt. He couldn't look at her. "Katira, I heard you scream. And I enjoyed it. Then I calculated when your pain would draw their attention fully, and used it as a diversion for murder."

"And that was wrong."

This surprised him. "You're not going to patronize me, and tell me I was insane with the injection, and couldn't think?"

"No, I'm not. I know you wanted revenge, and that was wrong."

"So what now? I got my revenge, but it was empty. I have no fines to pay, no deeds to fulfil. By whatever standards I try to measure myself by, I fall short. Do I keep living under this guilt?"

"No. There is hope."

Derek had watched the recordings—the whole, unedited recordings—until he had them nearly memorized. "Are you quoting Bridget?"

"Aye."

"What do I have to do?"

"Nothing."

"No quaint little speech, no declaration?"

"No. You simply have to believe that God has forgiven you. When you want to pray, that's between you and Him."

"Oh. As they say here, wow."

"Yeah." She gave a small smile. "It's pretty amazing."

"Wait—so you weren't just bluffing to rebel against Vivian?"

"It started that way, but it didn't stay there. We need hope; we were created to."

"For the hope God can give."

"Yeah. I'm not super knowledgeable about it all yet, but Miss Eillah's been taking me to church. You can come too, if you want."

"I've heard about church—from the television, that is. Do you like it?"

"Oh, yes. And the singing. The singing is amazing."

"I think I'd like to go, if you'll take me."

"I'd love to." She smiled again, then looked down at her fingers and twiddled them. The silence stretched for a bit, then she slapped her hands to her knees and stood up. "What is that awful smell?"

He waved a hand at the table. "The package says gourmet, but it's not. I think Oregga spoiled me."

"Yeah. She was a really good cook. Biatre in general made good food. Do you ever plan on going back?"

"I don't think so. I never really wanted to be king."

"Then what do you want?"

"I got my three out of three, and now I've got to find something else to live for. There was nothing for me there."

"I guess that makes sense."

"I do still miss the food, though."

"Well, if that's your only problem, I can fix it. I didn't work in that kitchen so long and not learn a few tricks." She walked to the kitchenette and swung open a cupboard door, and another, then looked into the fridge. "Do you seriously only have packaged foods?"

He gave a sheepish grin. "Um… yes?"

"We're gonna have to go to the grocery store then. It's only a block away from here, right?"

"I'm actually not sure. I've only been to the variety store across the street."

"We'll have to go for a walk then." She stopped. The expression on her face reminded him of all the times she used to shrink away, afraid of offending His Majesty. "If you want to, I mean."

He shrugged and grabbed a hoodie, answering while pulling it over his head. "Hey, I mean, if this is what I've got to do to get some decent food around here, I'll do it."

145

Atila withdrew her spoon from the cauldron of stew and tasted it, then walked to the next fire and repeated the exercise. The results were satisfactory. She turned to the fire behind her and wiped the sweat from her brow. Marie and Jenny were flipping corn cakes on large rocks placed halfway into the flame, making stacks of finished ones. Marie happened to glance up, and Atila quirked an eyebrow. Marie nodded.

"Supper!" Atila yelled. No one heard. Then something bumped into her legs, and she looked down to see a little mass of red curls tipping back, and a mischievous, dirty face revealed itself. He shrieked and dodged behind her as Heather, Hale, and Gina darted past. She scooped him up and tickled him.

"'Tila! Stop!" he giggled, writhing in her arms.

She did, and grinned. "Alright, Ronnie. Let's go get everyone for supper?"

He nodded and jumped from her hold, running ahead to the row of new cabins. The third one was nearly finished, and Rati was marking out the grounds for a fourth. Ronnie found Lato, carrying one end of an armful of freshly cut timber, and threw himself around his legs.

"Supper time! 'Tila says!"

Lato nearly tripped, but Captain Gresham, holding the other end of the load, stopped in time. "Ronnie, just let us put these down, okay?"

Ronnie obliged. The men placed the wood next to the rising wall and turned towards the cooking fires. Lato caught Atila's eye just as several more people, men and women alike, passed between them with their loads. She cupped her hands around her mouth and mimed shouting. He grinned and hollered. Of course, the people heard him. Together they surged towards the hope of food.

When supper was over and everyone's muscles had had a chance to stiffen, someone shouted for a story. The shout was picked up by the children and carried to the adults, who joined in. All turned to Lato.

"Would you tell us the story again?"

He stood up and raised his hands to quiet them, then took his place in the middle. It was a well-worn story by now, and most everyone knew it by heart, but everyone wanted to hear it again. Ronnie scrunched himself into Atila's lap. Heather and Hale fidgeted, but Gina and Quinn sat quietly. Rati slipped back into the crowd, leading Regina by the hand. Even Asa harrumphed in begrudging agreement as he sat on the ground beside his father.

Lato began the story. How God had created a perfect world, and placed a man and a woman inside. How they had gone against His one command, and how He could no longer associate with them. "Generations came and passed, but no one could restore fellowship with God. They had done Him wrong. Only a perfect sacrifice could appease Him."

The crowd exhaled.

"But no animal's blood could be enough. And no human had ever been perfect."

She felt a smile grow on her face as Lato's voice lowered.

"But God seen their plight. He sent His own Son, who had never done wrong, to come to this earth and die for the people. He was a perfect sacrifice. Those who loved him buried him, and mourned for three days when"—he threw his arms in the air—"He rose from the dead!"

Everyone gasped.

"Now He offers life after death to all who believe in Him!" His hands lowered. "Some people did not like this. Queen Vivian was one of them. She tried to destroy our knowledge of Him, but she failed. His word will always triumph. And now we wait for Him to return and take us home to heaven!"

A resounding cheer went up, but Lato did not sit down. Instead he scratched the back of his neck, and Captain Gresham let out a knowing chuckle. Atila glanced at him, perplexed; he usually didn't make noise unless it was forced out of him. A cough brought her attention to Lato, who now stood directly in front of her. His jaw flexed, and he held out his hand. She instinctively took it. He pulled her to her feet, dropping Ronnie to the ground.

"Atila?" he asked, lifting his eyes to hers but then dropping them again. "While we wait for Him… Would you like to climb the mountain with me?"

Somewhere in the back of her head, Atila could feel the stares pointed her way, but they all vanished when her eyes caught Lato's. "I'd love to."

A chorus of whistles and shouts were raised up, and Lato finally sat down, next to Atila. Ronnie immediately began demanding to be brought with, but they both laughed and shook their heads.

146

Nelda relaxed her fingers after translating the whole story so Ronald could read it, and sighed with contentment. An elbow jabbed her side and she jerked to the right to see her brother, Samuel, mimicking wiping a tear from his eye. She wiped her own and stuck out her tongue at him. He grinned, and so did Micheal. Then her father ruffled both his sons' hair as if they were little boys and knocked their heads together. Her mother swatted him while smiling at her daughter and future son-in-law. They were together again.

147

Regina's hand was soft in Rati's as he led her back to her home.

"I guess I should have known it would get so loud," he said.

"It was worth it," she smiled. "The headaches are better than they used to be."

"I'm glad."

They walked in silence for a while, then Regina asked, "What is it?"

"Well, I was thinking about Lato and Atila."

"What about them?"

"It seems kind of strange, because we grew up together. And now—"

"They're leaving you."

"Yeah. But at the same time, I guess I knew it all along. They've always had this… thing. And I—well, what I'm trying to say is that I—I think—"

Regina stood on tiptoe and kissed his cheek. "I think I know what you mean."

He pressed her hand in his. "That about sums it up."

148

Mason Blackwell meandered through his garden, kept neat and clean. It was incredible how much time he had for this now that he had stopped tinkering. He didn't miss it.

His step faltered, and he sat down in the raked path. Around him were rows of vegetables and herbs and flowers. Above, the sky was blue, and somewhere beyond it, there was a voice, calling him home.

ACKNOWLEDGEMENTS

Mr. Lama, for reading my stories in the teachers' lounge. You encouraged me and made me believe I could accomplish great things.

Hallie, for beta reading everything I write and listening to me rant about plot holes.

Sara, for editing my book and pointing out things I would never have noticed.

Dad, for teaching me that nothing would come of anything without hard work.

Mom, for teaching me how to read and write in the first place.

And everyone who doesn't know I stole their names or personalities to use in this story.

I owe you all so much. Thank you for the parts you have played in my life.

QUOTATIONS

All quotations are taken from the King James Version of the Bible.

"And we know that all things work together for good to them that love God, to them who are the called according to his purpose"
Rom 8:28.
Chap. 4, page 12
Chap. 8, page 25
Chap. 10, page 36
Chap. 15, page 49
Chap. 17(indirectly), page 54
Chap. 70(indirectly)

"The Lord is my shepherd. I shall not want. He maketh me to lie down in green pastures: He leadeth me beside the still waters. He restoreth my soul: He leadeth me in the paths of righteousness for His name's sake"
Psalm 23:1-3.
Chap. 49, page 144

"Yea, though I walk through the valley of the shadow of death, I will fear no evil: for thou *art* with me; thy rod and thy staff they comfort me"
Psalm 23:4.
Chap. 49, page 145

"Thou preparest a table before me in the presence of mine enemies: thou anointest my head with oil; my cup runneth over."
Psalm 23:5.
Chap. 49(indirectly), page 145

"Surely goodness and mercy shall follow me all the days of my life; and I will dwell in the house of the Lord forever!"
Psalm 23:6.
Chap. 49, page 145

"Intreat me not to leave thee, or to return from following after thee: for whither thou goest, I will go; and where thou lodgest, I will lodge: thy people shall be my people, and thy God my God; where thou diest, will I die, and there will I be buried. The Lord do so to me, and more also, if ought but death part thee and me."
Ruth 1:16-17.
Chap. 75, page 214

The Book of Ruth.
Chap. 77(indirectly), page 218

The Gospel of Mark.
Chap. 77(indirectly), page 219

The Epistle to the Hebrews.
Chap. 77(indirectly), page 219

"How shall we escape, if we neglect so great a salvation"
Hebrews 2:3a.
Chap. 77, page 219

The Book of Genesis
Chap. 141(indirectly), page 345

"In the beginning, God created the heavens and the earth"
Genesis 1:1
Chap. 141, page 347